GAME OF GAMES

Mavra and Joshi, breathing hard, stopped and turned back toward the compound. There was a glow from the fire there.

"What the hell is going on?" Joshi gasped.

Mavra shook her head. "I don't know. But it's the end of *our* world, that's for sure."

"What do you mean?" he asked, genuinely puzzled. "Those Parmiters sure won't be back."

"Oh, yes they will," she said grimly. "Them or somebody worse. They weren't just pirates, Joshi. They landed here just to get us—kill, kidnap, I don't know what. But they were pros. Somebody's put a price on my head."

"But—why?"

"Somebody's finally found the way to that northern spaceship and they're eliminating the competition." Her eyes were shining. After all these years —the great game was on again, *the game she was born to play . . .*

Quest
FOR THE
Well of Souls

Part II of
THE WARS OF THE WELL

Jack L. Chalker

A Del Rey Book

BALLANTINE BOOKS · NEW YORK

A Del Rey Book
Published by Ballantine Books

Library of Congress Catalog Card Number: 78-67181

ISBN 0-345-29337-1

Manufactured in the United States of America

First Edition: November 1978
Fourth Printing: October 1981

Cover art by Darrel Sweet

And for the dead as well . . .

John W. Campbell, Jr.
  who taught me to write the stuff

August W. Derleth
  who was always interested

Clark Ashton Smith
  who dreamed strange, infectious dreams

Seabury Quinn
  who cared as much for his friends as they did
  for him

Edmond Hamilton
  a wonderful man who liked the Well

Ron Ellik
  who should have lived to see this

H. Beam Piper
  who was never too busy

and to those two incongruous, ghostly specters,
H. P. Lovecraft and Stanley G. Weinbaum, who
have haunted this field since before I was born.

CONTENTS

THE WARS OF THE WELL, PART II

Part I of this very large novel may be found as *Exiles at the Well of Souls* (Ballantine/A Del Rey Book, 1978). A prequel, *Midnight at the Well of Souls* (1977) may be read before or after this book. *The Wars of the Well* was conceived as a single novel but published in two books because of its tremendous length. In order to accommodate the split, each novel has been written to stand alone. But in an ideal world *Exiles* should be read before this book.

JLC

H Bahaoid
S Yaxa
N Koorz
Avenue
N Harbigor
S Muré
H Kwynn
S Leba
N Fleisch
Avenue
H Birsk
S Aklak

N Karlbarx
H Lamotien
N Ruxton
N Nodi

H Hawyr
S Bache
H Teliagin
H Jiihn
H Porigol

N Dahir
H Godidal
S Kromm
SEA OF STORMS
S Slath
N Galidon

S Kleinglom
S Cebu
N Boidol
H Lata
N Tuliga

N Awbrl
H Parmiter
H Agitar
S Djukasis
H Zhonzhorp
S Olborn

H Kzuco
N Makiem
S Wygon
N Domien
N Klusid

S Vergutz
S Ogadon
H Itus
N Hookl
S Buta
S Simjim
S Folkla
N Yimsk

N Ronbondz
N Gekir
S Cibon
N Jol
H Rolga
H Zanti

H Durbis
H Kalibu
H Waynir
S Nocha
S Wuckl
S Wasdamahda

S Gilcres
N Ginzin
N Everod
SEA OF TURAGIN
S Ecundo
N Hadiza

S Flotish
N Ambreza
N Glathriel
S Usurk
H
H Giml

N Bahabi
H Abigosth
S Drika
N Zumerbald
S Quastador
N Ficarb

N Erdom
S Hadron
H Romeny
S Orarc
H Mastarx

GULF OF ZINJIN

x

WORLD
Southern Hemisphere

S Voxmir	S Cotyl	Avenue	H Mourgal	N Ivrom	N Ghlmon	Avenue	S Ekh'l	H Ulik

A map divided into hexagonal regions. The regions, each marked with a technology-level letter (H, S, or N), are:

S Voxmir, S Cotyl, Avenue, H Mourgal, N Ivrom, N Ghlmon, Avenue, S Ekh'l, H Ulik, N Dasheen, S Istssl, S Kagir, N Slelcron, H Qasada, N Jaq, N Umiau, H Qast, H The Nation, H Frick, H Czill, H Ilg, H Lewok, S Xoda, S Tsfrin, S Pia, S Agston, H Azkfru, N Dymek, N Murithel, N Dolom, N Huft, H Palim, H Dunhgran, H Staxsir, H Kymbol, H Jocir, N Gedemondas, S Slongorn, Rognel, S R'cot, N Alestol, S Dillia, N Xymk, **OVERDARK OCEAN**, Potocki, H Bilburg, S Mucrol, N Nidol, H Argest, N Chalidang, H Kuansa, N Kluberia, N Quacksa, S Laskein, H Shamozan, S Rustol, S Yzus, N Turek, H S Twosh, N Matusik, Alexist, H Suford, H Patpotz, N Susafrit, S Wisteria, N Aderleth, S Jirminia, N Nanzistu, S Yoribol, S Dolgiland, H Bliston, H Frodrum, H Pasnir, N Kyrbizmyth, N Tubrikon, N Smoire, S Virigod, H Bucht, N Nyarlath, H Oolakash, N Imtré, N Hovath, S Traglidon, S Calimande, S Urifraud, H Ivor, H Maldimir, S Pakiwa, H Mijistir, N Oslogo, N Regeis, N Chelan

H—Highly technological
S—Semitechnological
N—Nontechnological

xi

THE WELL WORLD
Detail of Northern Hemisphere

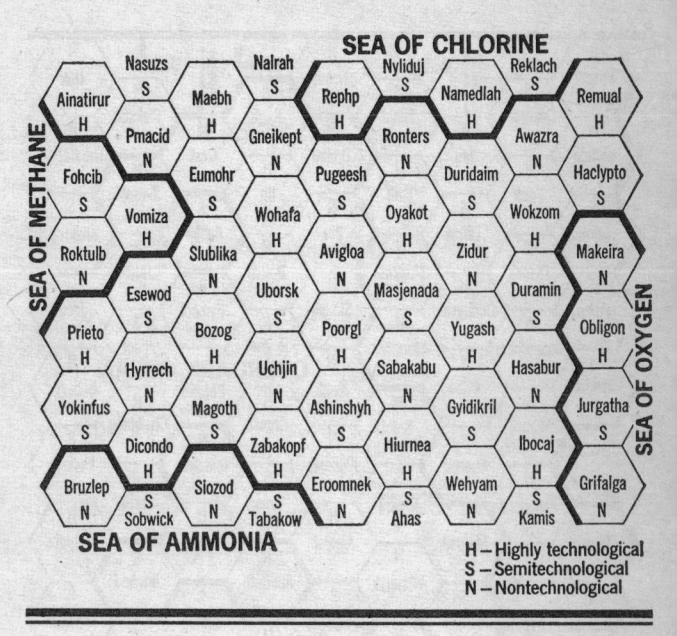

SEA OF CHLORINE

H – Highly technological
S – Semitechnological
N – Nontechnological

Quest
for the
Well of Souls

Kyrbizmith, a Hex to the South of the Overdark

A DARK ROAD IS DANGEROUS ANYWHERE; BUT HERE, on the Well World, in a nontech hex whose diurnal creatures literally became comatose after sundown, it was moreso. The atmosphere was as close to average for the Southern Hemisphere as it could get, and, unlike many other places, almost any race could exist here—all easy prey. Internal defenses protected the Kyrbizmithians; one could not even touch them and hope to remain sane and whole. But nothing protected the traveler so foolish as to tread the well-marked but unlighted lanes after sundown.

The Tindler was such a fool. Resembling a giant armadillo with long, clawed hands used for walking and for grasping, he moved down the road, confident that his thick shell could protect him from any inhabitant of a nontech hex. His night vision would alert him well in advance of any traps.

"Help me! Oh, please! Someone! Help me!"

There it was again—a strange, high-pitched voice pierced the darkness. From its sound, it had obviously been processed by a translator. The Tindler, himself a far-traveling trade negotiator, used one. When both speakers wore them the voices sounded slightly more artificial.

"Help me! Please! Somebody! Help!" The mysterious voice pleaded just ahead of him. The Tindler grew wary, automatically suspecting a trap set by brigands reported to be in the area. Worse, he feared someone had somehow inadvertently touched one of the great trees that abutted one another across the whole hex. These were the immobile Kyrbizmithians themselves, who moved by swapping minds with one another and who would absorb the mind of anyone touching them without approval.

Suddenly he saw it, a tiny thing lying in the roadway. The creature was more than seventy centimeters of bright-red fur tinged with gold. Its bushy foxlike tail was almost as long as its body, and its build was something like that of a small monkey. As the Tindler drew cautiously closer, the creature, a kind he'd never seen before, emitted a low moan; then he saw that one of its hind legs seemed set at an odd angle—almost certainly broken.

The Tindler's bulk made it impossible to conceal his presence; the little creature's head, lying in the roadway, turned and stared at him with beady little eyes from a curious face that resembled an owl's, complete to a tiny beak.

The Tindler stopped, looked around cautiously. Although his night vision was excellent, he could see no other life forms about except those of the hulking, ever-silent tree-creatures. From those he had nothing to fear if he stayed on the road.

Slowly the Tindler rumbled up to the stricken creature. Surely a being of his bulk had nothing to fear from one so tiny and frail.

"What's the matter, friend?" he called, trying to sound as concerned and helpful as possible.

The little creature groaned again. "Brigands, sir! Thieves and scoundrels set upon me a half-hour or so ago, took my pouch and everything, and twisted my leg right out of its socket, as you can see, leaving me to die here alone in the dark!"

The plight of the poor creature touched the Tindler deeply.

"Look, perhaps I can lift you atop my shell," he suggested. "You would be in pain, but it's not far to the Bucht border and a high-tech hospital."

The little creature brightened. "Oh, thank you *so* much, good sir!" it exclaimed happily. "You have saved my life!"

The two eyes at the end of the Tindler's long, narrow snout lowered to the little thing.

"Tell me," the Tindler asked, not a little nervous himself, "what did the monsters who would do this look like?"

"There were three of them, sir. Two of them were huge—and just about invisible. You couldn't see them until they moved!"

The Tindler thought that a little hard to believe, but so were the Kyrbizmithians. On the Well World, anything was possible somewhere.

"And the third?" the Tindler prompted. "Was it different than the other two? We have a long way to go, remember."

The tiny creature nodded, and tried to raise itself a little. It looked the Tindler straight in the eyes, only a fraction of a centimeter from its round nostrils. "It looked just like me!"

And before the great shelled creature could react, the owl-monkey held a strange-looking pistol in its prehensile left foot. The furry animal pressed the trigger, and an enormous cloud of a yellowish gas gushed out. The movement was too sudden and too close; the Tindler's nostril flaps didn't close in time.

As the Tindler lost consciousness, two huge shapes detached themselves from the landscape where nothing could be seen before and moved toward them.

The last he heard was the little one yelling to somebody, "Hey! Doc! Get ready! This one's got a translator!"

Makiem

HIS NAME WAS ANTOR TRELIG AND HE LOOKED A LOT like a giant frog. Nothing much unusual in this; in Makiem, *everybody* looked like a giant frog.

Trelig's chest bore the tattoo of the Imperial Household. From his office in the palace he could look out across the great city of Druhon—a lively, medieval center for 250,000 Makiem—to the great lake beyond that reflected the city's gaslights and the fairyland lighting of the castle. In the lake the land-dwelling Makiem could wet down their bodies as needed, swim underwater for long periods for recreation, and there, for one glorious week a year, the otherwise nonsexual Makiem bred.

Looming like dark shadows on either side of the lake were high mountains that provided an irregular frame for the great starfield mirrored in the lake. The sky of the Well World was spectacular to an unimaginable degree; from the Southern Hemisphere it was dominated by a great globular cluster and clouds of swirling gas, punctuated by an impossibly dense starfield that reflected the Well's position near a galactic center. Trelig often reclined on his balcony seat, looking out at the vista on clear nights. There was no other sight quite like it.

He heard a noise behind him but didn't turn away from the view. Only one person could enter his office without challenge or concern.

"You've never given up, have you?" The voice just behind him was somewhat softer than his, but with a toughness that showed that his wife, Burodir, was not just another pretty face.

"You know I haven't," he almost sighed. "And I never will. I can't when—now, for instance—you can actually see the damn thing tantalizing me, almost mocking me. Challenging me." He pointed a clawed and webbed index finger out at the dark.

She sat beside him. Theirs was not a romantic union. She had been married off to him because her father was the power behind the throne and needed a watch kept on this stranger. Though rumor said the old man had choked to death on a bad *mork-worm,* she knew deep inside that Antor Trelig had somehow arranged his demise, and then moved into the vacated place.

She was her father's daughter, though, so revenge

4

was out of the question. She would remain loyal and faithful to Trelig—unless and until she could increase her own powers safely by knocking him off.

He understood that. He was the same way.

She peered out into the darkness and the U-shaped starfield showing through the Mountain Gate. "Where is it?" she asked.

"Almost at the horizon," he gestured. "About the size of a twenty-*nug* piece. See it, all silvery in the reflection of the sun?"

Now she had it in sight—it was huge, really, but so low down and so oddly colored that it would often escape detection if one had a limited view of the horizon.

"New Pompeii," he breathed. "It was mine once—it will be mine again."

Once he'd been what he called human—resembling the folk of Glathriel far to the southeast. He'd been born unguessable billions of light-years from this spot, born to rule the Comworld of New Harmony, where everyone was hermaphroditic and all looked the same, but where party leaders like him had been larger, grander, than the rest.

He loved power; he'd been born to it and raised to wield it. Wealth and position meant nothing to him unless they served his lust for power. That was why he was content for now to be Minister of Agriculture, an anonymous lower cabinet position. Few knew him even in Makiem, except as the Entry who'd crashed there in a spaceship.

"Up there is all the power one could want," he told her, for perhaps the nine-thousandth time. She didn't mind; she was just like him. "A giant computer is the entire southern half of that little world," he continued. "It's a small-scale Well of Souls, able to transform physical and temporal reality on a scale that might be planetwide. See that sparkle, about halfway down? That's the edge of the big dish, locked on the Well of Souls at the equator, frozen in place. But if freed, it would be able to transform a world as large as this one. Think of it! A world! With the people designed to your pattern, the land and resources laid out to your specifications, and everything absolutely loyal to you—you who can be made immortal. And that computer can accomplish it all merely by adjusting reality in such a way that nobody would even know anything had been done. Everyone would just accept it!"

She nodded sympathetically. "But you know there is nothing on the Well World that could build an engine with sufficient thrust to reach New Pompeii," she pointed out. "You and I both saw the engines tumble and explode in that glacial valley in Gedemondas."

He nodded absently. "Fourteen thousand already dead from the Alliance that warred to get that fragmented ship, perhaps another forty thousand dead in the war itself—and the same number from the opposition alliance that the Yaxa and Ben Yulin headed."

He talked as if he were sincerely pained by the waste and futility the war represented, but she knew it was the compulsive politician in him that made it sound so. He couldn't care less about the dead and crippled, only that the war had been for nothing and had cost Makiem its friendship with its allies and neighbors, who took a dimmer view.

"What about Yulin?" she asked. Yulin had been the brilliant engineer who had kidnapped Gil Zinder's daughter, Nikki, and forced Zinder, who had designed the computer, to move and expand the project to New Pompeii, Trelig's private little world. Yulin was the only other creature who knew the code to bypass New Pompeii's computer defenses and could get in to operate the great machine. Not even Gil Zinder, who had somehow totally vanished on the Well World, as had his daughter, could get in without the passwords.

The mention of Yulin brought a chuckle to Trelig's great reptile lips. "Yulin! He's a semiretired farmer in Dasheen. He's got a hundred minotaur cows bred to adoring slavery for him. He's done some engineering work for his former allies, the Yaxa and Lamotien, but the Well math is beyond him—a great engineer, a so-so theoretical scientist. Without Zinder he can run, even build, some of the great machines, but he can't design one from scratch. They've tried! Besides, I think he's rather happy in Dasheen. It's the kind of place he's always fantasized about, anyway. The Yaxa had to drag him kicking and screaming into the war."

She was thoughtful. "This Zinder, though. *He* could build another such computer, couldn't he? Doesn't that worry you?"

He shook his head. "No. If he was in a position to do so, he'd have done it by now, I'm sure—and such a massive undertaking would be impossible to hide. No, with all the searches that have been launched over all this time, I'm certain that he's dead, or locked in one of those mass-mind worlds or nontech immobile-plant hexes. Nikki, I'm sure, is also dead. I doubt if she could survive *anywhere* on her own." First one, then the other of his huge independent eyes seemed to fog a bit. "No, it's not Yulin or Zinder I fear—it's that girl who troubles me."

"Humph!" his wife snorted. "Mavra Chang, always Mavra Chang. It's an obsession with you! Look, she's deformed—she couldn't run a ship even if you put her in charge. No hands, face always looking down. She can't even feed herself. Better face it, Antor, dear. There is no way of ever returning to that glittering bauble of yours up there in the sky, and no way anybody else can, either—particularly not Mavra Chang!"

"I wish I had your confidence," he responded glumly. "Yes, it's true I'm obsessed with her. She's the most dangerous antagonist I ever faced. Tiny little slip of a girl—not much bigger than Parmiter's owl-faced apes. And yet, she managed to get devices of incredible complexity past my detectors—and they were the best you could buy! Then she slipped into Nikki Zinder's prison, past all but a couple of the guards, talked one guard into deserting with her, and managed to steal a ship and not get shot down by my robot sentinels—they're still up there, too, you know—by knowing a password based on a system only I could possibly know. How? Because she was in league with that goddamned computer of Zinder's, that's how! It's self-aware, you know! It's the only answer. That means I haven't the slightest idea whether or not she really could get back through to that computer if she ever managed to get back up there! Even Yulin might have problems getting by the sentinels, but she won't! And her mind's so strange, so unfathomable, that no one knows what she'd do with that kind of power. She's vicious and vengeful, I know that. I lost a number of good syndicate hit men once when they killed her husband. I *know* what she'd like to do to me!"

Burodir shifted. She'd heard it all before. "But she won't!" she pointed out. "There's no way for anybody to get up there!"

"There's a perfectly preserved ship in the North," he retorted. "I ought to know—Ben and I crashed in it."

"But in a nontech hex populated by beings so alien they don't even understand what it is, and won't permit any other race to move it," she continued. "And, besides, it's impossible for a Southerner to go beyond North Zone. You know that. Any Zone Gate on the Well World, North or South, just brings you back to Makiem. You can't get beyond North Zone!"

That thought didn't bother him. "I'd have once said what Chang did was impossible," he pointed out. "I'd have said the Well of Souls, the Well World, Makiem, and all the rest were impossible, too. Besides, I've been reading the histories. A little over two centuries ago a Northerner *did* make it to the South, here. If it can be done that way, the same thing can be done in reverse."

She nodded. "I know, the Diviner and the Rel, or something. That whole story is so mucked up in distortion and legend, few believe it anyway. You know that. There was also supposed to be a Markovian then —still around a million or more years after the rest of his race died out—and the Well was supposedly opened, entered, and then sealed for all time. If you believe those kinds of fairy tales, you'll believe anything!"

He considered what she said. "Well, back where I came from, there were myths about weird, intelligent creatures in the dim past—centaurs and mermaids and pixies and fairies and flying winged horses and minotaurs and more. I have seen every one of those here. This Markovian—this Nathan Brazil, as he was called, from my sector of space—*was* a real person. There are records and descriptions of him in places like that plant-research center, Czill. Those people are not likely to accept fairy tales. And Serge Ortega believes in him, even claims to have known him."

"Ortega!" she sniffed. "A scoundrel. A prisoner in Zone because of his own quest for immortality, and centuries older than any Ulik has a right to be. He's a senile old man."

"Ancient he is," Trelig agreed, "but senile he is not. Remember, he's the one who has kept Mavra Chang on ice and protected, until such time as he finds his own solution to this Northern mess. *He's* the one who brought up that Diviner and Rel business. He was *there!*"

She tried to change the subject. "You know, it'll be our season in less than two weeks," she pointed out. "Have you cleared everything for it? I'm already starting to feel the urges."

Trelig nodded absently. "We've got twenty brats now. The worst curse of the war—this extreme fertility the Well imposed to replace the dead." But he continued to look out into the night, even though New Pompeii was now obscured by the western mountains. "Mavra Chang," she heard him mutter under his breath.

Burodir hissed in disgust. "Damn it! If she bothers you so much, why not do something about her? You're supposed to be a big plotter and dirty thinker. What would you do if some slip of a cripple was a threat to your power here?"

His great reptilian head cocked slightly as he considered her challenge. "But killing her wouldn't be enough," he responded. "No, I have to know what sort of things that computer put into her, and how much of it she's revealed to anyone else." His mind raced now. "A kidnapping, though. She's helpless to resist, given the situation she is in, and she's even isolated from Ortega's meddling. A kidnapping and a thorough hypno job in some high-tech hex that could be bought or blackmailed. Of course!"

"It took you all these years to figure that out?" his wife responded sarcastically.

He didn't recognize the tone. "Nine years to get a position here, almost the same to get the diplomatic mess straight, to repair and rebuild," he replied seriously. "Plus all the work on the Northern problem. Priorities. But—why not?"

"Want me to arrange it?" Burodir asked, thankful that, perhaps, this obsession could finally be cleared up. "Makiem will have to be well out of the affair on the surface, or we undo the diplomatic ties and bring Ortega and the rest down on us. But, it can be done."

Trelig nodded idly. "Mavra Chang!" he breathed.

South Zone

THERE WERE 780 RACES IN 780 HEXES IN THE WELL World's Southern Hemisphere. In each self-contained little world was at least one Zone Gate—a yawning hexagonal blackness that would instantly bring any of the hemisphere's creatures passing through it to an area around the South Pole known as Zone. Around a huge central Well—the input staging area for Markovians who had taken part in the great experiment to repopulate the stars by becoming lesser creatures of their own design, living, reproducing, dying so the children could go out again to a universe their parents had abandoned—were 780 small areas. Airlocks and atmospheric controls adapted each to one of the 780 life forms of the South; they were all connected by long corridors.

Here and here alone, all the races of the South could meet. Here most technology worked—as did magic, too, for some of the races had powers given by the Well to simulate some condition on the real planets their races were designed to inhabit. However, high-tech pistols would not fire, a diplomatic nicety.

Zone, too, was halved, with one half for the water races and the other for the land races. But high-tech hexes had long ago rigged intercoms among them all, and it was here that senior ambassadors with translators could conduct interhex business, try and keep the peace, deal with common problems, work out trade negotiations and the like.

Not all the embassies were manned, or had ever been. Some hexes remained complete mysteries, trafficking in nothing to no one. One such was the snowbound, mountainous hex of Gedemondas, where the war had ended in a fiery display as the spaceship's engine module plunged into a valley in full sight of the warring parties. It exploded as it pierced a thin floor of solidified lava masking volcanic magma. Other creatures, such as those Antor Trelig would once have called "human," also went unrepresented. The Glathriel, for instance, lost a war with their nontech neighbors, the Ambreza, who had secured a Northern Hemisphere gas that reduced the humans to the most basic primitive tribalism and then took their hex. The Ambreza controlled both Zone Gates, and made certain that, if humanity rose again, it would do so in ways they, not the humans, chose.

Ambassadors came and went in the 679 currently manned offices. Time went on, people grew old, or they got tired of the monastic life the embassies imposed, or they got promoted within their own hexes, which were their countries.

All but one—the ambassador from Ulik, a hex that lay along the Equatorial Barrier. Ulik was a high-tech hex, but one with a harsh, desert environment. Its people were great reptiles, snakelike to five or more meters beyond the waist, with humanoid torsos to which were attached three pairs of muscular arms with broad hands, the bottom four on crablike ball sockets. Their heads were squarish, thick, and both males and females had huge walruslike mustaches. Egg-layers who nursed their young when hatched, to non-Ulik eyes the only difference between males and females was the breast between each pair of arms on the female.

Serge Ortega was a male, and an Entry. Long ago he had been a freighter pilot for the Com who, old and bored, had unknowingly opened up an ancient Markovian Well Gate that had transported him to the Well World, which had in turn transformed him into a Ulik. He liked being a Ulik; the Well, while never changing one's memories or basic personality, made you feel comfortable and normal as whatever creature it made of you. Thus, Ortega was still the scoundrel, pirate, freebooter, and manipulator he'd been before.

The Ulik usually lived for about a century; none had ever lived past a century and a half. Serge Ortega, however, was already over three hundred years old, and he looked about fifty. He had blackmailed a race capable of magic into giving him immortality, but that, too, had its price. Such spells were effective only inside the hex of the casters or in Zone. Since the only way out of Zone was back to the nonmagical Ulik, Ortega was a prisoner in the embassy, but an active one. Zone was his world and he made the most of it.

In his time there he'd foiled many plots, helped defuse several wars, combined hexes into effective alliances, and, by fair means or foul, learned from his bugs, blackmail, and agents pretty much everything that happened in the South. Data reached him in mountains of paper, in reports, computer printouts, and photographs. He lived in quarters behind his huge office, with its communications devices, computers, and other marvels giving him the data and the means of correlating it.

In his own way, by his own labors and unique position, he was the closest thing to a head of government the Southern Hemisphere had—a Chairman or coordinator. And for every favor done, eventually a favor was asked in return. Some liked him, some admired him, many hated and feared him—but he was there and everyone had almost begun to take him for granted. He was *de facto* Chairman of the Southern Hex Council, an informal body of ambassadors called by intercom when matters of extreme gravity, such as the long-dead wars, threatened them all.

And now he sat, coiled on his serpentine body, rocking slightly back and forth, looking things over.

One report among all the others caused him to pause. It was the Ambreza's annual report on Mavra Chang, the one item he hated to see.

Serge Ortega in his time, and always for what he believed to be the best of motives, had lied, cheated, stolen, and committed practically every other offense. Since he always believed he was working in a good cause—whether true or not—he regretted none of it, felt no pity or remorse.

Except in this matter.

His mind returned to the time a new satellite had suddenly appeared around the Well World. One ship, launched from it, had approached too close to the Well over hexes where the ship's technology just wouldn't work. The craft divided into nine modules, and each came down in a different hex. Sometime later a second ship, one not designed to break up, managed a dead-stick landing in the North, where the locals had shoved the passengers through Zone Gates to get them to the South where they, being carbon-based life, obviously belonged.

That Northern ship had carried one Antor Trelig, would-be Emperor of a new interstellar Rome controlled by a home-built miniature version of the Well World, and Ben Yulin, his engineer-associate and the son of the sponge syndicate's number-two man. Trelig was number one. Also on that ship had been Gil Zinder, the scientist whose incredible mind had actually solved the basic principles of the Well World without even knowing of the Well's existence. He had built the great self-aware computer, Obie. They had come disguised as innocent victims—something Obie had managed—and they were through the Well before their true identities had been revealed.

Gil's naïve and pudgy fourteen-year-old daughter, Nikki, had been in the second ship along with Renard, a rebellious guard. Both were hooked on the mind-destroying, body-distorting drug called sponge. And there was Mavra Chang.

He sighed. Mavra Chang. Feelings of guilt and pity arose whenever he thought of her, and he tried to think of her as little as possible.

With the Northern ship barred to them, some Well World nations had allied to seize the engine module in the South. The coldly inhuman Yaxa butterflies, the resourceful high-tech metamorphs of the Lamotien, and Ben Yulin, now a minotaur living in Dasheen's male paradise, had marched and killed and conquered. The froglike Makiem, the little satyrs of Agitar, who rode great winged horses and had the ability to store in their bodies and discharge at will thousands of volts, and the pterodactylic Cebu had marched and triumphed and killed in their own war. They were confident in Antor Trelig's ability to lead them back to New Pompeii and Obie.

All so long ago, he reflected.

He remembered Renard, the guard, cured of sponge by the Well when it turned him into an Agitar. How the man had rebelled when he found he was still serving his old master, Antor Trelig! He then sought the woman who had never given up the struggle to survive on this hostile world and had kept him alive until he was rescued.

Odd that Mavra Chang affected him so, Ortega thought. He had never met her, and quite possibly never would. But he owed her, and he could repay that debt only by inflicting misery. He was the one who had dispatched the small party to Gedemondas, high in the silent mountains, where the engine pods lay. Whoever reached them first would get the one thing the Well World had not the resources nor the skills to manufacture. The team consisted of two Lata, flying pixies, because they were friendly to him and he knew one well. Renard on his great pegasus Doma, and Mavra Chang, because, as a qualified pilot, she would be the only one able to recognize and evaluate the engines.

And she had completed her mission, he reflected, as he did every year when that report came by. She had witnessed the destruction of the great engines. Along the route, she was captured by fanatical great cats of Olborn. Their unique power was derived from six stones that somehow allowed them to turn their enemies into mulelike beasts of burden. Unfortunately they'd done a halfway job with Mavra before the others rescued her.

He felt a certain satisfaction that Olborn had been practically destroyed in the war, and its own leaders turned into little mules.

Some satisfaction, but not much: a ship lay intact to the north in far-off, unreachable Uchjin. Furthermore, Obie was very much alive and active, though currently held captive by the unwitting Well of Souls computer, which had concluded that Obie was to be its replacement, that a new master race had finally arisen. It kept trying to give Obie control of the master equations stabilizing all matter and energy in the finite universe. But that was like feeding the sum total of human knowledge to an ant—all at once. Obie just couldn't handle the input.

So the Well wouldn't let Obie go, and Obie could not even talk to the Well. That stalemate had been unbreakable for many years now.

But there *was* a way for Obie to break contact. Obie knew of it—and Serge Ortega knew, too. To do so would require a good deal of modification deep in Obie's core. But as long as Obie was tied up in the "defense" mode, it could not create its own technicians to go down there, for it couldn't open its own door. Only Trelig or Yulin knew the words to cancel the safeguards, for they alone created them—and the passwords were not in Obie's conscious circuits.

15

Ortega had considered, as had others, kidnapping Yulin or Trelig and hypnoing the code out of them. But both had undergone extensive hypno burns to lock the magic words away from everyone, even from themselves, until they were once again physically on New Pompeii.

And that thought brought him back to Mavra Chang. Like Yulin and Trelig, she was a qualified pilot. As a professional, she was the best of the three, and she understood the sophisticated systems of the downed ship and could possibly get it aloft. More important, she also knew the code Trelig used to get by the killer satellites of New Pompeii that still guarded it.

At first, Ortega had kept her under wraps and out of the Well because of the war. Then, when it all came apart in Gedemondas, there she was—thanks to the Olbornians a freak, a one-of-a-kind creature on a world with 1560 types of creature. And yet he still had to keep her from the Well, which would have cured her physical problems, because he had no say in what she would become. She might easily awaken as a creature under the control of a Trelig, or a Yulin, or some ambitious third party who suddenly realized what a prize it possessed. Or perhaps she'd turn into a water-being, unable to pilot when the need arose, or something that could not move or had no individuality.

There were too many variables.

So he did the only thing he could do. There was the awful possibility that Antor Trelig or Ben Yulin, or someone they could enlist, would find a way to the North—and a way through the diplomatic tangle—to get that ship moved to a high-tech hex and properly set up for a takeoff. Against that, he had to keep her under his control, in that wretched condition.

He had made life somewhat easier for her. He'd put her down in Glathriel, the hex of the primitive, tribal humans. It had a tropical climate, and was watched over by the friendly but wary Ambreza, who resembled large, cigar-smoking beavers. She had her own specially designed compound, and once a month a ship brought supplies in forms she could manage. He had also hypno-burned her, so that she considered her current form natural and normal.

Ortega had hoped for a solution to the Northern-ship problem long before now, hoped that it would be solved or that the ship would be destroyed. Neither had happened, however. He had condemned Mavra to life as a thing, not for the short period originally intended, but for a long, long time.

He took out the thick folder with her name on it to add the new brief form to it. As always, he couldn't help glancing through the file.

She had been born on a frontier world that had gone Com. Her parents had fought the conversion and been condemned. Only the tiny five-year-old Mavra, so small she was easy to smuggle out, had been rescued by friends of the family. They had surgically altered her appearance to resemble the Oriental features and coloration of her stepmother, the freighter captain Maki Chang. After a lonely eight-year childhood in space, she'd been abandoned on a primitive, savage world at thirteen when her stepmother was arrested. She had coped, becoming a beggar—by sixteen, the queen of the beggars—and totally self-sufficient.

She had been raised in a freighter, though, and craved a life in space. Trying to raise enough money to get out, to get to Pilot's School and earn a rating, she'd sold her body in spaceport dives. In due course, she'd met and married a spacer captain who made his real money at sophisticated burglary. He'd given her that life in space, a ship, a rating, and a career in burglary along with a thin veneer of culture. When sponge syndicate bosses killed her husband, tiny, beautiful Mavra Chang tracked down and killed them all, one by one. She then continued alone on her freighter and on her burglaries.

Because of that record, she was picked by a moderate Comworld to represent them at Trelig's unveiling of Obie's powers. Hired was the better word—she was

hired to get Nikki Zinder out, in order to break
Trelig's hold over the older scientist.

Trelig had run all the spectators through Obie,
giving them all horse's tails so they would be living
proof of his power. But Obie had also given Mavra
the means and methods to allow escape with Nikki.
She almost made it, getting away with Nikki, a ship,
and even the computer's formula for an arresting agent
that would break the sponge syndicate's stranglehold
on its addicts.

But Trelig had moved up the test, whereupon they
had all been translated to the Well World along with
New Pompeii, and there they crashed.

A tremendous tribute to her ancestors, Ortega
thought approvingly. She always coped with adversity,
never quit in the face of impossible odds, never admitted defeat—and she always came through.

But her life had been ten normal ones, and rough
as no one person should ever have to endure. No
wonder she was bitter, no wonder she was unable to
relate much to other people.

How Ortega longed to talk to her, to reveal to her
her true history and heritage, which he alone completely knew—but he couldn't. He couldn't be sure
of its effect on her, and he needed her to remain as
tough, nasty, and self-confident as she was. *She* needed
that strength to survive, and he would need it if he
ever needed her.

He checked the sheet.

"Subject was given annual check by Dr. Quozoni
13/12," it read. "Had minor skin and dysentery problems from not taking proper care of herself, easily
correctable. Although a balanced diet is mandated,
subject tends to obesity, apparently from unauthorized
foodstuffs. Her apparent obesity is aggravated by permanent curvature of the spine resulting from body
adjustments to the deformities and from the fact that
breasts and fat hang as dead weight. However, over-
weight is not considered serious enough to jeopardize
life as yet. Major organs in excellent shape considering the obesity, probably from the forced heavy ex-

ercise she gets when walking. Hearing has deteriorated with age, but normally and not seriously, considering that she started with above-normal acuity. Eyesight, which is not a serious factor considering her condition, is far above Type 41 norm at night but very poor in daylight, partially a result of her adopting a nocturnal schedule. Thankfully, aging has brought on near-sightedness, which does not warrant correction considering her three-meter maximum range due to head limitations.

"Mental state appears to be continuing in that odd new track. There have been no attempts at escape in the past eleven years, which had us worried; but she also seems to have developed a total alienation from humanity. She can no longer even conceive of herself as anything but what she is. To watch her one would swear that she is, indeed, a truly natural creature. Recently she has taken an abnormal interest in biology and genetic structure and has talked of founding a race. We find that optimistic, and yet psychologically and scientifically intriguing. Of course, she had herself sterilized at an early age, but this blossoming maternal interest and the continuing relationship between her and Joshi bears watching. One cannot but think of the possibilities of designing a part of one hex, either Glathriel or Olborn—which owes it to her—into an ecosystem in which such creatures as she would survive on their own. We are sufficiently indebted to her that we are looking into this."

Ortega looked away from the sheet, reflecting. Odd how she was changing, yet, somehow, still in character. Escape—even if it could be attained—was futile: where could she go and for how long could she survive on her own? So she'd turned to a different form of coping, a dream of founding a race of her own kind designed, like a minihex, for its physical requirements. If it could be done, Ortega decided, it would be.

He sighed, filed the report without reading the rest, and pulled out a communications device from a drawer with his middle right hand.

It was on an odd circuit, and so could not easily be

intercepted, he felt, by anyone else. The office itself was debugged daily, so he was confident about its security. The line went directly from his office across to the other side of Zone, to the embassy of Oolagash, deep in the Overdark Ocean.

The connection buzzed a number of times, and, for a moment, he felt that he'd picked the wrong time. But, finally, he heard a click, and a hollow, high-pitched voice answered him via a translator. What with the water, the connection, and the double translator, it sounded eerie, as though made by an electronic instrument, yet it was intelligible. He wondered what he sounded like to the Oolagash.

"Tagadal," said that voice.

Ortega smiled. "Tag? Ortega. I have a little ecology problem for you to run through Obie, and a genetic question, too."

"Fire away," replied Dr. Gilgam Zinder.

North Zone

LIKE ITS COUNTERPART IN THE SOUTH, THE NORTHern Hemisphere, with 780 noncarbon-based life forms, had its Zone and its own embassies and ambassadors. In all, 702 hexes maintained permanent or semipermanent representatives in Zone, and had their own interzone council with rotating chairmanship. Yet the North had more problems than the South, which, though it had races so alien from one another as to make identification difficult, had more of a sense of unity. The Markovians had been carbon-based, and they naturally devoted much of their energies to other forms also based on carbon.

But they couldn't overlook a bet. In their suicidal

project to find for their children the glory their fore-bears had missed by attaining a stagnant godhead, the Markovians could not afford to miss the slight chance that they were doomed because they were car-bon-based.

North Zone was the true experimenter's paradise. There were no rules or restrictions on the 780 North-ern hexes, and some of the life forms were so wildly alien that they could not even find common ground with one another. Such had been the way with the Uchjin, in whose nontech hex Trelig and Yulin had crashed. *They* had an ambassador on station—it was the only reason the refugees had made it to the South —but few could talk to them. Their utterances just didn't make sense; their frame of reference, concepts, and the like were so totally alien that it would have been impossible even to convey to them what the ship was or what it represented.

"No," however, translated quite well, even to the Northern races who had themselves tried to gain con-trol of the ship—and some in the North were fully as greedy and Machiavellian as others in the South—and they had really tried.

To no avail.

The creature standing in the Well Gate at North Zone did not belong there. It was large—over two meters, not counting the vast orange-and-brown spot-ted butterfly's wings now compactly folded along its back—and its shiny rock-hard body rested on eight rubbery black tentacles, each of which terminated in soft, sticky claws. Its face was like a human skull, jet black with small yellow half-moons making it a devil's mask; two feelers rose interminably from it, vibrating. Its eyes were velvet pads of deep orange, clearly mark-ing a visual system different from the common one of the South.

The Yaxa never felt comfortable in North Zone, fearing that a sprung seal or some overzealous con-trolling hand might admit whatever atmosphere boiled on the other side of that door. For lack of interest and proper equipment, this was as far as Southerners usually came.

The Well Gate would zip a Northerner to South Zone or the reverse, and that's what made traveling so frustrating: there was just no opening from either Zone to the outside world; only the Zone Gates provided transportation in and out of the hexes. And any Zone Gate, North or South, always brought one back immediately to his home hex.

This time the Yaxa wore no pressure suit, which was one thing that made it nervous. The other was what it was about to meet.

The Yaxa had been among the originators of the Wars of the Well that had ended so futilely, and they had never given up on the North. Once, long ago, a Northerner went through a Southern Zone Gate—and had come out in that Southern zone's hex. The evidence was irrefutable.

How?

The Yaxa had worked on that problem for years, with very little to go on. They knew the Northerner had been a symbiont called The Diviner and the Rel, who came from the Northern hex the translator reproduced as Astilgol—none of the Northern hex names really translated, but that's the way the sound always came out.

The Astilgol were interested in the ship; they had already tried to talk to the Uchjin, but failed like everyone else. Floating just off the ground, the Uchjin looked totally alien to any Southerner—just a long stream of glistening silver chimes suspended from a crystal bar with a series of tiny lights glowing atop it, like fireflies caught in a round bowl. Yet no bowl was visible—only the sense that one was there.

The Astilgol ambassador had been interested in the Yaxa's contacts; they were in the North, and the Yaxa controlled Yulin. They'd also listened to Trelig's Makiem, and to Ortega as well.

But they could not help with the basic problem: the Diviner, it seemed, had been born a bit of a mutant, able to tune in occasionally on the internal processes of the Well. Sometimes it could prophesy when the Well calculated probabilities on new input—but this was not common. Only three Diviners had been born in known history, and the one that journeyed south had never returned. It was the last.

Why had the Well allowed the Diviner and the Rel through? Nobody knew. The Well was a computer but not an entity; it didn't *decide* to let the Diviner through —somehow the fused creature had interacted with the Well's transport system in a way no other could.

The Yaxa had theorized about this for years. The solution had boiled down to how the Well classified a creature. It had always been assumed that this was determined from its physical makeup, but what if that wasn't so?

Had the Diviner's relationship to the Well somehow jammed the normal translation process? Or had the Diviner somehow simply informed the Well that it was a different kind of creature than it actually was? Did the Well recognize an individual by its self-image? Could the Well, then, be fooled? Had the Diviner said to the Well, then, be fooled? Had the Diviner said in the South, "I am an Azkfru," and wound up not in Astilgol but in Azkfru?

They'd tried some experiments using deep hypnos on other creatures to convince them that they were Yaxa. They'd done the hypnos well, but the creatures continued to pop out in their true hexes.

Northern races maintained some trade with the South. The translators, for example, were actually grown inside the Northern creatures in Moiush and traded for iron that the Moiush needed. Thus, some Northern races had Southern contacts, just as some Southern races cooperated with the North. Word gets around on any project after awhile.

Finally it even got to the Yugash.

They never manned their embassy at Zone; they were neither liked nor trusted; they apparently had nothing of value to trade, and they generally treated the other races as mere animals, beneath their notice. Their physical structure was just bonded energy.

Wild creatures of unimaginable shapes and sizes inhabited their crystalline hex; the Yugash *grew* an organism to order—and then they entered it in some way, possessed it, and controlled it completely.

Physical creatures were but tools to the Yugash, things to be used until they were broken or no longer useful. As natives of a high-tech hex they were aware of the spaceship in Uchjin; it had passed over them on the way down, but crashed three hexes away. Some of the Yugash had even risked traveling to Uchjin, although the surrounding races hated and feared them and made it difficult.

Then suddenly the Yugash appeared, for the first time in any memory, at North Zone. They received reports of the Southern wars and read them avidly. They too started working on the problem, for their agents had told them that, though they could grow a creature to fly the ship, there was no one in the North who understood its operation. It was too alien for even the Entries.

They had tenuous contacts with Trelig, Ortega, and Yulin, and that last had referred them to the Yaxa. The people of his own hex—mostly farmers—would have lynched him if they knew he still contemplated getting that ship.

Suddenly, it had all come together. Yaxa theoretical research with the potential the Yugash believed they needed.

The airlock door opened, and the Yugash walked in.

Floated in was a more apt term. The creature looked strange, almost invisible in the light. Suspended a good fifty centimeters above the floor, a series of horizontal and vertical lines formed what appeared to be a red-pencil outline of a great hooded cloak—with no one in it.

Even the Yaxa, whose vision had the best resolution of any on the Well, had trouble keeping the creature in focus. The creature might be very visible in total darkness, but almost any light, let alone the bright ones here, washed it out.

The Yugash seemed to nod, but said nothing. It was one of the few creatures for whom a translator was totally useless; there was no place to affix it, for the Yugash had no material being.

The creature floated slowly by the Yaxa and up to the blackness of the Well Gate. It turned, nodded again, and drifted into the Gate, sharply visible as a strange specter before it was swallowed up. The Yaxa followed, more nervous now than ever, and emerged from the South Zone Well Gate instantaneously.

The Yugash floated up to it, touched it. The Yaxa felt an eerie, uncomfortable tingling, but nothing else. It was suddenly chilled, stuffy, nervous. Blending into the Yaxa body, the Yugash had now vanished.

There were a few other creatures about in Zone, but none gave the Yaxa much notice. The huge butterflies were cold and aloof always, and they inspired fear in some others. Only another Yaxa would have noticed how awkward the creature seemed, how unsure of itself.

It entered the Yaxa embassy, almost bruising its wings on the doorway. Inside were the ambassador and several other Yaxa leaders—all females. The male of the species was groundbound, a soft, pulpy caterpillar designed for only one purpose, and it responded with abandon. The males were kept dormant until needed. The Yaxa female always ate her mate after.

The ambassador looked concerned. "There is something wrong?"

The newcomer stopped and wobbled unsteadily on four tentacles. Its voice was hard to understand, and it was unlike anything they had ever heard before.

"I am the Torshind of Yugash," it mumbled. "You must forgive me. I am still learning to use this body. In Yugash we grow the bodies we need, and they are of good crystals and bred to their tasks. Yours is an incredibly complex creature, and there is also a great deal of resistance from the host."

"Do you mean," one asked, "that you are a Northern creature currently occupying the body of our sister?"

The strange Yaxa nodded. "Yes. Will you please instruct the creature not to resist me so? We cannot complete this test until I am in complete control of the cranial area."

They all looked nervous, uncomfortable now, both from the implications of what they were seeing and hearing and from being called "creatures."

"Please!" asked the Torshind again. "Do so or one of two alternatives will result. I shall either have to abandon the body, or there will be permanent brain damage!"

That last got them. "Hypno!" one ordered, and soon a syringe to Yaxa requirements was produced.

The doctor, if that was what she was, looked uncertain. "You're sure this won't put *you* under, too?" she asked, worried. "And a total takeover—it's reversible?"

The Yaxa-Yugash nodded. "Totally. The creature will simply not be able to recall more than dimly the possession. Come! It is becoming more difficult!"

The syringe was inserted through a joint, and in a few minutes the jerking ceased. The Yaxa was in a deep hypnotic sleep. Suddenly it became animated. It rose on all eight tentacles confidently, flexing its wings and tentacles. It donned a Yaxa pressure suit.

"That is much better," said the Torshind. "I am in complete control now. I would have to spend several days in a body as complex as this to learn it all, but I think I can manage. Shall we go?"

They left, the whole party, and walked to the nearest Zone Gate. Everyone, including the Torshind, was tense.

The ambassador and the project leader entered the Zone Gate first, then the Yaxa-Yugash, followed by the rest.

In his office far down the corridor, Serge Ortega cursed. His monitors had told him everything except whether the experiment had worked. Was the Torshind now in Yaxa or in Yugash?

Only the Yaxa knew, but Ortega would fix that.

Glathriel

The Gedemondan, almost three meters high, of
white fur, with padlike legs and a dog's snout,
chuckles.

"But the true test of awesome power is the ability not to use it." He looks toward her and points
a clawed, furry finger.

"No matter what, Mavra Chang, you remember
that!" he warns sharply.

She feels puzzled. "You think I'm to have
great power?" she asks skeptically and a little derisively, reflecting the way she feels about such mys-
ticism.

"First you must descend into Hell," the Gedemondan warns her. "Then, only when hope is
gone, will you be lifted up and placed at the pinnacle of attainable power, but whether or not you
will be wise enough to know what to do with it or
what not to do with it is closed to us."

Vistaru, the Lata pixie challenges it. "How do
you know all this?" she asks.

The Gedemondan chuckles. "We read probabilities. You see, we see—perceive is a better word—
the math of the Well of Souls. We feel the energy
flow, the ties and bands, in each and every particle
of matter and energy. All reality is mathematics, all
existence—past, present, and future—is equations."

"Then you can foretell what's to happen,"
Renard the Agitar satyr points out. "If you see the
math you can solve the equation."

The Gedemondan sighs. "What is the square root
of minus two?" it asks smugly.

Mavra Chang awoke, the words of the snow-giant echoing as always in her ears. She'd dreamed that dream a thousand times since the actual event. How long ago? Twenty-two years, the Ambreza doctor had said.

She had been twenty-seven then; she was approaching fifty now. All those years, she thought, lying here on her cushions. A lifetime.

She stretched, and thought about it for a bit. About herself, how she had changed so much in the years.

She no longer thought about the time she'd been human. She knew they'd hypno-burned that impression into her twenty-two years before, but it had worn off, in time, with the dreams and the thoughts.

And, for a while, it had mattered. She remembered the Gedemondans, even if they'd made sure nobody else did—their power and wisdom, the way one of them had simply pointed a finger at the engine pods and they had toppled and exploded.

She remembered being captured by the Olbornians —great bipedal cats in ancient livery—and taken to their temple, where they had touched her extremities to that curious stone. But she couldn't remember what life was like before that.

Oh, she remembered her past, but somewhere, years before, something had snapped inside her. She remembered that part of her life only in a lopsided, distorted way: everyone she remembered looked like her—the beggars, the whores, the pilots, her husband. Mentally, she saw them all as the kind of creature she had become—even though she knew she was a freak and that the people of her past did not resemble her present form.

That was right after the last time she'd tried to escape, to run for the border, to somehow find out what the hell the Gedemondan meant.

Doing so didn't seem so important, either, anymore.

She had brooded and dreamed and sunk into a tremendous, suicidal depression after that, and then the change had come over her. She didn't understand it, but she accepted it.

On a world with 1560 races, there was room enough for one more, a Chang, if you will.

And Joshi had come along just after that, as if in answer to this new feeling inside her.

She rolled over and got up unsteadily. It was no simple task, yet she'd done it so often it had become second nature. She stretched again, and her long hair swung down over her face. She didn't mind that it reached the floor both in front and behind her ears; no more than she minded that her horse's tail was now a great broom, trailing behind her.

She walked over to a low, two-meter-long mirror, and turned her head, shaking it a bit to clear the hair from her eyes.

You've changed in more ways than one, Mavra Chang, she told herself.

The creature that stared back was a strange one indeed to all but her and Joshi. In fact, it had been years before she even asked for a mirror. Not until after she'd changed.

First, remove the limbs from the torso of a small woman; then turn it face down, elevating the hips about a meter off the ground, the shoulders about eighty centimeters. Now attach a perfectly proportioned pair of mule's front legs on the shoulders. Add two hind legs, also a mule's, but keep it all "human," perfectly matched to the hairless orange torso—except for the hooves on all four feet. Replace the woman's ears with meter-long jackass ears of human skin. The result is even more impressive when one realizes that the woman was originally under 150 centimeters, head and legs included, so that the ears are actually longer than the torso. Now, as a final touch, add a horse's tail at the base of the spine. The last was a gift from Antor Trelig's New Pompeii party so long ago. Thus had Mavra Chang been transformed by the cats of the Olborn.

She didn't worry about her hair blocking her vision; at maximum head lift she could see less than three meters ahead, anyway. She had learned to rely less on her eyes than on other organs, the ears in particular.

Although they gave no better hearing than the originals, they were independently controllable from small muscles in the scalp. These she used as an insect would use its feelers.

She walked to the outer, roofed part of the compound, lowered her face to the ground, and grabbed a sheet of leather in her teeth. She pulled it back, to reveal a crude leather bag, which she then lifted with her teeth. The Ambreza kept her teeth in good shape.

Her neck mucles were the only aid she needed to lift the heavy sack. Placing a foreleg on either side of the bag, she worked at it with nose and mouth until it was wide enough open for her face. Inside was chopped cooked meat, cold but still fresh. She ate as a dog might. Afterward, she managed to close the bag, replace it in the hole, and cover it again.

The Ambreza left nice little tabbed plastic bags of tasteless trash every month. But she'd never accepted that. That routine made her dependent on others, and she had not stood it for long.

She walked over to the small fresh-water spring that ran through the compound on its way to the nearby Sea of Turagin. She lowered her face into the water and drank deeply. Its coldness refreshed her completely.

No dependencies, not for long, she thought with satisfaction. The dominant culture in this hex was primitive human. The natives were a dark people with Negroid facial features but compact build. Their hair was straight and black like her own. Originally, the locals panicked themselves with tales that the Goddess of Animals lived in her compound and that they would be turned into animals if they so much as caught sight of her.

And, of course, for quite a while she wanted no one, preferring to sulk in self-pity. But, eventually she would leave the compound, sometimes for the beach where she would prop herself up so she could see the magnificent starfield. Eventually she also explored inland, but always by night to minimize possible problems. Except for the mosquitoes and other pests she no longer felt, there were no predators that could bother her, and the natives feared the dark.

But, of course, she had eventually run into a couple anyway, and the first encounter was a disaster. They knew immediately what they saw—the very animal described in their tales—and it so terrified them that one actually *did* drop dead on the spot and the other became insane.

The most powerful voodoo is the one one's mind believes in, she found.

And so, at first, she was cautious. Having a translator meant she could understand them and they her—although the device added an eerie tone to her voice.

Just the right effect. Ambreza-like, but not Ambreza. Something else: The Goddess!

And, of course, finally she announced to the local natives that if they served her she would show herself once without their suffering any ill effects. When she eventually walked into the firelight, ghostly and eerie, they did what she had hoped. They fell on their faces and worshipped her.

But, she warned them, to tell the Ambreza was to risk her wrath. Even to tell other tribes would bring down upon them a fate worse than death. Her tribe had kept the faith. They were the People of the Goddess, and they reveled in that knowledge.

Mavra demanded offerings, and offerings she got. Hoards of food dumped at the door of the compound. Tobacco, too. Rare on the Well World, the substance was much prized; the Ambreza took most of the crop, of course—but now she had some to trade with the monthly supply ship for things she wanted more than the now largely unneeded provisions.

For tobacco, the ship's crews would bring what she asked. Since Glathriel was a nontech hex, machines were out; but books, geographies, and grammars were useful. She learned to read several related languages and waded through everything in their published histories.

She was, by her eleventh escape attempt, probably the greatest living expert on Well World life, geography, and geology. And she reread the books frequently, turning pages with nose and tongue until the volumes were almost unreadable. Even after she changed she continued to read voraciously; it was one of the few activities that kept her properly stimulated.

She also gave native hunters advice on game traps, which increased their yields, and suggestions for the manufacture of new nontech weapons. The Glathriel, of course, worshipped her all the more. The Ambreza became suspicious, but there was little they could do. The situation had gone too far.

Then, one night just after she changed, she noticed a strange glow in the direction of the village. Positioning herself nearby, she watched as one of the huts burned and people screamed. They got only one out alive, a young boy with massive burns on hands and feet.

She ordered him brought to the compound and launched one of her little rockets to signal the Ambreza. More Goddess magic.

And the Ambreza doctor had come, and looked at the boy.

"There's no hope," he told her. "I can get him to a hospital, yes, but not in time to do any good. He's horribly burned. I might save his life, but never his limbs, and he'll bear those tremendous scars his whole life as a cripple. Best I put him out of his misery."

Something rose in her, looking at the burnt and pitiful boy of ten or eleven. "That's *not* a pet to be put out of its misery!" she'd shouted to the beaverlike creature. "That's a *person!* If you won't save him for yourself, save him for me!"

She didn't know why she'd said that, it just seemed *right,* somehow. The helpless, disfigured boy in some way reminded her of her own differences, and she took the Ambreza's comments personally.

She accompanied the boy and the doctor to Ambreza and saw him later, still sedated in a high-tech hospital. He was a mass of scars, and both hands and feet had been amputated.

They argued with her. Ordinarily they wouldn't

have paid any attention, but the Ambreza felt a special guilt and a special responsibility for Mavra Chang.

"But what can he do?" they had asked. "The tribe would kill him. *You* can't help him. Make sense!"

And, suddenly, the solution had risen, unbidden, in her brain and come out. Such intuition was uncharacteristic of her; it was the change.

"He's a male!" she'd shouted back. "If the Olbornians still have those yellow stones, take him there! Touch his shattered arms until they change, then his twisted legs until they change! Make him a Chang like me, and give him to me!"

They were stunned. They didn't know what to do. So they did what she had asked, with a little push from their psychiatric technicians and a lot of nudging from Serge Ortega.

They hypno-burned his tortured brain clear of memories and then adjusted him for his new existence, with Mavra doing the instructing. She was like a maniac as she went at it, but the Ambreza indulged her because they owed her something and because, for the first time, she had a passionate interest beyond escape.

Joshi was the first step in the project that had been forming in her mind, a project she was now frantic to live to see: the establishment of their own independent little world.

He wasn't as bright as she by a long shot. That is not to say that he was stupid or retarded, merely average. She taught him to speak Confederation, in which she still thought, and to read Ambreza and the old Glathriel tongue, no longer used but still enshrined in prewar books maintained by the Ambreza. Most of his knowledge had to be force-fed; the studies didn't really interest him, and he tended to forget things he didn't use, as most people will.

Their relationship was an odd but close one; she was both wife and mother to him, he her husband and son. The Ambreza, who followed her activities off and on, believed that she had to play the dominant role,

33

that she had to feel and actually be a little superior to one close to her.

Joshi stirred behind her. It was getting dark, their natural time to be active established by long routine. The helpless ten-year-old had grown and matured; he was larger than she, and almost coal black, although the pinkish scars of the fire marked him all over.

He came up to her. They had been careful in transforming him; too long an exposure to that Olbornian stone made one a docile mule in all respects.

In some ways, despite the scars and darker coloring, he resembled her—same type of legs, ears, and downward angle to the body. But he had no tail, of course, and his hair was quite different. Some of it had been burned away in the fire, but he still had a fairly full head and a manelike growth down the spine to the waist. He was also fat. The native diet was not the world's best balanced. His scraggly beard was tinged with white, although he was still in his twenties.

They were used to each other. Finally, after drinking, he asked her, "Going down to the beach? Looks like a clear night."

She nodded. "You know I will."

They left the compound and cantered down the trail. The sound of the pounding surf grew very loud.

"Must've been a storm out there," he remarked. "Listen to those breakers!"

But far-off storm or not, the sky was mostly clear, obscured here and there by isolated wispy clouds that lent an almost mystical atmosphere to the scene.

He lay down in the sand, and she settled more or less atop him, propping herself up enough so she could see the stars.

In many ways, she had changed less than she thought. She had genuine affection for Joshi, and he for her. But Joshi was, in the end, part of her project, one designed as a means to gain independence from others. Dependency she hated more than anything else. She had never been dependent for very long on anyone, and the state to which they'd reduced her was intolerable.

But her brain had compensated for most of that; if she lived long enough, one day it would redress the balance.

But it was only coping. Mentally and emotionally she had acclimated to her physical condition and limitations, but never had she abandoned the stars, the great swirling gulfs that shined so brightly all around her on nights like this that you could almost leap forward into them. So close, so visible—and yet, so far.

That was where she belonged, and she never gave up.

First you must descend into Hell. Then, only when hope is gone, will you be lifted up and placed at the pinnacle of attainable power . . .

But hope was never gone, she thought to herself. Not while she lived. Not while the stars shined so.

Joshi turned his head upward a little, looking out at the northeastern horizon.

"Look!" he said. "You can see your moon!"

She lowered her gaze toward the horizon. It was there, a large silvery ball looking unreal and out of place, like a huge chunk of silver.

Surely they're all long dead now, she told herself. All but Obie—poor, isolated Obie. The computer had been much more than any self-aware model she'd ever known. Obie was the son of Gil Zinder, and regarded himself that way. His own tragedy was that self-aware personality; how lonely he must be, she thought.

Lonely. That was an odd term for her to use, she thought. All her life it had been her normal condition, except for those few years of marriage. And yet, she was better off than Obie now. She had Joshi, and the tribe.

After a while the salt spray from the incoming tide started to reach them, and clouds obscured the view, so they got up and headed back to the compound.

"The *Trader*'s due in some time this week, isn't it?" he asked her.

She nodded. "I hope they brought the bio references I asked for, and those books on seine fishing techniques, too."

He sighed. "The fishing stuff I can see—for the tribe, anyway. Got to keep the faithful faithful and all that. But what's all this interest in bio? You know we're a race of two, sterile. If we weren't, we'd have had some by now."

She chuckled. The logistics of that had been a real tangle, since their sexual equipment was not in the best places, but it had been accomplished. She wondered whether her renewed appetite for sex after so many years of abstinence was due to middle age.

"Well, I'm sterile, anyway," she responded. "Even if I weren't, we'd have Glathriel children. But there may be ways, somewhere. I've seen crazier experiments in genetic manipulation. It might be too late for me, though; I'm getting too old for that sort of thing."

He snuggled up to her. "You're not too old for *me*. A little frazzled and fat and big-assed, but I like 'em that way."

She snorted mock-contemptuously. "You just say that because I'm the only woman you've got. Besides, I know about that sacrificial virgin bit you've been working on the tribe."

He laughed. "I had a good teacher," he pointed out. Then he grew serious. "But I'm not a Glathriel. Not any more. Not ever that I can remember. I'm a Chang and you're a Chang and nothing can alter that."

That pleased her. They went back into the sleeping compound together, and Mavra felt confident that, before she died, once again she would control her own destiny and manage her own fate.

But destiny had always controlled Mavra Chang.

Dasheen

BEN YULIN WAS NERVOUS. YAXA WEREN'T VERY welcome in Dasheen, not since the days of the wars, when peaceful, agrarian Dasheen had been dragged into the Northern campaign by his presence and the Yaxa's insistence.

The Dasheen were minotaurs; they numbered about eight hundred thousand at the moment, only eighty thousand of whom were males. Their large, thick-bodied, muscular shapes were coated with fine fur; their heads, those of streamlined bulls: immense, almost neckless, with short snouts, broad pink noses, wide brown eyes, and tremendous curved horns.

From the males' view, the only worm in Dasheen's apple was the fact that Dasheen bulls lacked the ability to digest calcium directly, causing a deficiency that could only be counteracted by the milk of the females.

The Yaxa had arrived at the great farm unannounced, panicking the cows. Its great wings cast a tremendous shadow across the fields of oats and wheat, like some great, multicolored predator. It landed near the main house—a huge structure that included silos, storage facilities, quarters for Yulin's 117 wives and daughters, and his own quarters.

It was not that he'd been totally out of contact with the Yaxa. But such meetings were usually carried out surreptitiously, with him going to a neutral high-tech hex to test his theories, or arranging a rendezvous in Zone.

Yulin calmed down his family and went to meet the Yaxa.

The great butterfly, impassive as always, seemed to

bow slightly. Yulin motioned for it to enter his own living quarters, and it did, clearing the doorway with some difficulty. Yulin took his seat in a broad rocking chair and waited for the creature to speak.

"I am Racer," the Yaxa said, using its nickname. Their names were untranslatable, so they generally adopted and stuck to translatable nicknames when dealing with others.

Ben Yulin nodded. "Well, welcome, Racer. But isn't it a little risky coming here like this? I mean, I know the border's not far from here, but I doubt if you could avoid being seen. There will be a lot of questions."

"What I have to say is much too important to keep. Zone itself is far too risky for it, and there wasn't time to get you out plausibly. The questions may not matter, anyway, when you hear what I have to say."

"I'm listening," he said, a growing feeling of unease mixed with the excitement rising within him. He suspected he knew why the Yaxa had come.

"We have placed Yaxa in a Northern hex. We can place anyone there now—with difficulty, but with complete certainty."

A thrill shot through him, but it was tempered by his engineer's mind. Like them, he'd worked on the problem for many years to no avail.

"How is it possible?" he asked.

"A Northern energy creature, the Yugash, grows crystalline creatures tailored to its needs and then operates them by entering the creatures' bodies and controlling them," Racer explained. "Finally a Yugash, who are high-tech, got together with us. They, like us, thought that the Well used mind-set rather than physical form to regulate transfer between Zone and hex gates. We allowed a Yugash called the Torshind to possess a Yaxa completely while the thought processes of the Yaxa were heavily sedated. The Yaxa body entered the Yaxa embassy Zone Gate—but walked out in Yugash!"

Yulin thought about it. "You mean these things can

take over your body? And the Well switches them—and whatever body they're in—to Yugash?"

"It is so. A bit unnerving, but, thankfully, they cannot enter hexes in the South. The Well is called the Well of Souls for good reason—it recognizes you by your mind, not your form. We firmly believe that we can now move a party of our choosing to Yugash, only three hexes, straight line, from where you crashed in Uchjin."

The news was incredible. He could hardly believe it—there had to be a fly in the ointment somewhere, and he thought of one immediately.

"What's to prevent these creatures from not just letting us go once they take us over?" he asked cautiously. "I've seen enough Well World life to know that my own people's legends of centaurs and mermaids and ghosts were more than racial memory—some of those creatures must actually have gone to the home world of the humans in the early days. There are also legends of people being possessed by demons. I can't but wonder if the Yugash . . ." He left the uneasy thoughts incomplete, but the Yaxa got his point.

"We think you're probably right," Racer agreed. "Surveys of many Entries have indicated this possibility, and the stories are remarkably similar. It's entirely possible that Yugash roam in many areas of space, the descendants of those who occupied the bodies of prototype colonists leaving the Well eons ago. However, we have pretty well determined that, while a Yugash can control your body, it cannot read your mind. Thus, for lack of knowledge, it still could not fly the ship, nor could it gain the means of entering Obie."

Yulin nodded. *That* was a relief. But practical problems remained. "I'd still feel better if we could find some way to be in control of ourselves at the critical point, when we're inside Obie. The old legends mentioned ways of warding off evil spirits. If the legends of the spirits are based on fact, then the protective spells probably are, too."

"We are ahead of you," the Yaxa assured him.

"We have compared the legends of many Entry races for common factors, and, more important, we wanted to know why none of the six hexes surrounding Yugash were open to their takeover. We think we have found it—a common factor. First, protective amulets of some sort were always worn—though a few were vegetable matter, the ones that were not were frequently made of copper or a copper alloy. We checked into this, and, indeed, in all the hexes surrounding Yugash we found enormous quantities of copper, copper oxide, or copper sulfide, either in the physical composition of the creatures or in the atmosphere itself. *And there is no copper at all in Yugash!*"

Ben Yulin's bovine face could not smile, but satisfaction was evident there, and relief.

"But there's still the political problems," he pointed out. "The Uchjin will block any attempt to move the ship, and, besides, we don't have the means of doing so."

"We're working on that," the Yaxa assured him. "I doubt if we can ever get to the Uchjin, but between the Yugash and a Uchjin neighbor, the Bozog, we may have the means to seize the ship by force. The Bozog have the methods to move it, and their high-tech hex could be the launch site. The price would be their inclusion in our little party, of course, and they are not a very trustworthy race. We recently learned they have also contacted Ortega and Trelig. They will work with the first group to reach the ship."

Ben Yulin exhaled slowly. "So it's to be a race, is it? But, tell me, why didn't the Bozog just swipe the ship themselves?"

"Because they have no way of flying it," the Yaxa snapped irritably. "To the first one who provides the methods, they will provide the means."

Yulin considered this. "The logistics? Air supplies, food, and the like?"

"Already being quietly constructed," Racer told him. "And with the Torshind's help, we are mapping the best route there. It will be longer and more dangerous than the direct route, but it will keep us basically in high-tech and semitech hexes so the breathing apparatus and life-support systems tailored for this mission will operate." The Yaxa hesitated for a moment, considering its next questions carefully.

"Our biggest doubt," it went on, "is you. Can you still pilot after all these years? Can you get by Trelig's robot sentinels after such a long passage of time? And can you open that computer?"

Yulin took in what the Yaxa meant and thought about it seriously.

"As to piloting, I'm rusty, sure, but the system's basically automated. It's a matter of knowing what to push in what sequence. I think I can handle that, as long as there's no fancy stuff or crash landing required. As to getting into the computer—oh, I'm sure of that. And as long as I have eyes, fingers, and a voice, I can control it. The sentinels present a hairier problem. Of course, Trelig never knew it, but I ran the problem through Obie for my own benefit—that is, I think, how he knew which signals to give to Mavra Chang—and got the code. It's based on books in Trelig's New Pompeii library. We'd have to work out a long computer problem—I know the titles involved, but there are fifty-seven key ones and the thing was changed daily on an oddball progression. A little hypnosis should bring them back clearly. But— twenty-two years' worth. That's where either Trelig or Chang would have the advantage. They'd be 100 percent sure, we'd be about 90 percent."

The Yaxa nodded with its body. "It is sufficient. I gather you do not wish to reach an agreement with Trelig?"

"Good God! No!" Yulin shouted, then got hold of himself. "Never—you don't realize the depths to which that man's capable of sinking. I do."

"It will take about two months to get the hardware built and tested," the Yaxa said. "During that time, others will not be idle. Ortega already *has* the hardware—he's had it for years. And he may know more than any of us. Radio signals of a strange type, directed toward New Pompeii when it is visible, have been intercepted coming from some point near the Overdark Ocean. We have been unable to decipher them or get any idea as to what they contain. But it is certain that similar signals have come back from the satellite. *Someone* is talking with that computer!"

Yulin was aghast. And yet, it made sense, somehow. Obie *did* have broadcast capability, put in so that it could be remote-controlled from space when Trelig's big projects started.

"But they still won't be able to get him out of 'defense' mode," he pointed out.

"If it's Ortega, he wants the thing destroyed, not used," Racer retorted. "It's too great a risk! And the Yugash are a bunch of freebooting anarchists. If the Torshind can do it for us, some other Yugash might get ideas and contact that Ulik Ortega. Suddenly, after all this time, every second presses, works against us."

Yulin considered this. "But Ortega is by nature conservative," he pointed out. "He won't move until he's absolutely ready if he's sure he's ahead of us. The solution is simple—kill the Chang girl before he picks her up and gets her to a Zone Gate."

"Ahead of you," assured the Yaxa.

Glathriel

IT WAS A SMALL ROWBOAT, WITH THREE OCCU-pants, though the two straining at the large oars bore a marked resemblance to a cloudy sky and could only made out with difficulty. At the bow, looking into the gloom, was a tiny creature easier to see. A little owl-faced monkey, a Parmiter from the northwest, peered anxiously toward the dark shore.

"You sure we're far enough up from that compound

and those villages so that nobody will see us?" a deep voice behind the Parmiter asked.

"I'm sure, Grune," the Parmiter replied in its squeaky tones. "The natives around here are pretty scared of the dark, and they light torches and fires to ward it off. As for the others, well, you saw the pictures. We'd almost have to beach *on* them for them to see us."

That seemed to satisfy Grune. "Getting near the beach," it said. "Hear the surf?"

"Let it carry us in now," cautioned the Parmiter, "but keep at the ready. You too, Doc. It won't do to crack up on the beach. We have to get back out to the ship with her, you know."

Doc sighed. "I just don't understand why we bother. I mean, it'd be simple enough to kill her—and these primitive places are great pickings. They grow tobacco here, you know. Know what that's worth over near the Overdark?"

The Parmiter got upset. "Keep your mind on the job, Doc! For this job, they're paying fifty times what we've made in the last two years, but it's got to be a cinch! None of that petty-robbery business with my double-jointed hips! This is the big time!"

When they reached the beach, two large ill-defined shapes jumped into the water and grabbed the boat, pulling it onto the sand, to where the beach met the underbrush. For a very short time the big creatures were fully visible—long lizards with sharp, horny shields around their heads and tough, leathery skins. And then they started to fade again, automatically adjusting their skin coloration to the background. They pulled a camouflage-mottled tarp over the small boat and left it at the edge of the beach. In the dim light one would have to stumble over the thing to notice it, and they didn't intend to be there by morning.

Carefully, the threesome walked down the beach, the little Parmiter hopping atop Doc's head just in front of the horny guard plate.

The Parmiter reached into its marsupial pouch and

brought out its gas gun, checking it for pressure and load.

"Everybody got their filters in?"

Joshi grabbed a meter-long match from a large compartment with his teeth and struck it with a quick motion of his head, making sure that his long ears were well out of the way. Carefully he touched the burning end to a small pot filled with a foul-smelling liquid, and it burst into flame, lighting up the interior of the compound. He then dipped the match into the sandy soil, extinguishing it, and pulled on a long rope, raising the burning pot until it was high enough to spread its light. Then, rope still in his teeth, he walked around the post supporting the pot a few times and looped the end around a little nail twice. It held.

Mavra never touched fire because her long hair was too vulnerable; but he, born in fire and scarred by it, had no such fears.

They began cleaning up the compound. Their supply ship, the *Toorine Trader,* was due in sometime the next day—the hour varied, but it always came on the right day, sometime between dawn and dusk.

Mouth-held brooms swept the wood floors and smoothed out the sand in the outer areas of the compound. Looking at Mavra and Joshi in isolation, one would have thought they were helpless, pitiful creatures; but at work they seemed normal, natural, and able to do almost anything.

True, they depended on others to make the matches, the pots, and many other necessities—but so did everyone depend on others to some degree. Once Mavra Chang had worn clothing and used sophisticated gadgetry, but she could never have made those clothes or built those gadgets. She was once a spaceship pilot, but she could never have built the spaceship nor fueled and provisioned it. She had sought those who could and paid for what she'd needed, just as she used the tobacco stores to pay for what was needed in Glathriel.

Suddenly her ears caught some odd sounds. "Listen!" she hissed to Joshi. "Do you hear anything?"

Joshi stopped and cocked a large ear. "Sounds like somebody coming up the beach," he replied, puzzled and curious. "Somebody big, too. You don't suppose the *Trader* got in early?"

She strained, shaking her head slowly. "I don't think so. I know all of them well, their steps and sounds."

"Not Ambreza, either," he said. "I don't think I heard anything like it. They're sure trying to be quiet about it, too, aren't they?"

She nodded. Old instincts, unused and unneeded these twenty-two years, began to return. There was something wrong here. Something unpleasant was up; she was sure of it.

"Want to fire a distress flare?" Joshi whispered, catching her mood.

She shook her head again. "Takes too long for the Ambreza to get here," she responded in a tone so soft it was almost a wisp of breath.

"Whoever or whatever it is is just outside the door now," he pointed out, moving so close to her that he merely had to mouth the words into her long ears.

"If they get in, escape through the stream gate," she told him. "I don't think anybody will anticipate that."

He nodded. They edged as quietly as possible into the shadows.

"I wish we could risk putting that light out," she hissed. "Wait—see if you can unwrap the rope and hold it," she suggested. "Anybody coming in will have to pass right under the pot. Drop it and the place would be splashed with burning oil."

He nodded and carefully undid the rope from the nail.

"Help me!" cried a wailing, plaintive voice just outside, a voice much too small for the creature or creatures they'd sensed. "Please! Somebody help me!"

Joshi couldn't talk with his mouth full of rope, and he mumbled something.

Mavra caught the idea. "A trick to draw us out," she whispered. "So its big friend or friends can grab

45

us. Damn! I wish I knew who it was and why they were doing this."

She looked around, spotted a roof support that had long needed attention. She had intended to have the *Trader* crew shore it up the next day, but now it might come in handy. She had a mule's hind legs; mules had a mean kick, and so did she. She considered just where to hit the bottom post so the falling roof wouldn't also catch her.

"Help me! Please help me!" the voice, so pitiful and sincere, repeated.

Quickly she whispered her plan to Joshi. Head turned, mouth full of rope, he didn't risk even a nod, but he got the idea. He tapped his right foreleg three times. Younger than Mavra, Joshi had better hearing than she did. Mavra understood. Three of them. Two big, one little by the sounds. They had underestimated the Chang race.

There was a crawling sound. The little one was crawling up to the door flap, and, now, they watched it slowly open inward, top hinge squeaking slightly. A strange little creature crawled in, legs dragging behind as if broken. Mavra knew from her Well World studies that this was a Parmiter—a Parmiter a hell of a long way from home, two or three thousand kilometers, at least.

The legs really *did* look useless, and the thing was a truly pitiful sight. For a moment the Changs almost doubted their suspicions, and no noises whatsoever marked the larger creatures they'd heard.

The Parmiter looked up at them, genuine surprise in its face. The creatures were very strange-looking indeed, even if it had studied purloined drawings and photographs. They looked so *helpless*.

It glanced up after noticing that Joshi held a rope in his teeth. Its beady little eyes followed the rope, through pulleys and across the way, until, almost above it, they arrived at the pot of burning oil.

"Holy shit!" The Parmiter screamed. It jumped up, quickly drawing an odd pistol from a natural pouch.

At that, the parmiter's two companions decided not

to waste any more time on subtlety. They hit the log walls of the compound on the run. There was a tremendous shudder, and the logs gave a little, but not much. Mavra screamed "Hold it!" to Joshi and ran straight at the Parmiter, who suddenly felt itself trapped.

It raised the gas gun but she leaped, coming down on top of him, all sixty-six kilos of her landing directly atop the fifteen-kilo Parmiter, stunning it.

"*Ulg!*" cried the Parmiter, as all the air in its body was suddenly squeezed out. The pistol fell from its grasp.

Doc and Grune hit the wall a second time, then a third. And that did it. Not only did the wall splinter and give way, but it collapsed the unstable half-roof as well.

As they lumbered into the compound yard, Joshi released the rope.

Mavra rolled as no one would have believed possible and got back on her feet. "The stream!" she screamed to Joshi, and he turned.

The boiling pot landed directly on the back of one of the great lizards, which bellowed terrifyingly in its sudden agony and rolled over, tumbling the other lizard, too.

Fed by the dry straw that was all over, the flames ignited the collapsed roof of the compound.

With tremendous speed, Joshi and Mavra jumped into the icy stream and, trying not to slip, walked along its pebble-strewn bottom to the forest outside.

Inside the compound, the Parmiter gasped. It was sure a couple of bones were *really* broken now. Blood trickled from a corner of its mouth. It looked around, stunned.

"Let's get out of here!" it screamed to its companions, one of whom was still groaning in agony from its burns. "If the natives get here with their spears and bows, we've had it!"

They had not survived so long following so crooked a path to let injury or failure trap them. The Parmiter, with difficulty, jumped on the unburned lizard and the two dashed out of there, fast—followed, almost immediately by the injured lizard.

Breathing hard, Mavra and Joshi stopped and turned toward the compound. They could see the fire's glow, but it seemed to be localized. They watched as the two great shapes dashed out onto the beach, and they saw that while one seemed almost to blend into the beach, hard to see, the other had big dark spots on it that made it easy to trace.

"What the hell is going on here?" Joshi gasped.

She shook her head. "I don't know. But it's the end of *our* world, that's for sure."

"What do you mean?" he asked, genuinely puzzled. *"They* won't be back."

"Oh, yes they will," she retorted. "Them or somebody worse. They weren't just pirates, Joshi. They landed here just to get us—kill, kidnap, I don't know what. But they were pros. They wouldn't go after us with a village full of cured tobacco just a little ways off. Somebody's put a price on my head."

He shook his head unbelieving. "But—why?"

"The only reason I can think of is that somebody's finally figured out the way to that Northern spaceship, and they're eliminating the competition," she replied in a strange, coldly professional tone he'd never heard in her voice. He was experiencing the true Mavra Chang for the first time, and she bewildered him.

But her eyes were shining. After all these years— the great game was on again, the game she was born to play.

"Fire's already down, probably almost out," he noted, uncomfortable. "Want to see what we can salvage?"

"We'll keep away, spend tonight here in the bushes," she responded, tone still businesslike but with that same excited undertone.

"The natives—" he began, but she cut him short.

"Won't come close on Ship's Day, no matter what. *You* know that." If they did, they would risk the wrath of the Ambreza.

"What about the Ambreza?" he pressed, trying to

find some way to return to the comfort of his old situation. It was all he'd known since the fire that scarred him.

"No flares were fired, so they're not alerted," she pointed out. "If they don't have a random patrol in this area they might not find out about what happened until it's too late."

He looked at her strangely. "Too late for what?"

"I haven't tried to escape in so many years they take it for granted now," she pointed out. "No tight watches any more. But even though I long ago gave up on the idea, I always kept a trove, just in case. You know that. The dried tobacco in the back shed and the little gold bars I've collected over the years by bartering the stuff through the *Trader*."

He nodded. "I always thought that was all it was for —petty bribes. I never thought—"

"Stay alive, think of everything," she said evenly. "Now, if we're lucky, our little bank account there will buy us a smuggle on the *Toorine Trader*."

The *Trader* arrived in early morning. Mavra and Joshi could see its sails as it rose from the clear horizon, great masts holding weathered white clouds.

It was hardly the only ship on the Sea of Turagin, but it was one of only six packet-boats to make a complete circuit, servicing all the hexes who cared to, or needed to, get trade and transportation. It was a grand ship, almost a hundred meters long, made of the finest copper-clad hardwood. The crew would have preferred steel, but that proved too heavy for fast movement under sail.

It was a three-master, with odd bowsprit and gunwales through which a wicked-looking cannon could peer if needed. But its central housing also bore twin black smokestacks over an engine, which, in all but nontech hexes, could power huge twin screws in the rear. Everod, the sea hex adjoining the coast of Glathriel, was nontech; its denizens, huge clamlike beings with masses of tendrils piercing their shells, were deep-water types, and there was never any real contact between them and the land-dwellers, nor did they seem to mind the surface commerce that the *Trader* represented. In fact, they, too, used the *Trader,* placing orders with its Zone broker and having what they needed weighted and dropped to them.

The *Trader*'s crew of thirty-four was an amalgam of Turagin races. Batlike Drika stood the night watches and occasionally scouted ahead for storms. The scorpions of Ecundo climbed her rigging deftly and managed the sails with claws of amazing versatility. The captain resembled a great tangled ball of nylon twine, out of which spindly limbs appeared as needed.

They took in sail, and stood to, anchoring on a reef that was marked with yellow buoys. Not good for business to anchor in deep water and maybe conk an Everod on the shell.

The longboat was lowered off the stern, and large oars raised and lowered in cadence as it headed toward the compound.

The first mate, a shiny triangular Wygonian, whose six tentacles looked like huge, furry pipe cleaners, scanned the shore through his small stalk-mounted eyes, occasionally muttering instructions to his muscular Twosh oarsmen. When he finally noticed the crushed wall of the compound, he shouted to the oarsmen to slow. A few wisps of smoke still rose from the interior, and he knew something was wrong.

Mavra and Joshi trotted onto the beach just upshore from the longboat and walked to the landing. The sight of them put the mate more at ease, and the longboat turned and docked easily.

They were old friends by now. Many of the *Trader*'s crew had been with the ship, off and on, for a decade, and their contract had always called for this supply stop.

"Mavra!" Tbisi, the mate, called to her. "What in the world happened here?"

Quickly she explained the previous night's visitation and her own fears. The crewmen nodded sympathetically; they knew why she was here and why she was the way she was.

"So, you see, we can't stay here," she concluded, "and we can't go back to the Ambreza. You know what would happen. Ortega would just take us to Zone and lock us up in a nice little cage for the rest of our lives." Tbisi was pretty low to the ground, and Mavra could almost look into its strange face and eyes. "Imagine what that means, Tibby! Think about if somebody told you that they were going to take you off the *Trader* and put you in a nice dark hole for the rest of your days!"

Not only the mate but the Twosh as well nodded sympathetically. "But what can we do to help?" the mate asked, feeling his tendrils were tied.

She gestured to the compound with her head. "There's almost a half-ton of vintage tobacco and about thirty pounds of gold in there. It's yours if you get us out of here."

"But where will you go?" Tbisi asked in a tone that was more an objection than a question.

"Gedemondas," she replied. "Oh, I know it doesn't have a coast, but you serve Mucrol next door. A little detour?"

He shook his incredibly thin head slowly. "True, we could do it, but not directly. We have our own jobs, our own livelihoods to consider. It'd be at least a month, maybe more. If Ortega or anybody else is looking for you, the *Trader*'s going to be pretty obvious."

She considered what he said. "How about this, then. Take us across to the island, to Ecundo. I know you stop there. We'll make it overland through Ecundo and Wuckl and meet you on the other side, say at the Wuckl port of Hygit. Then it's only a short hop across."

The mate was still dubious. "I don't know. It's true we have some Ecundans, good people, in the crew; but that's a nasty bunch generally. The ones we have are mostly wanted men back home. Those Ecundans are a vicious bunch who don't like outsiders."

She nodded. "I know that. But they herd *bundas*, and, if you think about it, *bundas* look something like us with hair. A lot of it's open range—we could make it across, I think."

"But the Ecundans eat *bundas*," Tbisi pointed out. "They might just eat you, too. And what will *you* eat? You're talking about 350 kilometers across Ecundo, then all the way across Wuckl—almost a thousand kilometers in all, on foot."

"These Wuckl," Joshi asked, "what are they like?"

"High-tech hex. Kind of hard to describe. Nice folks, really, and vegetarians. I'm sure you'd have no trouble if you explained your problem, although they might not help much. But—wait a minute! I'm talking like this crazy thing is going to work! Hey, look! If you're right, Mavra, and somebody is trying to get rid of you as a threat to that ship, won't Ortega need you then?"

She laughed derisively. "For all I know Ortega's gotten impatient and decided to kill off all three pilots. Besides, even if not, it might just be that one side or the other has a lead and has decided to act just to foreclose any potential threat. It doesn't matter—I have to act as though that's the case. Please! Won't you help me?"

They would, could, and finally decided to. Any good seaman would chance the unknown rather than sit waiting for death to creep in.

They understood her.

South Zone

SERGE ORTEGA STARED CURIOUSLY AT THE CRYSTAL-line crablike form that had just entered. Though there was no face, and no eyes, ears, or other orifices, it could speak, the operator modulating small crystals inside the creature, which in turn modulated a translator.

"You are the Ghiskind?" Ortega asked, genuinely curious.

"At your service, Ambassador."

Ortega considered the Northerner. "I—ah—take it that this is not exactly your normal form, but is for my benefit?"

"That is so," the Ghiskind acknowledged. "It is one of my worker modules, which I have modified with the necessary speaking devices. Our own form of communication is, shall we say, nonverbal. I do wish to thank you for providing the translator; it is a fascinating device."

"My pleasure. And now, down to work. You know about this business with the Torshind and the Yaxa and the ship, of course."

"Of course. The authorities have tried to keep things quiet, but I had the good fortune to be near the Zone Gate when the Yaxa materialized. Its nature was immediately apparent—it radiated carbon. I guess that is the best way to put it. It is so difficult, putting these concepts into a form easily understood by you."

The Ulik nodded. "Never mind that. The real questions are more basic. For example, why have you chosen to contact me instead of one of the others, and

53

why are you going against your own government? And, of course, can you do the job we'll require—and why?"

"A- long series," noted the Ghiskind. "As for why you, the answer is that you are on record as opposing the Yaxa all along, which means, as well, that you are against the Torshind."

Ortega's bushy eyebrows went up Ah ha! he thought to himself.

"As for going against my own government," the Ghiskind continued, "well, first it is rather much of a tradition in Yugash to go against the government. A silly game in any event—the government has no true power, only the business clans. No, the government is quite out of this, really."

"The Torshind represents a commercial rival, then?" Ortega guessed.

"Not at all," the Yugash replied. "The Torshind represents the—ah, let me see . . . concepts, concepts —I suppose the closest thing I can get to it, although you will probably misunderstand, is a church. At least, an organized cult that has rigid dogmatic beliefs and is rather fanatical about them."

Ortega thought it over. "Cult is good enough for me. Doesn't matter much what it believes—or is that relevant?"

"Relevant, yes," the Ghiskind responded. "Once they had great power. Once, when the Markovians were supervising departures, they managed to go out in the bodies of some of these people, to spread the faith and power of the cult, so to speak. They are the reason for much of our social and political isolation, for they regard all other creatures as tools, like this device, for their use and pleasures."

"I thought you couldn't read minds, even when occupying a host body," Ortega interrupted nervously.

The crystal creature shook. "You misunderstand. Knowledge, no. But they can disrupt the brain, of course, cause damage, cripple, induce madness. They can feel—as all Yugash can—what the host body senses—sex, masochism, sadism, whatever, at no risk to the Yugash inside. And they can trigger such sensations by stimulating the centers responsible for such feelings in the brain. It is only a matter of experimenting to find where each is and what each does."

Serge Ortega shivered. "But you are not like this?" he prodded, somewhat discomforted.

"Most Yugash are not," the Ghiskind assured him. "Overall, the percentage of basically good to basically bad people is probably about the same as with any other race. I can guess your thinking. Some terrors of your own people's past—particularly the institutional ones—*may* have been caused by Yugash, but we have never been many and we reproduce slowly or not at all in hostile environments. Possibly my most terrible suggestion is that most such activities are not Yugash-derived but native-born."

He made a good if uncomfortable point. Ortega did not belabor it.

"So that cult is no longer the dominant factor in Yugash, and the government's a nothing. This means that you represent—who, then?"

The Ghiskind had no trouble with this one. "As I said, Yugash is divided into and ruled by business clans. Some, like my own, are at their saturation point in Yugash. We can not expand, we can only stagnate at present levels. My own business is enough removed from your kind of life that even explaining it is impossible. But there are a great many hexes—Northern mostly, but a few Southern as well—who can use our skills. However, with the cult still around—and the embargo has been in effect for so long it's an institution taken for granted—we cannot deal with anyone. My company, therefore, has sent me on a twofold mission. For one thing, to deny the Torshind and its kind any new outlet to other worlds and races. Second, to restore Yugash's credibility by working in joint operations with others, in the North and the South, to a positive end and in an honorable manner—and, in so doing, to reopen those long-dead channels of communication."

What he said was plausible. "But what guarantees

do I have?" Ortega asked, apologetic. "I mean, I have only your word . . ."

The Ghiskind had a ready reply. "There are ways to prevent a Yugash from entering and controlling a body," it replied. "We will reveal these to you. Also, occupation isn't as simple a matter as you think. Were I to try and seize your body now, you would fight me —and the stronger mind would win. Even if I gained control, it would take practice to learn your nervous system properly so that I could control you and not kill you. And, remember, we do not have a spaceship pilot!"

That, of course, was the clincher.

"All right, then, Ghiskind, I think we have a deal. I had the pressurized hardware made up a long time ago, but it'll have to be checked out, possibly refitted." He paused for a moment, as if in thought, then added, "You realize, of course, that if we can not get into the computer I intend to destroy things so that nobody else will ever get there, either."

The crystal shook again, apparently nodding. "Of course. Were it not for the potential threat to the Well itself I would say blow the ship now and be done with it."

"The Yaxa group is at least two months from completing its hardware," Ortega noted. "Shall we say— thirty days on this spot?"

"Done," replied the Ghiskind. "In the meantime, let me acquaint you with the terrain and logistical problems involved. I assume you have already talked to the Bozog?"

Ortega smiled. "Oh, yes. Those little rolling bastards shouldn't be underestimated. If we can get them a pilot, they can get the ship."

He sighed, suddenly deep in thought. Then he reached over with his lower right hand and pulled open a drawer, taking out a thick file. CHANG was written on its cover.

Now, after all these years, I can pay my own debts, he thought. He punched an intercom button with his middle right hand.

"Sir?" came the crisp voice of a female Ulik.

"Zudi, tell the Ambreza to bring Mavra Chang through the Zone Gate to me. They'll know what it all means. And tell them to bring Joshi, too, if she and he want."

"Right away, sir," the secretary replied.

He felt better. He'd been wanting to give that order desperately for twenty-two years.

Glathriel

THE PARMITER GROANED. IT WORE A PARTIAL BODY cast. Grune, the big lizard who'd been burned, sympathized from beneath the massive bandages on its back and side.

"Oh, shut up, both of you," snapped the other great lizard known as Doc. "Damn it, if Grune, here, hadn't rolled onto me, I'd still have had her!"

"You didn't happen to be on fire," Grune responded angrily. "Want me to put a torch to you and see if you roll right?"

"Take it easy, both of you!" the Parmiter responded. "This bickering gets us nowhere. We're still alive, we've still got this ship and a well-paid crew of nasties, and we've still got the problem of snatching this Chang."

"Why don't we just drop it?" Grune snarled. "Hell, piracy and robbery might not pay as well, but I sure never got fried doin' it."

"We can't and you know it!" the Parmiter retorted. "There's big money behind this job. You know the only ones with enough to outfit a ship like this in nothing flat and put up the kind of front money for a crew and expenses we got is a hex government. A *govern-*

ment, dummy! One crooked enough that it knew who we were, where to find us, and that we'd take the job. If it knows that and is indeed a government, we'd have to emigrate to the Northern Hemisphere to save our necks anywhere on this world—and even that might not be enough."

That thought quieted them, so the Parmiter was again able to concentrate. "Look," it said, "let's think this through. We've already gone back in and seen that the compound's deserted. The natives were in an uproar, so they don't know what happened. No sight of any Ambreza yet, so they haven't got her. So, where is she?"

"Hiding out in the woods, most likely," Grune suggested. "Or on the run for some hex."

"Right!" the Parmiter responded. "Now, we must go on the idea that she and her boyfriend don't like the Ambreza. After all, they cooped 'em up there. So south's out. Ginzin's over two hundred kilometers north, and it's a holy hell of a mess anyway. They'd be picked up by the Ambreza before then for sure, or dropped into those boiling tar pits if they made the border. They got brains. That's why they're still free and we're wracked up. Now, if we suppose that maybe they didn't go *any* of those places, what's left?"

Doc considered the question. "There's only water otherwise," he pointed out. "And they can't lift their noses far enough to keep from drowning."

"We are on the water, aren't we?" the Parmiter replied patiently.

Grune brightened. "They had a boat? Or took one?"

The Parmiter nodded. "Now you're gettin' there. Remember that big boat we had to dodge yesterday? I bet it was their supply ship. If it was, it stopped, saw the mess we made, and maybe . . ."

Doc nodded. "But that's a hell of a monster ship," he pointed out. "This is a nice yacht, but it's a row-boat compared to that thing."

The Parmiter sniggered. "Yeah? Maybe so, but did you see those launchers on the front and back? They're rocket launchers. And they shoot neat frag-

mentation bombs. They come down, hit something—
like a ship's deck—and go *bam* in all directions, blow
a hole a kilometer wide."

"What good's that here?" Grune asked. "This is a
nontech hex. You know that."

"Idiot!" snapped the Parmiter. "So the launchers
are spring-loaded, see? With a boost from a fuse and
gunpowder charge underneath. They blow up by
chemical action triggered by the shock. No power supply, see? *They work here,* and they'll blow a hole we
can sail through in that damned packet."

"Oh," said Grune.

The Yaxa drifted across the shoreline, its strange
eyes searching the ground. It had been a difficult journey; almost twenty days' worth. Now it was over; now
the Yaxa had reached its goal. True, there would be
some journeying back, but not as much. It needed
only to make a Zone Gate it could use without attracting undue attention. Its prize was destined for Zone,
for the Yaxa embassy.

It had been a hard and grueling flight over territory
not very friendly or hospitable; she knew that her su-
periors had been against her going because she was so
involved in the forthcoming expedition. But she had
insisted and had managed to communicate through
friendly Zone Gates to assure her compatriots that all
was well.

But, in the end, this had been her part of the project
from the beginnings—the long-ago beginnings, when
the wars were fought. As the only Entry in Yaxa history from a "human" world, she had special qualifica-
tions. The others didn't understand human nature, no
matter what its forms. She did, in all of its variations.

To her sisters' credit, they recognized her unique
capability and had given her the prized task. Her loyalty was unquestioned, her dedication unmatched.
Through her influence and authority, she had kept
them from sending out a squad or commissioning a
gang to kill Mavra Chang. Not Trelig—no, they'd

tried to get at him ten times or more, but that slippery frog was always too smart for them.

She'd told them that Chang was loyal to no side but her own, which was true, and that the strange woman was valuable as an alternative to Yulin, just in case. They had accepted what she said. To some extent, it had been the truth. But she had other reasons, ones they, perhaps, would never understand, but ones that Mavra probably would in time.

Now as she circled the compound, she saw immediately that something was wrong. The front wall had been smashed by something huge and powerful, and there had been a fire afterward. Part of the compound was in ruins, and a storage area behind stood open and empty. She felt momentary panic. Robbers? Pirates? Was she, then, too late?

But, no, as she studied further she saw Ambreza and signs of a frantic search through the area.

Dead? Or—?

She swung out to sea, to avoid Ambreza eyes and to think, gliding lazily on updrafts high above the whitecapped, blue-green waters.

She couldn't believe Mavra Chang was dead, wouldn't allow herself to believe that—not until she saw the body, or the grave. Not after all this, oh, no.

But—if not dead, then what? If pirates did hit the place, and she got away . . . where would she go? To the Ambreza? No. The Ambreza below looked too much like search parties, even the one out in a small boat.

Not south to Ambreza, nor north to deadly Ginzin, either. By water, then?

But that would mean—kidnapped?

Who would want to kidnap Mavra Chang except her, the Yaxa wondered? Not Ortega, certainly? He had her. Then—

Antor Trelig.

It had to be, she decided. Maybe to make a deal with Ortega, since Trelig was the only player in the game still without his own access to the North. If that were so, he'd hardly take her to Zone. The Makiem didn't have the defenses of a Yaxa, and he could hardly be expected to shield her presence for long from Ortega.

They would have come by ship, she decided. And that's how they'd get away—probably north, then, to Domien, which was neutral enough and would allow Trelig a hiding place to bargain with.

No, no, she reprimanded herself. You're thinking too straight. That's where Ortega and the Ambreza would look first. They'd surely sail south first, to avoid patrols, then maybe up along the middle coast of that double-hex island until they felt in the clear, then shoot over for Domien.

The Yaxa turned southeast, praying she was right.

Agitar

IT WAS AN UNUSUAL HORSE FARM. TRUE, IT HAD MUCH of the look of such places—rolling acres of lush, green grass, a large stable, and a ranch-style house. But there were no fences, no track, either. The saddles were strangely shaped to accommodate the instruments in them—wind-speed indicators, altimeters, and the like. Even the casual visitor to Agitar didn't have to wait long or wonder why, if one of those horses came around. They were huge beasts in pretty lavenders and blues and greens and yellows and all the other colors of the rainbow. And they had wings.

Wings, like those of a great swan lay folded in two parallel lines along the length of their great bodies. And, yes, they flew, for they were only externally equine; their internal construction included the ability to shift their center of gravity, hollow bones, and a host of other refinements. The creatures were more fragile than they looked, too, for they weighed less than half what anyone would guess.

The lord and master of this, the only major breeding farm for pegasi in all Agitar, had gone there to work over twenty years earlier as a trainer. Thousands of Agitar had learned to ride the beasts in the Wars, but only a special few possessed the affinity for them that made for good trainers. He was one.

His judgment, skill, and plain hard work had been rewarded. First he became Chief Trainer, then Master of Livestock, and now he was General Manager. The government owned the place, of course, but *he* lived in the big house and he was the boss.

He was also about 140 centimeters tall. Below the waist his body resembled the hindquarters of a goat —thick muscular calves draped in heavy, curly hair of deep blue became incredibly thin legs that terminated in small cloven hoofs. Like the pegasus, he had a great deal of control over his center of gravity and moved with the grace and ease of a ballet dancer always on point.

Above the waist he resembled a muscular human, skin still deep blue and very porous, whose triangular face sported a blue-black goatee flecked with gray. Between two small, pointed horns, close-cropped salt-and-pepper hair sat atop a demon's face.

He looked over the place with satisfaction. His name was Renard, an unusual name for an Agitar. Once he was librarian back on a Comworld called New Muscovy. Then he had been picked up by one Antor Trelig, who needed a classicist for his neo-Roman library on New Pompeii and addicted him to sponge. Renard was the one who'd helped Mavra Chang escape and who had originally crashed with her in among the giant cyclops of Teliagin. Mavra kept him alive until rescue, when Ortega ran him through the Well to cure his addiction. He came out an Agitar. The ship he'd crashed in had started the wars, and, before he knew what happened, he was drafted, put atop a pegasus, and sent off to fight—in alliance with none other than Antor Trelig.

Renard deserted, of course, and found Mavra. With two Lata they flew across the seas on his pegasus Doma. In Olborn he kept Mavra from being transformed completely into a mule, and eventually they all witnessed the destruction of the spaceship engines in Gedemondas.

Renard accompanied Mavra Chang into exile, but she drove him off. Even after all these years, he still worried about her. He occasionally received word of her from Ortega, although, because of his responsibilities he had never returned to see her. He felt guilty about that—and knew he should—but it just hadn't happened.

Mavra had predicted the Agitar would welcome him back as a hero. Well, they hardly did that, but they had dropped the desertion charges because he was a new Entry and did, after all, owe Mavra Chang something. They'd been impressed with his odyssey on Doma, too, and his ability to walk the beast on mountain trails when flying was impossible.

And so the job and the new career. And, except for the lingering guilt about Mavra, so little and helpless and alone, he'd done just fine.

"Renard!" a female voice called to him from the office area. He turned and saw a junior clerk waving at him.

Female Agitar were upside-down males; they resembled a goat in the face and torso, and a more human type below. But that never bothered an Agitar, and it didn't bother him, either. He'd had a lot of kids by a lot of them.

He ran briskly up to the office. "What is it, Guda?" he called good-naturedly. "Did they raise everybody's pay?"

She shook her head. Like all Agitar females she was incapable of facial expression, but her eyes reflected something serious. She handed him a telegram just off the government wire. He read it, growing serious himself. He skipped the address and routing codes and read the message:

RENARD, MAVRA CHANG ATTACKED, PROBABLY KID-

NAPPED. TRELIG SUSPECTED. SIGNS SHOW THEY MAY
HAVE BOTCHED JOB. CAN YOU FLY SOUTH GLATHRIEL
ASAP TO HELP SEARCH? CHECK AT ZONE GATES ALONG
WAY FOR FURTHER INFORMATION. AM ALSO DISPATCH-
ING VISTARU SAME LOCATION. GOOD LUCK. ORTEGA.

He was stunned. It was the last thing he expected.
He hesitated a moment, thinking. Leaving the farm,
perhaps for weeks—they weren't going to like that
back in the capital. But, then, it was for Mavra ...

"Guda, honey, will you saddle Domaru with at
least a two-week field pack? I'm going on a trip," he
said to her. "Tell Vili he's in charge until I get back."

He turned and trotted out, leaving Guda behind,
her long mouth half-open.

Everod, off the Ecundo Coast

THERE HAD BEEN FOG THROUGH MOST OF THE NIGHT,
and they had been drifting southward. They knew it,
but decided to ride with the tide as long as there was
deep water, at least until they could get a fix from the
sun, which they hoped would burn through after dawn.

And the sun did cooperate a little—a barely visible
splotch of light off to starboard and just ahead. After
gently rubbing the tubular proboscis jutting from its
middle, the captain decided to hoist sail and move a
little westward, on the chance that the fog was hugging
the coast of the Island. This was likely; land heats up
and cools down faster than water, which caused early
fogs over many seacoasts in warm weather.

Mavra was enjoying herself, was more animated
than any of them could remember her. She spent a
good deal of time pumping the crew for current information on Ecundo and Wuckl. Joshi, for his part,

could not remember a time outside Glathriel and the compound. So after his initial misgivings, he welcomed the sea voyage as a great new adventure, and was all over the place, asking questions, examining the equipment, and enjoying the smell of the sea and the cool gentle caress of the fog.

The crew was especially helpful; the sailmaker had been working for two days on jackets that the Changs could use to carry with ease their most necessary supplies. Though the crew hadn't neglected to remove Mavra's valuables from their storehouse, they were really cooperating not because of the big bribe, but because they sympathized with the fugitives.

Tbisi worried constantly, not only about their impending overland journey but also about what would happen beyond that. He was a chronic pessimist, but Mavra endured his attitude because the concern was genuinely for them.

"All right, so suppose you make it through Ecundo, a remote possibility," he argued, "and you also get through Wuckl and manage to link up with us or with one of the other packets we'll alert. If we get you to Mucrol, you still have to cross that hex before you get to this Gedemondas. Then you have to climb into the cold mountains—for which you are not in any way prepared and for which, in any case, you have no provisions. Then what? What will it get you?"

She had thought about it often. "Perhaps help—they know me there, and they are sympathetic to me. They seem to regard me as the coming center of their mystical beliefs. Whether you accept that bullshit or not, *they* believe it. They will give us sanctuary. I feel certain of that. Once we get there, *then* I can plan for the future."

She was adamant; Tbisi couldn't talk her out of her plan, and eventually he stopped trying—partly out of a healthy respect for her mind and the resourceful ingenuity it represented. He secretly suspected that there was a streak of masochism in her, that she was only happy when surrounded by insurmountable obstacles and hopeless odds just so she could figure a way out.

An odd way to live, but it commanded respect, for she was alive and still going strong after a life filled with such challenges.

That not a single member of the crew regarded either of them as helpless or unnatural was a measure of her tenacity. They were simply another life form on this strange world of multiple life forms, no more unusual than the others, and no less able to do what they needed to do.

The captain had guessed correctly about the fog; it was thinning, and a bright haze of thin swirling orange developed. The sun was still mostly obscured to the northeast, but it was possible to take a sextant reading.

"Ship ho!" called a lookout from midway up the forward mast. Mavra and Joshi had the same thought: the pursuing Ambreza had been patrolling the edge of the fog, waiting for the inevitable emergence of the *Toorine Trader*.

They trimmed the sails until they were balanced against the strong southerly current and stood almost still in the water. Mavra and Joshi ran to the side and jumped up to the low ship's rail. Their forelegs were near the top and they were almost vertical, supported by their hind legs. It wasn't entirely comfortable, but it gave them vision.

Tbisi came up to them silently on his padded pipe-cleaner legs and looked out with them.

"A little ship," he muttered. "A small black cutter. Fast, but no threat to us, I shouldn't think."

"Ambreza?" she asked nervously.

Tbisi extended his long, impossibly thin neck and peered into the mists. "No, I think not. Not the kind of ship they use. Aluminum hull and armored, it looks like. The ship is Oglabanian—don't ever see 'em over on the west side—but it's been heavily modified. I'm afraid I don't know exactly *what* it is."

The small black ship suddenly seemed to explode in a series of bright, blue-white flashes.

"Signal to *Trader!*" yelled the lookout. "Stand to for board and search! They're using standard customs codes, but it's not a government ship for sure!"

The voice of the *Trader*'s strange captain came through its translator sounding like a cross between a foghorn and a steam whistle. "Board and search be damned!" it yelled. "Not *my* ship! Signal: *We are in mutually neutral waters. Go about your own business!*"

A huge lantern was mounted forward, filled with something that glowed brightly but didn't melt the interior of the lamp. A weasellike creature perched to one side moved a lever back and forth several times, unmasking the forward section of the lamp and projecting a blazing glow into the haze. "Done, Captain!" it yelled.

The *Trader* waited tensely, wondering what the small cutter would do next.

Mavra, as tense as any, turned to Joshi. "You know, they could be the same ones who attacked us the other night. They must have come by ship—I bet that's them."

Joshi nodded without taking his eyes off the unknown ship. His throat was dry, and he could hear his heart pounding. An idle part of his brain hoped that his fear wasn't all that apparent to Mavra; it never occurred to him for a second that she was feeling the same things.

"Cannoneers to station, pump ballast to port side," the captain ordered. The crew was experienced; in short order the cannons were manned, loaded, the hatches through which they fired were lowered, and the cannons themselves were pushed up on small rails.

Joshi suddenly became disconcerted. "I think we're sinking!" he exclaimed.

Tbisi laughed. "No, we carry large tanks of liquid as ballast and pump water into them selectively to balance the ship when we have an uneven cargo load. Now they're hand-pumping all of it to this side of the ship, so that we'll present the least hull for them to hit."

"But that tilts the deck into them!" he noted. "Isn't that worse?"

Tibby laughed. "No, we can stand a lot of direct hits on the superstructure. Messy, but it won't sink us or drive us out of control. A shot below the waterline that got between two watertight hatches might send us to the bottom, though." He turned to face them. "Better take cover, you two. It could get nasty around here. I have to get to my command station in the auxiliary bridge."

Mavra nodded and then said, "Come on, Joshi. We'll be no good later on if we're in bloody pieces."

He was reluctant to leave; he wanted to watch the battle. However, he never questioned her judgment or common sense. He went.

"They're angling bow into us, Captain!" shouted the lookout. "Looks like we got a fight!"

"Trim sail completely!" ordered the captain. "I'm going to let the current carry us back into the fog. Hard port! Man stern bridge!"

The sails came immediately down; at the same time, the *Trader* turned slowly to present the least profile to the challenger. It also started to move slowly backward, at the mercy of the southern current now.

"All aloft, below!" the captain yelled, and everybody, lookouts included, got down fast and went to their stations. Large barrels of water were made handy to wash down the cannon deck. Torches were lit.

The cutter, seeing their maneuver, had matched it. The same current that carried the *Trader* would carry it, and as long as both were current-propelled, the big ship could not make any speed on the little one.

There was a bright yellow flash and a boom from the foredeck of the cutter, and a smoky plume rose from its bow, then angled toward them.

"Steady as you go . . . steady . . . steady . . ." the captain murmured. They had now turned completely around, bow away from the cutter, the captain on the stern bridge. The smoke plume looped, started to come down.

"Hard port, now!" yelled the captain.

The ship's massive rudder turned under heavy, trained muscles, the chains that controlled it groaning and the masts swaying as it suddenly turned to present its profile.

There was an explosion about thirty meters out, a tremendous blast as the rocket hit the sea in front of them and struck the surface at a velocity sufficient for spring-loaded detonators to ignite.

Fragments of metal ate into the ship even from that distance, but it was a clear miss, and nothing flew but a few splinters.

The cutter turned sharply now, so that it was apparent that they had only two launch tubes, bow and stern. In the time it would take them to get the stern tube in position, they would have to present a brief but inviting broadside to the *Trader*.

The second mate, who was in charge of the gun crews, waited his moment. Then, suddenly, for a brief period of time, both ship's sides were parallel.

"Fire all guns!" he shouted, and immediately bright-burning torches were touched to fuse holes in the rear of the cannons. There was a repetitive series of explosions that shuddered through the ship as sixteen cannon shots went off in series.

They were short. Though great plumes of water rose all around the cutter, and it looked as if the smaller craft had been completely destroyed, as the water calmed, it became clear that none of the missiles had come within fifty meters of the attacking craft.

The *Trader* continued to turn, bow now facing the pursuer's stern. The exceptionally strong current allowed the smaller craft to close, but, with the cannon-washes from the salvo, it wasn't any easier to turn than the much larger vessel.

Ordinarily the *Trader* would accept such a challenge and engage at a fixed distance circularly, ship-to-ship, but the cutter's rockets gave it added range, and the captain dared not let it come in too close. That was frustrating; the rocket mines obviously had a greater range than the *Trader*'s cannon, and, although the big ship could stand some hits, it could not do so without casualties, and if they didn't immediately disable the opposing craft they'd soon be at the attacker's mercy. The captain wasn't one to take such risks if he could avoid them.

Looking out at the attacker, whose second missile was already in the air, the eerie face and glowing eyes of the captain never wavered, but he shouted to the navigator, "Did you get me a fix?"

Before the navigator could reply, the grenade struck, closer this time, metal fragments flying from it and causing a series of nasty gashes in the *Trader*'s side and forward superstructure.

The captain shouted corrective orders; the fog was becoming thick again, and the cutter was becoming harder to see—as was the *Trader*. In a matter of minutes they would be invisible to each other. This, oddly, favored the cutter, which would continue to close because of its smaller, lighter nature as they both followed the current.

Joshi peered out from under a tarpaulin. "God! I wish I could see what's going on!" he complained. "Fog's getting thick again!"

"You're better off alive!" snapped Mavra Chang. "Get back under here and stay here! This captain knows what he's doing!"

I hope, she added silently to herself. There was no way that she or Joshi could swim.

The navigator on the bridge had waited for a short interlude in the exchange. Now it gave the information. "34 south, 62 west!" it called.

"Exactly!" snapped the captain. "How close are we to the Ecundan hex point and Usurk?"

The navigator brightened with the light of understanding. "At this speed," it replied, "maybe ten, twelve minutes' time at the most!"

That satisfied the captain. "All aloft!" he yelled. "Full sail!" Their bow was angled away from their pursuer at this point, the proper angle, and there was an eight- to ten-kilometer wind blowing.

The cutter, which, even though it was closing, was having increasing difficulty locating the bigger craft in the fog, got enough of a glimpse to see the sails unfurling.

The Parmiter, on a watch platform midships, cried out, "They're putting on sail! We have to catch them fast or we might lose them! Com'on, you bastards! They can't see us but we can still see them! If you can't hit something that size from this distance, we're all lost!"

The Parmiter was right. The early morning light of the sun occasionally revealed a small part of the *Toorine Trader*. Coming out of the still-darker northwest, their craft, of black aluminum, was indistinguishable from the water.

The bow tube fired again, and this time it was a close call. They were not only closing, they were getting the range; had they been able to use two bow tubes, they might have hit the *Trader* dead on. The constant turning, however, made aiming more chancy, for each time a tube came up the angle had changed slightly.

On the bridge of the *Toorine Trader* the captain was becoming worried. The last shot had blown a gash in the stern and blew open a hatch cover. Obviously the cutter was getting the range while managing to keep just out of cannon's reach. The captain resolved that if he got out of this, the company was going to pay for some of those rocket mines for *his* ship.

"We must be getting close to the border!" The captain shouted to the navigator. "Man boiler room! Preheat coke! Man Type A defenses!"

Two Twosh bowling-pins scampered across the deck on bright white-gloved hands, then hopped atop a tarpaulin-covered shape at the bow. The tarp came off, revealing a device resembling a small telescope with a dome-shaped housing. The Twosh poised before a control board with form-fitting indentations to the rear of the device, huge oval eyes staring at the dead controls.

Another rocket mine soared, then struck amidships, blowing a huge hole in the side of the *Trader*.

"Shift ballast to compensate!" screamed the captain. *Come on, you bastards, where's that border?*

Then suddenly, as if someone had lifted a dirty curtain, the *Toorine Trader* came out of the fog and stood clear to the pursuers, a sitting duck.

"We got 'em!" screamed the Parmiter in triumph. "Now let's finish 'em off!"

The rocket crews sniggered and loaded for the kill. They were aiming at the midsection, hoping to strike the central mast. That would leave the big craft at their mercy.

The Parmiter's crew took its time on this one, no longer worried about the problems of fog and elevation. They were so busy making sure of their shot that they failed to notice faint wisps of white begin to rise from the *Trader*'s twin stacks.

On the bow, the two Twosh at the strange console suddenly yipped in glee as sophisticated control panels came to life before them. A radar mast flipped up and started its slow back and forth sweep, and a large grid in front of one Twosh showed the cutter clearly.

The captain had won his gamble. Now, in the fight and run, with the current carrying most of the load, they'd drifted back over the high-tech hex border, into Usurk. That had activated all their technical devices.

They could see the flare in the hand of a ghostly shape on the cutter deck prepare to touch off the rocket mine that would administer the *coup de grâce* to the *Toorine Trader*.

But the Twosh suddenly elevated their platform to proper height, locked on, and fired with computer-aided accuracy.

The odd-looking telescope was better known as a laser cannon.

At the same time the *Trader* turned; sails came down in record time and when the master gauge on the bridge read ready a slim tendril shot out from the captain and pulled a lever, activating the great engines and twin screws.

Huge clouds of smoke billowed from the *Trader*'s stacks before the sails were even down, and it turned with astonishing speed and bore in on the small cutter.

"Fire!" screamed the Parmiter, but at that moment a blinding beam of greenish-white light struck them full force. The grenade rose a half-meter, then exploded. The laser beam swept down, slicing off a part of the cutter's bow.

The small ship exploded.

There was a blinding flash and roar as the balance of the rocket grenades ignited, and a great plume of water shot up, then fell, leaving only fragments where the ship had been.

A collective sigh of relief traveled the length of the *Toorine Trader*.

The captain surveyed the scene, its odd, transparent head cocked a little to one side. "Maybe they're right," it murmured to itself. "Maybe those grenades *are* too damned explosive to carry."

Damage-control personnel started cleaning up, patching, and repairing, taking advantage of the high-tech hex to use their best equipment.

The *Trader* approached the now-visible coast of Ecundo, which looked wild and forbidding this far south. Shortly she'd head north, back up that coast, almost all the way under sail.

As the ship headed toward the land, it moved away from a single, tiny figure drifting south in the current. It was too small, and soon much too far away, to be heard or noticed except by a few curious seabirds.

"Help me! Oh, please, god! Somebody help me!" came the anguished voice of the Parmiter. "Doc! Grune! Somebody! Anybody! Help me!"

But there was no one to help the Parmiter this time.

Nocha

THE *Torrine Trader* HAD BEEN PATCHED WELL; ONLY the fresh wood on parts of the bow, midsection, and superstructure hinted that something had been amiss.

A week later, the *Trader* was several hundred kilometers out, steaming across the Sea of Turagin to the northwest, on its way to deliver to Wygon huge crates of things whose function they couldn't fathom and couldn't have cared less about.

It was cold in Nocha, slightly above freezing. The crew stayed belowdecks as much as possible; the sea was extremely rough, and one could easily fall overboard into the chilly waters. Nobody wanted that— not in Nocha, where, only a few meters below the raging surface, thousand-toothed insects waited for just such a bonanza.

They were definitely not company customers, anyway, and no crewman wanted to give them anything for free.

The storm and cold had driven a tiny airborne figure farther west. She was almost exhausted, and had begun to doubt her ability to continue. No land had been in sight since she'd flown out over the sea to intercept the *Trader* before its landfall in Wygon three days hence—according to the schedule obtained from the company office in Damien.

She had no broad, great wings to maintain herself on comfortable updrafts above the storm. Her powers of flight were tremendous and included the ability to zig and zag almost at right angles with no effort as well as to stand still. But doing so meant that her wings had to work constantly to keep her aloft.

And right now all four pairs were sore as hell.

In desperation, she climbed as high as she dared, letting the gusts carry her tiny, frail body along like a leaf in the wind, allowing her some rest and forcing her to use her own powers only when she lost altitude. The system was working, yes, but it was a stopgap measure and not one that could be maintained for long periods. It was also taking her westward, although southwest, northwest, or due west she had no way of knowing.

The westward drift almost did her in. Hardly able to see, desperately fighting the elements, she was not prepared when the storm suddenly ceased and a wave of warmth washed over her. The atmosphere was also quite calm and at very low pressure, and she began dropping like a rock before she knew it.

Straining painfully to pull out of the fall, she realized she'd been blown across a sea-hex border. She pulled out just before hitting the waves and managed to maintain a low altitude. That was not enough; a gleaming silver fish that looked to be half teeth leaped from the water to grab at her. In panic, she managed to gain a little more.

Too exhausted to think straight she began to allow sensations of impending doom to penetrate her consciousness. She realized that, if she didn't find some place to land soon, she would drop into the suddenly placid sea. And wet wings would incapacitate her, leaving her easy and tempting prey for those silvery appetites below.

She had no idea where she was, or how far it might be from one place to another. Hookl, probably, since it was so warm—certainly not Jol, where icebergs abounded.

She'd settle for an iceberg right now, she thought longingly.

She drifted as best she could, certain that any moment now her wings would fall off from sheer overuse, berating herself for being such a fool. There'd be islands, she'd told herself, or other boats to use—but Jol was in no condition for shipping right now, and Nocha had been cold and rough and barren of land and traffic.

And then she saw it. Yes, there it was—a speck near the horizon. In hopeful desperation, she flew toward it with her last available energy.

It *was* an island, she saw. Not much of one— a crooked, twisted spire of rock jutting from the water, its glassy sheen partially obscured by low vegetation.

For a moment those growths worried her; she had no idea what sort of creature might live there, nor what it ate—those hungry fish weren't its prey, that was certain; but anything that could coexist with them had to be a little nastier than they. It didn't matter, though, she told herself. Her alternative to landing was to become a sure snack for the toothy beasties in the waters.

The island was a bit larger than it had seemed at first, and she could see bird nests tucked among the mossy growths, so she decided to take a chance on it. Not much larger than some of the seabirds herself, she chose a big nest on the cliffside that definitely looked deserted, and settled down into it thankfully.

It was hard and brittle and had a lot of sharp places, but she felt none of them. Within seconds, she was asleep.

It had been a dreamless sleep, hard and overly long. She stirred with difficulty; her head pounded, and her eyes felt as if they had weights on them. She sat up and groaned and opened her eyes that burned like fire, and gave a gasp.

She was not alone on the island.

A creature three times her size stood watching her. The thing clung to the sheer and slippery face of the rock effortlessly, as if it were level.

She uttered a short cry of panic, then rose immediately to her feet.

She had never seen a Yaxa close up before.

The giant creature's shiny death's head turned toward her. "Don't try flying out," it advised. "I took the precaution of temporarily disabling your wings."

Immediately she tried to flex them, and they felt like

lead. She looked over her shoulder, and saw that small clips had been placed on them, linking them together at their tips. The wings were too fragile to try and work the clips off, and the clips were out of reach of her hands.

The Yaxa was satisfied with her demonstration, and for good reason. Lata were tiny, delicate-looking creatures, but they were also very dangerous to most warm-blooded life forms.

The prisoner looked like a small girl of ten or eleven; it was impossible to judge a Lata's age, for they looked almost the same from a few years after hatching until they died. Aging was an exclusively internal affair.

But the little-girl image was enhanced by the fact that Lata were less than a meter tall and incredibly slender. Externally humanoid, internally they were more like insects, able to eat and digest literally anything organic. Even their soft, creamy skin was illusion, for it covered a flexible chitinous inner skin. Lata were almost impervious to temperature changes because their metabolism was flexible enough to keep them comfortable under all conditions except extreme cold and extreme heat.

They had tiny pointed ears, and tough, black hair which grew in a rough pageboy cut. Their four pairs of transparent wings kept their light bodies aloft much in the manner of a bee and gave them their exceptional maneuverability.

This particular Lata was a pastel pink. Her stinger —a wicked point of striped red and black descending from the spine down to the floor of the nest, was set on a hinged joint—it could be stiff and straight, its normal position, or bend back, allowing the Lata to sit. Her venom could paralyze or kill organisms many times her size. It was the poison that the Yaxa feared and respected.

"How are you called, Lata?" the Yaxa asked.

"I am Vistaru of the Deer Grove," she replied, trying not to show her nervousness. Never had she felt so helpless in the face of an enemy.

Yaxa never displayed emotion; they had no way to, and their voices translated hard and icy-brittle. And yet, there seemed to be a note of genuine surprise in the creature's voice when it responded. "Vistaru? The one who aided Mavra Chang in the wars long past?"

She nodded slowly, amazed that her name would even be known after all this time.

The Yaxa seemed hesitant, somehow, as if trying to decide what to do. It was uncharacteristic of the great insects. Its enigmatic eyes studied her closely.

"I should have thought you'd be in the male mode by now," the Yaxa said.

"I would have," she told the Yaxa, "but I've kept putting that off. To be a male is to have the responsibility for raising a child, and I have not yet been in a position to do that properly."

The Yaxa remained motionless, impassive, still thinking unknown thoughts. Finally, it said, "Ortega sent you here to help find Mavra Chang." It was not a question, it was a statement.

Vistaru nodded, but volunteered no additional information: their races were old enemies. As odd as this Yaxa was acting, she still did not expect to survive the encounter.

"Then I was right," the huge butterfly murmured aloud to itself. "She is missing, not dead."

"What is that to you?" Vistaru challenged. "If you didn't have anything to do with her disappearance, it was only because Trelig or someone beat you to it."

"Brave talk," the Yaxa noted coldly, but almost approvingly. "Still, I'll strike a bargain with you. Answer truthfully my questions, which will only make us equal in knowledge, and I shall make certain that you have the opportunity to experience the male mode."

Vistaru stared hard at the creature in wonder, but could not fathom what he was talking about. Although they were biochemically closer to each other than either was to the humans, mentally the Lata were much closer to humans.

"We'll see," Vistaru said cautiously. "Ask your questions."

"Do you know who smashed the Chang compound?" the Yaxa asked.

That was an easy one. "No. But we think it was a gang hired by Antor Trelig."

That answer seemed to satisfy the Yaxa. "I can assume that the Ambreza have activated all their antiescape plans and followed every conceivable procedure?" the Yaxa asked.

Vistaru nodded. "She is almost certainly not in Glathriel or Ambreza, nor does she seem to have crossed the border into Ginzin."

"Then she went by ship, as I suspected," the Yaxa said. "The question is, willingly or unwillingly."

"Trelig would have no use for her male companion, Joshi," Vistaru pointed out. "With hypnos available, one doesn't need any other pressure on a source of information. But he's gone, too. We assume that they got away." The Lata stopped, suddenly not sure that she hadn't given away too much.

"You needn't concern yourself," the Yaxa told her, as if reading her mind. "I had already come to similar conclusions. I assume that you are out here, in the middle of nowhere, for the same reason I am—you are hoping to intersect the *Toorine Trader*."

The Lata didn't reply, but her expression told it all.

The Yaxa continued to think hard to itself, its overall intent still a mystery. But its next statement stunned Vistaru.

"Lata, I could kill you, but I will not. Yet if I release you, you might try to sting me, or we will continue to parallel each other's movements in hunting the *Trader*, which should not be far off to the north now —and eventually we will come into conflict some other way. I could just leave you here with your wings tethered, but while you could eat the moss, eventually you would die. This bleak rock is off the shipping lanes, and only the *Trader* brought us together here by chance. So I propose an honorable truce. You will agree not to sting me, and I will agree to do nothing to you and remove the clips. We shall seek out the *Trader*

79

together, and remain together until we ascertain the whereabouts of Mavra Chang. Do you agree?"

She considered it. She had no hope of removing the clips on her own, and without her wings she was trapped. On the other hand, could she trust the Yaxa? What was its motive? Why was it here?

Still, she had no choice.

"All right, I agree. A truce. At least until we find out what is happening here. You have my word I will not harm you."

"Your word is good enough." A long sticky tongue emerged from the Yaxa's curved proboscis and gently lifted the clip from one pair of wings and "handed" it to a front tentacle, which replaced it in a small pack glued to the creature's underside. The same procedure was followed three more times, freeing Vistaru. She flexed her wings gratefully, and stretched.

The Yaxa remained frozen, motionless on the cliff wall, watching her. Vistaru knew that, if she suddenly took off or tried to sting the creature, it was ready for her.

She wouldn't. Her word was good, at least until they found where Mavra Chang was. After that—well, there was venom, and it would keep.

"You know where the ship is?" she asked the Yaxa.

"Follow me," it replied, and took off from the cliff, great orange-and-brown wings spread wide to catch the breeze. Vistaru followed, having to work hard just to keep up with the great creature.

"Slow a bit!" she pleaded, and the Yaxa complied. She moved up, just a little under and to the right of that black, shiny death's head. "What are you called?" she asked it.

"My name is Wooly," the other replied.

Ecundo

THEIR BASIC PROBLEM WAS THAT THEY COULDN'T DO the logical and safe thing—stick to the beach. Obviously, anyone looking for them would eventually come upon the *Toorine Trader* and put everything together.

"But didn't we blast those things that were after us?" Joshi complained as they headed through low brush, which caused a lot of discomfort despite their toughened skin. "Why are we running away?"

Mavra considered the question. How could she explain the situation to him in a way he could understand? That they were running from captivity toward freedom, the right to determine their own destiny? The concept was too abstract for him. Glathriel was the only home he had ever known. Except for an occasional visit to Ambreza, which was for him adventure, the compound and village were his world.

And yet, she reminded herself, she had almost been lulled into that complacency herself. She, the bride of the stars and free spirit of many worlds, had been enmeshed in a trap that had almost made her content with what amounted to routine domesticity, almost forgetting her commission and her goal.

She had been hired to do away with the threat of New Pompeii, and still it was there in the night sky, a dagger directed at the very heart of existence. That commission, given so long ago, was still unfulfilled. And too, what of her ultimate goal, which she could see from the beach on those clear nights. The stars!

Why are we running, Joshi, she thought to herself. From what and to what? From stagnancy and eventual death to adventure on our own terms, that's what!

Aloud she answered, "We don't *know* that they were the ones who attacked the compound, and even if they were, they were just hired hands, not the people who really wanted us. Those behind that attack will try again and again to get us until one day they do. We can sit and be a target until they bullseye us, or we can try and change the rules of the game. We're going to change some rules."

He considered what she said, even accepted it, but he didn't quite understand. The compound had always represented peace and security; to have those boundaries permanently shattered would take a little time to accept.

They wore garments provided by the sailmaker. Pockets contained some food, some vitamins for the rough times, and a few supplies they might need. Anything they could carry without undue weight or imbalance they had packed, and the jackets were covered in a dark fur that might be mistaken for hair at any distance.

Days were warm in Ecundo, but nightfall inland from the coastal ranges brought an uncomfortable chill to the air. They slept covered in brush, and often awoke cold and wet from dew.

Ecundo had five major cities, four along the coast and one in the center of the hex near the Zone Gate, but they were avoiding those completely. The Ecundans were long, tubular creatures with rubbery claws and nasty stingers on their rear ends. Their cities were great artificial mounds where thousands lived in burrows.

To feed the population, most of the country was given over to ranching; they were carnivores, who fed primarily on the bundas, creatures that bred like rabbits and roamed in large wild herds.

Two days in, they saw their first. They felt a rumbling in the ground, and they pressed back against some rocks and watched and waited. Soon the herd came by—hundreds of them, it seemed, some coming close enough to kick dirt into their hideaway, but the bundas showed no particular curiosity if, indeed, they noticed the two travelers at all.

Mavra counted on the bundas to help them through the hex. They ran in herds except when mating; then pairs went off alone to mate, breed, and supervise the first few weeks of their numerous young. As a result, the Ecundans always went for the herds and generally ignored pairs, which, after all, were what kept the food supply going.

Part of her instructions to the sailmaker used this information. They were to look as much like bundas as possible from a distance. Ideally they could stay far enough away from curious stalked eyes to avoid being recognized as alien intruders.

Seeing the bundas now, Joshi finally understood her plans.

The creatures were actually slightly larger than he, and moved, like the two of them, on four hooved feet. The hooves were black instead of off-white, true, and of equal length, but they made similar tracks. In other ways the creatures rather resembled giant guinea pigs. Short black hair covered all but their faces and outlined ears that, though not as long as the Changs', were plenty long enough. Their faces resembled that of the pig, with large brown eyes and a rounded snout below which a short hinged jaw drooped. They were primarily herbivores, eating grass and bushes along the plain, but they also ate insects that looked like a cross between ants and cockroaches and lived in small mounds all over the plain. The bundas never worked finding the insects or bothered the mounds. Instead, at night, after a day of foraging for fresh grass and leaves, they'd simply lie down and go to sleep, sticking out incredibly long sticky tongues that appeared to be coated with white hairs. The insects would then obligingly crawl out of their mounds and onto the waiting tongues, and get caught. Without waking up, the bunda would reel the tongue in, gulp, and then out it would come again.

Several characteristics of the bunda became apparent as Mavra and Joshi made their way across the plains. The beasts were lazy, complacent, easily spooked, and so dumb, Joshi concluded, that should a bunda come upon a three-meter fence section attached to nothing else, it would turn around before figuring out how to walk around it.

The bundas probably weighed sixty or more kilos on the average. Fat hung off them everywhere. And they certainly bred—four per litter every five weeks, weaned only two or three weeks, and full-grown in about a year. They had no natural enemies except the Ecundans, who managed them well.

From a distance an Ecundo would, they hoped, see only a pair broken off from a herd, maybe odd-looking and long-eared, and with perhaps a little less fur than usual. Two bundas not to be disturbed, for more food was on the way.

On the sixth day their theory was put to the test. They were getting used to the herds thundering through the plains on trails made by generations of bunda herds tramping the same ways, and, except for staying out of their way, Mavra and Joshi paid them little mind. This time, however, the herd seemed in a panic. Ordinarily Mavra and Joshi would travel by night, but if one is going to pretend to be a bunda, one can't be moving when bundas sleep, and so the sun shone warmly on them around midday when the stampede occurred. They barely dodged it, moving off in a hurry, but there was something in the animals' manner and almost frantic blind rush that made them pause.

The two lay down in the tall grass and waited several minutes before they saw the cause: five Ecundans, each standing on six two-meter-long crab-like legs, were coming down with amazing speed after the fleeing bundas. Their beady stalked eyes looked ahead—long tail-sections raised and nasty stingers dripping venom, the two claws raised at the ready before them.

The Ecundans intersected the herd near Mavra and Joshi. The two pressed into the ground and held their breaths as one passed almost over them, its eyes following the game ahead. It smelled lousy.

The Ecundans fanned out, driving the herd first one way, then the other, and, finally, almost in circles. Having tired the beasts, they closed in, claws grabbing, stingers flashing with incredible speed.

But those stung initially were just to help as barricades, to limit the frantic animals to a single avenue of escape, which was, in turn, covered by other Ecundans with great nets. The herd ran right into them, and even as the leaders stumbled and fell squealing into the trap, the others mindlessly followed, until the controlling Ecundans considered the haul sufficient and drew the net tight. Two nets held at least twenty bundas apiece, and the great scorpions carried the heavy load as if it were nothing.

Satisfied, the Ecundans let the rest of the herd pass, and all hands fell upon the paralyzed bundas that had formed the living corral, cutting with sharp claw-teeth and eating them, bones and all, in large gulps through mouths that opened wide in four directions. The Changs could see no chewing motions; either the Ecundans digested the chunks whole or their teeth were far back beyond the thorax.

"Oh, boy," Joshi breathed unenthusiastically as the Ecundans rumbled off with the day's catch. "I'd rather talk to them than have to argue with them."

"Wouldn't do much good," Mavra responded glumly. "Those hard cases on the ship said that Ecundans are very nasty about strangers they don't invite. They eat them or just paralyze them and send them home by ship as object lessons. No, we'll not get any help from the Ecundans, believe me."

On the ninth day their food supplies were running low. It concerned them both.

"How much farther to this Wuckl border or whatever?"

"Shouldn't be far," Mavra replied. "We've been making damned good time." Particularly since seeing that Ecundan roundup, she added silently.

And they *had* made good time. The interior valley

was mostly flat, there were few obstructions, bunda trails were everywhere, and they had had the sun at some point every day to keep their bearings. The flat land and trail had allowed them to trot; they were making forty to fifty kilometers a day, by Mavra's figuring. If they'd been keeping to the correct direction, the border should be close by. She told Joshi so.

"It better be," he replied. "Damn! What do they eat in Wuckl, anyway?"

"Pretty much what we do," she replied. "A lot less meat, though. They are a really funny people, as I recall. You'll have to see one to believe it—I won't even try to describe it. Mostly vegetarians by choice, they do some fresh-water fishing in interior lakes. They're high-tech, but slow breeders with a small population. And if the *Trader*'s information is accurate, they have a lot of parks and game preserves just for enjoyment."

He nodded. "But won't it be risky asking for food?" he wondered. "After all, a high-tech hex. The people who want us are bound to look there, too."

"We won't ask unless we have to," she told him. "There's a lot of wild fruit and vegetable stuff growing in those parks and lake areas, and I don't think we'll have to hustle long."

She was right. They made the border near dusk.

It was a forest, but not a dense one, just a parklike wood, complete with pebble-filled trails. The place was beautiful—they could see wild berry bushes and even several citrus trees bursting with fruit. It looked like the land of milk and honey, and the Wuckl were neither antisocial nor deadly.

But there was a hitch.

"Look at that," Joshi grumped. Four strands of coppery barbed wire about two meters high, the fence was attached to metal poles every four meters or so as far as the eye could see.

"To keep the Ecundans out?" Joshi wondered.

She shook her head. "To discourage a bunda invasion of the Wuckl parks and an attack on their goodies, I'd say. Probably put up by both countries in their mutual interest."

"That top line of barbs looks kind of nasty. How are we gonna get over it?"

"We're not," replied Mavra Chang. "We're going *under* it. There's a good fifty centimeters clearance, and I think I can stand a barb or so to get through. Game?"

Joshi looked at the little barbs, which didn't seem all that sharp, then thought about the Ecundans chopping up bundas. "Who's first?" he asked.

"I'll go. With any luck I might just wriggle right under it. Then I can help you through."

He nodded and she approached the fence. "Funny," she said thoughtfully. "A little humming sound. Vibration?"

He heard it but shrugged. "Who knows?"

"Here I go!" she announced, and crouched down as low as she could. The exercise was painful, and she started regretting that extra fat she'd laid on over the years.

She still made it about halfway under when her hips touched the bottom wire.

She screamed and Joshi heard a loud buzz as activators were tripped; she yelled and jerked spasmodically.

"Mavra!" Joshi cried in panic as he rushed to her aid. As soon as he grabbed at her twitching hind leg with his mouth he felt the shock, too.

Ecundo was a semitech hex, but, unfortunately, Wuckl was a high-tech hex, and the fence was one meter inside Wuckl.

And it was electrified.

Hookl

THE SKIES HAD CLEARED, THE WEATHER WAS WARM-ing, and all was right with the world for the crew of the *Toorine Trader*. Seas were under two meters, and she was under a full head of steam heading north-northwest, great clouds of gray-white steam leaving a kilometer-long double line from her twin stacks. They had lost some time in Nocha's storms; now they were making it up.

On the back hatch, two pinkish Twosh were relax-ing, enjoying the feel of sun on their bowling-pin shapes. With ten cigars in little holsters on its belt, one Twosh was balancing itself well on one broad hand while its other hand removed a cigar and stuck it in a tiny, almost circular mouth. It never lit one; it just kept sucking and nibbling on the cigar until it had in-gested the whole thing.

"Big thing, in flight twenty degrees off the star-board bow!" the lookout suddenly shouted from the radar console.

The Twosh with the cigar looked up and located a faint, faraway shape, then turned big lemon eyes to its twin. "Not *another* one!" it groaned.

The other Twosh strained. "I'll be damned if it don't look like a horse this time. That's all we need. A stampede on the high seas!"

"And you know who'll have to clean up the deck," the first one added ominously.

The great deep-purple horse, swan's wings spread wide to take advantage of the updrafts, circled the ship several times as if making certain that it was the one sought and, if so, allowing its rider to figure out how to land. It was a tricky problem. An Agitar pegasus didn't just land like a bird; it had to have a little room to run on the ground, to break its momentum. It could land in water, of course, but while the sea was calm enough for the *Trader,* it was pretty rough for anything smaller.

The captain and crew stared at the newcomer, wondering what he was going to do.

"Be damned if I'll slow for him," the ghostly captain growled in his fog-whistle voice. "If I'd known we were gonna get all this company in the middle of the ocean, I'd have taken up something more peaceful, like the Army."

Tbisi nodded his long, thin furry neck. "Maybe we're missing a bet here, Cap," he said half-seriously. "I mean, charge 'em landing fees, heavy fees for each question asked, fifty times the fee for each answer given, and five hundred times for the truth."

Renard decided that the starboard deck was clear enough and long enough for a try at least, and he brought Domaru, grandson of Doma, in.

Domaru refused the first pass; unlike his distant cousin the horse, the pegasus was neither a stupid nor foolish animal. There was not only the narrow and possibly too-short lane, probably filled with obstacles, ropes and stuff, to contend with, but also the yaw and pitch of the ship with the rolling seas. A second pass was refused by Renard, who cursed that no one below seemed to have the slightest inclination to help him or even move, but on the third try both horse and rider committed, and it was a narrow success. Once down, the pegasus, on a trot, had to fold its wings to clear the area between rail and superstructure. If Domaru couldn't stop at the bow, it would probably break his neck.

The sight of the fast-approaching bow chain seemed to help. The horse put on the brakes with barely fifty centimeters to spare and managed a turn.

Taking a little time to recover his breath and his nerve, Renard looked around at the crew, who were watching him curiously. For the first time he wondered whether or not he should have asked permission or something to come aboard. Two nasty-looking Ecundans were sunning themselves atop the bridge, stalked eyes staring at him; the two Twosh eyed him with expressions more bored than hostile.

He got down and nervously approached the Twosh with the cigar. "Uh, excuse me, but is this the *Toorine Trader?*"

The Twosh took a bite of its cigar, chewed, and swallowed. "Since you took so much trouble to drop in, I'll have to say yes to that."

This reply embarrassed him a little. He wasn't sure how one greeted a little pink brown-eyed bowling pin. Shake hands? No, then what would it stand on? Oh, well . . .

"My name is Renard," he tried. "I'm from Agitar."

"That's interesting," the Twosh responded helpfully.

Renard cleared his throat and tried again. "I'm, ah, representing Ambassador Ortega of Ulik."

The Twosh surveyed him critically. "My, my! Where's your other four arms?"

He sighed. "No, I'm just working with him. I'm searching for a woman, a person named Mavra Chang, who disappeared from Glathriel."

"Does she do other tricks?" the second Twosh put in.

Renard felt frustrated, and the sniggers from the rest of the crew didn't help any.

"Look," he said earnestly, "I'm an old friend of hers. I heard she was in trouble, and I've come to help. We've traced her to this ship, and I'd appreciate some help in locating her. It's extremely important."

The Twosh with the cigar eyed him suspiciously. "Important to whom?" it asked.

"To me, mostly," the Agitar replied. "And to her."

"I'll bet," the other Twosh said under its breath. "Well, if you've traced her to this ship, she must be on it someplace, eh? You're welcome to search away, although I'm afraid that on a ship at sea the crew is a bit too busy to assist you." Its black, straight eyebrows suddenly dipped until they touched the upper part of its eyes. "But I'll tell you right now it won't do any good," it whispered. Its small head gestured to the two Ecundans perched atop the bridge housing. "They ate her, you see."

For an uncomfortable moment Renard thought the little creature was telling the truth. But he dismissed it with a queasy feeling and was certain now that she was not aboard. They were trying too hard.

"You've only made landfall once since Glathriel," he told them, "and that was in Ecundo. Did you drop her there?"

The Twosh looked shocked. "Of course not! When we disembark someone, we lower him *gently* over the side!" it huffed.

Renard threw up his hands. "How you people can be so flippant about all this is beyond me!" he fumed. "That's a dangerous hex for someone like her!"

The Ecundans on top of the bridge suddenly got up on their six legs. "Say, goat-man! Are you insulting us?" one sneered. Two stingers rose.

He felt total defeat. "I give up!" he said, disgusted.

"If you think she's in Ecundo, then you'd better go there," one Twosh suggested. "The way everybody's looking for this person or whatever it is, you will have us covered in Domien. Watch it in Ecundo, though. Those two up there were thrown out for being such *nice* guys."

"Wait a minute. The way *everybody* is looking? Have others been here?"

The answer to that question the Twosh saw no reason to disguise. "Sure. Big bastard with pretty orange wings and a little bitch about as big as your knee flew in this morning. We weren't as helpful to them as we were to you, you bein' such a *nice* guy."

He was learning to ignore the sarcasm. "A Yaxa and a Lata? Did they run into each other?" He was concerned for Vistaru, from whom there'd been no word for several days.

91

"Considering one was perched on top of the other, I'd say they would have a hard time running into each other," the Twosh observed.

That bothered him even more, and he took great pains to describe a Lata to them to make certain they weren't putting him on some more. A Yaxa and a pink Lata—almost certainly Vistaru—*together?* It seemed almost impossible.

"Did either one seem in command?" he asked them. "I mean, did it look like one was, say, a prisoner of the other?"

The Twosh thought about it. "Nope. I wouldn't say they were buddies—but, then again, I don't think anybody could be buddies with that orange iceberg. But they sure seemed to be working together."

That bothered him. Had the Lata, for some reason, deserted Ortega after all this time and joined their old enemies? That was unthinkable—and yet, it had been so many years. People change, he told himself. Governments change, individuals change.

It didn't sound good.

"Hey, mate!" one of the Ecundans called.

He was startled. "Huh?"

"How you gonna take off?" it asked in an amused tone.

The question brought him up short for a moment. He just hadn't thought about it. The sea was too rough, and Domaru definitely needed as long a runway to take off as he did to land—and with wings spread.

He was stuck until landfall at Domien, another day in the direction opposite to where he wanted to go.

They were all snickering now. Finally it was left to Tbisi to administer the *coup de grâce*. "Passage is twelve gold pieces a day," he said, approaching Renard.

The Agitar sighed and mentally kicked himself. "I'll get it out of Domaru's bags," he said resignedly.

"That's another thing," Tbisi added. "The horse is freight. One piece per kilo."

Wuckl

THE CHATTER OF A FEW BIRDS FLITTERED BACK AND forth between the shady trees and sometimes, although rarely, back and forth between the hex border and the forest. There was something in the air of Ecundo the Changs didn't like and soon learned to avoid if possible.

The underbrush crackled as something inordinately large moved in this placid world of bird and leaf. Whatever it was, it was not in a hurry. It moved steadily and deliberately toward the electrified fence bordering Ecundo, a sentinel in response to a silent alarm.

The creature that reached the fence was a large biped. Its body, an almost perfect oval covered with thick, wiry black hair, was suspended on enormous birdlike feet, each with five long, clawed toes. The legs looked like long helixes, making the creature appear as if standing on springs; those thick meter-long legs could bend in any direction.

The Wuckl stopped and looked at the fence and at the two unconscious creatures with curiosity. Then it walked over to the fence and almost touched it. Its head swung this way and then that on its long, golden-ringed neck, as it studied every angle of fence wire and trapped creatures.

The Wuckl was plainly puzzled by them. From a distance they had looked like bundas, but close up they looked different from anything in its experience —bundalike, but distorted somehow.

It finally decided to leave its wonder for later. The fence was not loaded with enough charge to kill a bunda, Ecundan, Wuckl, or any other large creature likely to blunder into it. It was supposed to drive intruders away, not knock them out—but one of them had tried to crawl under the fence, got stuck, and became the focus of a series of jolts. The second had grabbed the first firmly and been subjected to the abnormal shocks too. By now, the cumulative effect had knocked them out.

Although the Wuckl wore no apparent clothes, a long, thin hand reached into the side of its body and pulled out of an invisible pocket a pair of insulated gloves. The right hand re-entered and came out with what looked like large wire cutters. Donning the gloves, it carefully cut the wire strands around the unconscious creatures so that there was clearance.

The first one was then easily dragged over to the Wuckl's side of the border. The second, however, caused more trouble, since the Wuckl didn't want to cut away the entire fence. For a while it considered leaving the other one behind. But clearly, beneath their bundalike garments, these were two of a kind and should not be separated—at least not until the mystery of their origin was solved.

Finally, by reaching over and then pulling from below, the Wuckl managed to drag the unconscious Joshi across as well. Then it removed the gloves and placed them, along with the cutters, in its invisible pockets and picked up one creature with each hand as if they were weightless. It walked back down the path with them.

Toug was a forester; injured animals were not its specialty, so it headed for the house of the gamekeeper, who had a graduate degree in Animal Skills. In the almost ten minutes it took Toug to make it to the gamekeeper's, the two beings it carried never stirred.

The gamekeeper, after some initial clicking of its beak and grouching about being disturbed at dinner, grew interested when it saw Toug's burden. Quickly, all thoughts of food gone, it bade the forester to bring the two into the surgery.

The room had an operating table more than three

meters long that was almost infinitely adjustable and some vats, bins, refrigerators, and the like. Special lighting was brought into play, and while Joshi was placed carefully on the tiled floor, Mavra was placed on the table, which was then adjusted to the game-keeper's convenience. It was smaller than Toug and obviously a bit older, but otherwise looked much the same.

"Where did you find these two?" it asked the forester.

"By the fence, as you see them," Toug replied. "I received a buzz alarm at Post 43 and went down to investigate."

The gamekeeper seemed bewildered. "Were they trying to get into Ecundo, then?"

"No, Senior, they were by all appearances trying to get into Wuckl," the other responded.

The gamekeeper's long neck moved as it surveyed the unconscious body. Long thin fingers probed this way and that. Finally it said, "Return to your duties. This will take some thought."

"They are not dead, then?" Toug responded with obvious concern.

The other Wuckl wagged its head in a circular motion. "No, not dead. But their systems are far too delicate for what they have received. Go, now, while I solve this riddle."

Once Toug was gone, the examination of Mavra and Joshi began in earnest. The Wuckl simply could not figure them out. As animals, they did not make sense.

The brain seemed inordinately large and complex, but there was little for it to do. With such limited limb movement and a total lack of prehensility, these creatures could not possibly be of a high order. They were clearly hoofed animals. They were shaped like bundas, but their internal construction was all wrong, and their faces faced downward. The legs, muscle tone, and the like were too obviously correct to be constructs; therefore, these must be mutants, it decided. But mutations of what?

They were strange, that was certain. The Wuckl pulled down its Well World Catalog and looked through it, but nothing matched up. There were centauroids, yes, but these were not like those. In some ways they were similar to those of Glathriel, yet far enough different that the gamekeeper rejected that possibility. The others were even more remote.

It replaced the books, satisfied that these were animals, not intelligent creatures, brain structure notwithstanding.

But what to do with them? Their nervous systems had suffered tremendously. The creatures needed help or they would surely die, and though it didn't know exactly what they were, the Wuckl had not devoted so much time to becoming a senior in Animal Skills to let animals die when it was within its power to save them.

Mavra's reproductive system brought the Wuckl up short. Someone with Skills had operated on it, crudely but effectively. These were not, then, something wild.

It thought about this, and reached the only conclusion it could think of that fit the facts. It remembered that five of its fellow students had been expelled, sent to disgrace in Manual Skills for their efforts. Though quite different in result, what he had before him reminded the Wuckl of their experiment. Taking a basic animal as a start, the five had added and subtracted with abandon, rearranging limbs, taking organs from other animal stocks. They created a pair of monstrosities.

What if recent students had done the same? And, fearing discovery, they'd taken the poor creatures and left them in Ecundo to be eaten or otherwise lost to Wuckl authority?

No Wuckl could deliberately kill, so that solution to the hypothesized dilemma never occurred to the gamekeeper.

That, of course, is what these creatures must be. Hideous creations of students. It explained a lot, but the implications were even uglier. These brains might have come from high-order creatures, implanted, perhaps, in the fetal stage, growing with the creatures for—how long?

Death might be a mercy for such as these, it thought sadly, but, then, these two would never know that they were what they were, and surely would not and should not suffer for the horrors growing from the minds of others.

It would report this butchery, though; the perpetrators would be caught, and their minds adjusted to Manual Skills. Even that was too good for them, but compassion was in all Wuckl.

But what to do with these two?

To leave them as they were was unthinkable; they were not in the Catalog, they could not assimilate into the Balanced Environment. To cast them out, as had been obviously tried, was equally unthinkable.

The only answer was to readapt them to the Catalog. The problem was that the life forms of Wuckl were, on the whole, quite different from those in other hexes, except for bird and insect life. The bunda would be the easiest, of course, but much time and effort had been expended in keeping bunda out of Wuckl; adding two more would hardly be good for the ecological balance.

It went once more to its references. In a preserve, some exceptions would be tolerated. If a form in the Catalog were chosen, it could be explained and rationalized as were the animals in any foreign-animal compound. Basically, the changes would be cosmetic, of course. An animal was a complex organism, not easily built from scratch. Some needs would have to be satisfied, however; special food would be out of the question, so some modification of the digestive system would be in order. And acclimation, of course, which would be tricky with brains so complex.

And then the gamekeeper had it: a native of several hexes, biologically compatible, requiring far less work than would be needed to recreate other forms. Straightforward modifications.

Joshi, who had received a much weaker shock than Mavra, groaned suddenly and stretched a bit. The

Wuckl, not ready for this, quickly grabbed a small device, checked it, and placed it gently against the Chang's neck. Joshi suddenly went limp. To make sure, the gamekeeper gave Mavra Chang a dose of the sedative as well. The substance would do the job. No sense in their coming around before modifications were finished, the Wuckl thought nervously.

It called several assistants by phone, then started setting up equipment.

Three hours later, four Wuckl stood in the surgery. Three were quite young, apprentices learning their craft. Quickly the gamekeeper had explained to them its theories, decisions, and plans, and they had concurred in its diagnosis. Electrobaths, instruments, and associated equipment were arranged, and all shared a sense of excitement. This was to be a genuinely creative series of operations of the type few ever got to perform; they might even get into the books for it.

The gamekeeper, as a senior, would actually perform the operations; the others would assist. Mavra, to be first, was stretched out on the table. The lighting was odd and surfaces polished; all of them could follow the operation with their trained and special optics from any point in the room.

The long Wuckl hands with their thin, sensitive fingers started in, kneading and prodding the skin, much in the manner of an extremely strong masseur. As this action continued, the movements grew faster, more furious. A second Wuckl stood by, ready with the necessary replacement organs and tissues.

And now the gamekeeper's hands were *inside* her, incredibly, with no incision apparent, no blood, nothing. The right hand retracted quickly—drawing with it a bloody organ—and was immediately back in. Now the left retracted, grabbed small clamps and slices of doughy flesh from liquid-filled containers, and returned. Its speed was fantastic; the student Wuckl watched in admiration at internal manipulation literally too quick for the eye to see. The senior had the gift in tenfold amounts, and they marveled at his sureness and skill.

The operation lasted some time, and then hands flew and small plastic clamps covered with small bits of bloody tissue were withdrawn from the body. The gamekeeper relaxed for a moment, rubbing its hands together.

"Internal modifications are completed," it told the others. "Next, the cosmetics." A new set of replacement organs were substituted for the old, and the apprentices double-checked their equipment.

On her body there was no sign of incision or wound, no blood, scars, or other traces. Mavra looked the same.

"Much of this is being accomplished with synthetics," the senior explained to the apprentices. "They are organic, of course, but manufactured. I compliment Yuog on the abundance of supply. As we have no way to replace the blood supply except naturally, and the two are of different blood types, speed is of prime importance. Now, let us begin the second phase."

Again parts were removed, parts added from the bins of assorted foul-smelling liquids, with blinding speed. Head done, it moved to the body, molding, kneading, altering, all the while taking care to preserve all neural connections so there would be no problem in adaptation. With a university's money and a computer's guidance, a complete remake was certainly possible, but the Wuckl in the preserve surgery did not have those advantages. This was more a case of adapting form to function, and, in a way, that was more satisfying.

Finally, it was done. They admired the work; it was incredibly good. Parts removed from the animals were preserved; they would be subject both to later study and to analysis by better labs and then used as evidence in its case to find the perpetrators of the biological crime.

"Electrobath!" the senior ordered, and Mavra was quickly lifted and placed in a tank of foul liquid. A face mask was hooked to an air supply so she could be submerged totally. Power was applied, and the fluid was energized to seal what had been done and to revise the genetic information in the affected cells so that they would maintain the new shape without forming scar tissue or rejecting what had been added. A small computer fed the instructions via the fluid, adding final developmental instructions as well.

"And now the male!" instructed the senior, and Joshi was placed on the table.

"Note the scar tissue. Long ago this one was severely burned, perhaps tortured." They murmured in shock. "We will address ourselves to that later."

It began, and, after several rests, was completed. Joshi was placed in a second electrobath.

A final step was necessary.

"You noticed the highly developed brain," it lectured. "My first inclination was to trim it to what was needed, but it is too complex; there is too much room for error there. However, it will be necessary that they acclimate to their new situation. Animals are creatures of habit and instinct, and since these two have the wrong habits and no proper instincts for their new existence, this must be provided. You are familiar with the principles of hypno-programming; it is my belief that these two are developed enough to absorb it on a basic level."

"But, Senior!" one young Wuckl protested. "These are still not of any life of the island, let alone Wuckl. How will you do this?"

"The creature is common, however, and in the Catalog," the gamekeeper replied. "I had its Catalog requirements transmitted by phone from the University. A bit esoteric, of course—I had to trade on an old friendship or two and will owe some explanations later, particularly for those who compiled the two modules at this late hour, but they are here. We will administer the treatment while they are in the electrobath. I will keep them sedated until certain that all the work is progressing satisfactorily."

"Then what?" another asked. "What will you do with them?"

The senior's bill opened wide in all four directions, the Wuckl equivalent of a smile. "They will awaken in their new and permanent homes, happy and cared for. I will arrange it. Do not fear. What we have done is ethical and right."

Mavra Chang awoke as if from a total absence of prior sensation. It was almost like being born; it was the beginnings of consciousness. Her mind was a complete blank; no words formed there. Then suddenly her senses brought input. She opened her eyes and looked around. It was dark, and hard to see. She got up and walked around the area with aimless curiosity. It was a straw-floored enclosure; over to one side, the only thing present, was a large male.

She sensed somehow that he was male and she female; the concepts were natural, like walking, sleeping, eating—not verbal concepts, just what was. The male was still asleep.

She found an opening and walked to it. She sniffed at it briefly, then walked through. At the other end lay the outside.

She looked around with that same nonintellectual curiosity, seeing a clipped grassy hill that smelled good and, nearby, a trough of aromatic stuff and, surrounding it all, a moat that was clear to its artificial rock bottom, perhaps four or five meters down. At one end of their compound, beyond the moat, a stone wall rose a meter or so higher than the hill; from the water, though, it was three meters to the top, effectively blocking any exit.

Although that wall was a bare fifteen meters from her, she had trouble seeing beyond it. Close-up things were sharp and clear, say, a few meters around, but then things started to blur. Beyond the wall she could see indistinct forms but no recognizable shapes. For some reason this seemed wrong to her, but she didn't dwell on it.

She was thirsty, incredibly so, and walked down to the water, sliding in easily and without fear, moving effortlessly in it. She opened her mouth and let the water enter until she had had enough, then headed back to the little hill. The smell from the trough was overwhelming, and she went to it quickly and started eating.

She heard a noise behind her and saw the male emerge sleepily and repeat her actions almost exactly. As soon as she saw what it was, she went back to eating. Soon he, too, was eating hungrily, greedily. An enormous amount of food lay in the trough, but they did not stop until they had eaten it all, even pushing each other for the last morsel.

Each then spent some time searching around the trough and eating what they had spilled in their feast. Finally, satisfied that there was no more, they returned to the water, drank some more and swam for a bit, then sauntered up the hill and reclined in the grass to bask in the warm sun and listen to the unfamiliar sounds that came from all directions—sounds of different animals and others.

Over the next few days the routine was unvaried. The male marked the island, the hut, the food places and the water with his scent which she accepted. It defined the limits of their territory.

The food was delivered by a strange-looking and stranger-smelling thing that entered by lowering a ramp from the other side of the wall; it would pour more stuff in the feeding-place, then leave, allowing the ramp to fold out of sight. At first they had challenged the thing, but the food was too strong and soon its function was obvious, so they left it alone. Beginning to look forward to its brief visits and its occasional odd noises directed at them, they would strain to catch its scent.

Always hungry, they left nothing. When there was no food, they would rest, or chase each other playfully, or swim in the moat. At no time did they have a verbal thought, at no time a memory, at no time even a curiosity as to where they were.

But the Wuckl's shock and conditioning had not really touched the brain; their intelligence was all there, and, as time passed memories slowly crept back to both of them, first as odd dreams, funny pictures of unfamiliar creatures making odd noises, then as whole sequences of events. At first it was too much for them to comprehend, but time, inactivity, and the total absence of anxiety healed them more and more.

Thoughts became coherent. Strange things in their disjointed memories started acquiring names, meaningless but definite. Then came the big hurdle: self-awareness. He. She. I.

For Mavra Chang there came visions of a cold and mountainous place, a place populated with huge two-legged creatures of white fur with doglike faces and kind eyes, beings she knew, beings who knew her, beings who perhaps knew everything, beings who could help her, although she did not as yet remember why she needed help.

She knew, somehow, she had to reach them. It was an imperative, like eating and sleeping. It was something that had to be done.

For Joshi, there was a different sense; he knew as the male it was his job to mate with and protect the female. He had no visions of strange beings with white fur and kind eyes, but he also sensed that he had to follow his mate wherever she went.

Escape became Mavra's mania. She searched all over the little island for a way out but could find no means of going over that wall.

Finally, when the feeder lowered the ramp and brought the food over, she had an idea. The thing was confident that the food smell would keep them next to it, away from the bridge—and for the first couple of times she did find the smell irresistible. But while the thing brought food to the trough, the ramp was down. Here was a way to get over that wall.

Vaguely, she was certain that they were in a zoo, though the concept was a hazy one. It was hard to think, to form plans, to plot on many levels or be very subtle about it. She tried running as fast as she could, and discovered that, despite being fat and low to the ground, she had short bursts of remarkable speed when she needed it. She felt she could withstand the food odor if she really tried and make for that bridge. She wished she could convey this thought to the male. But although she'd tried—and he'd tried—they could manage only deep grunts. But he followed her around, ran when she did, stopped when she did, and that should be enough. If he didn't follow, it would be bad, but she knew that she had to reach the strange place that haunted her dreams.

The Wuckl, a very young feeder, came by near dusk as usual. It had been working at the preserve for several months and had its routine down pat. When it got to the new ones and picked up the heavy buckets of food for them, they were there waiting for him as usual, and the female was grunting more excitedly than usual, but that was all right.

The feeder stared curiously at them for a moment. From a hex far to the northeast of the island, they filled a gap in the zoo's displays, although the Wuckl had wondered why such a grandiose place—once the pen for a large group of domestic animals—had been picked for only two of them.

They were curious creatures to see. Fat, they ate whenever and whatever they could—including the organic garbage from the city, which was their standard fare. They stood on four funny little legs that were set far back on their bodies and ended with small cloven hooves. They could not see their own legs because their heads took up the whole forward part of their bodies, allowing only a relatively inflexible neck.

The quadrupeds were not to be taken lightly, though; although almost bare when they arrived at the zoo, in the days that followed a brown growth sprouted all over their bodies except on the underside, legs, and face. The brown coat was deceptive—it was stiff, sharp, and needlelike, and to pet one would risk getting multiple punctures.

In fact, they looked like large pigs covered with porcupine quills, although the Wuckl, never having seen a hog, would not have recognized the analogy. There were some differences. They were tailless, and their ears were tall and pointed. The male was neutral pink in the face and legs, contrasting with the bitch's burnt orange.

A kick of its taloned leg and the ramp flipped up and over. The Wuckl hopped up before it swung back, holding it down with its weight as it crossed. Across the moat but still on the bridge, it put down one of the food buckets and reached down and put a small hook in an eye socket in the ground, thereby anchoring the bridge.

Mavra looked at her mate and gave a loud grunt that momentarily took his mind and eye off the food. As the Wuckl walked to the trough, she ran for the bridge, then crossed it with a clatter of tiny hooves. Joshi looked about, confused for an instant, then ran after her.

The feeder turned at the noise, shocked. "Hey!" it screamed, and started running after them. It was so upset that it tripped on the edge of the bridge and fell into the moat.

In the precious minute or two this mishap bought, Mavra was away. Her vision was limited, but she smelled the scents of numerous things like the feeder, and wherever the scent grew stronger she followed it.

The preserve was closed; the staff on duty were busy at their tasks or eating, so they went on unimpeded. She'd guessed right; the stronger the scent, the more Wuckl had passed the more likely she would find the entrance or exit. There was a chain across it, but it was too high to block them, and they were soon out into a parking area. They ran to the left, toward some trees barely visible in the growing darkness. The scent was strong, and it seemed a natural place to go. Behind them, the feeder had by then pulled itself from the moat and raised the alarm. But the fugitives were away and running, even though Joshi hadn't the slightest idea why.

Even though she thought she was a pig, and for all intents and purposes *was* a pig, and still couldn't think clearly or remember why, Mavra Chang was heading to Gedemondas.

Oolakash

THE CITY RESEMBLED A GREAT REEF OF BRIGHT-colored coral stretching out in all directions. It was not wholly natural, though; it had been formed by the biological processes of the inhabitants and by an advanced technology.

Inside, vast halls were connected by long, narrow tunnels; living units, offices, everything was communal. One knew where everything was and who was in charge of what.

The inhabitants of this high-tech hex were themselves long and thin, with bony exoskeletons. One such, tall and still very young, emerged from a passage into the clear dark waters. Its head bore a slight resemblance to that of a horse, but was actually a bony shell in which two tiny, unblinking red eyes were set atop a long snout that was actually a tube. As a result, the facial expression seemed one of permanent surprise. Two small ears, hardly more than folds in the exoskeleton, and two tiny horns over the eyes instantly relayed data on the water through which the creature moved effortlessly. Below its head was a body like an elongated turnip, from which a series of armored tentacles covered with suction cups emerged. The body ended in a long, curved tail that coiled and uncoiled as it moved.

Dr. Gilgam Zinder, despite so many years as an Oolakash, still marveled at this life and these—now his—people. Movement was like floating at will in thick air, a slight flick of tail here or there taking you up, down, or wherever else you wanted to go. It was wonderful, a feeling of total freedom and command.

In many ways he was a totally different person from the middle-aged human who had cracked the Markovian code.

Unorthodox, dogmatic, egocentric, and eccentric, nonetheless he understood the mathematics of reality better than any before him, and he had landed in a high-tech hex—albeit a water world.

This took a lot of new education.

It was an incredible world, though, a world with every modern convenience, even high-speed tubes in which water pressure could propel one to the various points of the hex. Oolakash had somehow attained a limited but efficient atomic technology adapted to underwater use, having bypassed some of the intermediate stages.

When Zinder arrived, he thought he was isolated, forever cut off. He had no idea where the others had gone, or if they had even survived.

Culturally, Oolakash had taken some getting used to. There was little privacy, but the people were good, honest, and serious. They were organized into guilds, which trained and developed their own and were interdependent for services. Each guild elected one member to a governing guild, which in turn elected a leader, who held absolute power for a two-year term, after which that person could never hold any office again.

Essentially their society was a matriarchy. Women did the majority of the work, dominated the guilds and the leadership. Males, with the ability to control their body coloring, were prissy peacocks who spent a good deal of time trying to attract females.

But the Oolakash had recognized an exception in Zinder; they'd known who and what they had, and they had erected a wall of secrecy and silence around him. All who knew of his origin had such knowledge erased from their minds when their need to know no longer was necessary—even the leadership. To the others, he was just Tagadal, a scientist who was exceptionally bright even if he was a male.

The island lay ahead. Below, it was festooned with

marine life; above, it was a barren rock in a smooth sea; inside, it was a communications center of a very unique sort.

The hardest part had been placing the transmitter above the surface and disguising it. But they had managed it, with remote devices, partially of Zinder's own design. The communications system itself was an ingenious hybrid of Zinder and Oolakash design. The surface of the sea was used, making possible the reception of a strong signal at a distance, but one too diffuse, close up, for proper triangulation to locate the ultimate source. In effect, the signal was unintelligible to any except the one for whom it was intended.

Zinder nodded to the technical people as he floated into his office to check a few reports before swimming up to the transmission chamber. Devices had had to be constructed just to allow his voice to be used; the Oolakash used a series of very rapid high-frequency pulses for communication. Instead of placing a translator on him, the solution was to wire it into the transmission circuitry itself. He talked normally; in Zone, a device was used to slow the speech to other-race norms, although it was often frustrating for an Oolakash to hold a conversation with such slow-thinkers. He figured it was something like talking between planets in a large system with an enormous time-lag. There was no problem, however, with the party to whom he talked using the big transmitter above.

Tentacles laced through controls with lightning speed. Lights and dials spun, power built up, and it was time to begin.

"Obie?" he called.

There was a slight delay, a real-time lag this time, and then a reply, in his own language, at his own speed.

"Yes, Doctor? I am here," came a distant voice.

"Do you have any way of calculating the progress of the Northern expeditions?" he asked.

"No one has left yet, if that's what you mean," the computer responded carefully. "I have been monitoring the Yugash Zone Gate inputs. Only the norm so far, and nothing from the South that correlates. I have also managed to pick up some Yaxa transmissions as you requested."

Zinder nodded. Those he needed. Obie was a great computer, true, but it was a minor toy compared to the Well of Souls. The Well, of course, was not self-aware, but its contents were open to Obie—who, unfortunately, hadn't the capacity to interpret such a mountain of complex data. Over the years, however, Obie had learned how to utilize subsets of the data from the Well; the Yaxa transmissions were low-volume enough to be usable, but it had taken Obie weeks to isolate them.

"So how far along are they?" Zinder prodded.

The computer didn't hesitate. "Many problems have cropped up. For one, the poor initial suit tests; the rebreather apparatus didn't work well, and almost caused two deaths," he reported. "They've started over from the beginning. Their error is fundamental to the limitations of semitech hex requirements—I could solve it in an instant—but they are still stuck awhile."

That was good, Zinder thought with satisfaction.

The problem, of course, was that while Yugash was fairly close to Uchjin, where the downed ship had sat these many years, it was not next to it but several hexes away. In none of the Northern nations was there atmosphere a carbon-based life form could use. An ordinary spacesuit would not do; a Southern native would need a truckload of oxygen canisters just to travel the 355 kilometers of a nontech hex side. Electrical rebreathers wouldn't work in a semitech hex either; some solution had to be found or, even if the Yaxa and Ben Yulin could get to the North, they would be unable to live to reach Uchjin.

Ortega no longer had such a problem. Obie had long ago solved it, and the devices, now secreted in safe and ignorant hexes, had been manufactured according to Gil Zinder's specifications. Ortega could get to Uchjin, but he could not fly the ship. Nor could Zinder go along; the Oolakash were almost invulnerable in their own environment, but they could not leave it. Besides, the available types of power on the Well World could not develop sufficient thrust to overcome the Well's effects on the hex and adjoining nontech and semitech hexes to allow such a cart to get into space.

Gil Zinder was a participating bystander.

"What of this Chang woman and her companion?" he asked Obie.

The computer emitted a very human sigh. "You know that since she has never been through the Well she does not register at all," he reminded the scientist. "As for Joshi, her companion, well, you know the number of life forms on the Well World. If I had his type's pattern to begin with, yes, I could trace him—but, now, even if I were directly monitoring him, I would have no way of knowing it was the correct individual."

The news meant that it was increasingly likely that the Yaxa and Yulin would be the first to reach New Pompeii—Yulin, who had supervised the building of Obie and who, Zinder now deduced, had access to circuitry in the computer that would make Obie do his bidding regardless. Of them all, Yulin was best able to use Obie and best able to thwart attempts by the computer to free itself or foul its controller up.

Gil Zinder sighed. "I greatly fear, Obie, that we will have to do the unthinkable. If the Yaxa get on the right track, we *must* beat them to New Pompeii, even if we have to do it with the devil himself."

"Which is increasingly likely," the computer responded glumly.

Wuckl

AFTER THEIR ESCAPE, THINGS DIDN'T SEEM SO SIM-
ple. Mavra's mind continued to increase its working
capabilities; there were gaps here and there, and how
the present situation had come about was beyond her,
but she continually found it easier to remember things
about the past.

As she and Joshi hid out in the hills from the sun's
revealing light, now just starting to flood the horizon,
she took stock of what she knew and what she had to
do. She wished she knew how much time had passed
between first hitting the fence and this moment.

The last thing she remembered was that fence.
Somehow it had knocked both of them out—and
they'd awakened as odd pigs. Why and how was
something to be discovered much later, if ever.

So she was a pig, she thought unemotionally. In
some ways it was a distinct advantage. Her breed
was obviously born to the wild; it was therefore
equipped with survival mechanisms heretofore denied
them.

Considering the swill they'd eaten in the zoo, food
would not be a problem. The Wuckl, for all their
strangeness, ate foods rather similar to that consumed
by the humans of Glathriel; as such, they had garbage
cans and garbage dumps. Mavra wasn't proud; if the
stuff was something she could eat without ill effects,
she would eat it. And, all the life forms of the South
were carbon-based; some were herbivores, some carnivores, some omnivores, but in general the food of
one would not kill a member of a different race, although it might not do much good.

Most important was the new head angle. For the first time in long memory she was looking straight ahead, not down. The tremendous sense of confidence in movement this brought was a fair tradeoff for the nearsightedness, which was still a better range than what she'd been able to manage in the old form. Finally, the sharp quills provided a defensive weapon that might come in handy.

All in all, it was better to be a pig, she reflected. In most ways, the Wuckl or whoever had done this to them had done them a favor. The only major problem was communication. She realized that their bodies had been highly modified, not changed, for she still had translator capability from the tiny crystal surgically imbedded in her brain. The implant allowed her to understand the Wuckl and others, but it didn't allow communication with them. Joshi, who had no translator, remained very much in the dark.

Either their larynxes were paralyzed or they had been removed; the pigs had only the classic grunt of the hog.

She wondered just how much Joshi remembered. Was he better off than she, mentally, or worse? Was there some way to communicate? She would have to try. They could hardly move about in broad daylight, and the appearance of the animal life in their vicinity convinced her that in this hex pigs belonged only in zoos. They would continue to be forced to move by night.

She considered what he knew. Universal code, yes —he'd learned that in order to help signal the supply ships in foul weather. If she could manage to regulate her grunting, and if he got the idea, and if he was mentally capable of understanding it, then it might suffice.

A lot of ifs.

She nudged him with her snout and he snorted, more in curiosity than annoyance. Time to begin.

She tried a simple phrase—"We are free"—to see if she could get something across. It was slow going, and she did it endlessly, hoping he'd catch the repetitive pattern.

Several minutes of this passed, and he seemed confused. She was afraid he hadn't gotten it when suddenly his ears twitched.

In truth, Joshi had received far less of a shock than she and so had recovered earlier. He simply did not have her drive or ambition. Now, though, he caught a word after first realizing that she was trying to talk to him. The group for "we" was brief and basic. He picked it up, repeating her grunt-pulses aloud. She became excited, tried it faster, and he followed again, excited himself now.

Now she stopped, and he did, too, a moment later. It was his turn.

"We are pigs," he grunted.

Breakthrough! She would have hugged and kissed him if she could.

"We will go on," she said to him.

He groaned in a more universal code. "What can we do now?" he asked her. "We are pigs."

"Chang pigs," she retorted. "We think. We know. We are still we. If we stay free, we can still make it."

He seemed resigned.

They worked out a short series of sounds for important concepts and practiced them until both had them down. The messages were basic, a few grunts and squeals, but they could signal "stop," "go," "run," "danger," and other basics whenever time would not permit the length of a conversation. A sentence could take close to a minute.

Eventually, Joshi signaled, "I'm hungry."

She sympathized. They were always hungry. But they had reason, and reason said they would wait until eating was less risky. He accepted her logic and decided to sleep instead.

Mavra Chang couldn't, though, not right away. Watching Joshi, thinking the way he was thinking, and knowing her own feelings she realized that there was a split here, a dichotomy that craved resolution in her mind.

Joshi looked normal. She felt hunger as a pig would, felt all of the things a pig would feel. In a way, she realized, this latest transformation had snapped the last bands connecting her to humanity. These past decades she'd clung to her humanity; she had still been human, just a different and unique variety that in an odd way had pleased her. She no longer felt that. For a while she wondered if her new attitude was part of what they had done to her. She doubted it; it wasn't like being hypnoed to accept her new life as a being on all fours. No, it was something else, yet something familiar. Rather, it was like that change when she had stopped thinking of how she would one day regain humanity and had accepted herself as she was, when she stopped thinking as a human woman and started thinking as a Chang female. Once again, her mind was split and she was trying to reconcile the opposing halves. She did not fight it, she let it happen this time.

Pig—all the elements that made up the animal to which she was now akin—struggled with human personality and point of view. What, after all, did she owe humans? What had they done for her? Even in the old days, as one of them, she'd been apart, different, an odd element that felt itself somehow superior to, alien to the "normal" people around her. They hadn't done much for her, only a lot to her. In turn, she had used them, as one would use a tool in completing a task. She had been among them but not of them, always, for as long as she could remember. They had made her an animal; very well. She would be one. A pig or whatever this was. A very smart pig, to be sure, but a pig just the same.

The competing elements inside her mind stopped their warfare. A pig she was and would always be, and it was all right.

Dusk found them both feeling as if they were starving to death. Cautiously they made their way toward some lights in the distance. This was a high-tech hex; the Wuckl were obviously creatures of the day, but, like humans, they could exist at night and were active then.

It was a small town; not the major population center, no, but a community of several thousand. They would be on the lookout for two escaped animals, so Mavra Chang and Joshi had to be careful. They circled the town, searching with the heightened senses of their new noses for the telltale smells that had to be present. Had to. These people had garbage cans, but she preferred not to nose into them if she could avoid it—too much noise and clatter. But garbage cans meant a garbage dump, and they spent half an agonizing night looking for it.

What they found was a landfill—lots of trash and garbage all around and mounds of dirt that were being bulldozed to fill in a marsh. Some of it had been chemically treated to avoid contamination, but their noses led them to the untreated garbage. They managed to gorge themselves on material that in their former existence would have revolted them. As wild pigs, it didn't bother them in the least, and the thought barely entered their minds.

Unfortunately, their hunger was omnipresent; even when it lessened they found it difficult to leave a sure source of food, for they knew they would soon need it as much as ever. They had to make time for traveling, though; Mavra knew that to remain in the area would mean inevitable capture, and at best a return to a much more secure compound, even a cage—a horrifying thought.

Earlier, the sun, now long gone, had indicated which way was east, and they headed overland. Much of the area was marshy, but they did not mind; their breed of pig was a tireless swimmer in the deep places, and neither dampness nor mud bothered them. In fact, mud smelled rather good to them, indicating to Mavra that their kind was originally from a swamp like this.

Things seemed to break their way. The second night found them near what appeared for all the world to be a near-ripe corn field, and this was like Christmas to them, particularly since an ear eaten here or there would hardly be noticed, and the standing vegetation provided excellent cover.

On the third night they could hear the roar and pounding of the surf from afar, and it was almost too much for Joshi to bear, particularly when they reached a cliff and looked out into the darkness and smelled the mildly salty air. This was the eastern side of the Sea of Turagin, but it reminded them of home.

Blinking lights not far offshore marked dangerous reefs, and powerful lighthouses warned of more extensive dangers.

They savored the sights and smells for some time, but Mavra did so with mixed emotions. The sea represented a curious contradiction. There was freedom, salvation, and escape—and a nearly insuperable barrier to such things. Beyond were the water hexes. This was probably Zanti, which led to Twosh. That was too far from their goal. Beyond it was Yimsk, which led to Mucrol, next to Gedemondas, but also next to the spider hex of Shamozan, which was in league with Ortega. To the north was Alestol, with its deadly gas-shooting plants. They still had hundreds of kilometers of swamp to get to Mucrol, and at least one hex side to Gedemondas. Yet somehow their goal seemed so very close, just beyond her reach.

Joshi seemed to catch her thoughts. "Now what?" he signaled.

Now what, indeed, she asked herself. They couldn't swim. If her memory served her, as it always had, those lights meant that they were just north of the chief Wuckl seaport, the very place where they were to meet the *Toorine Trader* once again if all went according to plan.

But how long had it been? What day, week, month was it? And, even if they were still in time, how could they board without attracting attention, and then convince the crew of their true identities?

Well, there'd be garbage there, and a place to sleep.

They started south along the beach, and as they did she could almost hear the voice of the Gedemondan coming in on mystic breezes and roaring seas.

You will descend into Hell, it whispered. *Only then, when hope is gone, will you be raised up . . .*

Hope was only gone when you were dead or might as

well be, she thought. Two pigs would tell that to the Gedemondans in their ice-covered volcanic caverns, and throw it in their smugly all-knowing faces.

Near the Ecundo-Wuckl Border

HE HAD SEARCHED FOR WEEKS, KNOWING THAT THEY had to be there. The *Trader*'s course, speed, and location assured him that Mavra could not have been dropped off anywhere but in Ecundo.

Renard cruised low over Ecundo, searching as he had for more than two weeks. He knew her well enough to guess her plan; he'd seen the bundas. He had also seen more than one vicious Ecundan roundup, the first of which had made him violently ill. There would be no defense against those great, fast scorpions and their deadly stingers and chopping blades if Mavra and Joshi were caught. He himself had discovered how nasty the Ecundans were when he'd sent Domaru down and tried to question some of them.

They had attacked, snarling curses and epithets at him, and he was forced for the first time in many years to use the great power of the Agitar in combat. The little satyrs were masters of electricity; they were immune to its effects and could store charges of thousands of volts in their bodies, discharging selectively at a distance using long, copper-clad steel rods called tasts. They always maintained quite a charge; it was required for proper health and was built up when their wooly blue fur generated static electricity as they walked.

The Twosh on the *Trader* had been right; the Ecundo in that crew *had* been nice people compared to their brethren back home.

What kept Renard going was his confidence in that

strange woman he'd not seen in over twenty years. *She* wouldn't change; her successful flight and demonstrated resourcefulness proved it. He wondered how they had managed to keep her down so long.

A glance at a map had convinced him that she would have only one goal: Gedemondas, a fixation of hers. He'd been in that cold hex with her and watched as the engine module was toppled by the echoes of the observers who crowded the valley; he had watched the unit break through the lava crust and melt. But none who had been there could remember seeing the mysterious Gedemondans themselves; only Mavra insisted that they not only saw them but were their guests, and that the strange snow creatures had somehow doctored or hypnoed all the minds but hers.

Sometimes in his dreams, Renard seemed to see them, and occasionally it worried him that she might have been right—she'd always been right before. An Agitar psychiatrist using the most sophisticated mind-retrieval techniques had been unable to expose any blocked memories, though, and had finally convinced Renard that he, not Mavra, was right, and that his dreams were reflections of *her* delusions heightened by his respect for her.

Still, Gedemondas was the only destination that made sense in light of her route; she never panicked, never gave up, and never did things aimlessly.

The only land connection between Ecundo and Wuckl was a 355-kilometer border lined with an effective electrified fence. He'd started at the southeast end and traveled by land and air along the border, looking for any signs that might indicate passage. Few Wuckl lived near the border itself; he didn't blame them, considering the nasty dispositions and brutal table manners of their neighbors.

Then, just a little more than halfway up, Renard noticed that a fairly large area had been landscaped as a park or wildlife refuge, and there was a small complex back in the woods. Just before that stood a relay house, which managed the current and monitors for the next kilometer of fence. He'd stopped at many and talked to the strange creatures who serviced them, all to no avail.

Suddenly he caught sight of a Wuckl emerging from the relay house; it had been about twenty houses since he'd found one manned, so he descended for another talk.

Like all the others, this Wuckl's bill opened all four ways and its head bobbed back and forth in amazement as the great flying horse flew in low and landed.

Quickly Renard jumped from the saddle onto his two thin goat legs and walked over to Wuckl, which towered over him.

"Good day and service," he called to it in the manner he had learned was common to Wuckl. The language of Wuckl contained no gender, although the people had three.

The Wuckl stared curiously. "Good day to you as well," it replied, a little uncertainly. It glanced at Domaru, a little awed.

"I have traveled long and far in search of one who looks like this," Renard told it, pulling out a photograph of Mavra Chang that had been supplied by Ortega.

The Wuckl took it, looked at it, suddenly becoming very agitated. Renard understood that it was excited and upset, even though it appeared to be undergoing convulsions.

"What's the matter?" he asked, concerned. "Have you seen her?"

"T—two such," Toug stammered. "About a ten-six day ago. I picked them up from when they hit the fence."

Renard was both excited and nervous. "They—they weren't killed, were they?"

The Wuckl's head made a circle, which meant no. "I took them to the gamekeeper." It seemed uncertain. "You mean they were—were not—not—animals?"

Renard was suddenly filled with foreboding. "No— people. Like you and me. Just a different form."

"Oh, my!" Toug managed an almost whispered exclamation. "You better come with me to the game-keeper pretty damn quick."

Renard took Domaru's reins and followed the anxious creature, not certain what the Wuckl's distress was all about, but feeling that whatever it was, it was bad.

Toug's reaction was as nothing compared to that of the gamekeeper, who, after it had heard the whole story, realized just what it had done.

"I didn't touch the brains," it told him, somewhat relieved. "If there was no permanent damage from the shock, then the conditioning would wear off in a few days—it's mostly to establish an animal routine or to change old habit patterns."

"Can it be reversed?" Renard asked, worried.

The gamekeeper thought about it. "More or less, yes. A thorough set of photographs or some good sketches, and, yes, I suppose so. Not exactly, though. I suppose it would be up to them."

Renard accepted that, and sympathized with the gamekeeper. It was a big world, and a complex one, and Wuckl was very isolated. The veterinarian still seemed beside itself with guilt. "I'm so sorry," it kept telling him. "I just didn't *know*."

Arrangements were made, and the gamekeeper called the preserve in the capital to prepare the way. It was then that he learned for the first time that his two specimens had escaped.

"It's to be expected, I suppose," the Wuckl sighed. "I should hardly like to be kept cooped up in such a place myself. Here! I'll give you a map that will get you to the preserve, and you can start out from there. A notice has already been placed about them in all the papers; the fact that they are sentient beings will have to be added in case they fall into the hands of another bumbler. But *they will be found!*"

Renard doubted it. "You haven't had much luck so far," he pointed out.

"But that was for two harmless animals," the game-keeper retorted. "Now the search will be intense."

He nodded, still more confident of Mavra Chang's abilities than the well-meaning but unknowing Wuckl.

"If they're found, get word to Ambassador Ortega of Ulik at Zone," he instructed. "Then get them into the Gate as fast as you can."

These instructions were noted, and Renard took his leave of the strange creature. He still didn't understand how it was possible for the gamekeeper to have done so extensive a job with such limited facilities.

As he walked toward Domaru, a huge shadow fell over him. Suddenly nervous, his internal charge coming to the fore, he whirled and looked up. A Yaxa was descending almost on top of him.

Fully charged, he reached out his arm to ward off the expected attack, but the Yaxa flapped its wings, lifted a bit, and called, "Wait! Do not fear! For the moment we are not enemies!"

Renard hesitated, but maintained full charge. He didn't know the true capabilities of the Yaxa, but they were a tough bunch who'd led a war and come out whole. He'd rather listen than fight if he could, for his own health.

The Yaxa put down between him and the pegasus Domaru, who started and stared suspiciously at the newcomer.

"You are the Yaxa who the crew of the *Toorine Trader* said was looking for Mavra Chang," he surmised. "A long way from home, aren't you? Trying to eliminate the competition?"

The Yaxa's cold, impersonal voice did nothing to reassure him, although all the Yaxa, he'd been told, sounded this way.

"I would not harm her," responded the great butterfly. "I give you my word on that. My sole interest at the moment is her welfare and safety. I can assure you that over these many years I have been the one who has safeguarded her from plots by my people and their allies, not threatened her."

Renard was skeptical. "Why?"

"I can not say for now. One day, perhaps. I know it is ridiculous to press this matter with you. Shall we place it in more exacting terms? I and my people are bitter enemies of Antor Trelig, as are you. For now, will it not suffice to say that the enemy of my enemy is my friend?"

Renard looked puzzled. "Trelig? How does he enter into this?"

"It was Trelig who made the attempt on her in Glathriel. It was Trelig's hired killers that drove her to this escape. He has no way into the North. This was the only way. It is in our mutual interests to see that she does not fall into his hands."

Renard still doubted. "You think Trelig will try again, then? From what I got from the *Trader* crew, they'd blasted the raiders to bits."

"That is true, but they were mere hired hands—a few among tens of thousands who would do his bidding for gain. Some are even now combing this place for her. My associate is currently trying to gain some knowledge of their plans; she is small and can get into places neither of us could."

That interested him. "Your associate is a Lata?"

"You have good information. Yes, a Lata—like you, not one of the trusted friends of the Yaxa, nor the other way around; but we have decided to work together rather than battle each other. You should join with us. It will avoid needless violence and duplicated effort—and you will be two to one against me in case you still mistrust my motives."

Renard did in fact totally mistrust the motives of the creature, but there was some sense in what she said. "All right, for now we'll be a threesome. I am Renard."

The Yaxa's death's head nodded slightly. "I know. I am called Wooly. The Lata I believe you know—Vistaru."

It was still a surprise, even though he'd guessed it. Vistaru, too—after all this time.

"When will she join us?" he asked.

"She will meet us here as soon as she can," Wooly replied. "In the meantime, we will share our information and try to narrow the search."

There seemed little point in holding back. If he refused, the Yaxa would simply go to the gamekeeper and ask the same questions. He told.

Finally, Wooly asked, "If she is making for Gedemondas, then undoubtedly by now she is at the coast.
How will she cross the Sea? She can not even talk."

Renard considered that for a moment. "If there's a
way to do it, Mavra Chang will figure it out."

Hygit, Chief Port of Wuckl

THE SMELL WAS OF DEAD FISH MIXED WITH STRONG
salt spray. The narrow strip of beach had been pretty
much covered by wharves and piers, most made of the
pliant but tough local woods. Some had buildings of
wood and aluminum on them. This was the port of
Hygit, where the unique vegetables and fruits of the
country were shipped elsewhere in exchange for raw
materials.

Mavra and Joshi had lived for a few days beneath
one of the more commercial piers—under a fish market,
actually, where small boats brought their catches from
the sea hex of Zanti to market around midday. Pickings
were pretty good around the pier. First, there were always dead fish around as well as the debris of commerce left in an area seldom cleaned.

The sturdy pylons and struts that supported the
structures provided a natural haven for the pigs. The
sand, what there was of it, was a gray-black, the woods
a weathered brown, affording them protective coloration. No one except a building inspector was ever likely
to visit, either. Furthermore, this was a commercial
location, not a likely spot for recreation or idle sightsee-
ing.

It was also a good place to eavesdrop. Squatting beneath the small sidewalk bars frequented by seamen and

Wuckl longshoremen, Mavra picked up the kinds of information she needed.

The date amazed her the most. It had only been a little over three weeks. The *Toorine Trader* was still four days from due, plenty of time. A sister ship was in. Mavra knew that crew, too, but they didn't have the story or the bribe and might not be as useful to her needs. The ship did allow them to scout, though; Wuckl was an exceptionally honest place, and holds were left open, side ramps down, when workers took breaks.

The Changs could have just stowed away. It might be possible to do so, if they could be assured of some food and could find some way of knowing where they were at any given point. She considered a better way.

Late at night she sneaked into the warehouse, treading softly to keep the clatter of her hooves on the smooth floor from echoing through the building. The cargo was identified with standard tags, large cards that fitted in slotted clips on the containers. Since so many races were involved in interhex trade, each with its own written language, pictographic hex symbols were used to show destination. On top of each card a color code or pictogram was placed for special instructions.

Live cargo was sometimes carried; there were cages of various shapes and sizes about, and she and Joshi checked one out. It had a straight, double-bolt lock, no provision for something more formidable. Joshi locked her inside the cage, and she worked hard for several minutes standing against the door, working at the bolts with mouth and tongue. Opening the cage from inside was harder than it looked; other animals might figure out simple bolts as well, and this one was designed to guard against that.

Still at work, they heard a sound echo against the walls of the warehouse. The watchman was making its rounds, and Mavra was still inside. Briefly Joshi considered trying to free her, but he realized that the noise would bring more attention than it was worth, and he opted instead to hide behind some wooden vegetable crates. Mavra could do nothing but huddle in the rear of the cage, in shadow, and hold her breath.

The Wuckl walked by on its great clawed bird's feet, pacing slowly, steadily, but relaxed. It shined a portable spotlight here and there at random. Clearly it was not expecting trouble, just checking on things.

Feeling helpless, she hunched up as much as she could and waited as the footsteps approached. The light swung from one side to the other, and as it seemed that the watchman was almost upon her it shined directly on her for a moment. Mavra felt panicky, exposed—trapped. But the light swung away; the Wuckl was swinging it to and fro idly, and hadn't been looking.

Soon the Wuckl was gone, out the door and out of the warehouse. They breathed again, but Mavra was shaken by the encounter. Being caged and helplessly cornered was new to her; she hated it, and feared it.

Still, there was the problem. She went back to working on the lock. Finally, she grunted in their code, "It won't work. Get me out and we'll try something else."

The bolts were easily slid with Joshi's flat snout from the outside, and she almost leaped out in relief. After a few moments to get hold of herself, she examined the rest of the warehouse.

One major problem was that everything was so high and they were so low to the ground. Even in her old form she had been more than a meter high; now, with the shorter pig's legs, her fat stomach almost rubbed the floor, and even a normal table appeared a giant obstacle.

She found the manager's office, and started looking around on the floor. It was dark, and the light switch might as well have been a light-year high on the wall, but she'd lived by other senses for almost half her life and those senses were much sharper now.

Finally she caught the smell; like all smells, it seemed different than she remembered, but it was unmistakable. Crawling half under a file, she struggled with, then managed to roll out a big grease pencil.

There were lots of paper scraps about, and they managed to find some fairly large sheets. Then Joshi took

them in his mouth while she held the pencil in hers.
They left.

Over the next day, in their hideout beneath the pier,
Mavra tried holding the pencil in her mouth while he
held paper with his hooves. It was tough, and there
were several false starts until she managed an intelligible message. It was shaky, uneven, a terrible scrawl,
but finally she made one that was readable. Wandering
in frail lines all over the paper, it said: I AM MAVRA
CHANG HELP ME DONT TELL

She hoped it was good enough.

Now she had to wait; the ship then in port was heading in the wrong direction. For her only the *Trader*
would do.

The streets of Hygit were crowded with Wuckl of all
sizes scurrying to and fro. The clamor of trams, some
motorized traffic, and all the rest of the sights and
sounds indicated a big city in a high-tech hex. The
foursome making their way down one of the streets
drew a great deal of attention even in a city used to the
strange life forms of passing ships.

Vistaru, perched on Domaru's rump, grumbled,
"You could hide an army in a place like this." Her soft,
tiny voice was almost drowned out by the sound.

Renard, leading the great horse through the crowd,
nodded in agreement. "It *does* look rather hopeless,
doesn't it? But she's here, I'll bet on it. This is the only
east coast port."

"She will be down by the docks," Wooly added. "It
may not be as hopeless as you think. Consider how long
and involved a journey it has been to this point, and
now we have closed the gap. I feel that the search will
end here. Come, let us go to the wharves."

The city's low hills dropped off abruptly at the coast;
a cliff had been smoothed mechanically and they descended a steep, final incline to the piers, one of which,
from the top, afforded a panorama of the port complex
and the rough seas out to the horizon.

"Look!" Renard noted, pointing. "Smoke. A ship's
coming in!"

"Going out, more likely," the Yaxa replied. "It draws a bit farther away. I should not like to be on it—that sky looks very threatening."

It did indeed, but the dark clouds and occasional distant lightning contrasted with the warmth and sunshine they enjoyed. Another hex lay in that direction; Wuckl's slightly pinkish atmosphere and somewhat darker water marked the border between Wuckl and the next hex.

Of course, such differences existed between each Southern hex, but they were usually minor—a matter of humidity, carbon-dioxide content, the addition or subtraction of some trace gas. In only a few was it necessary for visitors to use respirators or protective gear. Nonetheless, all hexes were slightly uncomfortable for nonresidents.

"It *is* disappearing," Vistaru noted. "Look—you can't see the smoke any more. They're making speed."

"Zanti is high-tech," the Yaxa reminded them. "They will have full power and speed."

Ordinarily two high-tech hexes did not adjoin, but there were exceptions. For their part, the Wuckl swam poorly and could not tolerate more than a dozen or so meters depth; the Zanti, nearly immobile plants few had seen, could not stand depths of *less than* one hundred fifty meters. In this case the two hexes were well balanced; neither had anything the other wanted, and in the few matters—like fishing rights—that required interhex cooperation, they got along well.

Renard had a funny feeling all of a sudden about that ship. "You know," he said glumly, "wouldn't it be a bitch if that's the *Toorine Trader*, or something, and they're on it?"

Theirs had been a long and tiring hunt; suddenly all three felt that he was right. Their pace accelerated.

At the docks they found tired longshoremen packing their gear. The Wuckl were fascinated by the strange-looking foursome, but pleasant enough.

"Excuse me—was that the *Toorine Trader* just left?" Renard asked with grim foreboding.

The Wuckl gave that shake of assent. "That's right.

You missed her by a good half-hour. Next boat in three days."

There was not a shred of doubt in the three aliens' minds that Mavra Chang was somehow aboard her.

"We can fly out and overtake her," Vistaru suggested.

"Wouldn't recommend it," the Wuckl longshoreman put in. "That's a hell of a storm brewin' out there. If Zanti weren't a high-tech hex, they'd never have put to sea at all, I think. They're built to take it. But there are winds over eighty kilometers per hour in it, and a good deal of sleet. That's *cold* water—dip your feet in it if you want to see how cold. It's why we're fogged in here almost every night."

"How long before the storm passes?" Wooly asked the Wuckl.

The longshoreman wagged its neck a bit. "Hard to say. Meteorology up at the Port Authority Building could probably tell you. Not before midmorning tomorrow, though, I'd say."

The Yaxa thought a moment. "Any idea how fast the ship moves in a high-tech hex?"

The Wuckl cocked its head and considered it. "In a calm with full power, maybe twenty-five, thirty kilometers per hour, more or less. They got the storm with them, though, so make it thirty, I'd say."

Renard looked at the other two. "If the storm lasts as long as our friend here estimates, that's about fourteen hours. Four hundred twenty kilometers head start." He turned back to the Wuckl. "This is near the hex border, isn't it? I mean, Zanti and the next water hex."

The longshoreman nodded. "Yep. But they won't go over into Simjim if they can help it. It's nontech. They're headin' for Mucrol, and they'll keep to the high-tech side unless the storm's too bad to deal with. A straight line's always best, you know."

They thanked the Wuckl and Renard quickly got the map from Domaru's saddle bags. They all peered at it intently.

"All right, here's where they'd have to land in Mucrol," Renard pointed. "Now, there's Gedemondas, possibly two hex sides overland. If we assume she's a stowaway, then she'll have to get off at the Mucrol port. So that's where we head to begin with. If, on the other hand, she's managed to communicate with the crew, and if they're willing, I'd bet on them dropping her as far north in Mucrol as possible, giving her only a hex side to cross, here, near Alestol. If there's nothing at the Mucrol port, that's where we head next."

Vistaru stared at the map in concern. "I don't know about this Mucrol—but I hope she doesn't cross into Alestol. Those nasty barrel-shaped plants can gas you in seconds."

"The Yaxa are friendly with Alestol," Wooly pointed out. "If we can get to a Zone Gate somewhere I can send a message to watch for them but not to harm them."

"Not much chance of that," Renard responded. "We'll be sticking to the borders, and the water hexes are out for that. No, we'll stick to Mucrol. She'll be aware of the dangers on the other side."

Vistaru was thoughtful. "I wonder, though, about the dangers on the Mucrol side."

Renard's head shot up, looked straight at her. "You know about the place?" he asked sharply.

She shook her head. "Not a thing. Do you? Or you, Wooly?"

None of them did. It was a complete mystery.

Mucrol

TI-GAN STARED INTO THE MIDDAY SUN FROM HIS POST atop the caravan. It was bleak country; a desert of reds and oranges and purples, badly eroded and with occasional clumps of brush, cactus, even a few trees where ground water approached nearer the surface. It was like this for much of the year, except in early and mid spring when melting snows from the north-eastern mountains sent floodwater—in its own way, as dangerous as any enemy—cascading through the canyons.

There *was* water, though; it was locked beneath the surface, and brought up by steam pumps into basins, which then had to be jealously guarded. To control a pack's water was to control it completely.

Ti-gan looked like a cross between a dog and a weasel; his face came almost to a point at a moist black nose, under which a huge mouth opened to reveal a nasty set of long, sharp teeth. He had rounded, saucerlike ears. His body was disproportionately small for a creature with a head the size of Ti-gan's. His arms and legs ended in stubby black five-fingered paws with equally dark claws, somewhat like those of a raccoon. When he moved he moved on all fours, but when seated, as he now was, he sat back on thick rear legs, resting on his tailless rump like a humanoid.

To the first-time viewer, a Pack Guard Unit was a strange sight—a massive armored platform supported on rows of giant balloon tires, each with an independent axle so that it followed the subtle contours of the harsh land like a treaded vehicle. On top was a wall of

130

metal with gun ports, and a smaller structure atop that was also well armored. Five progressively smaller decks terminated in a huge sooty smokestack that belched great plumes of steam and ash to be sucked up by the dry air.

It was the driest of seasons, and therefore the most dangerous. Some packs had only mudholes now, with the prospect of four weeks or more until the melt started. So it was a time of desperation. Particularly during this period, all were loaded into Pack Guard Units except those in the water village that were needed for essential services. Expecting a last-ditch attack at any moment, they patrolled in a circle around the oasis that was the key to their power.

It was hot as hell in the Pack Guard Unit, although some relief from massive fans was possible. Ti-gan's pack had once managed to trade for some precious freon produced across the waters-that-cannot-be-drunk, so steam-powered air conditioning cooled the upper tiers. The effect was almost self-defeating, though; so many bodies gathered in the cooler areas that their natural body heat was overcoming the advantages.

Ti-gan preferred the outside, the steady wind and occasional cool breeze from the far-off mountains. None of the Mucrolians, as much as they felt the heat and discomfort, considered the conditions intolerable. They had been born in this environment and perceived it as one of life's normal burdens. Flies buzzed around him, and he idly swatted at them, not really caring what they did nor even blaming them. It was a hard country, and all life had an equal right to struggle.

He leaned over, blew into a speaking tube, and was rewarded when a little mechanical gauge near him twitched and rang a bell, informing him that someone was still able to move in the engine room.

"Cut to idle, all stop," Ti-gan commanded, and the PGU ground to a halt. There was still vibration and some engine noise, of course, but not nearly the roar there had been. He didn't know why he'd ordered the halt; just a sense developed in him after long years of experience. Something not quite right, something he had to check out. He reached over and picked up his field glasses.

Although his race was almost color-blind, seeing everything in a nearly completely faded set of textures often allowed better visual discrimination than did true color sense. His eyes were extremely sharp and the field glasses made them almost phenomenal. He surveyed the hills to his right, looking for he knew not what.

He was almost ready to admit to himself that he was simply jumpy or getting too old when he noticed movement—very slight, almost lost among the shades of almost-gray among the low hills to his right.

Two figures, going fairly slowly. He adjusted the focus to try to see what they were, but they were just too far off. Nothing familiar, that was for sure. Not scouts from an attacking PGU, but not desert animals, either.

"Left nine degrees and full speed," he called into the speaking tube. The PGU roared to life, hissing and moaning, and by the application of power to only one side at first, it waddled off. "Full speed" wasn't all that fast, but it would do.

At first the two figures seemed unsure when they heard the sounds, then they tried to hide in a small wash. Ti-gan nodded to himself in satisfaction; they were making pursuit too easy.

"Give me a five-man squad, pistols, and nets."

There was a lot of sound and movement inside the PGU, and within a minute the squad was on the third tier, ready. He nodded to them and gestured in the direction of the two strange objects.

"Two of them, some kind of animal, not anything I know," he shouted to the squad leader. "Try and take them alive if you can. I want to see just what the devil we've got there."

They strained but could see nothing. Finally Ti-gan shouted, "Get up on the jump platform. I'll give 'em a panic flare that'll star⟨ 'em running!"

They climbed to the second tier to a flat area of

metal flush with the armored sides. They waited, more excited than tense. They rather welcomed this little break in the tedium of the slow roast below.

Ti-gan loaded a pinpoint flare, attached a high-compression gas cylinder, and, using the rail as a brace, fired where he knew the two mystery creatures to be hiding. He didn't care if he hit them, but he hardly expected to; at this range a flash and bang within ten or fifteen meters would be sheer luck.

The flare struck the gully wall and exploded with a roar that rolled across the flats. And it did the trick. Two creatures suddenly darted from the shadows at a pretty good clip.

The squad saw them. "Jump and run!" yelled the leader, and they were off, their small bodies showing incredible speed. The Mucrolians could sprint to almost sixty kilometers per hour.

The PGU slowed to a crawl and a number of people came out on deck to watch the chase. This was against procedure, but Ti-gan didn't have the heart to shove them back into those conditions, not for the length of time he anticipated the hunt would last. It would be time for a break soon, anyway.

The squad fanned out, forcing the fugitive animals first this way, then that. Although the quarry were fast, the squad was faster, and they also seemed able almost to change direction in midleap. They toyed with the animals for a bit, then two suddenly rushed them. As if from nowhere a spring-loaded net expanded over the animals and into the hands of a squad member, who grabbed it and did a back flip, bringing the net down with a twist that caught the animals perfectly. They were struggling, but the net was designed to hold tougher beasts than they.

The squad closed in, taking up the slack in the net as they did, and were now standing around the no longer struggling captives.

"They're pigs!" one exclaimed. "Giant pigs!" There were pigs of a sort in Mucrol, but they were much smaller and had no hair at all.

The squad leader was puzzled. "They are and they

aren't. Some kind of relatives, I'd guess. Not from Mucrol, that's for sure. Wonder how they wound up here?"

"Wonder if they *taste* like our pigs?" another mused hungrily.

"Maybe we'll find out," the squad leader replied. "You know the squad gets the first share of a catch. Looks like a male and a female, though. Might pay to breed 'em if they're that big and if they *do* taste like ours." He shrugged and sighed. "Not ours to say. Pack 'em up and take 'em into the Springs."

Still in the netting, they were professionally trussed and loaded on a small round platform. Guide bars were erected, and the squad squirmed into small harnesses, then wheeled the cart across the desert toward some distant trees.

The Springs proved to be a settlement of multitiered buildings like red adobe variations of the PGU spaced around a marketplace with a small pool of muddy-looking water in the center, flanked by a palisade of palm trees.

The two captives were taken to the livestock pens in the marketplace and penned in a large wire cage. When removing the net, two of the Mucrolians discovered that to touch the creatures' long coat was to be stuck deeply and painfully. One had to be restrained by his fellows from killing the pigs on the spot. Finally, a small padlock secured the cage, and the squad members left; two went to the first-aid station, the others back to the PGU. They were in no hurry, and stopped for a drink before returning to duty in what was generally referred to as the "hothouse."

Mavra Chang erupted with every curse she had ever learned in her life. These were considerable in number, but all were issued in a long series of grunts and squeals that conveyed to the uninitiated only the emotion, not the sense, of her words.

Joshi let her rant and rave. He felt just as disgusted, but it was too damned hot to let off emotional steam.

134

He simply stayed out of her way until she was through.

After she'd calmed down and was panting from heat and exertion, Mavra took stock of their situation. The cage was firmly bolted to the wooden floor but was out in the open; fine steel mesh surrounded them, floor and top as well as sides, and the only opening was the door on slightly worn but still durable steel hinges.

After a while she and Joshi tested the padlock, trying to ram it or butt it with head, rump, whatever they could. Their attempts shook the cage and made a lot of noise but accomplished little else except to give them both headaches and pains in the rear end.

"Face it," Joshi grunted. "We're stuck."

She knew he was right, but she refused to accept it. Not after all this time, not this close, not with the mountains that led into Gedemondas only a few dozen kilometers away. It couldn't end with her locked in a cage, finally to wind up as an experimental pork chop when it became clear to these people that there would be no breeding.

"Maybe we can work out a way to talk to them," Joshi suggested. "After all, we did it with those on the ship."

"With what?" she responded. "No pencil, no paper —and nobody here who could read what I wrote, anyway. Not even dirt to scratch out a symbol for them. But don't give up yet. Something will happen to give us a break." She tried to console him.

He wasn't convinced, and, truthfully, neither was she. The only trouble was, everything suggested they had pushed their luck once too far. Always in her colorful past when she'd gotten into hopeless situations something had miraculously happened to get her out. Even when she'd crashed on this world so many years ago by flying too low over a nontech hex, something had happened. She'd had Renard and Nikki Zinder with her, both sinking fast on sponge, their minds rotting before her eyes. Then, captured by Teliagin cyclopes who chewed on sheep and placed in a prison just as secure as their current cage—and with the same fate awaiting them—she'd been rescued by the Lata.

It had always been that way. Trapped on New Pompeii, she'd been given what she needed by the computer, Obie, to get her out—the complete schematics of the private little world in her head, still there somewhere. Obie also gave her the necessary codes to bypass Trelig's system of roving robot killer satellites.

All her life . . . When her native world had gone Com, that mysterious freighter captain smuggled her out, and Maki Chang took her to grow up in space. Kindly beggars had taken her in and helped her along when Maki was picked up. Gimball Nysongi took her out of the whorehouse in the spaceport dives of Kaliva and gave her a ship, the stars, skills, and a measure of happiness when all had seemed so hopeless. Then, even after Gimball was killed, and she'd continued on her grand thefts of the Com, there was always something whenever things became impossible, lucky breaks that kept her from ever being caught or convicted of anything. Always something.

She had again and again gotten away. She had come to expect it, waited for the improbable to happen, the nick-of-time hair's-breadth escape—even though, back in the darkest recesses of her mind, she knew that one day it wouldn't happen.

But this wasn't the day, she told herself, making herself believe it. She *couldn't* believe it.

However, she admitted ruefully, whatever was to save her would have to come from outside unless some better opportunity presented itself here. For now, she could only lie down and seek respite from the dry heat in sleep.

The sun was setting. In a few more minutes the long shadows would overtake the PGU as it steamed and lurched around the oasis-town and plunge the area into darkness. Already kerosene lanterns had been lit in the streets of the little town, visible as dull glows from the PGU watchtowers. There was little added risk from them. Any enemy would know where the town was by the smell of water. They would also know the general whereabouts of the PGU by its hissing, clanking, and belching; but there was no purpose in offering an extra bulls-eye for any eager cannoneers. The thing stayed dark.

Mor-ti had replaced Ti-gan on the con; she had much better night vision, although far less distance perception, than he, and so was better suited to the conditions. There was less threat at night, oddly enough. As Mucrolian night vision was so poor, an attacker would be approaching over unfamiliar terrain heavily guarded by the defenders. Though such an attack had been known to happen, the PGU relaxed a little; most of the people had been allowed to visit the water hole, leaving only the night guard aboard.

Again that sixth sense that marked the best lookouts came into play. Mor-ti couldn't put her finger on it, but there had been some sort of discord in the gathering gloom, and she signaled the engine room to slow.

A breeze was blowing from the west, off the distant sea. It was a bit stronger than the average sea breeze that cooled the length of the coastal plain at dusk, throwing the cloud of smoke from the stack almost at right angles to the stack lip.

Her ears strained to hear through the rumble of the idling engines and the hissing of the boilers. Something was out there, something both odd and wrong.

She blew into the speaking tube and got a response. "Two scouts up top," she ordered. "Something funny here. Keep pressure up. We may—"

Before she could complete the statement there was a series of reports to her right, quickly followed by a series of whistling roars all around the PGU.

"All crews to action!" she screamed into the tube. "We are under attack! Let's gun it! Zigzag pattern!"

The PGU roared to life and began a series of defensive course changes; Mor-ti pulled armored shielding around her spotter's perch and peered out from eyeslits.

More reports, and more explosions, closer now, all around them. Little bits of metal went *ping, ping, ping* as shrapnel bit at the steel flanks of the PGU. All around the huge steam tank the ground was erupting in explosive columns of heat and light.

Observers forward and aft tried to spot the flashes from the attacking PGU, for that was what it had to be. A spiked cannonball struck the PGU and detonated, causing tremendous concussion and vibration. The defenders screamed in rage and frustration.

"Hard right and scatter-shot!" Mor-ti commanded. "Let's see if we can smoke them out."

Ports fell with a clang from one side of the PGU, and as the vehicle turned sharply a series of cannon reports shook it again, this time the result of an outgoing volley of eight shots into the deepening night. They landed in a wide group and went off with a roar, their phosphor-gels load lighting up the countryside.

Mor-ti thought she spotted the enemy juggernaut in the dying light of the flare shells. She gambled on this and aimed her PGU where she felt the enemy was. The angle of fire showed her to be right; the new volley passed directly over her craft and struck a hundred meters to the rear.

Suddenly the enemy commander realized that he was being charged; he turned his black-painted craft and raised a nasty, sharp device on the front that looked much like a great can opener.

The defender was bearing down at full speed, which meant that he would need a good quarter-kilometer to turn fully, so the attacker slowed almost to a crawl and waited, his guns suddenly silent.

As the defender approached, it passed just to the right of the attacking armored craft. Suddenly, the attack commander screamed "Full ahead and hold!" into his speaking tube, and his PGU lurched forward with a roar.

The timing was almost perfect. The attacker struck the side of the defending PGU, not quite midships as he'd hoped but a bit behind, the great sharp corundum blade on the front ramming into the rushing defender.

The steam vents of the stricken PGU screamed as if living things; a boiler had been struck and Mor-ti's wounded craft jumped, then lurched slowly into the darkness. The attacker yelled "Feed kerosene!" into his speaking tube as his PGU lumbered immediately behind the slowed defender.

The enemy commander tried to keep pointing forward at the tear in the other's armor, angling for a good flamethrower shot.

The technique was tricky; the pressure in the flamethrower tube could not be held indefinitely, the PGU itself would have to do the aiming, and once the kerosene was ignited it would make them a perfect target.

The commander decided. "Ignite now!" he shouted. A small figure forward struck something against the side of the PGU and a glowing ember was suddenly thrust forward. The fuse was a target at which the defenders could fire, and they did. But the attacker ignited a stream of pressurized kerosene, and it passed through the torch and caught fire.

Suddenly a long, pencil-thin line of fire licked at the defender's gun ports, leaving a burning ichor as it crept toward the breech in the armor. It had to be done fast, for there was only so much kerosene, but the attack commander maneuvered against Mor-ti's equal driving skill to direct the jet of hot liquid fire into the gap.

Finally he could hear screams from inside the wounded PGU as the kerosene found the mark and the fire spread. Almost immediately the engine room, with its vulnerable rubber hosing and wooden superstructure, was engulfed, and the defending PGU ground to a halt, its boilermen unable to contain the flames and maintain boiler pressure simultaneously.

Sensing victory, the attacker rammed the now idle PGU and kept moving, its engines straining against the bulk of the disabled fighting machine. Slowly, with an agonizing metallic groan, the defending PGU was pushed upward, then over, falling on its back with a crashing roar.

The black attacker reversed. Already its infantry troops were off-loading from hatches in the rear and making for the town in the distance.

The defenders hadn't been idle. When the boiler room was evacuated, troops in the overturned PGU had scattered into the darkness, while others in the town fanned out. Kerosene lanterns winked out all over, leaving only a total darkness and the stars overhead.

Fighting erupted almost immediately, the skirmishers alone harassing the enemy troops until fixed cannon within the town suddenly roared to life.

The PGU turned and roared toward the flashes, then put its broadside to the town and fired.

Flashes from incoming and outgoing fire fitfully illuminated the scene, silhouetting hundreds of small, dark figures as they moved about.

Within the town the attacking PGU's fire rained down in deadly fashion. The bombardment knocked gaping holes in the adobe pueblos, and people began running to and fro, yelling and screaming.

Mavra and Joshi huddled in their cage, he with fear and she with frustrated rage.

Somebody ran into the square near them. "Scatter the livestock!" he commanded. "Defile the water hole! Out! Out!" he screamed.

Figures fanned out, determined to deny the attackers any fruits of their victory. Someone came down the line in the stockyard opening the gates, and panicked animals ran everywhere. He did not stop at their cage, though, but ran on.

A shell crashed very close to them, and some of the metal fragments struck the cage. They huddled as close together as they could, trying to get as far away as possible from the lethal bursts.

A second hit, then a third very close to them, struck the adobe building that loomed over their cage. A huge block of mud masonry tumbled, striking the side of the cage, ripping a great tear in it.

They neither waited for nor needed communication; they headed for the gap. It was hard to get out, part of the cage still blocked them, and Joshi found himself jammed painfully at his stomach, half in and half out. Mavra, seeing the problem, rushed at him and butted him in the buttocks, pushing him out, but not without cutting his belly.

He fell to the ground and she tried it. Her legs were just too short, her fat pig's body too balanced, and she got hung up as he had. Not even thinking of his own pain and fear now, he hobbled to her, and she rocked forward desperately, trying to lower the front of her body. He finally took hold of a foreleg with his mouth and pulled. The sharp teeth tore her flesh, but it was enough, and she tumbled over on top of him.

She picked herself up and found she couldn't stand on her injured leg. Three-legged would have to do, she told herself in an instant, and she started off away from the action, he following quickly.

Shells crashed and boomed all around them, and Mucrolians were running around, yelling, screaming, firing blindly into the dark, and, once in a while, dying.

The dark itself looked like a gathering of white-and-orange fireflies as the attacking force closed in. They made no attempt, however, to encircle the town —in fact, they actually hoped that the defenders would withdraw. The oasis was the target, not the people. Realizing this, Mavra and Joshi headed for the dark at the rear, where no flashes were evident.

Their biggest problem was to keep from being trampled by the frightened animals and retreating defenders. Another, once they had been completely engulfed by the dark, was to avoid being shot by panicky defenders.

Eventually the sounds of the battle faded behind them. The attack had succeeded; they were free once more—but a new problem existed: they would have to share the harsh land with a large number of refugees—for whom food would be a major priority. If the pigs were caught, there would no longer be thought of breeding.

Dawn's light revealed an eerie scene to the three aerial observers. From four hundred meters, the desert terrain showed in all its colorful glory, off almost to the hazy mountains in the distance. Below was carnage—bodies, the hulk of a PGU, the bombed-out buildings of the oasis, and by the water a large group of Mucrolians siphoning scum from the surface of the pool to make it serviceable again. The attackers' PGU stood silently nearby; alongside, a ramshackle machine labored noisily to filter water, then transfer it to the flushed boilers of the imposing war machine.

"My God!" was all Renard could manage.

"If they were in that wreck, I don't see how they could have survived," Vistaru said glumly.

"This Mavra Chang will manage," Wooley reassured them in that cold but steady voice of the Yaxa. "I would not land or long dwell here, though. It is clear even from this height that most of the animals are dead or have escaped. The sun is now up. I would still keep to the most direct line for Gedemondas. They will be there."

The other two wished they could be as confident.

To the northeast of the bombed-out oasis they could see occasional pockets of Mucrolian refugees, some obviously well armed, trying to regroup. Once or twice those on the ground noticed the strange creatures above. Some were agitated, and several shots were fired at them, but for the most part they were ignored.

Of the three, the Yaxa had by far the best vision. Her range went far beyond the others in color perception, contrast, depth perception, and just about every other parameter, and they relied on Wooley for a careful canvass of the ground.

Several times she spotted small animals and they descended for closer inspection but always the creatures proved to be just what they seemed.

By early afternoon the false alarms had started to get on the party's nerves.

"Maybe we should go on further," Vistaru suggested. "Work up a ways maybe all the way to the border and then backtrack."

That made sense, but Wooley was reluctant to leave. "If they are in those washes, the refugees will make short work of them," she pointed out.

They shifted a little to the north where one of the dry washes opened into a salt flat that would have to be covered by anyone heading for the mountains.

"This is a good compromise," Renard decided. "They'll have to cross this flat sooner or later, and we can see everything for a great distance."

"Unless they've already been through here," Vistaru responded, obviously worried.

"Better than more blind searching," the Yaxa noted, and they decided to act on Renard's plan. After putting down for a half-hour or so to give themselves a break, they went aloft again.

It was past midday when something finally happened.

"To the right!" Wooley yelled. "Mucrolians chasing something! Two objects!"

At first, neither of the others saw what he had spotted, for the Lata are nocturnal and Renard's eyes were only average, but they followed the Yaxa.

"There!" Renard finally called out; he pointed, leaning forward in his saddle.

A half-dozen or so Mucrolians were chasing two smaller dark objects across the yellow-white flats. It was no contest; the natives were much too fast for their prey.

"It's Mavra!" Wooley shouted, the rising tone generating the first emotion they'd heard from the normally impassive butterfly—excitement.

Renard reached over and pulled his long rod from its scabbard, which hung from Domaru's great neck.

"Make sure I don't get shot!" he told the others. "I'm going in!"

On the ground the six Mucrolians were tiring of

143

their chase and were closing in for the kill when they heard the beat of mighty wings just above them. One turned and looked up, and yelled to its comrades.

Mavra Chang also spotted them, and knew immediately who they must be, although the Yaxa was a surprise. She had no intention of being taken; she took the moment as the Mucrolians turned to face this new threat and dashed across the flats as fast as she could, Joshi following.

One of the Mucrolians raised its rifle and was suddenly struck hard by a small object. Vistaru came in feet first, hitting the creature in the snout, then plunging in the stinger.

This momentarily drew the attention of the pack from Renard, and they turned.

Domaru made a low pass and Renard struck out with his tast; the thousands of volts stored in his body flowed down his right arm and into the rod. It struck one and there was a bright flash as the warrior screamed and fell.

These were not well-coordinated soldiers, though; they were desperate refugees and the attack confused them. When Renard acted, they turned once again to deal with him; another rifle barrel rose, and Vistaru struck again.

Renard simultaneously leveled another of the beings with his tast. Although they had sidearms, the two remaining Mucrolians panicked completely and dashed for cover at full speed.

Renard laughed triumphantly and descended near the bodies. Vistaru landed daintily on Domaru's back.

"Whew!" she breathed. "Haven't done anything like that in years!"

"You should talk!" Renard laughed. "Just like old times again, though! We haven't lost it!" Suddenly his grin faded. "Where's Wooley?"

He turned and looked around, as did Vistaru. "There!" she almost screamed.

The orange wings were off in the distance now, heading for the Alestolian border.

"We've been double-crossed!" Renard snapped. "While we did the fighting, she got Mavra!"

Pursuit was automatic, but fruitless. The Yaxa was every bit as fast, if not faster, than Domaru, and Vistaru was good only for short sprints at high speeds. Every minute that passed increased the distance. They crossed into Alestol, where the country was green—and deadly. Below, huge barrel-shaped plants paralleled their course and waited for them to come down.

"It's no use!" Vistaru told him. "I know where she's headed, and we're being played for suckers!"

He didn't want to give up. "What do you mean?"

"She's heading for the Zone Gate of Alestol. Taking them to the Yaxa embassy at Zone. At the same time, we're being sucked farther and farther into Alestol, which was on *their* side in the war. We'll have to land sooner or later for water or rest, and those gas-shooting plants will get us and eat us, so we have to get out—now! Besides, she's already pulled us a tremendous distance from the nearest Zone Gate we can use!"

Renard resisted the obvious, but she was right. Their best move, as soon as it was clear that Wooley was uncatchable, was to head for a Zone Gate, alert Ortega, and get ready at Zone. Unfortunately, they were a good six hundred kilometers from a usable Gate, and they were almost exhausted.

Not only did the Yaxa have Mavra Chang, but they would have her for a day or more before that fact could be reported in by the only others who knew.

Cursing themselves for fools, they headed north toward Palim.

South Zone

ALTHOUGH THIS WAS IN FACT THE YAXA EMBASSY, only two of the technicians clustered around the tables were Yaxa. A Wuckl was present, and with it were several other creatures who were at least neutral—in some cases friendly—to the Yaxa.

A tall minotaur paused before the door, looking curiously for a moment at the symbol embossed on everything. Unlike his native Dasheen, which used a standard hexagonal symbol, Yaxa used an ideogram which he mistook at first for a pair of stylized wings. After a moment he realized that it was not so. Yaxa was a state along the Equatorial Barrier. It was composed of one half of a hex split horizontally joined to one half of a hex split vertically. Only twenty-four such hexes were so split on either side of the Barrier. The "wings" were, in fact, two half-hexes joined.

A Yaxa approached him from outside as he peered quizzically into the room. "Mr. Yulin?" she asked.

The minotaur turned and nodded his massive head. "Yes. I got your message and got down as quickly as I could settle my own affairs on the farm. What's going on in there?"

"I am Ambassador Windsweep," the Yaxa replied, introducing herself, with her official nickname. "Those two creatures are Mavra Chang and her male consort. We are performing minor surgery to make things easier for all."

Yulin was puzzled. "Chang? Why bother? If you've got her, just get rid of her and we have the field all to ourselves."

The Yaxa gave what might have been taken for a

sigh or impatience or both. "Mr. Yulin, I wish to remind you that we have a number of problems. First, we must reach the ship in the North. Second, we must depend on the Bozog to secure the ship in some way from the Uchjin and establish a proper launch platform. Third, once away, we must approach your planetoid of New Pompeii through Antor Trelig's robot sentinels. Mr. Yulin, what is today's codeword for the sentinels?"

He looked startled. "I—I'm not sure," he admitted. "We'd just planned to run through all of them on a fast tape."

"But what if the robots are programmed only for slow speech?" the ambassador asked him. "We have by your own account just thirty seconds to give the codeword. If the tape doesn't work, we are lost."

He didn't like that thought, particularly because it was true. "So?"

"Mavra Chang went to New Pompeii as a guest, is that not so? She had never been there before?"

"That's true," Ben Yulin admitted. "Get to the point."

"And yet Chang stole a spaceship—within the realm of possibility—but then she flew right through the robot sentinels without a problem! Tell me, Mr. Yulin—how did she do that?"

He had thought that one over a thousand times before. "I wish I knew for sure," he responded. "Best guess is the treacherous computer gave it to her when we ran her through it. But, hell, it probably only gave her the codeword for that particular day. They're changed daily, you know that."

The Yaxa bowed slightly on its four forelegs in acknowledgement. "But Trelig used the code when you took off, and that was a day later than Mavra Chang. You didn't hear it—you were too busy flying. Deep hypnosis proved that. So the only codewords we know for certain are for the exact day and time that Mavra Chang took off. Correct?"

"That's true," he acknowledged, beginning to see the point.

"So, we also know from you that there are fifty-one code phrases. But only one can be matched to a specific day. They are changed daily. Even over twenty-two years, we can start with the day of Mavra Chang's escape and project which day it will come up again this time. We know the standard Com calendar. Hence, by picking the time of entry we can be certain of getting through. Do you see?"

Yulin was uncomfortable with this line of thought. As long as he was the only pilot, it gave him absolute command. Mavra Chang was a threat to his power, an unknown quantity in that he did not know what else the computer had programmed in her brain. He didn't want her on New Pompeii again, that was for sure.

"But you can just deep-hypno the words out of her and leave it at that!" he protested.

"We've tried," the Yaxa told him. "So did Ortega long ago. It won't work. Whatever is within her brain by Obie's doing is accessible only in the applicable situations. She does not remember it until she needs it, and it's blocked to us as well as to her."

That was only partially true. Actually, the Yaxa had no love, let alone trust, for Ben Yulin, and they liked having a lever. They did, in fact, know the codewords, because she'd said them and used them consciously in the escape. It was the remainder of the programmed information that was blocked.

In addition to Yulin's basic amorality, his new culture was totally male-dominated; the women did the work, the men reaped the rewards. Yaxa society was more than the reverse: basically, male Yaxa were sex machines, killed and eaten by their mates after their performance. To an all-female society, Mavra Chang's additional knowledge was more trusted.

Yulin accepted the situation grudgingly. "All right, then, she's going with us. So what's all that?" He gestured toward the makeshift surgery.

"Chang and her companion were surgically altered by the Wuckl to look like pigs," the Yaxa explained. "Never mind why. But we have a lot of problems to solve: protective suits can't easily be altered; the reinstatement of vocal cords. Working on them are the Wuckl who did the original work and five surgeons from the best biologically advanced hexes we know who can be bought and trusted to stay bought. Some of their skills are incredible."

"You mean they're going to change them back?" Yulin gasped. "Wow! I'd think that was impossible!"

"Cosmetics," Ambassador Windsweep told him, "are easy. Form-fitting them to the spacesuits that we have is more difficult. I think you'll be amazed."

Yulin shrugged resignedly. He would be happier if they died on the table.

They entered the ambassador's office, and the minotaur took the huge fluffy chair there for his benefit. "So what's the timetable?" he asked.

"We've already contacted the Torshind," Ambassador Windsweep replied. "They'll be ready for us in another two days, which should be enough for the recuperation of our prisoners. All the equipment from our end is already here, and all of the major paraphernalia has already been transferred by the Torshind and its associates to Yugash." A tentacle snaked down and lifted a plastic cylinder holding a pale liquid.

"This is how you will survive. Taking four cows with us just to supply you with the needed calcium and lactose is an incredible expense. This will free you."

Yulin looked uncertainly at the container. "How much of that do you have?" he asked nervously.

"You need only a small amount per day, really," Windsweep noted. "We have a three-month supply. Even then, you could survive pretty well for another two months without it. If we aren't done with our business by then, we will be dead."

Yulin stared at the container and hoped the ambassador was right.

"You can always back out, you know," the Yaxa prodded. "After all—we can't *force* you into this,

149

even though we need you to gain access to the computer."

The minotaur threw up his hands. "You know better than that," he said, defeated.

The surgeons had several problems to solve. The cosmetic changes would be easy to reverse, of course, but not the legs, which made it impossible to fit them into any available pressure suits. Though the Yaxa had manufactured suits based on their old forms, these were now deemed unusable because of the very different shape of the pigs' limbs. To return them in any way to their original form would be to have them small, weak, slow, and facing downward—in other words, tremendous burdens on the expedition.

There, then, was the problem. Assuming that Mavra Chang could be snared and Joshi taken hostage, what to do with them to make them useful during the journey and to fit in a spacesuit that would have to be one removed from an Entry—someone who had fallen into a Well Gate out among the stars or on a deserted Markovian world and wound up in Zone.

The suit problem was acute. Though dozens of races had apparently reached space, many more had not. There were limits. The problem remained until the Yaxa themselves suggested a solution.

Over two centuries before, the near-legendary Nathan Brazil—perhaps the last living Markovian—had walked the Well World. Only a few who saw it were still alive, and a lot of propaganda had gone into convincing most that he was a legend, nothing more. Most of those witnesses were on Ortega's side—indeed, Ortega himself had been there.

But one witness was on the side of the Yaxa, and that was all that was necessary.

In the far-off land of Murithel, inhabited by the ferocious Murnies, who ate living flesh, Brazil's body had been battered and broken beyond repair, and the Murnies had somehow transferred his consciousness, that which was truly he, into the body of a giant stag.

Others knew of the process, although they couldn't study it, for the Murnies tended to eat anyone first and ask polite questions afterward. Still, it *had* been done, and at least another two races in the North knew about it.

A Yaxa stuck her head in the surgery. "The Cuzicol are here!" she announced. From the North, the Cuzicol were a race that traded with the Yaxa.

A strange creature, like a metallic yellow flower with hundreds of sharp spikes, stood on spindly legs. In the yellow disk that was its head several ruby-red spots flashed as it spoke. "Bring in the first one," it commanded.

The others would assist. Happily. Any of them would have sold his soul—if he believed in it—just to witness this operation, which most didn't believe really possible, for it did, in fact, presuppose the existence of something not quantifiable, but real and transferrable, nevertheless. And they witnessed it, not once but twice, the transfer into an animal which was part surgical, part mystical. It was not the same method the Murnies had used, and it depended a great deal more on technological skills, but it worked.

And all agreed that the twin problems of spacesuit fit and usefulness to the travel party were well served, while minimum disruption of the subjects' habits was observed. They were accustomed to being four-footed, hooved animals, and such they would remain.

The Wuckl's skill was used in constructing rudimentary larynxes for the two and in implanting a translator in Joshi. Their voices would have low amplitude and sound somewhat artificial, but they would do. The only thing the translator required was something to modulate.

Mavra Chang awoke. The last thing she remembered was running across the barren salt flats away from her rescuers when four powerful tendrils suddenly wrapped themselves around her and another two pairs snared Joshi, jerking them into the skies. Something had stung painfully, and she had blacked out.

Now she was in a room. It was definitely made for creatures different from those she knew—there were odd cushions, strange furniture and implements all about.

She was still near-sighted, and now color-blind as well. This disturbed her; much more than the very slight fisheye effect she was getting. She had enjoyed color, and that was now taken from her.

She knew that they'd transformed her again. It was obvious from the change in perception and also from the fact that her height and viewing angle were different.

For someone who had never yet been through the Well of Souls, never been made by that great machine into a creature of this world, she had been more creatures than anyone else on the Well World, she thought.

Whatever she was, she had a fairly long snout. Her eyes were set back from it, making that obvious. She tried to move, and found that shackles held her four feet in check.

A nearby noise attracted her attention. When she turned her head, she saw a small horse, perhaps the size of a Shetland pony, gold, and with broad, thick powerful hooved legs. The animal had a thick mane, and a clump of thick wavy hair hung from between its ears, reaching almost to the eyes.

"Joshi?" she said to herself, wondering, but she said it aloud.

The other stirred. "Mavra?" came a strange, electronic-resonant voice.

"Joshi! We can talk again!" she exclaimed excitedly.

He looked at her with his horse's head. "So we're talking horses now, are we?" he responded morosely. "What next? Horse flies?"

"Oh, come on!" she scolded. "We're no worse off

152

than before. We're alive, we're healthy, we're *together*."

That last got to him. It was the first time she'd really said anything so endearing to him, and it seemed to energize him. "All right, all right," he replied. "So who got us? The thing on the horse or the butterfly?"

She looked around. "The butterfly for sure. Why and for what I have no idea as yet, but I think we'll soon find out."

They talked on, more for the joy at being able to communicate again than for any serious purpose. Neither had really been conscious of how much their earlier isolation had affected them until they could speak once again.

After a half-hour or so, a door panel slid back with a whine. A Yaxa entered, looking no less huge and fierce and formidable in black and white and shades of gray than it had in color.

"I see you are awake," it began in the eerie, ice-cold voice of the Yaxa. "I am Wooley. You know who you are, and so do I."

"What's all this about?" Mavra demanded.

Wooley's death's-head looked at them. "Would you like to get back to New Pompeii?" she asked.

Mavra almost gasped. New Pompeii! Space! The stars! But— "I'm a hell of a pilot as a horse," she responded sarcastically.

Wooley showed no reaction to the comment. "We do not need you as a pilot, except, perhaps, as a backup. Do you remember Ben Yulin?"

Mavra thought a moment. The truth was, she had seen very little of Yulin—the young scientist at Trelig's test panels. Not even a picture of him came to mind. All her experience had been with Trelig, not Yulin.

"Vaguely," she responded. "Scientist who worked for Trelig. So? I know he's the one you depended on to get you to New Pompeii after the wars over twenty years ago. Kind of fizzled on that one, didn't you?"

Wooley let it pass. "We have Yulin, we can penetrate the North, we can reach New Pompeii, but it won't be easy. You are our backup. Would *you* trust a former lieutenant of Antor Trelig?"

She had to admit that she wouldn't. But, then again, she wouldn't trust Mavra Chang, either, who owed no loyalty to the Yaxa.

"It wouldn't have more to do with the fact that, if I'm with you, then Ortega can't use me?" she prodded.

The Yaxa's antennae waved a bit. "That is part of it, yes. However, we could kill you and accomplish that. No, we are interested in you as a check on Yulin. We want someone else who knows New Pompeii, and we want someone who can make certain he is not planning a double-cross. You are the best we can do."

"But why *horses*?" Joshi asked, a little miffed at being left out of the conversation.

"Relatives of the horse, yes," Wooley said, "but not horses. You are *extremely* strong, for one thing."

"So we help carry the freight," Mavra noted, understanding. "I can see that."

"Also, your new bodies are not strictly herbivores. Your breed is from a hex to the east, Furgimos, and you can eat almost anything, in much the same way you could as pigs. Your water-storage capability is excellent. Two weeks or more. You can see how this simplifies travel problems."

They did. "I take it that there's a long journey after we get North, then," Mavra guessed.

"Very long," Wooley admitted. "For one thing, the rebreathing apparatus necessary is only usable in a semitech or high-tech hex, so the shortest route is out of the question. The shortest route avoiding nontech hexes is blocked because the Poorgl are extremely nasty high-tech creatures who would be death to us. That means a seven-hex journey."

The horses started doing the math in their heads, but Wooley cut them off. "It's about 2,400 kilometers, all told. A huge distance."

Joshi was shocked. "That far in the *North?* Without air, without any food or water we don't take with us? It's impossible!"

"Not impossible," the Yaxa responded. "Difficult. You forget we have had a great deal of time to prepare for this mission, both diplomatically and logistically. A thousand or so of those kilometers will be hard traveling. In others we will obtain transport and be resupplied from established caches. Still, the going will be difficult, and dangerous."

"What about us?" Mavra asked. "How will *we* breathe and be protected?"

"I told you there were several reasons for your being horses. Well, the Dillians—you might remember them, they are centaurs—in whatever part of space their colony began, also attained space flight. We have obtained two of the suits and a spare from off-planet Dillian Entries and easily modified them," the Yaxa explained. "They are made for an equine shape, yet operate in the main as yours do—they are form-fitting when pressurized. It is all arranged."

"And when do we start this great expedition?" Mavra prodded, excited.

"Tomorrow. Early tomorrow," the Yaxa replied, and left. The door whined shut behind her.

They stood in silence for a few minutes, thinking. Suddenly Mavra became aware that Joshi was shaking his hindquarters, obviously agitated.

"What's the matter?" she asked. "Worried?"

"It's not that," he replied, certainly upset about something. "Mavra, will you look down between my hind legs and tell me what you see?"

She humored him, lowered her head, and looked carefully. "Nothing," she answered. "Why?"

"That's what I thought," he cried mournfully. "Damn it, Mavra! I think they made me a girl horse!"

Ortega's Office, South Zone

THE INTERCOM ON SERGE ORTEGA'S DESK BUZZED and he punched it.

"Yes?"

"They're here, sir," his secretary answered.

"They?" he responded, then decided quibbling wasn't worth the trouble. "Send them in."

The door slid back, and two creatures slow-hopped in. They looked very much like meter-and-a-half-long frogs, with legs in proportion, although one was slightly smaller than the other and had a lighter green complexion. On their whitish undersides elaborate symbols were tattooed.

"Antor Trelig," Ortega nodded. "And?"

"My wife, Burodir," the larger of the two frogs responded.

"Charmed," the snake-man replied dryly. He looked around. There were spaces for Uliks to curl and some chairs and a couch for visiting humanoids, but there seemed to be nothing appropriate for frogs. "Have a seat if anything fits."

The chairs did, surprisingly. As the frogs sat, they looked almost human, curved legs slightly crossed.

"You know what's up, I assume, so I won't beat around the bush," Ortega began. "The Yaxa have Mavra Chang, and they are ready to start any moment with Chang and Yulin into the North. We have to get there—if not ahead of them, then at roughly the same time as they do. It'll be a rough trip out, and there may be a fight at the end. It's very much like a miniature replay of the Wars of the Well on neutral turf."

Trelig nodded. "I understand. You have my complete cooperation, Ambassador Ortega."

"Cooperation, yes—but I think we understand each other, Trelig," the Ulik answered pointedly. "Don't cross me. I'm sending some people with you as my representatives. One is an Agitar, and you know what kind of power *he* has."

Trelig nodded.

Ortega continued, "Also along will be a Lata, whose sting works on Makiem, and who will have flying speed on New Pompeii—and some male and female Dillian centaurs to help carry supplies. In addition, one of the Yaxa who's along with the other side, goes by the name Wooley, is a former sponge-addict Entry."

Trelig, former head of the sponge syndicate, gasped.

"She has sworn to kill you at any cost and has tried several times," the snake-man continued. "She'll try again up North. The Yaxa are among the most cunning and deadly creatures on the Well World, so you can afford no mistakes."

Trelig nodded soberly. "I have gotten this far and this high by not making any. I assure you that self-preservation is a primary objective with me."

"All right then," Ortega said. "You brought two Makiem suits?"

"Already being worked on by your people," Burodir put in. "We will be set to go as soon as they are through."

Ortega sighed. "Okay, then. Get your supplies transferred as quickly as possible, and be back here for briefing at 0400."

The Makiem rose and made for the exit. Trelig turned slightly, and said, "You won't regret this, Ortega."

"You bet I won't," the snake-man replied, and watched them go out. The door closed. "You son of a bitch," he added.

Two figures emerged from behind a partition.

"So that's Trelig," Renard breathed. "Now he looks

just like he always was—slimy. Color matches, too. He hasn't changed a bit."

"I notice you didn't tell him *who* that Agitar was," Vistaru the Lata said.

Ortega chuckled. "No, and I think you better have an alias, Renard. Something that won't give you away —and he'd better not find out, so don't slip."

Renard's grin lent a particularly evil effect to his devil's face. "I won't slip. But nothing will stop me from electrocuting the son of a bitch once we don't need him any more. You understand that."

Ortega did. Trelig had picked Renard from a Comworld mental institution, fed him massive doses of sponge, and enslaved him on New Pompeii. More than anyone, Renard knew Trelig's basic evil, his degradation. The man was a monster. But Trelig did not know that Renard was Renard—and if there were no slips, he would not. While Trelig worried about a vengeful Yaxa, right next to him would be an enemy who knew him well, knew New Pompeii well, and hated him with a passion that defied description.

"I just wish it'd been Mavra," Vistaru said between clenched teeth. "That bitch Wooley! I'll get her if it's the last thing I do."

Ortega looked thoughtful, then sighed. "Renard, will you see to some of the final preparations?" he prodded. The Agitar turned to go, and Vistaru started to follow. "No, Vistaru, not you. Stay here a minute."

She looked puzzled, and Renard left. The door hissed shut again.

"I think," Ortega said slowly, "it's time to tell you a few things you don't know. Wooley knows—I had to tell her in order to save Mavra Chang's life these many years. Now it's time for you."

Vistaru experienced a creeping dread within her, as if she didn't really want to know what Ortega was about to tell her, but dimly guessed the truth.

Ortega sighed and pulled some papers from a desk drawer, a thick file marked CHANG, MAVRA in indecipherable Ulik, but the Lata knew what it was from the photo on the jacket.

"I better start from the beginning, all the way," he said carefully. "It begins fifty-four years ago, back when you found Nathan Brazil . . ."

Yaxa Embassy, South Zone

THE TORSHIND FLOATED A FEW CENTIMETERS ABOVE the floor, a pale-red cloak without a wearer, like a vision from a nightmare. Because it was essentially an energy creature, a translator had nothing to modulate, so it was also silent now as it watched the preparations underway. Yaxa guards armed with nasty weapons stood all about as insurance against attempts by Ortega or Trelig to interfere with the operation.

A drug was administered to the party; it made them sleepy, close to comatose. Because of the supply problem, the expedition was small: Wooley, of course, and Yulin and the horselike Mavra and Joshi and, of course, the Torshind. There had been some debate about it all, particularly the inclusion of Joshi and the exclusion of another Yaxa. But Joshi provided a handle on Mavra Chang and he was needed to carry supplies—and anyway, another Yaxa would consume more in food and water than he. Five were enough; none of them trusted Yulin, so that kept him in check. None trusted the Torshind either, but the Torshind could not pilot the ship. Mavra had no hands and her shape precluded her ability to activate the ship, particularly at an incline, so she would need an ally with arms—and for that Wooley was a better bet than Yulin. It wasn't perfect, but it was the best that could be done.

Most of the supplies had been shifted earlier; the suits in which the expedition would live in the North had been fitted with small but complex rebreather apparatus. For himself, Yulin adopted a "human" suit, of old design. The Yaxa had their own suites from Entries—and Mavra and Joshi used modified Dillian equipment. The Torshind did not breathe as the South understood breathing, and so needed nothing.

Transfer was simple. The Torshind simply glided up to the transferee, melted into the other's body, awkwardly took control of it, then moved down the hall and into the Zone Gate.

The drugs made the Torshind's task easier, and each transferee had undergone at least one test earlier.

Consciousness returned slowly.

Mavra Chang shook herself, stretched her limbs outward, and moved her head around as if clearing cobwebs.

They were in a strange chamber, a hall of some glassy substance. The light was poor but sufficient, and she could see the others struggling to one or another degree to regain control.

One thing seemed clear: the Well had been fooled. They were all in Yugash now, including the Torshind.

Other shapes moved about, as spectral as the Torshind but sharp and clear in the gloom. Mavra's color-blindness actually helped the contrast; to her the Yugash were sharp white outlines against a dark-gray background.

Another creature could be seen in the room, a thing apparently of the same substance as the walls, an angular crystal sculpture of a crab with glassy tentacles instead of claws. It wore an incongruous device around its midsection, a transmitter that enabled the translation device inside the creature to send to the radios in their suits.

"Welcome to Yugash," came the thin, electronic voice of the Torshind. "I shall keep to this ptir—this creature you see—for much of the trip. As soon as you all feel able, we will cross to a chamber prepared to your requirements. I suggest that we brief everyone on the route and problems and then get a good night's sleep. Tomorrow we will begin this epic journey."

They nodded in agreement. They sensed that history was being made, that they were to be the focal point for events that would shape the future.

Still slightly groggy, they followed the Torshind out of the Zone Gate chamber and into Yugash.

It was a dark hex; the sky seemed slightly overcast, the sun somehow much farther away. It was like this in some hexes, where the Well facets changed things to simulate worlds closer to or farther from primary suns. Each hex, after all, was a laboratory simulation of an actual planet onto which the creatures of the hex were to have been sent to establish, build, and develop a normal culture.

The city was built of twisted glass, or at least that was the way it looked. Huge spires rose to the sky, and even basic buildings looked melted, twisted, or otherwise malformed. Thousands of crystal creatures like the Torshind's ptir scurried to and fro on unguessable business. Grown to the specifications of their owners on great crystal farms, they were every combination of creature imaginable. Only rarely did the group see a Yugash in its natural form, though.

The large room prepared for them was extremely comfortable; rugs and drapes had been hung to mask its glassy structure, and quantities of provisions suitable for all their needs were neatly arranged. Only an occasional hiss from the pressurization system reminded them that this was a sealed room, and that here alone the atmosphere and pressure—a compromise of their respective hexes—were made sufficient for them to live without suits.

After Wooley and the Torshind had removed her suit, Mavra groaned. "I could sleep for a week," she told them. There were muttered assents.

Wooley managed to shake herself out of her stupor to inspect some of the leatherlike pouches. With mittenlike hands on her tentacles, she opened one, pulled out a large folding map, and spread it out on the floor. The others gathered around, and the Torshind took the floor.

"First of all, we have designed the breathing apparatus to work in semi- as well as high-tech hexes," it began. "That's fine—but no amount of storage will get you through even a full hex side of a nontech hex. There you would have perhaps eight hours at best. This means avoiding such hexes." It pointed a glassy tentacle at the map. "As you can see, we are only four hexes from Bozog, three from Uchjin. A direct route from here avoiding nontech hexes would be across Masjenada into Poorgl, then through Nichlaplod to Bozog. However, the Poorgl are not cooperative. They have refused us permission to cross and promised attacks if we try—and as a high-tech hex it's almost impossible to get by them for the distance we have to go. That means an indirect route."

The tendril shifted to the northwest. "Masjenada is easy and helpful; my people and theirs have not exactly been friends, but we have so little in common that we are not enemies, either. They value certain minerals as luxury goods, and my people were in a position to supply them from the South, thanks to the Yaxa. The Yaxa themselves have been helpful in dealing with Oyakot, which otherwise would never aid someone of Yugash. Pugeesh is an unknown quantity. We will have to tread carefully there, and we'll have to do things ourselves. Wohafa will aid us because they are friendly with the Bozog, and while Uborsk can't really help tremendously, they'll do what they can. Thus, it should be a fairly easy journey."

"Too easy," responded Ben Yulin, worried. "I can't help but think there's a joker in this deck somewhere."

"The distance is great," Wooley admitted, "and parts of it will not be easy, but it's the best route."

"What about the other party?" the Dasheen bull persisted, feeling ever more pessimistic as he looked at the distances involved.

"Ortega has his own friends among the Yugash," the Torshind replied. "We can not stop them here. But they will be at least a day behind us, and may well decide on a different route. If not, we will have to plan a surprise for them."

They understood what that meant. In totally unfamiliar terrain, with only the suits to protect them and the supplies to maintain them, both parties were extremely vulnerable. If one could surprise the other, there would be big problems for the defender. The suits were tough, but even in a semitech hex a bullet—even an arrow—might do the job.

Mavra filed that information in her mind for later. There was nothing she could do now, and she felt little loyalty to either side as long as she got to the ship. She would not like someone she knew, such as Renard or Vistaru, to be killed—but where had they been for the last twenty-two years? Did she have any more responsibility toward them than they had felt to her?

In the meantime, she would be totally dependent on these people for survival, and self-preservation was always the first priority.

Yugash, then Masjenada

SMALL FIGURES TRAVERSED AN EERIE LANDSCAPE; bleak gray-black rocks rose all around, and they made their way in, out, and around the jagged forms like ants in a granite quarry.

There were seven in the party: two Makiem frogs in stark white spacesuits; a small Agitar in a transparent, form-fitting model; a Lata wearing a suit of her people's design; two large Dillians—a male and a female—heavy-laden, with packs on their backs and pulling a wheeled wagon with more supplies; and the crystalline crab in which the mysterious Ghiskind rode.

"How much of a start do they have on us?" Renard asked.

"About six hours," the Ghiskind replied. "Not very much, but they are traveling lighter than we—we have only two resupply points, where they have five."

"Then they'll certainly beat us," Vistaru said unhappily. "Every hour they'll get farther ahead."

"Not necessarily," the Ghiskind told her. "We have advantages in travel they do not. My own company has established some better relations than the Torshind's ilk could, and Ortega has been skillful as well. I think we have a good chance. The main danger is our running into them. We will have to be prepared for a trap."

The Lata sighed. "I wish I could fly. It would make things so much easier." As it was, she was too small to keep pace, and so rode atop the supply cart.

The Dillians, Makorix and Faal, a male and a female who were married in the manner of their people, pulled the loads effortlessly and without complaint. Yugash had a slightly lower gravity than Dillia, which helped considerably, although they dreaded the idea that one or more of the places ahead might be just the reverse.

"How much longer before we reach the border?" Makorix asked the Yugash.

"Not long," the Ghiskind replied. "Just over the next rise."

Renard looked around dubiously. "Nice place for an ambush right here," he noted. Antor Trelig, peering around with his great independent chameleon's eyes, nodded in nervous agreement.

"They won't dare do anything in Yugash," the Ghiskind assured them. "The cult is not strong here anymore, and my own people have been with us, unseen, as guards and preparers. They know our strength, and they also know they'd face an attack on their main temple if they tried anything. No, an ambush won't happen here. And we'll outflank them in Masjenada, I think. If we don't jump ahead of them then, at least we won't run into them. The best place would probably be Pugeesh, about which we have been able to learn next to nothing. But—wait a minute! There! You can see the border now!"

They crested the hill. Although all on the Well World were used to sudden changes at hex borders, this one was more stunning than usual.

The dark bleakness of Yugash ran to that intangible line, and across from it the horizon exploded in light and color. The ground itself was ablaze with glowing light, iridescent yellows and greens and oranges that seemed to have a life of their own, and was dotted with thick pale-red plants, like exotic coral, all over the rolling plains. The sky was a bright green with clouds of wispy brown and seemed to reflect some of the colors radiating from the ground.

"Masjenada," the Ghiskind announced. "Do you see that outcrop of rock over to the left? That's our rendezvous."

They headed for it. As they crossed the border in their protective pressure suits, there was a slight gravitational adjustment downward to perhaps .8 Well World average, giving them additional quickness and buoyancy.

The plants proved as rock-hard as they looked, and the expedition avoided them as much as possible, for some of their growths were sharp and might puncture a suit. They reached the barren rock outcrop shortly, and the two Dillians unhitched the wagon.

Various supplies were unpacked, food and water cartridges were checked and changed if necessary. The rebreathers continued working normally; their action was primarily chemical, but the apparatus also had small power-storage cells that somehow worked within the semitech limitations.

Trelig and Burodir did little to help in the operation; they sat patiently and seemed to accept being waited upon as their due. Though this irritated the others more than a little, they could do nothing but grumble. Trelig was in the driver's seat and he knew it.

They didn't have long to wait for contact.

The Masjenadans were definitely unusual. Several

were soon seen flying nearby; then a small number circled around, finally approaching slowly and circuitously. Resembling the kind of swan a master glass blower would create, but three meters long and of a transparent material that caught and reflected the predominant colors like small starbursts, the creatures appeared to have no functional neck or head, nor legs. They were stylized crystalline forms flying effortlessly on nearly invisible wings.

The team watched them in fascination. Renard gasped as two of the creatures headed right at each other. "They're going to crash!" he yelled, and stood up.

But the Masjenadans didn't crash. They met and seemed to pass right through each other as if neither were aware of the other's existence—as if both were made of air.

"How the hell . . . ?" Trelig managed.

"I'm afraid they exist in a few planes more than we do," the Ghiskind explained. "I'm not certain I understand it. But they fly through each other all the time with no ill effect—and they can combine, too."

"What are they? Gas bubbles?" Vistaru shook her head.

"We're not sure what they are," the Ghiskind admitted. "One thing is for sure—they have mass, and all that implies."

The Masjenadans who'd flown through each other settled a few centimeters above the ground just before their visitors.

The Ghiskind approached to within a few meters of them. "The Lata hate snakes," it said mysteriously.

A bright yellow light suddenly glowed inside one of the creatures. "Unless the snake is a Lata," responded the creature, in a voice thin, high-pitched, and somewhat reverberant.

The sign and countersign properly given, the group relaxed. "I am the Ghiskind of Yugash," the crystal form resonated. "These are Antor Trelig and Burodir of Makiem, Makorix and Faal of Dillia, Vistaru of

Lata, and Roget of Agitar," it introduced, using Renard's alias, "all of the South."

The Masjenadans' bodies turned slightly, apparently to survey the others.

"We have just signaled others," the one glowing yellow said. "In a few minutes we'll have everything we need here. It is possible that we can transport you across in a day, a bit more at the most."

That was good news to all of them.

"What about the other party?" Burodir asked them. "Any word?"

The light went out for a moment, then returned. "They crossed well north of here," the Masjenadan replied. "They, too, are using friends to fly them. We would think we will maintain about the same distance, about a half-day's walking."

"Anything more about Pugeesh?" Renard asked worriedly.

"You will receive better information in Oyakot," the swan replied. "We know little."

They paused for a few moments. Suddenly the air was filled with glittering Masjenadans. The strange creatures began to fly into one another, weaving back and forth, into, through, and between one another in an intricate pattern. As they did, things started to happen.

First, each pass-through seemed to generate a long strand of glassy rope. The patterns became more intricate, and they wove the stiff substance into a single fabric, like a great net.

"Where does all that stuff come from?" Vistaru wondered aloud.

"From them, I think," the Ghiskind responded. "Parts of their bodies. Remember, in the North things might be totally different from one hex to another. Not merely different varieties of life, but different kinds entirely—one totally alien to the other. Yugash has bordered here since Midnight at the Well of Souls, yet we have no better notion of what they do, why they do it, or how they do it than at the start."

The eerie aerial ballet was completed now and a

great woven structure that seemed to have real flex was the result. The Ghiskind was right: the construction seemed actually to be a part of the creatures, attached to them.

Now swans not connected to the net looped and flew and crashed into each other—only this time they did not reappear on the other side, rather they merged into each other, into single Masjenadans twice the bulk of the original. These then repeated the process with other combined creatures, until eight huge swans perhaps twelve meters in length almost covered the group. These fanned out and paired on either side of the netting, flowing a bit into the webbing but not into the still normal-size creatures attached, and lowered the whole thing to the ground.

The travelers were a bit awed by all this, and it took the Ghiskind to snap them out of it.

"Let's get the equipment onto the net!" it ordered, and after a few moments they started, first rolling the cart on, then the loose packs. Finally they spread a huge skin rug to the rear and another forward, with the freight between. Some experiments with balancing freight and people were needed, but after a few false starts they had it.

Vistaru was nervous about the spartan accommodations. "Shouldn't we all have seat belts or something?" she asked uncertainly.

"Just relax," the Ghiskind said. "You will see that this is not as bad as it looks. Just keep from the edges and maintain the balance."

Before any of them could reply, the assembly took off. It was an odd sensation—no jerk, no sense of acceleration, as if they had suddenly become weightless and floated off. Only the eight huge Masjenadans, whose wings overshadowed them all, and the dozens of smaller ones expended any energy, their wings moving slightly up and down in graceful unison.

They were over a thousand meters off the ground before they knew it, and the land opened up beneath them.

Masjenada from the air looked like a rough, rocky

canvas on which millions of gallons of luminescent paint had been spilled. It was a stunning vista, particularly when contrasted with the drab darkness of Yugash behind them or the sickly yellow atmosphere and dark-blue carpet of the nontech Zidur to their right.

Although there was an uncanny lack of any sense of motion, the ground below had changed every time they looked.

Hours passed, vistas changed, a low mountain range was crossed effortlessly, and their only problem was arranging the slight shifts in load necessary when one or another of the passengers moved.

The sun dipped below the horizon and slowly faded, but their mysterious and enigmatic transporters carried on. By night the countryside was even more aglow in eerie beauty, and the swans added a ghostly radiance.

Renard looked around at them in wonder. "Don't they ever get tired?" he wondered.

"Or hungry?" Faal joined in, chomping on a thick material that oozed from a thick tube.

But there was no answer.

"What do they trade with the South?" Vistaru asked the Ghiskind, looking for a clue as to the mysterious swans' lives.

"Copper and coral, mostly," the Yugash answered. "What they do with it is anybody's guess. There is no oxygen here for combustion. Maybe they eat it."

The Masjenadans provided no information, so it was the best guess that could be made.

They slept, more from boredom than fatigue. Dawn broke again, flooding the landscape with new light.

Ahead was a hex border, that was clear. They had been paralleling it for some time, but now before them a three-point junction appeared.

"That should be Avigloa on our left." The Ghiskind pointed. "Oyakot ahead and to the right. We should be landing soon."

High mountains filled the skies in both hexes and even below them in Masjenada; indicators in the suits showed the temperature to be extremely low, as cold as eighty below, Celsius. Only the internal heaters of the suits kept the travelers comfortable.

They descended a little to land on a small plateau. Opposite, Oyakot presented a chilling vista: the snow was oddly colored and definitely not water of any sort, the rocks eroded into strange shapes.

The set-down was gentle, the unloading easy and quick. They watched them as a new ballet was performed; reversing the original dance the large Masjenadans produced smaller creatures, gathering up the net into their bodies.

All but two of the creatures immediately flew in the direction from which they had come.

The remaining swans floated near, and one turned its internal yellow light on again.

"We wish you good fortune. Oyakot borders the far edge of this small plateau. Someone should meet you there in a few hours."

The group thanked the strange creatures, and watched them take off and turn, flying back into the colorful glow to the east.

Suddenly they felt terribly alone.

Oyakot, Nearing the Pugeesh Border

THE OYAKOT CONTINUED THE RELATIVELY SWIFT AND comfortable passage the group had thus far experienced. The creatures resembled olive-green canvas bags with small, sharp spikes all over. They had hundreds of tiny legs beneath and a central network of long tentacles atop. The location of their eyes, ears, nose, or mouth was not apparent, and the mountainous landscape with its strong cold winds didn't seem to faze them.

But they had roads, and vehicles that traveled swiftly along single lines of light. The hex was criss-crossed with a tremendous transportation network, and the journey took them over massive bridges and through tunnels many kilometers long. Speed was constant and control automated; drivers only monitored progress and took over in an emergency.

The Oyakot were also talkative; a friendly, practical people, they had made the most of a harsh land. That oxygen was a solid to the Oyakot didn't dim the mental kinship the travelers felt for these clever, industrious people.

Wooley was worried, though. Word had come through the dispatching network that Trelig and his party were also well into Oyakot, and only a few hours behind them. Too, her party was already approaching Pugeesh, and information was still sparse.

"Can't tell much on them," their Oyakot driver admitted. "Much too hot over there. Sure death just to cross the line. Ugly-lookin' place, though, all boilin' and hissin'. I'm told they don't have anybody at Zone, neither—so your guess is as good as anybody's. There —you can see it ahead. Gives me the creeps just to look at it."

It was a jungle, that was for sure. A solid wall of purple plants rose before them, and tremendous vapor veils drifted here and there, between the leaves of thick growths.

As they unloaded, Wooley warned them, "The Sea of Borgun is just to the north of Pugeesh, and it's primarily liquid chlorine, so that will give you an idea of the place. The Oyakot think of it as hot, but it's still extremely cold to any of us."

Mavra Chang and Joshi surveyed the scene uneasily. "No sign of roads, either," she pointed out. "How are we going to get through that crap?"

"There's flat land slightly to the north," the Yaxa replied, looking at a topographic map. We can get around the mountains that way. As to crossing the jungle, well, we might have to cut a pathway."

Ben Yulin was uneasy. "Suppose the plants are the Pugeesh?" he said worriedly. "We start chopping through them and *zap!* And we've got a long way to go to fight our way through."

"I am fairly certain that they are not plants," the Torshind put in. "Exactly what they are I do not know —but we'll find out. In the meantime, we have the means to be pretty effective through there." The tendrils of the crystal creature it inhabited fumbled in the heavy packs on Joshi's back, finally coming up with several odd-shaped metallic parts. Assembled, these made a rifle with a long stock and a huge low-slung cylinder.

Mavra looked at the curious weapon with wonder. "What's it shoot?"

"Napalm," the Torshind replied.

To Mavra and Joshi, they rigged long flats that balanced on a single broad, spiked roller. On these the supplies could be carried. The travois were perhaps two meters wide, but balanced properly, they worked very well.

Mavra in particular resented the hookup, especially the halter bit, but the others were sharp with her. "It's why you're along at all," Yulin snapped irritably. "If you don't pull your weight, you're no good to us."

She finally relented, although she was always conscious of the contraption. A beast she might be, but a beast of burden was almost too much.

There *were* wide spaces once they reached the plain, and the going was relatively easy for a while. The ground was hard and covered with long razor-sharp purple stalks that reacted much like grass when walked on and offered no resistance to the rollers.

Maintaining the proper heading was often difficult, and Wooley frequently had to consult a compass when they had to detour from a straight-line route. The needle always pointed to the Equator, which was sufficient.

As to what kind of being the Pugeesh were, there wasn't a clue. No visible trails, no evidence of moving things. This made them nervous; they would have preferred vicious predators to something they could neither see nor identify until, perhaps, it was too late.

They had traveled a good distance by sundown, and they had to stop and rest. Yulin and Wooley agreed that the inhabitants had to be nocturnal, which meant posting a guard at all times. It was decided to stand in twos: Wooley and Mavra the first shift, Yulin and Joshi the second, with the Torshind—who did not need sleep but could selectively turn off parts of its brain for rest—as a backup.

Wooley and Mavra switched their suit radios to a different frequency—the Yaxa had to do it for the handless horse—so as not to disturb the others.

For a while there was silence between them, and of course little noise penetrated the suits, either. Finally Wooley said, "Sure is still around here."

Mavra nodded. "It's completely dark now. You can see some stars up there—and nothing down here but the plants. Of course, I don't have much vision now, but I haven't seen anything. You?"

"Nothing," the Yaxa admitted. "Perhaps we'll get lucky and it'll stay this way. There seems to be nothing at all alive here except the plants. The only things moving are those wisps of gas—I think they're chlorine from their color, but I can't be sure."

Mavra strained and did manage to make out cloudy patches here and there. "You don't suppose . . . ?"

"The clouds? I've been thinking the same thing. They don't seem to drift in any particular direction, as with a wind. But they're just wispy puffs. Even if they *are* the Pugeesh, they can't harm us much. Even the worst of these suits could take a bath in pure sulfuric acid without harm."

Mavra considered it. "But napalm wouldn't be very effective against them, would it?"

There wasn't much to say.

"You're an Entry, aren't you?" Mavra asked the Yaxa. "I can tell by some of your expressions."

The Yaxa nodded slowly. "Oh, yes. Not from any place you've ever heard of, though. I've been a little of everything—farmer, politician, cop. Finally I just got old, and rejuves take something out of you mentally each time, so we—I—decided the hell with it, I'd done all I could, more than most people ever do. I went out with that frame of mind, and wound up getting suckered by a Markovian gate. They're triggered by that, you know—a desire to end it all, despondency, all the things the Markovians would feel when they used it to come here. But it's been a good life since, too. I don't regret much of my past or present. You?"

Mavra was surprised at the Yaxa's candor; some genuine emotion came through, at least in intent, despite the ice-cold monotone. It was *because* she was an Entry, Mavra decided.

The once human horse chuckled dryly. "Me? Nothing much to tell that you wouldn't already know. As for regret—I don't know, really. Some individual things I would like to do differently. Stop my husband from that meet where they killed him. Not touch that damned stone in Olborn that changed me into a half-donkey. Maybe not have been so damned complacent these last years. I still don't understand why I stayed in Glathriel and accepted it so calmly."

"If it makes you feel any better, you had little choice in that," the Yaxa told her. "Every six months the Ambreza gave you a physical. One of the devices they used for checking you was also a hypno gadget. Bit by bit they carefully changed your attitudes—slowly this time, so you'd never even be conscious of it."

Anger grew within her. "So that's it," she said in a tone devoid of emotion. "That explains a lot."

"But in a crisis the old you returned in full," Wooley pointed out. "They didn't dare hypno too strongly or too deeply, or you'd have been no use to them later. And that brings up your stake in all this. Only that computer up there can restore you to humanity, you know—or the Well itself, which might make you something other than what you want to be. I guarantee that if you somehow escaped they'd find a way to keep you from the Well just so your knowledge wouldn't fall into others' hands. They'd do a full brain scan, maybe using a Yugash to keep you from Well processing. You'd *be* a dumb horse."

Mavra considered that. She wasn't sure it was possible to return to the South without Well processing, but a lot more impossible things had happened. "I'm not sure I care," she said softly.

Wooley was startled. "Huh? How's that?"

"I keep going over and over my life," Mavra responded, "and I keep wondering what I'm trying to get back to. Sometimes I feel like the Markovians—money, some power that money brings, skill, my own ship, although it's probably been sold for salvage by now. But for what? Somewhere along the line I missed something, and I don't know what it is."

They were silent for a while, each locked in her own thoughts.

Mavra felt a little groggy, drained. At first she thought it fatigue, but the condition persisted, a numbness increasing like a lead weight on her brain. She shook her head to clear it, but the movement didn't help. She felt herself drifting off.

She was a little girl, running across green fields toward a large farmhouse. An elderly man and woman stood on the porch, looking kindly and smiling as she ran to them.

"Gramma! Grampa!" she squealed in delight. Her grandfather picked her up and hugged and kissed her, laughing. Her grandmother was still a remarkably good-looking woman, and she seemed to have an infectious spark of life inside her. She tenderly brushed back the little girl's long hair and kissed her.

And they sat on the porch and played and talked, and Grampa told tall tales of a magical world where everybody was a different kind of creature and you could have wondrous adventures. He was a marvelous storyteller, and she was enthralled. But though only four or five, she sensed that something was wrong, something was different about this visit.

It wasn't anything they said or did, it was something else, something in the grim way they talked to her parents and older brothers and sisters, some seriousness they tried valiantly to hide from her but could not.

And she'd cried and wailed when they left; for some reason she was certain that they were leaving for good this time, that they would never come back.

And they didn't. There was furious activity in the house, people coming and going, all kinds of serious people who spoke in whispers and pretended nothing was wrong whenever she approached.

She started playing games to eavesdrop on them. Once she hid behind a couch while her mother was arguing with two big men.

"No! We won't desert this farm and this world!" her mother yelled angrily. "We'll fight! We'll fight as long as there is breath in us!"

"As you wish, Vahura," one of the big men replied, "but you may regret it when it's too late. That bastard Courile is in charge now, you know. He'll seal this world off in a minute when he's ready. Think of the children!"

Her mother sighed. "Yes, you're right about that, I suppose. I'll try and make some arrangement."

"Time's short," the other man warned. "Already it might be too late."

And it had been too late. Some of the political opponents had been allowed out, but not her parents, for they were the leaders of the opposition to the party takeover. Not them. Their children would be the example of the new conformist society, and they would be forced to watch. An example to the nation, to the world.

And, one night shortly after, the funny man had come. A small, skinny man who sneaked in a back window, her window. She'd started to scream, but he was such a funny little man and he had such a nice smile. He held a finger to his lips and winked at her, and went out her door.

Soon there was muffled conversation, and then her father came back with the funny little man.

"Mavra, you have to go with our friend here, now," he whispered to her. She was confused, hesitant, but there was something in the little man that made her trust and like him, and Daddy had said it was okay.

And the little man smiled at her, then turned to her much taller father, smile gone. "You were fools to stay," he whispered. "The Com is absolute once it wins."

Her father swallowed hard and seemed to be fighting back tears. "You will take good care of her, won't you?"

The smile was back. "I'm no father figure, but when she needs me, I'll be there," he assured the other.

They sneaked out the back, running from bush to bush, a game she was too sleepy to follow.

"Awake! To arms! Here they come!" A loud electric shout shot through her. Only vaguely did she identify it as the voice of the Torshind.

Woozily she managed to look up. Ben Yulin moved swiftly, grabbing the napalm rifle from Wooley's stunned grasp, turning, and firing.

A tremendously bright, pencil-thin line of flame shot outward, striking some objects nearby. There was a flash. Suddenly it seemed as if the very atmosphere were on fire, burning white-hot, burning and illuminating the Pugeesh, great huge spindly creatures standing on ten incredibly thin legs, with monstrous claws front and rear and large eyestalks that shone like rubies in the center of their round tiny bodies.

The napalm was effective. It struck the leading trio of attackers and clung like glue. There was no sound, but the two forward legs melted like molten plastic and the claws deformed. They retreated hastily, dripping fire.

"To your left!" Joshi shouted. "Something like a cannon!"

Yulin saw it by the flickering light and adjusted a dial on the rifle. The Torshind meanwhile had assembled a second weapon from the pack and shot a random half-moon of burning gelatin behind them, lighting up the surroundings.

Yulin fired again, this time in broad intermittent bursts, at a huge device that did indeed look like a cannon. When it went up, the whole area seemed to be melting.

"My God! They're all over the place!" Yulin screamed. "Get me a new cylinder!"

There was a report of some kind from the right, and a large stone landed near them with a crash and rolled, almost getting the Torshind on the bounce.

Wooley seemed to snap out of whatever trance she was in and grabbed a napalm cylinder, tossing it to Yulin.

Mavra looked around at the eerie scene, trying to see what she could with her poor vision. Napalm at least was the right weapon here; it seemed to set fire to anything it touched. Whenever it landed the stuff melted, burned, and bubbled—and it spread.

The Torshind covered the rear while Yulin zeroed in on a large and complex cannon device that shot huge rocks. He was good with the rifle; the third blob struck, disabling the machine before the Pugeesh manning it could fire again.

And suddenly they were gone. Moving so fast the eye had trouble following, they just faded back into the brush, leaving only the burning remains of eight of their number and the bubbling wreckage of two cannons.

The minotaur was furious and turned on Wooley. "Some guard! They damn near had us!" he snarled.

The Yaxa was slightly bewildered. "I—I don't know what happened," she stammered, the cool self-confident tone of the Yaxa breaking for the first time. "I just seemed to sink into dreaming without even realizing it. I just don't understand it—I never dream, normally."

"Me, too," Mavra put in, furious not only at her own lapse but also because in a battle such as this she had been totally helpless. "It just sank on me like a heavy, irresistible weight."

The Torshind considered this. "I think perhaps there is no blame here. It is entirely possible that the

Pugeesh caused those effects to take us off guard. I have heard of such things being done elsewhere."

"Oh, damn!" Mavra swore. "Not another *magic* hex!"

"Call it what you will," the Torshind replied, "I think we'd better be doubly on guard from now on. How many more cylinders do we have of this stuff? I don't think anything but chemical fire is going to stop them. They appear to be silicon-based."

Yulin, scared and still grumbling, looked into the ammo pouch. "Nine. That's not so good. I don't think we can fight more than two more battles like this."

The Yugash silently agreed. "Let's try diplomacy, then. What have we to lose? Reach over and switch my radio to external amplification, will you?"

Yulin was still too upset, and it was Wooley who made the adjustment.

The Torshind walked to the side of the camp. "Pugeesh!" it called, its voice booming now out into the night. "Pugeesh! We should talk! We are weary travelers, nothing more. We do not threaten you or what is yours. We need only to cross your land to reach the other side! No one else need die, on either side! We ask your permission to continue!"

They waited. There was no reply, but there were no further attacks, either. They settled back for an uneasy balance of the night as the fires slowly burned themselves out and black smoke rose into the night sky.

About forty kilometers back, the other group was fighting a similar battle with different weapons.

Trelig and Burodir were crouched behind rocks, shooting tracers at the attackers. They had some effect, but not much; although the Pugeesh were enormous, there was really very little to them. A wall of flame was much more effective than the odds of projectile hitting a vital spot.

The Dillians, acutely aware of how large a target they were, found concussion hand grenades much more effective. The shrapnel from the grenades found their marks in a wide spread.

One of the spindly creatures charged and a great claw reached out for Renard. The Agitar's suit was from an Entry of his race; it was designed at several contact points to allow the electrical discharge of which all Agitar males were capable. The claw grabbed him, and he reached up and fed the charge into it.

There was a hiss and a crackle, and the Pugeesh curled up into an impossibly small burning ball. This made the other Pugeesh pause, and they drew back cautiously.

The grip hadn't torn the suit, but it had been painful nonetheless. Renard hoped his shoulder was just bruised, not broken.

"Well, they're not eager to die, anyway," Trelig shouted optimistically.

The Ghiskind considered that. "Perhaps that works for us. Make sure this *ptir* doesn't wander away," it said, then abandoned the body, its red-cloaked visage floating into the darkness after the still-present but hesitant Pugeesh.

The creatures watched the Yugash's approach and hurled some rocks at it, which passed harmlessly through. One took a sharp spear and lunged at the Yugash, also to no effect.

The specter reached the spear-thrower's body and merged into it. The Pugeesh turned, convulsed, then charged into its fellows in the darkness.

Terrified, they uttered high-pitched screams.

The occupation was short-lived, however; too scared to do anything, the poor Pugeesh who'd been possessed simply dropped dead.

The Ghiskind emerged, satisfied with it demonstration, and headed for another. They pulled back in terror.

Frustrated that it couldn't talk to them at this point, the Yugash turned and glided back, then returned into the *ptir*.

"I have just given those savages a demonstration of my powers," it told them. "Perhaps now I can talk to them."

The ptir scuttled toward them, and this time they

were not hostile toward it. Their red faceted eyes had followed the fearsome ghost back to the camp and watched as it merged with the crystal being. They knew what approached them.

The Ghiskind stopped when it was convinced it had an audience, and turned its radio to external broadcast.

"Pugeesh! Hear me! We will cross your land. We will not harm or otherwise touch you or yours unless you attack us again. If you do, I promise you that not only you but your children will suffer for generations. Neither mind nor body of us shall you touch, and we will do the same. Is that agreed?"

There was no reaction for some time, then the sound of murmuring and mumbling. The Yugash received no formal reply, but soon heard the sound of many creatures moving off. Inspection revealed just one or two remaining, apparently observers.

In a way, they'd agreed.

Fairly confident now, the Yugash rejoined the others. "I don't think they'll bother us again. If they do, we'll have to come up with a really big power demo."

"Maybe they were luckier with the Yaxa group farther on," Trelig said hopefully.

Vistaru, totally helpless in the battle because she was too small to man a weapon and her suit prevented flying or use of her stinger, sighed. "Poor Mavra!" was all she could manage.

None of them slept the rest of the night, and they packed up and continued their journey at dawn's first light. None of the strange creatures had molested them further in mind or body, and they hoped it would stay that way.

A couple of hours later they came upon the camp of the Yaxa party, saw the charred remains of the battle, and Vistaru noted with relief the lack of non-Pugeesh bodies about.

"Too bad," Antor Trelig said sadly. "Looks like they're still in front of us."

Wohafa

WHETHER IT WAS THE PROMISE, THE FIGHTS, THE threat, or other factors, the Pugeesh interfered no more. Both groups felt they were being watched, but as time passed and the truth of their claim that they were simply passing through became more obvious, they felt less threatened.

Wohafa was an eerie scene. A bleak, copper-colored landscape set against a deep-pink sky through which wisps of anhydrous white clouds drifted. Lightning was so frequent that often the land seemed to be lit by a stroboscope, with everything moving in a jerky slow motion.

The Wohafans themselves were odd creatures, balls of bright yellow light from which hundreds of light-ninglike tendrils darted. A cross between creatures of matter and those of energy, they manipulated things with arms of energy, yet seemed to have mass and weight.

As a high-tech hex, Wohaja had a large number of machines and artifacts, but, for the most part, these, too, reflected the ambiguity of their makers' nature and seemed odd lumps working from no apparent source and to no apparent purpose.

They became aware that building in Wohafa was accomplished by matter-to-energy-to-matter conversion, when they watched rock worked by a number of Wohafans dissolve and reform in new and obviously planned forms.

The Wohafans were a group neutral to them, though, which helped enormously. Having close contacts with the Bozog and a number of other high-tech Northern civilizations, they had almost daily contact with the South, obtaining whatever a customer wanted by making it from the surrounding rock and rearranging its atomic structure. They accepted the waste of other civilizations and remade it to order, so they were a key economic link in the loose economy of the Well World as a whole.

They were also pragmatic. They understood the significance of the eerie silver moon that shined on the Southern horizon, and they appreciated its dangers, so they were willing to allow someone to reach it and remove the threat—for whatever purposes. As insurance, the Wohafans were willing to aid both sides so that, no matter who reached New Pompeii, they would bear the strange creatures no ill will.

Wohafans created huge platforms that stood atop a strange blue-white glowing energy field, and transported first the Yaxa group and then the Ortega group across the hex, scrupulously maintaining the time interval between the two groups as well. The six hundred kilometers or so they needed to cross were wiped out in less than a day by this rapid and cooperative transportation system.

A semitech hex, Uborsk was a bit more of a challenge but it bordered both Wohafa and Bozog and was partially dependent on them for some manufacturing. It could not afford to run afoul of the neighbors without causing long-range strains in which it had the most to lose.

The Uborsk were enormous blobs of jelly, perhaps four meters around, who lived in a sea of soft, granular material that twinkled in sunlight. It was obvious that the Uborsk civilization was almost entirely hidden from the Southerners' sight.

Out of the translucent blobs, however, could emerge tentacles, arms, anything they needed when they needed it. In order to facilitate commerce between Wohafa and Bozog, the Uborsk had allowed the two high-tech hexes to build an efficient railroad causeway along the Slublika border. The trains were an almost unending series of flatcars rolling on a continuous rail and powered externally by internal combustion engines at regular points along the almost four hundred kilometer route, like an enormous escalator. For allowing the construction and running the system, the Uborsk received raw materials they needed from the versatile Wohafans, manufactured goods their own technology could not produce from the Bozog. It was a good compromise that surprised the Southerners; interhex cooperation on a long-term basis was rare in the South, and it was all the more remarkable in the North because the three hexes involved were so different in composition that long-term stays even with protection were uncomfortable.

The politics involved in the transportation systems were somewhat frustrating to the two groups, however; a five-and-a-quarter-hour interval had been established when the second group had crossed into Wohafa, and it was maintained absolutely. The trailing group was not permitted to close on the leaders, and the leaders were unable to prepare anything to eliminate their rivals.

And thus, much more rapidly than they had dreamed, the leading group under Wooley and Ben Yulin pulled in to a strangely surrealistic station in Bozog.

It was a surprisingly bright land; the pale-blue sky was reminiscent of the South, at least at the higher altitudes, and nearby mountains had what looked like snow. Spindly gnarled trees dotted the landscape, the fact that they were purple with orange leaves not in the least disconcerting. Only the midday temperature registering on the suit gauges offered any strong indication of difference: it was minus thirty degrees Celsius.

But the Bozog were no distant relatives of the South. The Bozog were, if anything, more alien and enigmatic than any creatures they had met to date.

A Bozog official rolled up to meet them on ball-bearing feet. It was very thin, more or less round, and, except for the two orange circles on its back, rose no more than 30 or 40 centimeters from the ground.

"Welcome to Bozog," it said in its most dignified

voice, like a small-town Chamber of Commerce head greeting visiting dignitaries. "We are amazed and pleased at your rapid and safe arrival. If you will follow me across town, we will arrange for the final part of your journey."

They followed it, noting the liquidity of its movements; the official seemed to flow rather than roll down broad streets, and almost oozed around corners.

The city itself was low, and furnished with an incredibly intricate network of broad ramps. There were vehicles, too, resembling mechanical copies of the Bozog—low, flat, with two storage humps in the middle. A Bozog driver lay on a forward platform and seemed to have no means of control, yet the driving was perfect.

Observing the odd people at work showed how they carried on the business of a civilization. Beneath each Bozog were what appeared to be millions of sticky cilia, so that a Bozog who lay over something could manipulate it quite well. For elaborate or problem work, the two orange spots proved singularly versatile. Out of each could rise a large orange tentacle or many smaller ones—the orange material seemed to be a viscous liquid that the Bozog formed into any shape and then held it under strain—to the limit of the amount of mass in the body containers.

Another, final train took them to the launch site. It was in some ways similar to the Uborsk railroad in that it was a continuous line of flatcars, but it seemed to roll on soft noiseless tires or treads through a U-shaped channel, like a moving walkway, and was powered by a system much more sophisticated than the one used in the semitech hex.

As they rode, Wooley signaled that they were to switch to low-power radio only. They were nearing the end of the journey, and it was time to discuss what would come next.

"It's rather obvious that we haven't faced, or been able to face, our chief remaining problem," she pointed out.

Yulin nodded. "The others are only a few hours

behind. There's no way we'll launch immediately. The Bozog said they're still bringing the ship in from Uchjin. So we'll still be there when they arrive." He couldn't help wondering how the Bozog were bringing the ship from the nontech hex where he'd crash-landed it over twenty-two years before, nor how this was being done against the wishes of the Uchjin themselves.

"You could always compromise," Joshi suggested helpfully. "I mean, why don't we *all* go?"

"Compromise with the Ghiskind is impossible," the Torshind pointed out. "We represent totally conflicting views, goals, and philosophies. As for the rest—only Trelig counts there, of course. Would any of you like to reinstate him on the world that he designed? Yulin? Do *you* know everything there is to know about New Pompeii? Would you trust the rest of us there with Trelig around?"

Yulin shook his bull's head slowly from side to side. "You know the answer there. That place is built like a fortress. Not even the full weight of the Com could get in there with less than the full fleet and its terror weapons. Even I was confined for the most part to the Obie project underside—I was only allowed up for breaks, and then only to the luxury rooms. No, Underside I'm totally familiar with, but Topside and the little secrets, twists, turns, and traps I'm not."

Mavra suddenly had a headache. It irritated her, and she shook her equine head in annoyance. It was a sharp, local ache that felt as if someone had inserted a glowing wire in her brain.

And suddenly it exploded.

She remembered. Remembered it all. When she was first on New Pompeii, Antor Trelig had run his political guests through the great computer, Obie, giving them horse's tails as demonstrations of his power. The computer, designed and built by Dr. Gilgam Zinder, was not friendly to Trelig. It simply obeyed whoever gave the orders from the console—but it was like making a deal with the devil, as Yulin had complained. If there was a loophole, Obie found it—and one such was Mavra herself. When she'd been run through, Obie had decided that she was best capable of escaping New Pompeii, of freeing Zinder's daughter, Nikki, and getting her off-planet before Zinder and his near-human machine carried out their ultimate double-cross of Trelig and Yulin: the reversal of the field of probability that had transferred them all to the Well World.

She had almost made it, thanks to Obie. Obie had given her the complete plans and specifications for New Pompeii, down to the last nut and bolt. It had allowed her to foil Trelig's best defenses, nab Nikki Zinder, steal the ship, and bypass the robot sentinels. But it had been too late—they'd all crashed anyway after being translated with New Pompeii to Well World orbit.

And all that knowledge had been locked inside her mind since that time. It was there now—more than she herself could follow. She suddenly understood Obie's dilemma with the Well World—too much input. The computer was in contact with the great Well computer, but could not absorb the knowledge. She concentrated, found that if she wanted a specific thing it could be retrieved—but only if she knew the right question to ask.

The others ignored her.

"It is important, then, that we have our showdown at the launch site," Wooley was saying. "We will have only a short time to prepare, so we must be extra careful. Remember, though, that this is a high-tech hex, and everything works here."

Yulin was thoughtful. "What about the Bozog, though? Won't they stop us from doing anything?"

The Torshind answered that. "No. They are opportunists. They cannot operate the ship, but they want a representative on it when it goes. They do not care who the pilot is—or what. They are also far from stupid. They will know that this tension exists, and that it must be released. I would suspect that, as long as at least one pilot lives, they will not interfere."

"I wish we could be sure of that," Wooley responded. "However, we will act as if it were true because we have no other choice. Remember, we will have only hours at the launch site before they arrive. Not much time to assess conditions and prepare." Her voice seemed to grow even colder, sharper than usual. "On no account must Antor Trelig survive," she concluded.

The launch site itself was impressive. The Bozog had had years to prepare, and they'd made the most of it. Huge buildings stood out from a flat, desolate landscape, and a massive version of the rail system on which the Southerners were riding ran about a kilometer from one huge building to the site itself. Around the site massive cranes were positioned to manipulate the ship onto the platform, a tremendous black metal structure reaching into the sky, with a tilt toward the northwest.

"I'm not sure I like that angle," Yulin commented, surveying it from the train. "As it is, we'll have to build to full thrust before taking off, a tremendous danger to us even without other problems."

"You will need to clear sixty-three kilometers within the first minute of flight," their Bozog host responded. "Using information supplied by you and by others, we calculate that you will have nine seconds to spare. The slight angle is to give you maximum high-tech free flight. A perfectly vertical takeoff is impossible with the ship's design, anyway, and you would run the risk of a high-altitude wobble that might take you for a moment over the wrong side of the border. Any power failure during takeoff will result in insufficient speed to break free of the Well's influence before normal rotation takes you over semitech Esewod or nontech Slublika. You of all people should know what that would mean."

Yulin nodded soberly. He and Trelig had escaped New Pompeii in disguise to avoid being murdered by Trelig's former guards and slaves, who, seeing that they were now in an alien sector of space, realized they were dead people because they'd be deprived of their daily sponge supply. Trelig and Yulin had made the same mistake as Mavra Chang had a day earlier— they had flown too low over the Well World, so that the technological limitations of the hexes below had affected them, and they had plunged to the surface.

But Chang's ship had broken up over the South; attempts to recover the sections, particularly the power supply, had been the cause of the wars of the Well. That had ended in failure with the destruction of the engines in a volcanic crater in high Gedemondas.

Yulin's ship, however, was not designed to break up but was a smaller utility craft used mostly for in-system work. It had atmospheric-flight capabilities and collapsible wings, and he and Trelig had brought it intact to a dead-stick landing in nontech Uchjin.

"Are you certain of those figures?" Yulin asked, worried. "I mean, *absolutely* certain?" Whoever was in that ship would have one crack at it, and one crack only.

"We are," the Bozog assured him. "We have had independent channels of communication. We know as much about that ship as its designer. Only the lack of two key minerals anywhere on the Well World prevents us from constructing our own drive and building our own ships."

"Curious," Mavra put in. "I wonder if the lack was deliberate?"

"Probably. Makes no difference," the Bozog responded. "The fact is that nothing on the Well World so far discovered can power a plant with sufficient initial and sustained thrust to overcome the Well's effects. You might say we know how to build one, we just can't do it."

They were taken to a large square building that proved to have a very conventional airlock. Inside, it contained a suite of comfortable rooms complete with closets, manipulable lights, and an intercom to the Bozog launch control complex, and the project director's office.

It was also filled with a generic Southern atmosphere

that was maintained at a temperature of twenty degrees Celsius, comfortable for all concerned.

The atmospheric difference seemed to have no effect on the Bozog.

"We are rather versatile in this department," it explained. "In general, we cannot stand the presence of certain lethal gases, but none of them are present in your atmosphere. You will excuse me if I do not elaborate on which gases and other substances are not to our liking."

They understood. Why give a possible enemy the lethal weapon?

"How do you breathe, then?" Joshi asked, fascinated.

"We don't breathe, not in the sense you mean it," the creature replied. "What gases we require we obtain in our eating. There is as much gas in the rock we consume as in anything else. We just do not require constant respiration."

Left alone shortly afterward, they were thankful to get out of their suits. The Torshind, who had no such problems, left its crystal crab shell and explored rapidly.

"No locks," it reported to them. "Heavily bugged, of course, but I find nothing threatening. It is my opinion that, if the Bozog remain neutral and don't warn our adversaries, we can surprise them shortly after they enter the airlock."

The Yugash had used its crystal tentacles to draw a rough floor plan, and Wooley surveyed it critically.

"I disagree," she responded. "There is too much danger of hitting a Bozog, and *that* we can't afford. No, this second chamber across the way is obviously for them. I would suggest we let them in, allow the Bozog to leave, then hit them as quickly as possible, before they even have a chance to unsuit."

The Torshind considered it. "A bit more risky," it pronounced, "but politics is politics."

Bozog, the Launch Site
Five Hours Later

THE ORTEGA PARTY LOOKED AT THE BLOCK STRUC-
ture with more relief than apprehension. They had
been in their suits for several days; they were smelly
and itchy. Even Trelig and Burodir were uncomfortable: they needed an occasional rinse of water, and it
had been the same water over and over for some time.

Their number was greater, too; two large Dillians,
two Makiem, plus Renard, Vistaru, and the Ghiskind
made for an unwieldy assortment with different needs
and comfort levels. All were out of their element.

The Bozog stopped near the airlock. "The others
are inside, in their own apartment," it warned. "They
are out of their suits and have had a long time to prepare. They will do nothing as long as I am with you,
of that we're certain—it would force us to take a hand.
However, once I leave, you are all on your own. I will
tarry as long as possible to give you as much chance as
you can, but after that it's up to you."

They understood perfectly, and were grateful that
it bothered. The two Dillians pulled pistols and acted
as guards; they would cover the others until they
themselves could be guarded.

There was no sign of the Yaxa party when they
entered, went down a well-lit corridor, and through a
top-hinged panel to their rooms. As they passed a
similar panel on their right, the Bozog's rear spot had
formed a shaky tentacle and pointed silently, then re-
ceded back into the orange mass.

They understood. The enemy was there, ready,
and less than twenty meters down and across the hall
from them.

The Bozog did in fact linger with small talk for a while, allowing Vistaru, Renard, and the Makiem to unsuit and choose their weapons. Renard unpacked his tast and took a pistol in his other hand.

"I hope I remember which hand has which," he whispered in a half-joking tone he didn't feel. "It'd be a hell of a thing if I blew up the gun and shot the tast."

Trelig and Burodir checked out their own hand weapons. The centaurs managed to get out of their suits before the Bozog felt it had to leave. With a cheery, noncommittal farewell, it oozed out the panel, leaving them inside.

"Best to let them come to us," the Ghiskind said as low as possible. "Dillians to either side of the door. Makiem in the far corners. Agitar with me in the middle, just forward and a little out of direct fire from the door. Vistaru, can you fly in here?"

She tried it. She could and it felt wonderful to rise up and dart about, although her wings hurt like hell from their recent inactivity. She had a Lata pulse-pistol in her tiny hand, and now her wicked red-and-black-striped stinger oozed with venom.

"Now what?" Renard asked tensely.

"We wait," Trelig whispered from his corner. "As long as necessary."

Time passed. It wasn't productive, nor comfortable; they were all tired. The tension, too, was having its effect, developing into a sense of numbing lethargy.

Renard was sitting down now, pistol only half-pointed forward, shaking his head. Vistaru, too, was relaxing.

"Why don't they just come and get it over with?" he grumbled. "I figured they'd hit us as soon as the Bozog left."

"There are a lot of devious minds there," Trelig pointed out. "I'm sure that that was their first plan, but it will have been refined into something a lot more diabolical by now. This waiting is almost certainly part of it—designed to get us to let down our guard."

"It's working," his wife grumped from the other corner. "I can hardly keep my eyes open."

"Look who's talking about devious minds," Renard said wryly, looking over his shoulder at Trelig. "I've been told that nobody holds a candle to you in that department."

"Stop that!" the Ghiskind ordered. "It will simply get us killed if we start in on one another. Why do their job for them?"

"Relax," Faal the Dillian cautioned. "Remember, we outnumber them. Chang and her mate are no threat, they won't even be in on it. That's just three of them against seven of us."

Renard suddenly stirred and jumped up, looking around.

"What is it?" several of them said at once.

He looked around, a slightly puzzled expression on his blue devil's face. "I'm not sure," he responded carefully. "Something funny. You know how aware I am of electrical things. I'd swear the lights flickered for a moment, then became brighter."

They were all suddenly awake again, and tense, even though none of the others felt what he did.

Against the brightness of the lights, none had noticed a strange shape, faded almost to invisibility, flow under a room partition that was only two or three centimeters off the ground, and silently move along the baseboard toward the door until it reached the big male centaur, Makorix, standing pistol at the ready.

It flowed into the body of the Dillian, instantly striking at nerve centers, paralyzing movement. The Dillian brain was related to the human brain, and the Dillian central nervous system was a good compromise between human and horse. The Torshind had become familiar with equine movements while transporting Mavra and Joshi to Yugash; except in size Yulin's Dasheen brain was very close to the Dillian brain. The Torshind had no trouble locating the correct spots.

Slowly the hand holding the pistol moved and readjusted. A thumb kicked the little control lever up two notches. The energy density would be greatly lowered, but still enough to paralyze; the beam would now be much wider.

The barrel moved ever so slightly away from the door toward the left of the room, where Renard, Vistaru, and Burodir sat waiting.

Suddenly Vistaru noticed the new targets. "Look out!" she screamed, and took off straight up.

Renard's reflexes were tremendously fast; he kicked off on his powerful goatlike legs, soaring into the air as Makorix's pistol fired.

The beam sprayed the room, and struck the Ghiskind and Burodir full on. It had no effect on the Yugash, but the great female frog gave a strangled croak and pitched forward.

Suddenly, the door exploded as a huge orange shape burst through it, followed quickly by a squat, humanlike powerfully built form, shooting wide scatter bursts.

Vistaru reached Makorix in an instant and knocked the pistol from his hand. The Dillian reached up for her with a snarl, and she obliged, stabbing him with her stinger.

The centaur gave a surprised cry, then collapsed in a heap.

Faal, hardly comprehending what was happening or why, swung her pistol at the orange shape and was gunned down almost immediately by Yulin.

Renard had lost his tast and had almost run straight up the wall in his escape from the initial shot; fully charged, he whirled and leaped for the orange shape, but the Yaxa saw him and spit a thick, brown fluid, catching him in midleap. It burned like fire when it hit and he plunged helplessly to the floor.

The Torshind left the unconscious body of the centaur and was headed for the Ghiskind when Trelig opened up. He was like a madman, capable of leaping ten meters or more. Coming to rest on any surface—even walls or ceiling—for an instant, he would fire. Suddenly he dropped directly onto the Yaxa.

The Ghiskind's crystal form leaped now, crashing

into them, jarring them away from each other.

Vistaru, flying about, was afraid to move close in for fear of hitting a friend. She looked anxiously about and screamed, "Where's the damned Torshind?"

Wooley shouted something and Yulin ran out the door. Spitting and using fore-tentacles as whips, the Yaxa also retreated beyond the door, which banged back down noisily.

Vistaru looked around appalled. Both Dillians were either out cold or dead; Burodir was frozen stiff, Renard was unconscious and covered with sticky Yaxa stuff.

She looked at the two survivors with her. "Nothing to do but go get them before they try again!" she yelled.

"I agree," yelled Trelig, slapping a new energizer into his pistol. "Let's go!"

"Let me go out the door first!" the Ghiskind cautioned. "I'm harder to kill."

There was no argument, and out it went, the other two following a second or so later when they heard no sound of struggle.

The hall was deserted, but there was a thin trail of a pale-green ichor leading toward the other room. One of them, probably the Yaxa from the nature of the stuff, had been hurt.

"Take it easy," the Ghiskind cautioned. "No sense in playing their game all the way. We hurt one, yes, but they're still a whole party and we're down to three. It's even now. If we go charging in there dead on, they'll just wipe us out. Let's think a minute."

Although Mavra and Joshi knew the plan, they were helpless to do anything one way or the other. This was not their fight; they wanted only to survive it.

When Wooley and Yulin had come crashing back through the door, the horses knew that the plan had been only partially successful; there were some gashes in Wooley's tentacles, too, which slowed the Yaxa a good deal, and a few nasty welts on Yulin's back. The

Torshind entered by other means and slid back into its crystal shell.

"Be ready," the Yugash warned them. "The few remaining will come at us as soon as they can. It will be hours before they can count on any of their survivors, and they won't wait that long."

Wooley's death's head nodded. "If I were they, I'd be coming through that door right now. Check your weapons and be at the ready. Yulin! Dim the light so we can make sure the Ghiskind doesn't pull our own trick on us! Mavra and Joshi, stay back and out of the way!"

They waited tensely for the counterattack, and they didn't have long.

The door opened slowly, and they all trained their weapons on it, ready to fire as soon as the creature was visible.

It was the Ghiskind's ptir, against which they had only the energy pistols, but they fired anyway.

Which played right into the Ghiskind's hand.

The shots ignited a series of smoke and concussion grenades attached to the creature; these went off with a deafening roar that almost blew the door apart and filled the entire area with a dense, acrid yellow smoke.

Everyone was blinded, and Yulin started coughing. As he did so, something struck him hard on the back of the head and neck, knocking him down and rendering him semiconscious. His pistol skidded into the yellow fog.

The Ghiskind, its shell destroyed by the blasts, drifted across the room to the two horselike creatures it saw cowering helplessly against the far wall and entered the first one it encountered, taking control. Suddenly animated, Mavra made for the Torshind's crystal shell and plowed right into it, sending it sprawling. The horse reared and with its forelegs struck the fragile crystal form repeatedly, shattering it like glass.

The fog began to clear, allowing Trelig and Vistaru —who were wearing the breathers from their spacesuits—to join the action.

The Torshind abandoned its ptir for the body

nearest it—Wooley's. The Yaxa was surprised, but the Torshind knew the Yaxa system well and was in complete control almost immediately. It quickly turned on Trelig, spitting the brownish substance.

The material didn't devastate the reptile as it had the Agitar, but the goo did blind him for a minute. Wooley then turned to the horse, which was finishing the job on the Torshind's shell, and raised its pistol.

Joshi, still amazed at Mavra's jumping into the fight, noticed Wooley's threat to her, although none of the others did. Without thinking, he leaped to the center of the room, placing himself between the Yaxa and Mavra, who was just turning around.

The pistol fired full-force, enveloping Joshi in a blinding electrical light that flickered like a photographic negative and then faded into nothingness.

Seeing this, Mavra's mind suddenly exploded, expelling the Ghiskind with unexpected force. "Joshi!" she screamed and started for the Yaxa. Disoriented, the Ghiskind followed just above her, almost as if attached. Vistaru, who had managed to fly out of the smoke, saw what had happened and dived for the Yaxa.

At this moment, Ben Yulin was rising shakily to his feet and noticed a blur of motion from the corner of his eye. Lunging for a saddlebag, he flung it with full force at the shape. The saddlebag struck Vistaru straight on, knocking her to the floor and pinning her under it.

She looked up to see Mavra's horselike form bearing down on the possessed Yaxa, whose pistol rose to meet the threat.

"Kally! For God's sake fight it! Take control! *My God, Kally! She's our granddaughter!*" the Lata screamed.

A tentacle tried to squeeze the trigger, but could not. The Yaxa body convulsed, and Mavra Chang struck, knocking over the Yaxa and landing on top of the butterfly-creature.

Trelig, meanwhile, spied Yulin picking up his pistol,

and leaped for the minotaur. Yulin whirled, saw the frog, dived—and the Makiem sailed over him.

Like a swimmer in a sprint, Trelig didn't miss a stroke. He turned in midair, and his powerful webbed feet struck the wall, propelling him forward again. He landed, somersaulted, and rose with a pistol on Yulin.

And Yulin had his pistol on Trelig.

The Ghiskind, atop Mavra, regained its senses from the stunning mental blow it had received. No mind that strong had ever been experienced by it or any other Yugash.

In the meantime, Mavra extricated herself from the convulsing Yaxa to avoid being crushed. Clearly, a major battle was being fought within the shiny yellow-black head.

Trelig and Yulin looked at each other. "Standoff," Trelig chuckled. "How about a truce, Ben? We're old friends. Let's see how the rest of this comes out. You and me, together again on New Pompeii!"

Yulin's big brown eyes shined, his manner softened. The pistol dipped slightly. "Okay, Antor. Partners this time, though. Right?"

Trelig kept one of his eyes on Yulin while the other followed the drama being played out on the floor.

And it was clear now who was winning.

Slowly and unsteadily, the Torshind emerged from the body of the Yaxa; Wooley collapsed and was still.

The Ghiskind immediately hurled itself at the emerging ghostly red figure. As the two met, their forms became less distinct, just a blurry dull-red sheet of energy, a ball of dull fire suspended two meters or so above the floor.

While this was occurring, Vistaru managed to free herself of the heavy saddlebags and rose groggily to her feet. She looked around, saw Yulin and Trelig through the thin yellow haze not three meters apart, pistols half on each other but attention mostly on the drama now in the center of the room.

Mavra lay unnaturally on her side, still but breathing hard. Huge, thick tears fell from the horse's eyes.

The fight between the two Yugash had intensified.

The energy sphere grew denser, more compact, and more intense. Now, suddenly, there was but a single glowing bright-red ball, almost too bright to look at, in the air above the room. It was about the size of a grapefruit.

There was a sudden, violent explosion and thunder reverberated along the halls of the building, rattling partitions, doors, and anything else that was loose. The odor of ozone was sharp.

Then, so dim that it could hardly be seen, a figure dropped to the floor and seemed to inflate, like a balloon. It moved slightly, but was terribly weak and stunned, that was obvious.

One of the Yugash had survived.

"Which one?" Vistaru breathed. "I wonder which one?"

Trelig turned slightly to face her. "We'll only find out when it can get into a body," he said. "Until then—"

His words were cut short as Yulin, taking advantage of Trelig's preoccupation, suddenly dropped to one knee and fired directly at the frog. As Joshi's had, Trelig's form froze in fire, seemed to become a negative of itself, then winked out with a flash.

Antor Trelig had made the first mistake of his long life, and now he was dead.

Vistaru gasped and had her own pistol from its little holster in an instant. Yulin turned to face her, gun ready, and saw that she had him cold.

He paused, shrugged, and tossed his own energy pistol away to the other side of the room where it fell with a clatter.

The Lata was amazed.

"Why?" she asked him in wonder.

He laughed. "I'm your only way into Obie now," he reminded her. "And the only pilot with hands. I think it's time for a merger."

Vistaru didn't trust him, but was uncertain as to what to do. Mavra was apparently in shock; the Yugash, whichever it was, was badly hurt and unable to communicate; Wooley was out cold; Trelig was gone; the rest of her allies were out cold or dead.

She and Ben Yulin were the only whole and conscious people in the room, perhaps in the whole building.

Yulin stood up and looked around. His massive bull's head surveyed the wreckage of bodies, the charred and smashed equipment.

"God! What a mess!" he breathed.

The Launch Complex
Four Hours Later

BOZOG ATTENDANTS WHEELED OUT THE LAST OF THE problem cases, janitorial crews swabbed down the floor, and blowers cleansed the air. Several decisions had been made by the survivors, which had pared things down nicely.

Of them all, Renard had been the least hurt; the paralysis from the Yaxa venom wore off within an hour of the battle. Wooley was slower to recover; she had lost some blood in the first clash and had a debilitating headache as a result of the second. Burodir and the centaurs were sent to the Zone Gate for return home. The form of a Yugash still lay on the floor, indistinct but definitely alive. The survivors still had no idea which Yugash had survived; to most of their tastes, it would have been better if the two enemies had destroyed each other.

And now they sat—just Renard, Wooley, Yulin, Vistaru, and Mavra Chang—and the odd red form on the floor.

With Bozog help, they'd managed to get Mavra to her feet; she hadn't made any protest, just remained limp and glassy-eyed.

Ben Yulin looked her over carefully, trying to get some reaction, but none was forthcoming. "Think it was the Yugash battle that did it?" he asked casually.

Wooley, still nursing her head, emitted a sigh that sounded like metal scraping glass. "No, I don't think so. Certainly her experience would have been no worse than what I went through, which was bad enough—and I surely had the crazy one. The creature was totally insane, its thoughts flooded into my brain somehow. It hated us—it hated all of us, everything and everybody. It was incredible. And I almost lost. If Vistaru hadn't yelled . . ."

"So what is wrong with her?" Vistaru asked, perplexed. "Why won't she say anything?"

Renard, now cleaned up thanks to a chemical suggested by Wooley and provided by the Bozog, got to his feet and walked over to her.

Twenty-two years, he thought. She has changed more than I; she had a nasty life for that period while I enjoyed things. The guilt he felt was mixed with admiration for her. She was here, she'd come this far. He was also convinced that she'd survived because of her total egoism, her absolute belief in self, in the ability to do anything no matter what the odds.

He looked at her. "Come on, snap out of it!" he said sharply. "You're Mavra Chang, damn it. Perhaps you loved him, cared for him as wife or mother, but you've gone through that before! You never let it get to you! You survived! You triumphed! That's what life's all about to you! The chase is coming to a climax after all this time! Come on! You can't give up now!"

He sensed a flicker in her eyes, minimal animation, fleeting but nonetheless very real. She heard him and understood him all right.

"Don't you think you're being a little hard on her?" Vistaru asked, concerned.

"Let him be, Star," Wooley whispered. "Let's face it, he knows her a lot better than we."

The Lata nodded silently. "You feeling as guilty and rotten as I am?" she asked after a moment. Wooley didn't reply.

Renard threw up his hands in exasperation and walked over to them. "So much for psychology," he sighed and sat back down. They were silent a time, and Yulin drowsed off. Finally, Renard turned to Wooley and Vistaru. "Are you *really* her grandparents?" he asked.

Vistaru nodded. "Yes—although I didn't know it until Ortega told me. *This* bastard's known for over twenty years, but didn't even tell me when we met on that island and joined forces to find her."

Wooley chirped a dry chuckle. The Yaxa couldn't manage to change its cold voice, but there seemed an extra dimension of humanity, of warmth in it somehow. "You want to tell him the story, or should I?" she asked.

The Lata shrugged. "I'll start and you can join in any time you want." She turned to face Renard. "Let's see—where to begin. I suppose we ought to go way back, to the first of our three lives."

Yulin was suddenly awake and interested, too. "*Three* lives?" he said.

Vistaru nodded. "I was born on a Comworld, one of those where you are made into little plastic ten-year-old neuters and raised and conditioned only for a specific function. The theory's to produce a society much like an insect colony—and it works, after a fashion. I was called Vardia Diplo—I was a courier, a kind of human tape recorder. You understand this was two centuries ago."

"My background was much the same," Wooley put in. "I was a farm worker who didn't work out on a world that didn't work out, either. It was Com, but syndicate-controlled. I suppose you know about that, Yulin."

Yulin's bull's face could show no human expression, but the minotaur's bearing seemed to grow sheepish and apologetic. Yulin could show sincerity and conviction—whether he felt or not.

"I was never involved with that," the Dasheen responded defensively. "Look, I was *born* into the syndicate, the son of a major controller. Raised in luxury on a private world a lot more human and humane than Trelig's. Who knew? Educated in the best places as a scientist and engineer. You have to understand—when the big-shot villains of the galaxy are your father, mother, friends, family—everybody you know—then they aren't villains at all. Not to you. Not to me. It's true I had no particular regard for anything but family law, but, then, again, aren't freighter captains like Chang there just variations of the same attitude?"

In Mavra Chang's case it was particularly true; she'd been a rebel and a thief the first half of her life.

"Never mind the alibis, let's get back to the story," Renard snapped impatiently. Yulin shrugged and settled back down.

The Yaxa paused a moment and continued. "I was developed as a woman, put in a Com whorehouse for party bigwigs, and got so screwed up and was so abused by the men who came by that I became unable to relate, sexually or socially, with men at all. That made me wrong for the job, so they gave me to a bastard controller in the sponge syndicate to use as a sample—hook me on sponge, then decrease the dosage very slightly as a living example."

Renard nodded sympathetically. "Remember, I was a spongie, too—and I saw New Pompeii in its heyday."

"Well, the two of us found ourselves on a freighter bound for Coriolanus," Vistaru continued. "The captain was a funny little guy named Nathan Brazil."

Renard's dark eyebrows rose in surprise. "It's been over twenty years since I heard that name. I can hardly remember where. Mavra, I think. He's not for real, if I remember. The Wandering Jew."

"He's for real," Vistaru assured him. "He discovered that Wooley was on sponge and decided to make a run for the sponge world without us knowing. We got detoured by a strange distress signal from a Markovian world, discovered a mass murder, and wound up falling through a Gate and winding up here. Wooley came out a Dillian first, I came out a Czillian —you may have seen some. Intelligent plant creatures."

Renard nodded. "Seems to me I met one—named Vardia, come to think of it."

She nodded. "That was me, too. The Czillians reproduce by budding off. There are probably several of the original me still around, with memories complete to that point."

"Wait a minute!" Yulin objected. "You say she was a Dillian and you were a Czillian. That's not possible! You only get one trip through the Well and you know it!"

"*Most* people," the Lata corrected. "We got more. Brazil's immortality is easily explained. We accompanied him on a journey much like this one, to the Well of Souls itself—and it opened for him. He was a Markovian, Yulin! Perhaps the only one still alive!"

Yulin was fascinated, and so was Renard. "A living Markovian!" the Dasheen breathed. "Still around! Incredible! What did he look like? Did you ever see him in his natural form?"

Both Wooley and Vistaru nodded. "Oh, yes, for a while inside the Well. It looks like a huge human heart on six tentacles. Brazil—well, he claimed to be more than that."

"He said he was God," Wooley put in. "He said he created the Markovians and saw them go wrong, and he was waiting around to see if we did a better job of it."

The prospect was unnerving. "Do you believe him?" Renard asked.

Vistaru shrugged. "Who knows? One thing's for sure —he's at least a Markovian, and he could work the Well. Somehow, during the worst of the journey, the two of us had grown closer together—I guess I was learning how to be a real human being. As for Wooley —well, she kind of loved Nathan Brazil, but he was too inhuman, and she also hated being a woman. Nathan fixed it. We were transported from the Well World to Harvich's World, which was then on the frontier. He put me in the body of a beautiful but suicidal whore, and Wu—Wooley—well, became a farmer named Kally Tonge, a big, handsome man who'd just died in an accident. We became those people and got together—as Nathan had planned, I think."

"We ran the farm together for years," Wooley added. "They were great years. We had nine kids, too, and we brought them up right. Some got real big on their own—politicians and space captains and Com police, that level. Most left Harvich's World for greener pastures, but one stayed."

The Lata nodded. "Our daughter Vashura. She was smart as hell, and beautiful, too. Became the senator for the district, and would have been councillor if she'd had enough time. Kally and I went through one rejuve, and it took pretty well, I guess. Both of us went out-system, did a lot of work with the Com police on the sponge trade after selling the farm. Interesting work, but it grew increasingly frustrating as we got older. Finally we faced another rejuve and maybe some loss of memory or ability along with it. We decided not to. About the only thing we had to stay around for was helping Vashura fight the Com threat to Harvich's World. A local party apparatus had grown up, and it looked weak until suddenly lots of key votes switched. We knew sponge was the cause, but we couldn't prove it. Finally, the strain became too much for us. We decided to pack it in. Neither of us could bear to be around and see the world that had so much of our sweat and blood in it turn into another cookie-cutter insect world."

Renard understood. "What about your daughter, though?"

"We tried for the longest time to convince her to take the family and get out," the Yaxa told him. "She was stubborn—got it from us, I guess. Thought she could fight them. By the time it was clear she couldn't, well, it was too late to leave. We barely got out in time ourselves. We didn't know what to do. Vashura would fight to the death, but there were the grandchildren to think of. So, before finding a Well Gate, we used every bit of pull, contact, IOU, and subterfuge we had to locate Nathan Brazil."

"And did you?" the Agitar responded, surprised. "He actually returned to our part of the universe?"

Vistaru nodded. "Oh, yes. He promised to get the kids out if it were physically possible and if their parents would allow it. All he managed was Mavra." That last was spoken with incredible sadness.

"This Brazil—when you found him, almost two centuries later—how did he look?" Yulin asked, genuinely interested.

"Exactly the same," the Yaxa replied. "Not a hair different, not a sign of aging. I think he's looked like that since mankind was born."

"I wonder why he picked us to live among?" Renard mused. "Couldn't be our superior good looks."

"As a Markovian he'd helped establish the original Glathriel," Wooley explained. "As he described it, it wasn't his project, but he was—well, the manager. He arranged the transfer to Old Earth. But, unlike the others, he never transformed himself totally and irrevocably. He stayed a Markovian."

Yulin nodded. "A temporary line. When we built Obie, we found out all about that. The whole universe is just stabilized energy fields. How that energy is transformed and manipulated creates the different elements we know—and the Well—or on a smaller scale, Obie—stabilizes them. You can have a permanent change, literally writing an equation to hold the elements so thoroughly together that your creation becomes normal reality and is perceived as such by everyone around you. Using Obie, we changed a woman into a centaur long before we heard of Dillia, and, sure enough, everybody always remembered her as a centaur, there was even a logical reason for it going all the way back to her birth. That's how the Markovians recreated the universe."

"Clear as mud," Renard noted.

Yulin shrugged. "Then, at Trelig's bidding, we ran the people through Obie and gave them all horse's tails—it was supposed to be an example. So everybody had to *know* they shouldn't have the tails they had. We created a temporary equation, a local one, as it were. Their tails, which were *not* considered normal, are like Brazil's humanity. He is a Markovian, and reverts to it when in the Well. I wonder if he's the only one of them who did that?"

It was a thought, but not one that could be resolved. They didn't worry about that or dwell on it.

Renard looked at Mavra Chang. "Why the hell did you desert her?" he asked angrily. "Why didn't *you* stay around to raise and educate her?"

Wooley and Vistaru felt more than a little guilt on that score, but it was expressed in rather human terms, defensively.

"Why did *you* desert her in Glathriel and go home to Agitar?" Vistaru countered. "How many visits did *you* pay her in twenty-two years? After all, I didn't know about her until Ortega told me just before we left for here—but you owe her your life. Some repayment!"

He started to protest, to justify, but saw her point. "There's plenty of guilt around for everybody, isn't there?" he said sheepishly.

"The Yaxa had decided to polish her off," Wooley told them. "Ortega told me the story about her in order to get my aid. I managed to short-circuit those attempts all along. That's why it was *I* who managed to be the one who was finally sent to capture her. I couldn't trust anyone else not to take the easy way out." Her shiny yellow-and-black death's head turned to Vistaru. "As for you, I did *not* know then. Ortega made a couple of slips a few years ago and I drew the proper conclusions."

"If I remember, Nathan Brazil set the Well to summon him if anything ever went wrong," Vistaru pointed out. "Why didn't it call him when New Pompeii suddenly appeared overhead?"

"I can answer that," Yulin responded. "You see, to the Well nothing is wrong. The Markovians knew that at some future time one of their races would attain the ability to manipulate the universe as they could. At that time the Well was to transport the young race to it and receive new instructions, a changing of the guard so to speak. As far as the Well's concerned, it's just waiting for Obie or his operators to talk to it. Of course, that's like waiting for a monkey to quote the Koran. The Markovians blew it. We found the secret early, too early, and our artifacts can't even absorb its data, let alone talk to and order the Well. Obie, with some justification, refuses to try. Suppose it issued an incorrect instruction and wiped out humanity?"

It was a sobering thought. "You say 'he' often when talking about this computer of yours," Wooley noted. "Why?"

Yulin chuckled. "Oh, it's a person, all right, and it perceives itself as male. Self-aware computers have been around for a thousand years—I'm sure you ran into one or two. But never one like this one. It really is a person, as human as any of us. When you see and hear him, you'll know what I mean."

They let it go. Suddenly Renard's head came up, and his eyes blazed. He stood up and walked back over to the still-unmoving Mavra.

"All right, Mavra Chang," he told her in that same hard tone he'd used before. "You've heard it all now. Make up your mind. The ship will cross the border this evening and be ready in another day or two. Do you want to be on it? Because, by damn, you'll go through Well processing as you should have twenty-two years ago unless you snap out of it! Make your choice! Make it now! *What the hell is wrong with you, anyway?*"

Something seemed to penetrate. Slowly her respiration increased, and life began to flow weakly back into her.

"Why did he do it, Renard? Tell me why?" she asked, totally bewildered.

The tone matched his own. "Huh? Why did who do what?"

"Why did Joshi jump in front of that pistol burst? It's insane. I can't understand it. I—I wouldn't deliberately sacrifice my life for anyone, Renard. Why would he?"

So that was it. He looked into her eyes. "Because he loved you, Mavra."

She shook her equine head. "How can anyone love anyone else that much? I just don't understand."

"I'm not sure I do, either," he told her. "I'm not sure any of us can understand that. Welcome back to the land of selfish hypocrites." He sighed and smiled.

She turned and faced the others. "You two—you are truly my grandparents? The stories—your tales of the Well World, Nathan Brazil. They were all real? The old memories were all real?"

Vistaru nodded. "And Nathan cared, even if we failed," she said. "Ortega received occasional communications from Brazil in tubes sent from Well Gates. They were meant for us, but, perhaps wisely, the snake-man kept them. He felt it was better if we didn't know who or what the other was, or what had happened to you and Vashy and the rest. He was a lousy parent and he botched the job of finding the right one, and he knew it. But he never lost sight of you, Mavra."

She looked at the Lata quizzically.

"It was Brazil who, when he was unsuccessful in warning Maki Chang on the smuggling setup, made sure they didn't find you. It was Brazil who got old Gimmy the beggar king to look out for you. It was Brazil who steered Gymball Nysongi to you—supposedly just to check on you, although it developed better. He took the heat off you when Nysongi was killed. And so on and so forth. It's all in the dispatches in Ortega's office."

She was stunned again. Renard sensed something wrong, went to her again. "What's wrong? I think it's wonderful—to have someone do that for you, year after year."

"It's horrible, grotesque!" she spat back. "Don't you see? It makes my whole life a lie. I didn't do everything on my own. I didn't do *anything* on my own! I was being helped by an immortal super-Markovian all the way!"

And he *did* understand, although the others could not. The only thing she had, the only thing that had kept her going, was her enormous self-confidence, her ego, her total belief in her ability to surmount any odds and overcome any obstacles. When ego and self-image are suddenly kicked away, there's very little left. In Mavra's case, only a tragic little girl, lonely and alone; an intellient horse, but a dependent plaything.

"I understand," was all Renard could manage, softly, gently, somewhat sadly. "But you're on your own now, Mavra Chang. You've been on your own since you escaped from Glathriel."

She shook her head and turned away. It wasn't true. Joshi had put the final lie to it. Suddenly she hated him, hated him with a fury that defied reason.

For he'd given his life for her, the ultimate interference.

And now she was just Mavra Chang, a shell inside a shell, all alone, helpless, and dependent. In the dark, forever.

Bozog, the Launch Site
Next Day

"HEY! I THINK I CAN SEE IT!" BEN YULIN SHOUTED over the suit radio. He was like a little boy, wildly excited and animated.

Less than two kilometers across the plain lay the border with Uchjin, where he'd crashed so many years before. Since that time he'd wondered how, even if anyone got to the North, they could get that ship out. It was enormously heavy, off-balance, and could not be moved by mechanical power because it rested in a nontech hex. In addition, the flowing paint smears that were the Uchjin objected to its being moved.

"The biggest problem was physically moving it," the Bozog told him. "The Uchjin are nocturnal, absolutely powerless in daylight, so that's when we do most of the work. They don't have the mass or means to replace it, so the only problem was protecting the moving party from night attacks. We did this by turning night into day with phosphor gel. It was simply too bright for them."

Yulin nodded. "Like you'd build a campfire in the wilderness to keep the wild beasts away. But how are you moving it?"

"Slowly, of course," the Bozog admitted. "It's been several weeks of work. We actually started when we received word of the breakthrough in north–south travel. It all has to be done by manpower alone—we lifted it with chains, pulleys, and the like onto a huge platform, a feat that took nine days in itself, and since then over twelve thousand Bozog have been pulling it along in shifts. Today, the great project is nearing completion."

Yulin thought about it. "That's a tremendous cost in manpower and matériel," he noted. "Why did you do it?"

"It was a challenge, a great undertaking," the Bozog replied. "It was a feat that Bozog will sing of for generations. A tremendous technical problem that was solved, proof that any problem can be solved if enough thought and energy is expended on it. You might say it was an act of faith."

They began to hear rumbling in the distance, like the sound of millions of horses in stampede, or a violent storm. The huge ship, resting on its left wing and secured by chain and cable, was riding on thousands of giant ball bearings connected by some sort of mounting network. It was slow, but the thing moved, pulled by huge numbers of Bozog.

"It won't be long now until they are close enough to attach cable from the giant winches," the Bozog pointed out. "It can then be pulled into Bozog quickly."

"When do you think you'll be ready to put it on the launch column?" Yulin asked, genuinely awed by the undertaking and the casual way that the creatures seemed to approach it.

"Tonight," the Bozog responded. "Sometime late tonight."

Mavra Chang had avoided everyone and all the excitement of the arriving ship. She didn't want to talk to anyone, speak to anyone, could feel nothing for the expedition anymore.

The more she thought about her life, the less meaningful it became. Brazil had gotten her off Harvich's World, to Maki. Brazil had shielded her from arrest, arranged for her "independent" career, sent Gimball, watched over her. She thought of the mistakes she had made in robberies: yet, somehow, overlooked alarms failed to go off, or pursuit was accidentally diverted elsewhere. Even on New Pompeii, she realized, Brazil had been replaced, supplanted by Obie.

Obie had given her the plans and schematics for the planetoid. Obie had given her the codewords. Obie had actually used her as his vessel for his own ends. On the Well World she'd always been somebody's pawn. The Lata rescued her from the Teliagin cyclopes on Ortega's orders. Here she'd become an object in Ortega's plans, controlled, moved around, manipulated by circumstance and hypno to do exactly what the snake-man wanted. Protected, too, in the end, by Ortega and by her own grandparents. Even here in Bozog she was controlled by her captors, including her grandfather—and Joshi. During the fight, control of her had passed to the Ghiskind, yet when the mistake was made, and she should have died, Joshi had blocked the shot and died instead.

I'm Mavra Chang, I can do anything, she thought bitterly.

I can die, she reflected. That much I can do on my own.

But not quite yet. Lie or not, one small piece of unfinished business. One small attempt to salvage a tiny shred of her honor and self-respect was left to her . . . on New Pompeii.

"The Yugash is rising!" she heard Vistaru yell behind her. Idly she turned and saw the pale-red specter, still looking not quite right, rise and form its cloak a few centimeters above the floor.

They all watched apprehensively. Clearly their hopes for its demise had not been realized: one of the eerie creatures was still around. They all remembered Wooley's contact with the Torshind, and the horror she found there.

The Yugash looked around at them uncertainly. In its present form it could not talk or even grasp a material object; it needed a vessel. A ghostly appendage pointed to them, then both appendages rose in a very human shrug. They got the message. It wanted to communicate, and needed a volunteer. In its weakened state, it probably couldn't fight for control.

"Get a Bozog," Wooley snapped, and Renard ran from the room. The Yugash seemed content to wait.

Several minutes later Renard returned with not one but two medium-size Bozog. While neither of the creatures had vision as the Southerners understood it, all sensed that the Yugash was getting a good looking over. Finally, one said, "Yugash! You have my permission to use me as a vessel temporarily, but do not try anything. We are ready to assist in your dissipation if you do."

The hood of the ghostly creature nodded slowly, drifted to, and merged with the Bozog, which twitched slightly.

A minute passed before the Yugash traced the proper nerves and could activate the translator. It didn't even try for any other control.

"It is good to speak with you again," came a voice that was definitely not the Bozog's. "It is good, in fact, to be alive."

"Who—which one—are you?" Vistaru asked hesitantly.

"I am the Ghiskind," responded the Yugash. Several breathed sighs of relief, but Wooley was more cautious.

"Wait a minute," she said sharply. "How do we know that?"

The Ghiskind considered that. Like most creatures it considered itself a distinct individual. It simply hadn't occurred to the Yugash that others might not be able to see the differences.

They commenced a dialogue covering conversations on the trip, conversations with Ortega at which Renard and Vistaru had been hidden but present, details of the equipment and battle in Pugeesh. Finally, the Southerners were satisfied.

"It was an incredible battle," the Ghiskind told them. "Never before had I actually been forced to kill a Yugash. The Torshind was, like all fanatics, exceptionally strong; the final maneuver I used was sheer desperation—the Torshind was winning. I fully expected it to kill us both, and it almost did."

"So the final party is made," Renard said. "Wooley, Vistaru, the Ghiskind, the Bozog, Mavra, Ben Yulin, and me."

Vistaru nodded. "Such a group as no one has ever seen together before. But it's a highly important group symbolically."

They turned to her. "How's that?" Renard asked.

She glanced around at all of them. "Seven members, seven races. The Wars of the Well are over at last."

Aboard the New Harmony Shuttle

IT TOOK FOUR DAYS TO RAISE, POSITION, AND LOCK in the ship, and another two were required for Yulin to check out the systems. Some vital power systems had discharged over the years, but were easily replenished by Bozog technicians. The craft was banged up, but a lot less so than the engineer would have believed. It needed a bit of internal work, but the engines and command computer needed only reenergized secondary systems to come to life again. The atmosphere of Uchjin had preserved everything marvelously.

The ship had been designed for humans. This presented little problem to Yulin or Renard, and neither the Yugash nor the Bozog required much, but the bulk and odd shapes of Mavra and Wooley presented real difficulties, and Vistaru's wings could not be pressed into a seat for long without damage. Tearing out some seats in the passenger compartment and replacing them with heavy cushions held down by wide belts solved the larger problems, and Vistaru decided she could live strapped on her stomach for a time.

Yulin spent another day assisted by Mavra—who seemed to be taking some interest in things again—checking out computer operation, programming, and control functions. Both were extremely rusty, but they soon found that their remembered abilities were complementary. Between them they could probably work out what was necessary.

"I still wish we had somebody who has done this recently," Yulin told her worriedly. "Damn! After a twenty-two-year layoff, we're going to program this ship through a series of maneuvers beyond half the pilots we ever knew! I'm damn sure *I* wouldn't trust a pilot who'd been away that long!"

"Second thoughts?" she taunted. "I can always have Renard follow my instructions, you know."

He laughed. "No, I've come too far and waited too long for this. I'll go or die."

"Or both," she responded dryly.

In two days New Pompeii would be in the proper position and the proper code words Mavra Chang knew for the robot sentinels would come up. They'd go.

"Initial test, two percent thrust!" Ben Yulin broadcast to ground control and throughout the ship. He flipped a switch. A satisfying whine and vibration were the response. He held the power at that setting for four seconds. The instruments showed steady output to less than a thousandth of a percent, then cut back.

"Initial test on the nose," he reported. "Give me lift data."

A Bozog voice crackled back at him. "On our count, switch to internal at one hundred; build up at ten percent per decade count on our mark. Release restraints at the ten mark. Full boost on automatic within one second of our count. Link and synchronize."

"On my mark . . . one hundred," Yulin said crisply.

"Hold to our mark. Linkage established. Switch to internal. Mark one hundred."

Yulin punched a board. "Internal link, aye. Thrust ten at ninety." Slowly, eyes on the instrument panel, he flipped a series of switches. "Fifty-one at fifty, go," he told the control.

"Down, area cleared, all restraint away, thirty," replied the Bozog.

"Seventy-two at thirty," Yulin responded. "Stand by."

"Ninety at ten."

"Ninety at ten coming up. Mark!"

"Ten . . . nine . . . eight . . . seven . . . six . . . five . . . four . . . three . . . two . . . one . . . full boost!" called the Bozog launch control.

Yulin pulled back on a long lever. He didn't have time to think, which was good.

He was scared to death.

They felt a sudden impact, as if some huge thing had struck the ship, and a tremendous, crushing weight on them.

Mavra was in the prone position to absorb shock. Not designed to lie down, she blacked out in seconds; Wooley was not far behind. The others remained conscious although all, even the Ghiskind, were tremendously uncomfortable.

Yulin, pressed back into his seat so hard he could feel the metal support fifty centimeters behind,

watched the controls wide-eyed. It was out of his
hands now and up to the computer.

An eternity passed, and the pressure on him was
unbearable. He fought with himself to keep from
blacking out, even as he watched the displays, unblinking, fearful. The sequencing timer seemed to
crawl, the seconds ticking off in slow motion. Forty-
six . . . forty-seven . . .

He knew he was going to die now. He would never
survive the eternity until that clock reached sixty-one,
he was sure.

And then, finally, it hit sixty and seemed to hover
there for the longest time. It flipped, and the thrust
was reduced. Even though he was ready for it, the sensation of sudden release, like falling over a precipice,
caught him by surprise, propelling him forward. The
restraints bit into him.

He sighed, looked over at the screens. They were
still heading outward, into deep space. The indicator
showed an altitude of over one hundred kilometers
and climbing.

They had made it.

The screens flipped on. The group wasn't out of the
woods yet, he knew. Now he had to take the ship to
high orbit, loop, and approach New Pompeii, making
certain that at no point in his initial approach did he
fall to within eighty kilometers of the surface. The ship
swung around. The console screen showed the Well
World, projected trajectories, and the ship's current
position. A string of figures ran down one side, constantly changing, showing the computer working to put
them in the preplanned slot.

He activated the intercom. "Everyone okay?"

"Some bruises, and Mavra and Wooley are out cold,
but I think we all came through," Renard replied.

Yulin turned his attention to the controls. They had
made orbital insertion while he talked, and were only
a few kilometers per hour from the optimum and less
than a fifth of a degree off-orbit. Easily correctable,
and he told the computer to make the adjustments.

The large screen came on, providing a remarkably

detailed picture of what was ahead. The Well World filled most of the area below them, and, as he watched, New Pompeii rose. He would make one pass as a check before going final approach.

On the screen, columns of figures shot by at speeds barely slow enough to read, and graphics showed angle, speed, and destination. The computer was locking in for Phase Two.

But the critical human element was gone now. It was the computer's job to follow the carefully programmed instructions and do all the work. The passengers could only hope that the systems would continue to function as well as they had so far.

"How's it going back there?" Yulin asked over the intercom.

"All right now," Vistaru's soft voice answered. "We have Wooley back with us again, and we've undone Mavra's straps and got her to her feet. That's all right, isn't it?"

"Fine," he responded. "There will be only slight motion problems now that the ship's in its element. We're braking over North Zone, and the screens say it's a perfect intercept. All we can do is watch and wait."

"On track," Yulin announced. "Locked in. All right, people. Hold on. Here we go."

The big screen showed the Well World, ship, and New Pompeii clearly. Small dotted lines indicated the ideal and actual trajectories. The multicolor graphics were of no use to Yulin's color-blind eyes, but he knew which trajectory was which by the pattern of characters that composed each curve. He felt slight jerking motions as the computer adjusted speed and direction. Slowly but steadily the two traces were merging into a single perfect flight path.

Suddenly the radio popped on.

"Code, please," a mechanical voice demanded pleasantly. "Correct code within sixty seconds or we will destroy your ship."

Yulin almost jumped out of his skin; panic suddenly

rose within him. He'd been so intent on the takeoff and approach he'd just about forgotten about the robot sentries. He could see them on the screen, little dots moving to intercept and take him out. He gulped.

His mind was a complete blank.

"Fifty seconds," the voice said pleasantly.

He punched the intercom. "Is Chang awake yet?" he screamed.

"Still groggy," Renard replied. "Why?"

"I need the damned code!" he yelled.

"Forty seconds," said the voice.

"I thought you knew it," Wooley responded accusingly.

"I can't remember, damn it! Ask her the goddamned code *now!*"

"Thirty seconds," said the voice. The little dots were in perfect attack position now.

Suddenly a new voice came in over the radio on the same frequency. It was a man's voice, soft and pleasant.

"It's Edward Gibbon, Volume One, Ben," said the voice.

He was startled but he grabbed at it.

"Twenty seconds," said the robot sentry.

"Edward Gibbon, Volume One!" he screamed.

There was silence, and he watched the LED clock tick off. It passed ten seconds, and there was no new warning. Now it counted off the last ten. As it did he glanced up and saw the little blips break formation and resume their stations.

Ben Yulin almost fainted.

"It's Edward Gibbon, Volume One, Ben," Vistaru said pleasantly.

"I know, I know," he growled, out of breath. "If I had to depend on you we'd have died thirty seconds ago."

But who *had* given him the code? Not the Bozog. Though almost certainly they were monitoring the radio, it was too human a voice for that. A familiar voice, somehow, from the distant past. But this was a journey into that past, as much as into the future, he thought.

He flipped on the interspace radio and called, "Obie? Is that you?"

"Yes, Ben," came the reply. "How have you been?"

"Obie—how the hell? Are you alone down there?"

"Oh, yes, quite alone," responded the computer. "It's been a long time, Ben. A lot longer for me than for you. I've followed some of your progress through the Well, though. Who wound up on the ship? I can't tell that from here."

Yulin told him, then asked, "Topside—what are the conditions there?"

"You know I have no voluntary circuits Topside," the computer reminded him. "The atmosphere, pressure, and temperature have been maintained, and the electrical system is functioning normally. Beyond that I can't say. I've nothing with which to monitor."

Yulin thought for a moment. The ship was closing on the spaceport airlock as they spoke. "Obie—have you been incommunicado all this time? I mean, if you can talk to me, do you talk to others?"

There was silence at the other end.

"Obie? Did you hear me?"

"I heard you, Ben. We'll talk again when you get here," the computer said.

He tried to raise Obie several more times, but there was only silence. He sat back and thought for a moment. The computer was fully capable of deceit; it was as human as he in many ways. The fact that it had refused to answer his question was in itself an answer. The computer *had* been talking these past years with someone—and there was only one person who would know how to build the proper receiving equipment.

Dr. Gilgam Zinder, discoverer of the Markovian mathematics and creator of Obie, was still very much alive back on the Well World.

But back there, Yulin told himself confidently. He knew all the Southerners aboard, and Zinder would not have been processed as a Northerner. Zinder could talk with Obie, even consult the great machine, but he couldn't actually operate it, change the programming. Only someone at one of the control panels inside Obie itself could do that, and even if Zinder were *there,* he did not know about Ben Yulin's innovative circuit design. When he'd used it, he'd stunned Zinder to unconsciousness.

No matter what surprises Zinder and Obie had planned for him, they were in for a nasty shock, Ben Yulin thought confidently.

He watched the console. The ship closed gently. The first of the two locks was damaged; he probably had done that himself in his panic during the flight from New Pompeii, he reflected. The other was fine, though, and the computer headed for it.

A sudden scraping sound forward, and a wrenching jerk as the ship slipped into its berth and straightened itself heralded their safe landing.

They were back on New Pompeii.

He switched the ship to external power, drawing from the New Pompeii power plant. The instruments flickered briefly and it was done. The last step in the chain.

He undid his straps and stood, for the first time realizing the brutality of the takeoff.

Painfully, limping slightly, the minotaur made his way aft to see about his passengers.

New Pompeii

THE AIRLOCK HISSED, THEN THE BIG AMBER STAND-BY light flashed off and the green went on. Ben Yulin threw the levers, pulled open the hatch, and walked to the other side. The proper light was on, so he opened that end as well. A breeze wafted back at them as the slight differences in pressure equalized. The group followed the Dasheen into New Pompeii's spaceport.

To Mavra, despite her distorted, black-and-white vision, it looked very familiar. Renard, too, looked around in wonder at the familiarity of it all. To the others it was new; a plush, luxury lounge.

Yulin was cautious. "Funny," he said. "Looks almost like somebody cleaned up here, doesn't it? I'd expected it to be dirty. The carpet isn't even stained —and I know a lot of shit went on in here just before I left. I don't like this at all."

They took the hint. Wooley and Vistaru drew pistols.

"An odd construction," commented the medium-size Bozog. "I may have some problem getting my two-and-a-half meters through the door."

"I think it's wide enough for you to get through," Renard said.

Yulin, who was unarmed, declined to lead the way. Finally Wooley volunteered. The door slid open before her.

The rest followed cautiously. Vistaru took advantage of the atmosphere and uncluttered corridor to fly; her race was not really built for walking, and she was otherwise too small to keep up. The lower gravity, which made the others feel wonderfully relieved, proved a problem at first, but she found the condition tolerable as long as she didn't get fancy or ambitious. No use in slamming full tilt into a wall, she scolded herself.

Outside, the terminal looked like a Roman ruin. The grass was high, and the lawns were dotted with flowers. The walks were just about overgrown, and trees were more abundant and less perfectly manicured than those who had previously been to New Pompeii remembered. Ivy, ferns, and mosses had overgrown some of the buildings, giving them a haunted appearance. Antor Trelig had dreamed of a new Roman Empire with himself as God-Emperor,

Caesar. New Pompeii reflected this; its architechture was Greco-Roman, with lots of columns, arches and domes. As a ruin, it was in some ways even more impressive and awesome than it had been.

"It's incredible," Wooley breathed.

Yulin nodded. "In its own way a great achievement. Under the dome, this world is completely self-sufficient. The plants have probably added too much carbon dioxide to the air, but the animal-plant balance was about perfect in the old days. The air's clean, pure, and it's cleansed continuously. The automatic monitors keep the oxygen–nitrogen–trace-gas balance from deviating too far from optimum. Water vapor is injected from the subsurface tanks, and reclaimed. Trelig even had his own rainfall in there—on demand."

"That's a pretty thick forest over there," Vistaru noted, pointing to the left, beyond the buildings.

He nodded. "A nice forest, yes. And somewhere in there are glades where exotic fruits were grown. Some deer and minor wildlife have probably survived. Insects, too. You can hear them if you listen."

They could. It was eerie.

"Bozog, you having any problems?" Renard asked.

"None," responded the creature. "If necessary, I can feed on one of the buildings."

They walked on, heading for the largest structure in sight, the great hall where Trelig had held court and entertained guests—willing and unwilling.

"Yulin?" Mavra called.

He stopped. "Yes?"

"I'm sure it's occurred to you that at least a few people could survive here on the animals and fruit."

Yulin nodded.

"The sponge would have polished them off long ago," Renard retorted.

"You forget, Renard, there were others for Trelig's big show—councillors and councillors' representatives. Some of them were pretty tough people."

Yulin reconsidered. "Could be," he admitted. "If the spongies didn't kill them off."

"A couple of those people were professional agents

223

like me," Mavra noted. "They'd have been a lot harder to take, and time was on their side. I think we'd better assume that somebody's still around."

"That clean lounge," Yulin said softly, now suddenly alert again, looking around. "They sure haven't taken care of the rest of the place."

Renard agreed with her the more he thought about it. "That's true, but you have to figure that they'd be pretty normal for a while. But it's been twenty-two years now, without hope, without communication. Who knows what kind of life they'd develop, what would happen in their minds?"

"I think you're right," Renard agreed. "There are no bodies. No skeletal remains. Organic material decays slowly here because of the purification system used to filter out microorganisms."

"No graves that I can see, either," Vistaru pointed out.

"They'd be overgrown," Mavra responded. "No, I think we'd better assume we're not alone here and treat this as we would a hostile hex."

Yulin had a sudden thought. "The ship! It's not secure! Maybe we'd better—"

"Yes, maybe we'd better," Wooley agreed.

After securing the ship, they returned to explore the ruins. Power was still available, even the video equipment that spied on people everywhere. But aside from the fact that a kitchen area had been cleaned out, which was to be expected anyway, there was no sign of current use. The guards' quarters had been used, although not recently.

"Not many survived, that's for sure," Renard noted. "Maybe three, four people at best. That's enough for this place to support. I wonder where they are?"

The weapons locker had been sealed shut by an energy weapon. Mavra had done that twenty-two years ago, and it was clear it hadn't been opened since. A few weapons were found scattered about, all discharged and useless.

Some time passed before Renard, who knew the

world better than anyone else, discovered signs that someone had attempted to leave a message in a small room below the combination guests' quarters and library. The door had been broken in from the outside and whoever did it had fantastic strength because the ornate wooden doors were very thick. Inside Renard found signs of a struggle before the communications gear built into the far wall. A recording module was in place, and the panel still worked, so they anxiously crowded in as Renard ran it back to start.

"This was the monitoring room for Trelig's recording studio," he told them. "He sometimes brought in musicians for private sessions, and he'd listen here to what was being recorded. You can see the hundreds of modules in the wall case. Whatever happened, this module is the last one made here—and might tell us something."

It stopped, and Renard deftly manipulated the controls, then punched PLAY. A screen flickered, and a realsound field enveloped them.

The face was that of a young woman, very attractive and soft, with a gentle face and voice.

"Gossyn!" Renard exclaimed. It was all coming back, after all these years.

"I am Gossyn of Estuado," she said, her voice so true, the projected holoimage so clear, that they felt as if they were peering through a doorway at her. "One of Antor Trelig's former slaves. I am leaving this record in case one of the ships that left here returns, as I expect them to. No matter—it's too late. This afternoon we gathered all of the weaponry in the main courtyard, keeping the guests back. We are all addicted to sponge, and without it we will die painfully, and by bits and pieces. I can feel it eating at me even as I speak. We, the last of Trelig's slaves, will not face that sort of death. When the weapons were gathered, the others stood among them, and I—" her voice broke, and tears appeared in her eyes —"I fired full beam with the rifle beside me. Nothing remains of them now but a brown spot. Soon I will place the rifle charge on feedback overload, and go as well—the last slave, the last weapon." She paused, overcome with emotion, and then continued.

"I do not care what becomes of the guests. They know that this little world can feed only a small number of them. I leave it to them, with the hope that, if it is Antor Trelig who returns, those who survive will somehow rip him slowly limb from limb, as befits a demon and a monster. I don't even know why I'm making this . . . except—oh, hell, I guess I don't want to die." She muffled a sob. "I'm only seventeen," she managed, and pushed forward, blanking out the picture.

Mavra sighed. "Might as well switch it off," she said, but, at that moment, the screen flickered to life again.

It was a different person now, a strong-looking woman of perhaps thirty dressed in a utility uniform. She was not terribly attractive, but something extraordinary was revealed in her face and movements.

She was terrified.

"Anyone! Oh, Lord! If you came back and got this far!" She stopped as a hard thud reverberated behind her. It was so realistic that all the listeners' heads turned toward the ruined door. The ghost of a moment was very real in the room.

She hurried. "He's crazy! Listen! Yesterday the guards destroyed the weapons and themselves. Then somebody started killing the rest." The sound of pounding was clear in the background, and she turned again, then back, getting frantic now.

"One of us—Belden, his name is. He's a plant. One of Trelig's people, put in with us as a spy. When his boss deserted him he went crazy—if he wasn't already." More pounding and some slight splintering noises. "He's mad. Killing off the Comworlders, finishing off the men. Some of the women—Trelig has a Chamber of Horrors in mind-control devices here. He's using it, wiping their minds, turning them into animals. He's mad. I may be the only one left. No time. Watch it. Get the bastard in my name. Please! I—"

The screen went blank. Renard sighed, switched it off. "She ran out of module before he got in," he said.

"Well, now we know." Wooley added. "Did anyone else notice her as she turned around?"

"The tail," Yulin responded almost apologetically. "Yes, Trelig gave everyone a horse's tail."

"But that was twenty-two years ago," Vistaru pointed out. "Who knows what became of them?"

Yulin was thoughtful and concerned. "I think we better find out."

The natural spy was the Ghiskind. A thorough and careful search of the building complex showed no signs of recent habitation, but it was a large world. Yulin pointed out areas of abundant wildlife and groves of fruit trees on a map from the control room files, and the Yugash made for that area while the others camped out on the portico of the main hall, from where they could see anyone coming and prepare themselves.

New Pompeii's rotation was fairly rapid, and not a little disconcerting. The Well World filled half the sky, but it was eerie, distorted by the atmosphere and plasma skin through which it was viewed, and the stars in the brief night periods were equally nebulous.

It took the Ghiskind less than an hour to return. As agreed, it merged with the Bozog for communications purposes.

"They are there," it told them. "A small colony, mostly young and all looking and acting quite wild and animalistic. Two males, five females, four young. Very strange."

"No sign of Belden, then," Mavra noted. "Interesting. I wonder if he died? An accident, or maybe that woman took him with her somehow. I hope so. We'll leave them there. Did they seem hostile?"

"Frightened of their shadows," the Yugash responded. "But definitely without much more than rudimentary reason, which probably explains why there are so few young. Few would survive."

They nodded. Yulin sighed. "Well, then, I propose

we leave them, keep on guard just in case this Belden is still around someplace, and go Underside. That's safest anyway."

They were tired and still sore, but they agreed. Underside was much more defensible, and it was where they had to be anyway.

Mavra walked with them to the large stone structure to one side of what was once a park in front of the main hall. It, too, was overgrown now, but both the former syndicate scientist and Renard knew its operation.

"It's pretty cramped in there," Yulin warned them. "I'd say Mavra and Wooley by themselves, and we'll take the backup car. Bozog, you're going to have a rough fit."

The face of the seemingly solid marble cube vanished after a series of carefully spaced taps on the outside. The grass, moss, and vines didn't vanish, though, and had to be pulled off.

The car before them had eight seats designed for humans. Wooley managed to fit in back by scrunching down and flexing her wings uncomfortably. Mavra managed to sprawl across the front three.

"See you down there—and be careful. Belden would know about this, too," Yulin warned, and punched a new combination.

"*Now* I understand why Yulin wasn't eager to be on the first car," Wooley noted sarcastically. "Our big brave bull is about as cowardly as I have known."

Mavra said nothing. The drop was too uncomfortable. It was a long way to Underside, and although the rate of descent was controlled, it felt as if they were falling at all times—an uncomfortable sensation, and it was a long, long ride.

Above them the others clambered into the service car, which was not quite as roomy as the first one. The Bozog managed, with great difficulty, although if the Ghiskind had had feet or if Vistaru and Renard had been larger, it would have been stepped on the whole way. Yulin was scrunched up trying not to step on the strange creature.

Finally it ended, and the front of the car dissolved again. Mavra climbed out with difficulty, and Wooley almost snagged a wing doing the same. They found themselves in a sterile, brightly lit hall, resembling any of the tens of millions of halls in the stark technological centers common since the dawn of technical civilization. The others arrived almost immediately; the smaller car's speed was determined by the larger one, and let out a floor above.

Yulin's bull's head nodded and he looked around in satisfaction, tail swishing back and forth in anticipation. This was his element—the metallic walls and artificial lighting, the bowels of a great machine. He had helped design the place and supervised its construction. It seemed a part of him.

They walked along the hall, ready for anything. After a bit, it opened to reveal a broad platform and an overlook from which stretched a great wide bridge across a huge, impossibly deep pit.

"No bodies again," Yulin noted, surprised. "Then Belden has been here."

"Look!" Renard called. "Out there—across the bridge! Isn't *that* a body?"

They all strained. The Yaxa had the best vision, and her death's head nodded. "Yes. A man. Outlandishly dressed, too. Very dead, I think—maybe for an awfully long time. A good deal of decomposition is evident."

Yulin considered it. "Looks like he tried for the computer. In the defense mode he'd just about get across before the lethal charges hit him. Even at this end, it's got fifty volts as a discouragement, so he was nuts, driven, or determined. Probably all three."

"Think it's Belden?" Vistaru voiced the other's thoughts.

"Probably," Wooley replied. "The man has a horse's tail, he's big, and he's dressed in flowing robes, a wreath on his head. Looks like the new Emperor of New Pompeii finally got bored Topside and decided he was able to defy the computer. That explains everything, I think."

Renard was thoughtful. "Well, if it's just an electrical defense, I can walk right through it," he noted confidently.

"It's about ten thousand volts where Belden got," Yulin pointed out. "It's not on until needed, of course. The system senses a life form, then zaps it, then there's no life form any more and it shuts off."

"Ten thousand wouldn't bother me," the Agitar replied. "The excess would simply discharge."

"But only Obie can open that door," the Dasheen told him. "And it will defend as it has to. There are guns here, too, as a fail-safe. Lots of nasty stuff. No, it's got to be by proper code, everything done in the proper sequence, or no go," he said earnestly.

"Want to get it over with?" Mavra asked him. "What do you have to do?"

He was thoughtful. "All right, first I walk out on that bridge in a certain manner—that will cancel the voltage to a particular point. Then I say the password and advance in the same manner. The door will open as I approach it. Then I must go to the panel and cancel the defense mode or it will be reinstated."

"One of us will go with you," Wooley said suspiciously.

He shook his head. "No, it's got to be one, only. Don't worry. Even if I don't cancel the mode you'll know how to break into it, right? Hell, haven't I played square with you all up to now?"

He had, but he'd played square with Trelig for years, too.

"Perhaps the Ghiskind," Mavra suggested.

"No!" Yulin was adamant. "Nobody! Sure, it *might* be ignored, but then again it might not, and it sure as hell can't say the password—and the Bozog can't make the gestures. Neither could you. It's me alone." He threw up his hands. "Come on! What the hell are we arguing for? In five minutes we could all be inside and that would be that."

They were uncertain, and there were whispered conferences, but the conclusion was inescapable, as Yulin knew it had to be. Wooley voiced it.

"We haven't come this far to turn back now," she pointed out. "All right, Yulin. Go ahead."

He nodded to her, satisfaction and confidence mirrored in his manner. He turned and walked to the foot of the bridge, then raised his arms and turned palms out. He hesitated a moment, as if expecting a jolt, then stepped onto the bridge and started across.

A bit more than halfway he was a small figure that they watched anxiously. Wooley and Renard drew weapons and aimed them at Yulin without a word.

Yulin walked nervously, head bobbing, trying to look at both sides of the bridge. Long ago he'd shot a mark into it for the proper place. For a moment he was afraid that the mark had somehow been erased, or that his less efficient vision would miss it, but then— there it was! It was farther along than he remembered, but he hadn't been zapped yet, so that must be it.

Keeping arms upraised, palms out, he stopped and nervously cleared his throat.

"Obie!" he yelled at the top of his lungs, his voice echoing across the chamber and up and down the great shaft. "There is no God but Allah and Mohammed is His Prophet! Hear me, Obie? There is no God but Allah and Mohammed is His Prophet!"

He hesitated a moment more, took a deep breath, and walked on.

Nothing happened.

He reached the other end of the bridge, a tiny figure very far away and almost invisible to all but Wooley, whose pistol remained firm and dead on.

Yulin looked down at the body. It was badly charred and decomposed. Very ugly. That bastard Belden deserved every volt of it, he thought without pity.

The door slid back and he was surprised to feel a warm blast of air greet him. He stepped inside, then to one side and immediately to the control panel.

He flipped it on.

"Defense mode returned to my voice signal cancel only!" he said quickly, entering a series of numbers through the key pad on a control panel. The door slid rapidly shut.

"Defense mode on," Obie's voice said, as if from thin air. "You haven't changed a bit, have you, Ben?"

He chuckled. "Hello, Obie. Well, a little. I—" He stopped suddenly, noting that the dish—the platform used by Obie, the one from which the guests had received their tails and from which he'd received the disguises he used to escape from New Pompeii—was on ACTIVE, ready to energize.

"Cancel that energize!" he ordered into the operator's mike. He walked over to the rail and looked down.

He saw a large oval, more than a hundred meters across at its widest by about seventy. A railed three-meter-wide balcony on which were located three control consoles was elevated above it. From the balcony, stairs led to the lower level, in the center of which was a metal disk raised perhaps a half-meter. Above it Obie's dish hung from its boom.

Ben Yulin gasped. Someone was on the disk—two people in fact. Humans!

"Hey! You on the disk! I'm Ben Yulin! Who are you!"

They looked slightly fearful, glancing at the little dish above them.

"Obie can't help you," he called, his voice echoing. "I control him now. Who are you?"

One of the figures sighed. "Hello, Ben." It was a pleasant, soft female voice. "I guess we're back to the beginning again. I'm Nikki Zinder, and this is my daughter, Mavra."

"Well I'll be damned!"

The Other Side of the Bridge

RENARD HAD TRIED THE SYSTEM AFTER THE DOOR slammed shut, and Wooley had fired a shot, but it was too late, meaningless.

It took the Agitar only a few steps to discover that the bridge was indeed still energized.

"Renard! Come on back!" Wooley called. "Maybe he was lying about those guns, maybe not. But you'll never get that door open on your own! Why take the risk? The bastard's double-crossed us and we have to retrench!"

Reluctantly the Agitar agreed with her, turned, and walked back. The voltage pulses struck him repeatedly until he reached the center of the bridge, but to no effect—except that he was fully charged for the first time in many years. It was a heady feeling to carry over eight thousand volts; it made an Agitar male light-headed and gave him the feeling he could do anything. Still, he made his way back to the far end of the bridge.

"Don't touch me!" he warned them. "I'll have to discharge some of this, or I'll kill somebody!"

He finally found a section of metal rail that didn't seem to be connected by a conductive material to anything nearby, tried a short jolt, then discharged about two thousand volts.

"So, now what?" he asked.

The Ghiskind merged with the Bozog. "I will see if I can get in," it said. "The electricity and guns won't hurt me even if I am detected, and if I get inside I can take his body, I am certain."

They agreed to let the Yugash try. It floated over

the bridge and was soon invisible to them. They
waited for several minutes, then watched it return.

"No good," it told them, again through the Bozog.
"The place is solid. No cracks. That door has insulated seals. It's an entirely self-contained atmosphere
in there. And if that computer's a fraction of what he
claims, he can live in there almost forever, even wait
us out."

"This is a hell of a mess, isn't it?" Vistaru said. "So,
now what do we do?"

"I'd say go Topside again until we think of something else," the Agitar suggested. "For one thing,
Belden's dead. So we haven't that threat. Second,
that's where all the food and water is. And third, I
have to go to the bathroom pretty damned bad."

There was little else to do. Underside, they were in
Yulin's element. Defeated, they slowly made their way
back along the corridor.

To guard against Yulin and any tricks he might
pull, and because they were still not certain that Topside held no dangers, they slept in the open in shifts.

Mavra slept solidly, and awoke feeling much better.
Her head seemed clearer, her body did not ache so
much.

One last commission, she thought determinedly, one
I have to handle myself. Nobody else this time. Just
me, at least in the brain department. If I blow this
one . . .

But, no, failure was unthinkable. Frankly, she
didn't care what Yulin did with Obie or planned to
do, but she cared about this last opportunity, the
chance to prove to herself and to the others that
Mavra Chang was as good as she'd always believed
herself to be.

To succeed here would be to put the final stamp on
her life, the proof that Mavra Chang existed as a
unique individual, better than them all. With that she
could be content to die. Without it, she was already
dead. For she knew the moment she'd set foot on
New Pompeii that she would never leave it. She

would not return to the Well World, to be transformed at random into something absurd, a Krommian dancing flower, say, or a Makiem frog—perhaps worse. And if she succeeded, and they all still lived—return? As what? A horse? That would go over big in the Com.

No. Triumph or disaster, it would end here.

The architectural plans of New Pompeii kept flashing through her head. Something must be there, some key, some way to foul things up. She was sure of it.

Apparently unimportant facts kept occurring to her, and she tried to organize them like a great jigsaw puzzle. But she had far too many irrelevant pieces. Her mind raced—the mind the Ghiskind had called the strongest it had ever encountered.

Obie. Obie was the key. Something about Obie. Think, Mavra, think! No, straining's not the way. Slow down. Relax. Let it come.

And she had it—part of it, anyway.

"Renard!" she said sharply. He'd been dozing and his head came up slowly, sleepily.

"Huh?"

"Remember long ago, when we escaped from this hole? Remember, we stole the ship and started toward the Well World?"

He was still half-asleep. "Yeah, I guess so," he mumbled.

"Obie talked to us over the ship's radio. Remember?"

He was suddenly awake. "Yeah, he did, didn't he?" he responded, understanding.

"Let's get to the ship," she suggested.

It was frustrating not to be able to handle the controls. At least there was a central pickup transceiver, not the headsets in the ship they'd used. Quickly she instructed him on the procedures, the radio tuning, power check and the like. Finally, she was satisfied.

"Mavra Chang calling Obie," she said. "Obie, can you hear me?"

"I was wondering when you'd think of this," the

warm, human voice of the computer responded immediately.

"Never mind the quibbles. We're not computers," she responded. "Obie, what's the situation in there now?"

"Bad," the computer told her. "Ben has complete control. Oh, sure, I can do this sort of thing, but except on his command, I cannot act on anything that means anything—and I can't stop him. Worse, Nikki Zinder and her daughter did not move when I told them and they were still here when Ben got into the room. He has captured them."

"What?" they shouted at once. Both Renard and Mavra tumbled through sentences, and Obie let them run down.

Finally, when they had calmed, Obie explained.

"I spent most of my time trying to probe the Well," he told them. "I discovered early that if I asked a specific and very limited question, the Well computer would answer it. By that time Trelig, Yulin, and Dr. Zinder—who I was really after—had already passed through. I sensed them, trying to get data on Dr. Zinder, but I was too late. All I could do was suggest that he be placed in a high-tech hex. It was a simple enough idea; I could handle it. So, when Renard and Nikki came through several days later, I was ready. Renard I made an Agitar, mostly because I knew Trelig was a Makiem and the two were situated next to each other. I thought you would act as a check on him, Renard."

The Agitar nodded. That explained a lot, and eliminated the wild coincidence he'd had to accept.

"Nikki wasn't ready, though," Obie continued. "On her own she would be lost almost anywhere on the Well World, and I had no way of making her an Oolakash, like her father. The Well follows rather complex rules, and she just didn't fit the Oolakash requirements. So, I decided there was only one thing to do. I seized her, practically in transit, so to speak. She went from the Well Gate to a mathematical limbo; then I brought her to me through the big dish

Underside and produced her in the control center through the little dish. I cured her of sponge and most of the excess weight. She's really rather cute. About the only thing that surprised me was that she was pregnant."

Again there was a chorus of *"What?"*

"Your child, Renard," Obie answered. "In Teliagin, when the two of you were sinking from sponge and thought you were going to die. Remember?"

Renard had totally forgotten it. Even with Obie's prompting he could barely remember it now.

"I needed hands, and I needed people," Obie told them. "So I allowed her to have the child. A girl, which she named Mavra, after you, Mavra Chang. You made quite an impression on her."

Mavra felt slightly pleased. "She's been living in there for twenty-two years with you?" she asked, unbelieving. "And the daughter is almost that?"

"Oh, no," Obie replied. "Not exactly. Several years, yes. The child is about fifteen, and very attractive— I *did* remake her slightly," the computer boasted. "Nikki is about twenty-five. There was no purpose to their living a strictly linear existence in there. I could provide the growth-match and some of the upbringing in the same way I put plans in your head, Mavra. They've lived off and on inside me."

"I thought you were the god machine," Renard pointed out, a little upset at all this. "Why'd you need people?"

"I could make extensions of myself, yes," Obie admitted, "but not new life. The mathematics isn't right for that. Even the Markovians had to become their own new creatures. And, of course, there was the matter of loneliness. I needed companionship. They have provided it. And they've been even more helpful ever since Dr. Zinder managed to build his transmitter and contact me many years ago."

The surprised "What"s were getting monotonous.

"It's been almost like old times," the computer admitted. "Dr. Zinder was safe and well and happy— and could work with me. We coordinated with Ortega so that we'd know as much as possible what was going on with you all down there. It's worked out nicely, and we've been able to help Ortega and several others with problems. The major task was the study of the Well, which is an endless project, and quite beyond me—and, of course, how to free myself of the Well's hold. *That* proved to be relatively simple."

"You mean you're independent of it?" Mavra asked.

"Oh, no. I mean I know how to do it. The trouble is that only half of me is controlled by voluntary circuits—much like the human brain. The way to free the other half is to get into the shaft and short out a series of circuits. Harmless, but without them the Well and I cannot conduct proper communication."

"Then why haven't you?" Renard asked. "Involuntary circuit?"

"In a way," Obie replied. "You see, they had me in 'defense' mode and *that's* involuntary. In that regime, which I am still in, by the way, I can not open the door. I could make Nikki and Mavra into what I needed and give them the skills, or I could create a robot analog and do it myself—but I can't get out there to do it."

Mavra's brain was racing, questions shooting through her mind with blinding speed.

"Obie?" she asked. "Why did you pick *me* to give those plans to?"

"I didn't. I told the same thing to everybody I felt capable of doing the job," the computer responded. "You were just the one who made it."

That wasn't the answer she wanted to hear, and it clouded her thinking for a moment. She recovered with difficulty.

"Obie—Ben Yulin's going to find this out sooner or later," Renard pointed out. "And when he does, he'll free you of the Well's hold but still be in control. What happens then?"

"As soon as contact is broken, he can reverse the field," the computer replied. "New Pompeii would be back in normal, familiar space again—and the big dish would be operational. With my knowledge of the Well, and the big dish, he'd have the power to transform an entire planet into anything he wanted."

"And how long do you think *that* will take?" Mavra asked.

"Not long," Obie answered apprehensively. "He has Nikki and Mavra Zinder, and he has learned from them that Gil Zinder can be contacted by radio. Dr. Zinder built me into New Pompeii because of Trelig's threats to harm Nikki Zinder. Do you think he'll do less to save his daughter *and* grand-daughter? You know better. In a matter of hours Yulin will know it all. He'll break contact with the Well not long after —and he's very cautious and extraordinarily tricky. I calculate that Yulin will discover that I'm talking to you over the ship's radio within that period, too, and put a halt to it."

Plans and schematics continued to flash through Mavra's head. Something, the key to it all, was there, she knew. But what? I've got too much data, she thought in frustration. Can't get a handle.

"Then time's running out on all of us," Renard breathed helplessly.

"Except for Ben Yulin," agreed Obie.

Underside

BEN YULIN WAS SINGULARLY UNEQUIPPED TO BE A world conqueror. He had to order Obie to swing the dish to him, then create some tough rope in an energy-to-matter conversion before he could even tie up the two women. They presented very little threat; the Dasheen bull was extremely powerful, and they had no weapon to use on him. There had been a lot of chasing and yelling, but the result was inevitable.

Satisfied that all was well, he climbed the stairs once again and checked the control panel. For the first time, he allowed himself to relax and think about the past and the future.

True, he told himself, he'd planned everything each step of the way, knowing that he and he alone had to be the one to enter and to control the powerhouse. But he'd been like a prisoner in jail who dreams of escape: so much effort went into planning how to do it that little thought had been given to what was to happen after.

There were ghosts in this chamber all right, not the least of which was the living ghost of Nikki Zinder, whom he'd assumed many years dead. Now here she was—if not pretty, at least cute, and fairly trim.

Obie was a slippery character; you could force him to follow your orders, but if you left him a loophole he'd plunge through every time. That brought up one thought immediately.

"Obie?"

"Yes, Ben?"

"I don't want you telling anyone else by any means what I'm doing in here, or anything I might do in the future. Understand?"

"Yes, Ben."

That settled at least one big worry. Next was—

Suddenly Yulin was very dizzy and somewhat nauseous, and he grabbed onto the panel for support, steadying himself until it subsided.

For a moment he was fearful, and he took a few more minutes to calm down enough to think it through. What was wrong with him?

The answer was obvious. As a Dasheen bull he depended on milk manufactured by the female for deficiencies in his own system. How long had it been since he'd had some of the chemical substitute? A day? Two? More?

He was about to order some made up for him by Obie when he stopped.

Do I still want to be a Dasheen? he asked himself.

He liked the culture, he felt comfortable as one; it was practical on the Well World. He'd run enough through Obie to know that control of the Well of Souls computer was impossible unless a machine far greater than Obie was built, and that much was beyond him—at least now. Nor did he dare tinker too much by giving the Well new instructions; the Well was the stabilizing device not only for the Well World but for literally all living things in the universe. Give it improper instructions and one could wipe out civilizations, even oneself. At best summon that Markovian, Brazil—a being who could operate the Well, even cancel out Ben Yulin, New Pompeii, and anything else it wished. He had no desire to run into that character; still, Brazil was also subject to the Well. Handled carefully, he should never know.

But handle what? This was the new problem. To go out in space, looking into new civilizations? Perhaps, one day—but not now. Obie represented unlimited opportunity coupled to virtual immortality.

What he needed were people to do the hard stuff, people he could trust as he could trust his Dasheen cows back home.

There was only one source for such people that he knew of, and that was in the human sector of the Milky Way galaxy, now so far away. One world at a time, if need be, carefully, nicely, normally adjusted so precisely that nobody else would even realize things had been changed. Not Brazil, not the Council.

That meant being human again.

But what kind of human?

He thought it out carefully, sighed, and flipped open the channel to Obie.

"Yes, Ben?"

He punched several buttons on his keyboard. "Unnumbered transaction, file in aux storage under my key only."

The computer was amazed every time he did this,

and opened the section otherwise closed to him. Yulin and Obie always went through a complex exchange on it, which Yulin suffered through again.

"Now, Obie, I want you to listen carefully," Yulin said slowly. "You will carry out my instructions to the letter, neither adding nor subtracting anything on your own. Is that clear?"

"Yes, Ben."

"Recall subject Ben Yulin as first recorded physiologically."

"I have it, Ben," the computer responded.

"All right. That model shall be the subject, as modified according to the following criteria. First, subject shall be two meters tall and proportioned accordingly, with total muscular development. Got that?"

"Yes, Ben. You want to look like a body-builder," Obie replied in his sarcastic way. Yulin ignored it.

"Obie, do you have Mavra Chang's original encoding?" he asked.

"Up front."

When he'd first escaped from New Pompeii, Yulin used Obie to turn himself into Mavra Chang. At that time he'd discovered that Chang had surgically implanted tiny sacs and needles under her fingernails that could inject powerful hypnotic drugs. He'd had the opportunity to use them once in self-defense and he'd never forgotten them.

"Give subject Ben Yulin the hypnotic injector system found in the Chang encoding below the fingernails. Make it natural, self-refilling, and harmless in all ways to the subject, who shall himself be immune. Got that?"

"I've got it, Ben," Obie said. "It will take some work, but not much."

He nodded. So far so good. "Further modifications to subject. The best ocular vision system possible, including infrared and ultraviolet perception, full day-night capability with good color and excellent resolution even at great distances. Okay?"

"I have such a system design," the computer replied.

"Further modifications to subject Ben Yulin: the best hearing in all ranges you can design, wavelength selectable by the subject."

"Go on," the computer responded casually. "I'm fascinated by this superman you are constructing."

He had a few additional ideas. "Obie, you've studied the denizens of the Well World. I'm aware that the Lata and a number of other creatures can live off anything organic. Can you adapt subject's system to do that?"

"It's getting better," the computer noted. "Oh, yes. Do you want wings, too?"

Tempting as that was, he passed it up. "No, but can you design subject to be immune to Lata and Yaxa venom?"

"Done."

"How about Yugash takeover and even severe electric shock?" he asked, pressing it but at the same time truly reveling in this casual godlike activity at his command.

"The prevention of takeover by a Yugash is relatively easy," the computer replied after a moment. "Immunity to electrical shock is much more difficult. Since I assume that you are merely looking for a defense against Renard, might I just design in a tolerence for voltages of slightly greater amplitude and duration than the Agitar are capable of?"

"Good enough." Yulin's mind was racing again. Then he remembered one attribute of at least four Well races that would be very handy about now.

"Obie, among others, the Zupika can blend in with any background. Can this be programmed into the subject, usable on a voluntary basis? I assume true invisibility is impossible."

"Invisibility's impossible if you want to remain a creature of solid matter," the computer replied. "As for ability to blend—well, it might not be as perfect as the natural form, but I think it's possible. Yes, I can do it."

"Then add that attribute to subject."

"Is that all?" the computer asked mockingly.

Yulin's head cocked slightly to one side. "No, one more thing. Add that subject is male, will breed true in these attributes, and is capable of almost indefinite multiple male orgasms."

The computer actually sighed. "I should have guessed. That's three things, but they're locked in."

"Closing instructions," he concluded. "Subject will have all of Ben Yulin's current input memories and personality—nothing of that is to be changed! However, subject will feel comfortable, normal, and natural in the new body and will know its operation, capabilities, and limits."

"Coded," Obie acknowledged.

"This is a closed transaction," Yulin ordered. "You will be unable to complete any other transaction until it is completed, and your next transaction must be coded by me personally. Clear?"

"Clear," the computer responded. "Lock and run. Now."

Yulin walked down the stairs carefully, still dizzy, still nauseous for want of Dasheen milk. He made it to the circular platform and stood upon it. The overhead dish swung out, locked, then bathed him in a metallic blue glow. The image of the Dasheen bull stiffened, flickered, then winked out.

The two women tied up in a corner struggled to free themselves while their adversary was inside the machine, but could not.

Eight seconds later another image flickered in the glow, then solidified. The blue glow disappeared. The dish swung back.

The women stared. Ben Yulin had always been a handsome, somewhat exotic man; now, every muscle developed and bulging, he looked like an Adonis and a David wrapped up in one.

But this one moved, smiled at them, and checked his fingernails. He stepped down, walked over, touched a fingernail to Nikki Zinder's skin. A tiny needle, a hollow tube of cartilage, injected a clear fluid into her. She struggled a second, then stiffened, and seemed to sleep. Another finger flexed, and her better-looking daughter also succumbed.

He untied them, ordered them to rise. Nikki Zinder was first on the platform; her daughter stood zombie-like, in front. He returned to the console, punched some more numbers.

"New transaction, Obie," he said, feeling better than he ever had in his life, so confident that he was now a god that worries faded.

"Go ahead, Ben," the computer came back at him. "My, I did a nice job!"

Yulin actually laughed. "Yes, you did," he approved. "Now you have a similar set of jobs. Subject is Nikki Zinder. New encoding modifications for subject."

"You know Dr. Zinder built in a prohibition to prevent my doing certain things to her."

Yulin nodded. "Not strong enough. Not nearly strong enough. And some of it I can undo. Okay, new subject is to be 160 centimeters high, female, age seventeen standard, the following dimensions."

Slowly, carefully, he described his Venus. He gave her all of the modifications to sensory apparatus and immunities he'd given himself, including the camouflage ability and digestive-system versatility. Strength, too; great strength, but managed by an alteration in her internal structure and not something that would mar her exceptional beauty.

And a few things more.

"Mentally, subject shall retain all memories and sense of identity, *except* she shall look upon herself as my slave and my property, and she will consider this right and just and proper, normal in all ways. She will be totally obedient to my wishes, totally devoted to me and my wants, desires, and needs, to the exclusion of all else. Understand?"

"Sure, Ben. You want a human Dasheen cow," Obie cracked. "It is unfortunately within my limits. Is that all?"

"For now," he told the computer. "Lock and run. Now."

It took the same eight seconds or so. He stared down in anticipation, and he wasn't disappointed. She was absolutely the most beautiful woman he'd ever seen.

Her daughter he made a twin of the new Nikki, except he replaced Nikki's black flowing hair with auburn, so he could tell them apart at a distance.

He called for them to come to him, and they did, joyfully, almost throwing themselves on him in adoration.

"All right, girls!" he laughed. "First, I think maybe we'll explore our new bodies. Then you'll run a few errands for me while I work with Obie on getting us back where we belong."

"Oh, *yes,* Ben!" they both sighed in anticipation.

A few hours later he was ready; they had been intensely pleasurable hours, not at all wasted, but now to business.

"Obie?"

"Yes, Ben?"

"Are your external sensors still operable along the main shaft?" Although the computer was blind Topside, it could see the Underside area around the shaft leading to the big dish that still locked on the Well of Souls.

"Operational, Ben."

He nodded. "Okay. Any life forms Underside?"

"None that I can detect, Ben—although I don't seem to be able to detect the Yugash too well unless it's in visual range. My sensors weren't designed for energy creatures."

He understood that. "But we're all immune to its takeover, right?" The computer assured him they were. Yulin continued. "All right, then." He turned to the two women, unable to overcome his delight at their beauty.

"Girls, you know what to do now." They nodded in unison. He turned back to Obie. "Defense mode off, Obie. Defense mode will be off automatically on their return unless they are under coercion. Return to defense mode when they clear the door into the control center. Clear?"

"Clear, Ben."

"And Obie—don't forget. Not a word of this to anybody."

"You know I can't now," the computer responded grumpily. "Defense mode off."

The two women walked to the door, it opened, and they passed quickly out. It slid shut behind them.

Yulin returned to Obie. "You've been talking to Gil Zinder all along, haven't you?" he accused.

"Yes, Ben, I cannot tell a lie," Obie replied. "I thought you'd want to talk to him sooner or later."

"Maybe not," he said thoughtfully. "Obie, did the two of you work on the problem of freeing you from the Well?"

"Yes, Ben."

"Did you solve it?"

"Yes, Ben."

Aha! So much for problems, they vanished like magic, he thought smugly.

"Procedure?" he asked in anxious anticipation.

As Obie told him, he realized the logic of it and cursed himself for not having seen it himself. The solution was so simple it might have been overlooked for decades—of course, he was still rusty, he reminded himself. But there was a feeling of power in him beyond anything he'd ever known, and the confidence that he not only could do anything, he *would* do everything.

He would make no mistakes, he assured himself. Everything was to be thought out and carefully considered.

But he had already made one, and he didn't know it.

Topside

THE GROUP WAS DISAPPOINTED AND GLOOMY. THE products of diverse cultures and backgrounds, veterans of many campaigns—some in more than one form—most had fought, clawed, and schemed to be among those to reach the enigmatic New Pompeii. Six creatures of great potential and no little intellect, all totally impotent to solve their problem.

"We could always go home," Renard suggested. They looked at him impatiently, a little patronizingly. He shrugged. "It's an option, that's all," he added defensively.

"No, it is not an option," Wooley responded. "We know what is in there. A big machine. We can even talk to it. A machine that can talk to the Well, tell it what to do. If Yulin wishes to, he can do anything he wants to the Well."

"Perhaps he will leave it," the Bozog said hopefully.

Vistaru sighed. "That's even worse, and you know it. Well, maybe not so much to you or the Ghiskind, but Yulin's not going to rush off to some strange system or race. He's going to go home—to his original home. And he's going to have the big dish to do whatever he wants to with entire planetary populations. The rest of us—Renard, Mavra, Wooley, and myself —came from those people. We can't let him remake a civilization if we can prevent that, and we must do all in our power to prevent that."

"Not to mention that Yulin's a Dasheen," Mavra pointed out. "Three guesses how women would fare in his new order. But—we have to be committed, I think. I sense that at least in Wooley and Vistaru. Bozog, if you want to take the ship and return, I'll give you all the programming instructions you need. Renard could take you if he wanted, although your tentacles would do for what little control manipulation would need to be done."

The Bozog shifted its bulk. "You know that is impossible," it responded. "We knew it, too, before we took off. There is no return possible with that ship. None of us is capable of another perfect dead-stick landing, not even friend Mavra here, had she tentacles or arms. It was a one-in-ten-thousand shot that they made it originally. The odds are far worse now. No, we can crash into the Well World, but not land, not ever."

This surprised them. That aspect had never crossed their minds, although it should have. "Then why did you come?" Wooley asked.

"For myself," the Bozog said slowly, trying to choose its words, "because it was possible. Because it is a feat and experience beyond duplication. To be here, on another world! To see the Well World from afar! This, in itself, is worth a dozen lives."

Renard shrugged. "What about you, Ghiskind? You could survive a crash, I'll bet."

The Yugash flowed into the Bozog. "Perhaps. Perhaps not. But, if so, which of you will be the pilot willing to surrender its own life for mine? No, I, too, knew it was a one-way trip, unless the Obie computer can send us back."

"I think that's unlikely," Mavra put in. "I don't think any of us will ever see the inside of that control room. He's too well defended."

"If only there was some way to destroy it," Wooley said in frustration. "A bomb, perhaps!"

"Maybe we can crash the ship into the big dish," the Bozog suggested.

Mavra shook her head. "No, Obie's pretty firm on

that. Defenses are automatic since that was the weak point Trelig had to address. Fly into that beam and you're gone." Still, the *idea* of destroying Obie—which she rebelled against because, despite all, she liked and respected the thing—struck a chord. Schematics and plans flowed again, only this time with purpose.

Destruct. Destruct mechanisms.

The idea wouldn't gel. A corner of her mind remembered Obie's comment that, though he couldn't absorb the Well's input, he could do a few limited things by concentrating on a single, specific task. Well, Obie was to her what the Well was to Obie. She tried it, concentrating on destruct mechanisms.

And there it was.

Not a single one, but many, all over. Antor Trelig wanted to be certain that no one would ever be able to displace him as master of Obie or New Pompeii.

Excitedly, she told them about it. "Some are old—probably the original destruct mechanism for the whole planetoid. Others are new, in small pockets designed to blow vital parts of Obie in case Trelig was displaced."

"Can we blow any of it?" Wooley asked.

Mavra sighed. "Let's ask Obie—if he'll tell us. He might not take kindly to assisting in his own murder."

The elevator wall dissolved and the two women engaged their camouflage mechanisms. They blended well with the background. Though when moving, they could be made out with difficulty, they were generally undetectable to anyone not fully alert. The Well Worlder's camp still lay nearby the top of the exit so the two crawled through the grass, and only someone actually looking for them would have noticed anything amiss.

In the clear now, they made their way to the primitive little colony of survivors of the destruction of New Pompeii.

Though Ben Yulin had instructed Obie not to tell anyone what he was doing about the Underside operations and plans, he had neglected to prohibit Obie from talking with others and thus only limited Obie's informability.

"Hello, Obie, this is Mavra Chang," she called into the ship's radio.

"I'm here, Mavra," the pleasant tenor of the computer replied.

She considered carefully what she was going to say. If in fact Obie could not cooperate in this, he might well have the power to stop it. At least he could warn Yulin.

"Obie, when we all came here, it was either to join with you in a partnership or to die. You know that."

"I had concluded that you knew the only avenue home was through me."

She nodded. "All right, then. It turned out bad. Wrong. Ben Yulin's in there, and we can guess what kind of person he is. We're all agreed, even the Bozog and the Ghiskind, that we're willing to die rather than let him get control of the big dish. You understand that?"

He seemed to sense her direction. "I accept that, Mavra. Come to the point. I feel as you do, if that helps any."

It did. "Obie, in those plans you fed to me were the self-destruct mechanisms for New Pompeii. I've just picked them out of my mind."

"I'm surprised it took you all this time," responded the computer. "I am programmed not to participate in my own destruction, so I could not bring them to your attention, but I knew you'd find them sooner or later."

His casual attitude and acceptance made it easier.

"All right, then. Obie, how is the main destruct system for New Pompeii's power supply activated?" she asked. "Can you tell me that?"

"Phrased that way, yes," Obie replied. "However, it's a bust. It was coded to Trelig, almost literally built into him. If he were to die, so would the planetoid. But when he was transformed through the Well, the mechanism was removed. In effect, there is now no way to detonate the main power supply without a technical crew and a lot of work."

She was disappointed. "Can any of the secondary systems still be activated?"

"All such systems are controlled from the control room itself. They are voice-actuated, and I'm afraid Ben wouldn't allow something like that, nor could I give the codes to anyone not in the control room."

"Could any one of them be triggered by external action?"

"Some."

"Is there one that could be triggered by, say, the application of a strong electrical voltage to a specific message circuit?"

"There is at least one such," Obie replied. "It is in the area between the voluntary and involuntary circuitry, and it can be reached from the main bridge. However, it is 62.35 meters down, and 7.61 meters inside the circuitry. The panel opening is less than a meter wide at that point, and the access tunnel twists up and around."

Mavra concentrated. Diagrams sped by in her mind. She had it. She was learning that the more she used the implanted memory, the easier it became to find what she needed. Unfortunately, she had no overall picture. She knew the specific circuits, and she knew the general area, but she couldn't be sure which opening led to that circuitry, or exactly which connector to jolt.

"Thank you, Obie," she said sincerely. "We'll take it from here."

There was no reply.

She returned to the others with Renard, who'd sat there listening.

"There's no way I could get into an opening that size, or even down there," he pointed out. "Vistaru could fly down, and might fit, but she couldn't handle the voltages, and her wings and stinger would be in the way, even if you knew just which circuit to tell her to reach. We're probably dealing with a single microscopic line."

She nodded. "No, you couldn't. But the Ghiskind can certainly reach it. It could probably follow the circuitry all the way to the bomb."

"So?" he responded. "What good is that? It can't carry anything, nor generate a voltage."

"But the Bozog could," she pointed out. "I saw some traveling up walls at the launch site. Thousands of tiny, sticky feet. It's low enough, and can ooze around curves like it managed in the elevator. And it can carry a wire—if we can find a hundred meters or more of thin copper wire."

"Of course! Then all I'd have to do is touch the wire with a full charge after the Bozog carries it and the Ghiskind directs its placement!"

She nodded again. "But first we have to see if we have enough wire around. And, second, we have to lick the other problem—without Obie's help, I'm afraid."

He looked confused. "Other problem?"

"The Bozog is a living creature. It's not at all immune to severe electrical jolts, nor—particularly—to those guns the plans in my head tell me are no bluff. The key area is on the *far* wall of the bridge, Renard. As long as Obie's in his defense mode, we can't get the Bozog to it."

"Oh," he said softly. Suddenly he froze, and there was a quizzical expression on his blue devil's face. He cocked it slightly to one side, as if listening for something.

"What's the matter?" she asked. Though Wooley had the best eyes of the group, Renard had by far the best hearing.

"There's something moving over there, not far from the elevator," he whispered. "Fairly large, too."

She turned her head slightly, carefully, in that direction. Nothing could be seen.

For a while there was no sound, then even she heard it. A soft sound, as if something heavy were being dragged through the grass.

"Let's head over to the elevator," she suggested softly. He nodded imperceptibly and they strolled over, casual but alert.

"So that's it, then," Mavra said conversationally, in a normal conversational tone. "We're stuck here. Our only chance is to make a deal with Yulin."

He nodded. "If he'll make deals. He's got to come out of there sooner or later, you know. He'll have to deal with us or trap himself."

All sounds had stopped. Renard nodded slightly in the direction of the base, where an unconscious human form could be seen. It was naked, dirty, and scarred, and its hair was a long, twisted mess. It lay face up—a young boy, apparently.

Renard looked into the elevator and couldn't suppress an exclamation. "My God!" he breathed.

Inside were stacked six or seven bodies, all out cold, all as filthy as the boy. All had horse's tails.

When he turned to yell to the others, something struck him, hard, sending him sprawling. He was up in an instant and rushed back.

Another unseen thing hit Mavra broadside with such strength that it toppled her onto her side.

Renard saw something large and indistinct near her, and reached out to touch it. Voltage flowed.

Apparently it had no effect, for something landed hard on his head, bringing unconsciousness.

Though nearly helpless, Mavra struggled to rise as she saw two eerie forms, like women but green and grassy, step into the elevator and pull the boy in after them. As they started to change to match the elevator interior, the wall solidified.

Renard regained consciousness quickly and got unsteadily to his feet. Mavra managed finally to pull herself to her feet.

"Who the hell was *that?*" he gasped.

"The savages—Belden's people," she replied. "Probably all of them, I'd say. Snatched right in front of us."

"But *why?*" he asked, still holding his head. "And

254

who was it? Yulin? There were definitely at least two."

She nodded. "Two, and both female. I saw them, briefly. They have a way of fading into the background, like two creatures I once knew—but far different. I don't know who they are—but Yulin's obviously being creative with Obie. We've been suckered under our very noses."

"I still don't get it," Renard persisted. "Why the savages?"

"Here!" she said. "Get up on me. Ride me in. You're still groggy."

He was too woozy to resist her suggestion, and mounted her with difficulty. It was the first time a human being had been on her back, of whatever race. It was uncomfortable, but the Agitar was experienced and clung to her professionally. She slowly walked back, taking care not to throw him off.

"Well, Yulin needs or wants people, that's for sure," she said. "We know from Obie that he can't materialize thinking beings out of thin air. The savages were the easiest to get—just hypno them and carry them down. If he runs them through, he has at least nine slaves that we know of, with whatever powers he wants to give them."

"Whatever they were, one took a full jolt with no effect," Renard noted glumly. "But why so many?"

"Us," she replied. "Remember, he *is* trapped down there until he deals with us. He's a very clever and devious man. He knows there's nothing he can offer us, and certainly nothing he can do whereby we would trust him or he would trust us. Would you step under Obie's dish with Yulin at the controls?"

"Hell, no!"

"So, what does he do? I'm sure he doesn't want to risk feedback on Topside. The last time that was tried, Obie transported New Pompeii to its present place. So, he has to capture or kill us. For that he needs others—he can't do it himself and risk leaving the controls. See?"

Renard whistled. "So our time's even shorter than

we thought," he said nervously. "It's nine to six now."

"And you can bet that if he's got them immune to your electric personality he's got them guarded against the rest of us," she pointed out. "I'd say we have to blow that charge quickly or it's all over."

"I think—" Renard started, but he was suddenly cut off.

The whole world was cut off.

There was only blackness and the sensation of falling. No sight, no sound or other impressions, nothing. It was as if all but their minds had simply ceased to exist.

It lasted for a long time, then, suddenly, they were back to normalcy again.

Renard had fallen off Mavra's back and she'd stumbled herself. Now, for the second time they picked themselves up.

"Now what?" Renard groaned.

Mavra got shakily back to her feet and looked up.

"Events are quickly overtaking us," she said quietly. "Look up. No Well World. Just a distant sun up there, and a more reasonable amount of stars.

"He's done it, Renard! We're back! Back in the human sector of space! Back in New Pompeii's original orbit!"

"Oh, boy!" Renard said sourly. "And I told the breeding farm I was taking a short vacation . . ."

Underside

BEN YULIN WAS PLEASED WITH HIMSELF AS HE looked over his troops. He had changed all of them into his dream women, even the two boys. Each had a distinct hair and skin tone; but nine new names were a bit much to remember, and aside from the first two, Nikki and Mavra, he just decided to settle on numbers for a while.

The savages were really that, too, not very smart and at about an ape's level of experience. Each retained the horse's tail, as Ben Yulin thought they were kind of sexy, and they served to further distinguish the first two from the rest.

Obie did not give them a past, of course, but he provided language ability, demeanor, and all the other things necessary. Effectively, they were amnesiacs with needed skills, but that was fine. They too were love-slaves of Ben Yulin. All lay prostrate before him at his feet.

"You are my herd, my *hareem*," he told them. "You are a part of me and I of you. You are the most honored of women, and will sit at my feet as I sweep away the old order and establish the new."

"Yes, My Lord Yulin," they responded sincerely in unison.

He looked at them in extreme self-satisfaction. In truth, a new order, he decided. Long ago, in lands lost in time and space but alive in the tradition of Yulin's people, his ancestors had lived amid desert wastes in tent cities that followed the water and the blowing sand. Then great lords had grandiose *hareems*. Some of this would be restored, he told himself.

He would create human beings in all ways so close to perfection that clothing would be a sin except when needed for protection. Powerful Lords would rule not desert wastes but bountiful planets, holding sway over their own herds of beautiful, powerful, and adoring woman. Yet all would be subservient to him, the Supreme Caliph from whom all blessing and curses would flow, and for all time. A land of artisans, scientists, and engineers pushing back the ultimate frontiers.

A race to fulfill the Markovian dream of utopian perfectionism, a race to become gods.

All this was within his grasp, right now, here, to-day!

"Arise and go about your duties," he commanded, and they did so. Thanks to Obie, their living quarters were already quite comfortable, with great soft beds covered in silk and satin. Obie had also provided exotic fruits, vegetables, and meats indistinguishable from the originals. Though it was true that Yulin and his harem could now eat anything organic, even grass, there was no reason to.

Yulin returned to Obie and sat at a control console, flipping the transmitter switch.

"Obie? Have you plotted our position exactly?" he asked.

"Yes, Ben. We are back in the original New Pompeii orbit, along with the robot sentries. No sign of anything within a one-light-year scan. I suppose any curious investigators would have given up by now anyway. It's been over twenty-two years."

Ben Yulin nodded. "What about our movement capability, Obie? Can you move us to a different point, even a different sector of space?"

"Any area whose coordinates are precisely specified in my memory. That includes, of course, all Comworlds and frontiers as of the time we were last here."

Ben Yulin nodded in satisfaction, then shifted his

thoughts. Only a few things now stood in his way. Six things.

"Obie, is there any way you can change the atmospheric content Topside?" he asked. "Alter the balance, drain it, or introduce a toxic substance?"

"Those areas are controlled by totally involuntary circuits," the computer reminded him. "I can't do anything about them at all. You should know that. Antor Trelig didn't want you or Zinder or anyone else to have that kind of power—and particularly not me. For some reason he never really trusted me." There was a hurt tone in that last.

Yulin chuckled. He trusted Obie himself about as far as he could throw the thing.

"All right, then," he sighed. "I'll have to deal with the Northerners as best I can. Right now I need good knockout substances that will affect Agitar, Yaxa, and Lata."

Obie had the necessary information.

Topside

AN ARMED GUARD WAS POSTED NEAR THE ELEVATOR, and the camp was moved to the center of the grassy park. They didn't want to be surprised again.

"Why not take the ship and scram for help?" Renard suggested. "We sure as hell are living physical proof of what we say, and the Council could then move to blast this place."

"That's just what Yulin would want us to try,"

Mavra retorted. "Once out in the ship, he could swing the big dish on us and bag us all in one sweep. That's why he hasn't bothered to disable it."

Renard looked toward the elevator, perhaps a hundred meters away, now guarded by Wooley and Vistaru. "They're going to come for us sometime," he said flatly. "Soon."

She nodded. "Well, we have the wire from the technicians' repair center. Three hundred meters—that's more than enough. If we can only get close enough to use it."

"They have to relax the defense mode to get their people in and out," the Bozog pointed out. "That would be the logical time."

"Yeah, maybe we should wait by the bridge," Renard interjected. "Ready to go, so to speak."

"I don't think so," she replied. "No, the plans indicate that Obie can see the entire area from the end of the entrance corridor all the way across to his door. And if we stay in the corridor, our backs are to the elevator; Yulin can change his zombies into whatever he wants and nab us. No, I think—"

"Hey! Something's coming up!" Wooley yelled, and both she and Vistaru tensed and the others started toward them.

The elevator door opened and emitted a hideous-looking cloud of mixed orange-and-green gases. It was thick and enveloped them. A wild shot was fired from near the entrance, then nothing.

The others reached the area where the cloud hung but stayed back cautiously when the first whiff proved acrid. The Yugash and Bozog advanced, disappeared, then reemerged moments later. The huge ball of smoke started to rise up and away as the automatic circulation machinery caught it.

"They are gone!" the Bozog exclaimed. "Both of them! Vanished!"

Renard shook his head sadly. "Now we are four, damn it all!"

"And, more important, he's eleven, even without

including himself," Mavra responded. "This changes everything."

"We could give chase in the other car," the Bozog suggested.

She shook her head. "No, that's no good. It always stops at the upper door, remember? And it whines. So we get there, the door opens, and we're all taken." She turned to Renard. "Still got your energy pistol?"

"Here," he said, slapping his holster.

"All right, then. We'll give them some time, then we'll call a car. You'll spray it with stun fire before we board, and the Ghiskind and the Bozog will also check it out. When we get down, you'll spray again as it opens, and all the way down to the lower floor. We're going to go fighting!"

"But just that very activity will alert him," the Bozog objected. "Logically, he'll keep his people inside until he needs to send them out. Yulin will want to avoid something happening to one of them. He cannot know all our capabilities."

"I'm counting on that," she replied. "And on the fact that the lower car was down and they used the upper. If that is the case, we're safe for almost an hour. Ghiskind, you and the Bozog keep watch just in case. Renard, one last trip to the ship, and then it's do or die."

"Or learn to love Ben Yulin," he sighed.

Lights flashed, figures spewed forth under Renard's hands but Mavra's guidance. It took several minutes, but finally they were through.

"It's an automatic sequence," she told him. "If we manage the explosion, it's entirely possible life support will continue, at least for a while. If so, you might be able to get up here—with the others if you can—and get to the ship. Once you activate the fuse, *don't waste time!* If power goes, you'll be asphyxiated in the elevator. Get everyone you can, get inside, get up here, get into the ship, close the locks, and punch E-LIFT on the board. The ship will disengage and follow a course that will bring you within radio range of the

Council inside two days, so then you call for help. They will board you, see you, and believe. Tell them *New Pompeii must be utterly destroyed.* Atomized. Otherwise, some scientists will come here, and some politicos will get control, and it'll all be for nothing. Everything must go."

Renard didn't like the tone. "You're talking as if you won't be among us," he protested.

"Maybe I will, maybe I won't," she replied. "We can't take the chance on me being here. If you can, get into the control room and get the people out."

"But they'll all be Yulin's slaves!"

She shook her head. "No, they won't. Physically, yes. But any mental controls put on them will fail. Nikki Zinder was under a love-slave compulsion to Yulin when she was lured here, but when they disconnected Obie to relocate him to New Pompeii, the spell was broken. It should be the same this time."

"All right then, but I won't leave without you."

"If it's necessary, you must!" Mavra snapped. "Believe me, Renard. You're the only one now who knows these procedures. And don't let anybody else go for me or try to rescue anyone else if they can't be gotten to immediately. You can't kill all those people for me. Promise me you won't!"

He sighed. "All right, I promise," he almost whispered.

They left the ship, locks open, and rejoined the two Northerners.

"We're lucky it wasn't Renard they grabbed," she told them. "The three of you can still pull this off if one bit of luck shows up."

Even the Bozog was getting nervous. "What's that?"

"We've got to have them all inside the control room," she replied. "I hope he has enough ego to think he doesn't need guards, and enough insecurity not to switch off the defense mode unless he has to. If he doesn't know we're down there until we're ready, we'll make it."

"But how will I get past the defenses?" the Bozog asked her.

"Diversion," she responded. "Me. I'm going to be the bait. A little pony sitting out there watching the end of the bridge. It'll be too tempting to pass up."

"But he'll know we're around," Renard pointed out. "What if he makes a try for us, too?"

"It won't matter. You see, they'll have to switch off the defense mode just to send his slaves out. It's a long way across that bridge. When I've gone as long as I can stall, I'll charge them."

"And what happens to us while you're doing all this?" the Bozog prompted.

"Bozog, you'll take the wire and go along the *outside* of the bridge. Ghiskind, you'll lead him. Renard, keep that energy pistol firm and stay slightly back, out of sight. Yulin might see the wire but not figure out he's been had. Even if he does, he'll have a job getting at it. As soon as the wire is in place, tug three times. That will tell Renard to give it all he's got. Get clear after you tug, and make it back up if you can. All hell will break loose when that goes."

"And you?" Renard asked, concerned.

"If I get inside, I'll try and raise as much hell as possible," she replied. "No matter what, Yulin's attention will be on me, I think. You should have several minutes—more than enough time. If they *do* catch on, Renard, use your energy pistol on anybody and everybody. There's no way Ben Yulin can neutralize the effects of *that* on a living body!"

"But it might be Wooley, or Vistaru!" he objected.

"Even if it's me!" she snapped. "Renard, save as many of the living as you can, kill who you must. It's that or good-bye to us all! This plan's got enough holes in it, that it'll probably fail anyway!"

"There is no better that I can devise, not at this late stage," the Bozog added. "Shall we go?"

She nodded. "Renard, call the elevator and hold that pistol ready."

There was no one on the elevator.

"A good sign," the Bozog said, approvingly. "I think Mr. Yulin may yet be in for a shock. He does not know how fast a Bozog can run!"

Underside

THEY WAITED ANXIOUSLY IN THE CORRIDOR NEXT TO the elevator car for the Ghiskind to return, Renard's pistol at the ready. The Yugash had already been out once and verified that no living creatures were to be seen anywhere.

A tense fifteen minutes passed before the Yugash returned a second time and merged with the Bozog.

"I have located the explosive module," it told them. "Rather primitive, really. A thermal device. However, it will cause massive disruption of circuitry if it goes —including some in the involuntary sections that affect life support. Be warned of this."

"It'll do," she responded. "Those sections are the weakest point in Obie's construction. Through that tunnel runs the junction with its power supply and much of its operational circuitry. That's why the charge is there—it doesn't have to be big, it just has to go off."

"It will," Renard said grimly. He rolled the wire coil out in front of him. Although it wasn't copper, it was conductive enough.

"We shall have to run the wire a bit farther for insurance," the Ghiskind warned. "I should like to have it directly on the main junction, very near the explosives. That way, if triggering fails, the voltage generated might set the charge off directly. This will also give friend Bozog a better place to attach it, and perhaps a little additional time to get clear."

Mavra took a deep breath. "All right then. I guess there's nothing left to do but go and do it."

"I still don't like you being in the clutches of that bastard," Renard muttered.

"For the last time, Renard, forget about me! I'm not important. Remember, it's up to you to get everybody away, to blow this place to hell. And," she added, "do you remember that string of symbols and numbers I recorded on the ship's recolog?"

He nodded.

"A gift from Obie, Renard, twenty-two years delayed. It's the arresting agent for sponge. It will free millions and break the back of the syndicate. You of all people must understand what that means. You must get that to the Council! Remember your responsibilities, Renard!"

The Agitar nodded. He didn't like the order, but she was right. If only he could get out, then it was his duty to do so.

Mavra walked slowly, deliberately down the hall and they followed. Just ahead was the opening to the first platform, then the bridge over the great shaft that led to the big dish. Once they were framed in that archway, Obie would be able to detect them and would be forced to warn Ben Yulin and his love-slaves.

Renard ran out a few meters of wire, then sat on the floor, just out of view of the open area, his thin goatlike legs splayed in front of him.

The orange liquid inside the Bozog's forward hump swirled, then exuded a serpentine tendril that grabbed the wire and twisted around it.

Mavra scanned the area. Renard was in position, hands on his energy pistol—it was not on stun. His face was grim, and he was perspiring, but he nodded.

"Here we go," Mavra said tensely, and stepped out through the archway.

Ben Yulin was exceptionally pleased with his girls' catch on their first attempt. Wooley's unconscious form had been hardest to move, particularly to get down the stairs and onto the disk, but they'd managed, and the transformation was swift and complete. The tiny form of Vistaru was next; the transformation equally swift. Since they had names, he let them keep them, but he observed no other restrictions regarding them: he wiped their memories clean, reprogramming them as two more loving slaves, horse tails and all, only slight variants of the others.

And, after, he joined them and initiated them into his *hareem* as he had the others.

He was holding them both to him, patting one on the head, when Obie suddenly broke the mood. "Intruder on the far bridge," it announced.

Yulin immediately abandoned the two new recruits and bounded up to the control console. "Who is it, Obie?" he asked.

"One life form, very large," the computer replied. "It appears for all the world to be a horse!"

Yulin's eyes blazed. "Mavra Chang!" he grunted under his breath—the one person he still considered a threat to his dreams, for she had some sort of rapport with Obie.

And she was the only other pilot.

"What does she appear to be doing?" he asked the computer.

"Standing just in front of the bridge," Obie replied.

He frowned. Now why the hell would she expose herself like that? "You sure there are no other life forms on that bridge?" he asked, puzzled.

"No other," the computer assured him. "Unless the Yugash is with her. That one would have to be a lot closer for me to detect unless it was inside her body—then it would be undetectable."

Yulin nodded. That must be it. She was setting herself up as bait, and when he got her in, the ruse would also get the Yugash in.

"Obie," he asked, mind racing, "could the Yugash communicate with you?"

"Yes, Ben. Of course it could."

"But nobody in this room could be taken over by it."

"No, Ben."

He considered that. "Obie, basic programming line establishment." He tapped out a long string of numbers on his keyboard.

"Running," the computer responded.

"You are not to take orders of any sort from a Yugash, whether on its own or in someone else's body," he said flatly. "Further, you are to ignore all Yugash-generated information."

"Clear and locked," the computer came back.

The minotaur nodded in satisfaction. All right, he told himself. *Let* the Yugash get in. Without a body, and powerless to communicate with Obie, it would just have to compromise with him or float around aimlessly. Offer to send it home, somehow get it under his control.

He smiled. This might be the best break yet. He got up, walked over to the balcony, and called, "Wooley! Vistaru! Nikki! Mavra! Come here!" The honor, he thought with grim humor, should be theirs.

Four women scrambled eagerly up to him.

"There's a horse out there at the other end of the bridge," he told them. "It's more than a horse. It is a person inside a horse's body and it can talk. It is one of the people opposed to me. A very dangerous one, the most important one. We must get it inside here. However, others are waiting just out of our sight and may rush you." He thought furiously for a moment. "When you reach the horse, work your hypnos on it. Give it all you have. Tell it it is your horse and must follow you, then lead it, ride it, or in any other way possible bring it and yourselves back here."

"What of the others, My Lord?" they all asked in unison.

"Numbers one and three, up here with your weapons" he yelled. Two more women came. They held energy pistols.

Obie couldn't design an organic defense against energy pistols, but he could make them easily enough.

"You will follow the others to about halfway across the bridge," he told them. "Keep your pistols ready, and get into position so you can cover both them and the hall opening. If you see *anything* coming out of that opening, kill it. If the horse gives the sisters any trouble, stun the whole batch and bring them back. Understand?"

"We hear and obey, My Lord," the two responded.

He nodded, then turned back to the control board. "Obie, on my count, you will drop out of defense mode and open the door. You will reinstitute defense mode on my command the instant I order it. Got that?"

"Got it, Ben."

"Get ready, girls. All right, Obie—five . . . four . . . three . . . two . . . one . . . *now!*"

The door slid open and Wooley, Vistaru, Nikki, and Mavra rushed out. A few seconds later the pair followed, pistols ready. In two groups the six ran low and carefully out across the bridge.

Mavra saw them immediately. "Okay, Bozog, Ghiskind! Now!" she hissed.

Like a flash the Bozog was across the bridge and over the side. The women, still carefully keeping low, didn't see it.

Renard was almost dragged into the archway by the sudden force of the uncoiling wire and he struggled to keep his legs in position. He was afraid that he would lose the wire, or that the Bozog would pull him into the opening.

Mavra was acutely aware that the wire was visible and very noisy as it unreeled. Since she did not want it noticed, she was left only one choice. She reared up like a wild horse, kicked off, and charged across the wide bridge.

At first, the women were taken by surprise, but they recovered quickly and waited for their quarry to come to them.

Mavra got up so much speed that she decided to try to run right past them, into the open door of the control room. The four lead women leaped out of her way, leaving a path for her, which Mavra took. Just as she passed them she felt, first, a sharp series of stings and then the sudden force of a boy jumping on her back. Then more stings, this time in the neck.

She tried to throw the rider, but things suddenly slowed, her mind clouded, and she came slowly to a dizzy halt.

"Keep going, horsie," a soft, sexy feminine voice said to her. "Right through the door, at a trot."

She obeyed unthinkingly. The three other women jogged alongside, and the two backups followed last, ensuring that there was no pursuit.

"Defense mode on, Obie!" Yulin yelled. The door slammed shut as the bulk of a horse almost crowded him out. He managed to turn and asked, "Obie, any life forms now in the bridge and shaft area?"

"No, Ben," Obie responded. "No life forms in that area."

Vistaru still rode Mavra's back, smiling like a child with a new toy.

"Such a nice horsie," she said to Yulin. "Can we keep it? As a pet?"

He chuckled, but he liked the idea. The more he thought about it, the better it sounded.

"Take her down to the disk, my love. A pet you'll have, but a new kind."

The girls had some problems negotiating the winding stairs with Mavra, but they managed it. The horse-woman was taken to the disk, placed on it, and the girls stepped away.

Yulin chuckled to himself. He'd never seen Mavra Chang as an Olbornian mutation, but he had some notion of it, which he found erotic and exotic. A pet! he thought gleefully.

"Obie, you have Mavra Chang's original encoding still, do you not?" he asked, hardly able to suppress himself.

"Yes, Ben."

"All right. Encode subject on the disk," he ordered.

The little dish swung over, the blue glow enveloped the disk below, the horse flickered and disappeared.

"New encoding for subject," he said to the computer. "Body that of Mavra Chang with tail, as placed in previous run-through. Arms and legs are to be that of a small horse, body facing down and resting on them, length and muscle size in proportion to human body. Internal muscle tone and bone structure sufficient to support weights up to one hundred kilos, or pull even more. Ears will be as on a mule. All skin and body color to be human, but digestive system shall parallel mine, ability to eat and digest anything organic. Got it?"

"Got it, Ben. Has anyone mentioned that you are beginning to resemble Antor Trelig?"

"Who said it mattered to me?" he retorted. "Continuing instructions. Enlarge breasts so they almost reach the ground. Sensory perception human norm in all areas. Make the tail long enough to reach the ground, and establish hair on subject's head and neck to be thick but short. Okay? And make her hermaphroditic—self-reproducing by parthenogenesis. Identical copies. Got it?"

"Yes, Ben."

"Attitudinal adjustments: Subject is to be fond of humans, particularly those in this room, and to require constant love and attention. Totally docile and obedient, no memory before this point nor reasoning ability above the level of a highly intelligent dog. Got it?"

"I've got it. Ben, you are a true rat."

"Thank you, Obie," he responded. "Lock and run."

It took less than six seconds.

The Bozog oozed down the side of the shaft, following the Yugash closely and maintaining a tight grip on the wire. Finally, after passing what seemed like thousands of panels and openings, they reached one that the Yugash pointed to, then entered. The Bozog followed.

Just inside, the wire snagged, and the Northerner had to stop and gently free it, afraid that Renard might interpret any tug as a signal to fire away.

The shaft led past large humming modules for some distance, then up, back, and around. It was quite a maze, and the Bozog stayed close to the Yugash, knowing full well that should the other abandon it there was no way it would ever find his way out of there.

Finally the Yugash reached the correct point. Only a meter or so away was a very odd-looking cube with a lot of connections. It didn't match anything else around, and so it had to be the bomb.

With the Yugash guiding, the Bozog placed the wire on the proper module. The device was incredibly complex—millions of tiny hairs, each surrounded by countless tiny, perfectly round bubbles, protruded from the surface. At the proper spot, the Bozog emitted a sticky, glistening substance, then embedded the wire in it.

Hastily, the Bozog started to back out, following the wire. It got a fair distance when the Yugash started making anxious gestures.

For a moment the Bozog was puzzled, then it thought about it for a second and gave a slight tug forward on the wire.

It moved easily.

Retreating, the Bozog had pulled the wire from the jury-rigged connection. With a grunt that the translator would make a sigh, it followed the Yugash back toward the bomb.

"Oh, she's so *cute!*" one of the girls squealed in delight as a new Mavra materialized, looked around as best she could, and, catching sight and sound of people, scampered happily over to them, bushy horse's tail wagging.

The girls clustered around, petting and rubbing her. One of them held a piece of fruit under Mavra's nose. She sniffed at it, purred, and ate it as a dog might.

Yulin looked at his handiwork from the balcony. "Here, Chang! Here, Chang! Come on, girl! Come here!" he called.

Mavra was puzzled but delighted. An idiot's smile played on her face. She sought the source of the call, locating it when Yulin clapped his hands. She raced up the stairs to him. He stooped down and took her head in his hands, rubbing it.

She licked his feet.

The Bozog couldn't risk too much secretion on the module, or the current might not reach its target.

"It's in as firm as we dare, Ghiskind," it said to its silent companion. "You'll have to take me out a slightly different way than we came in so I don't disconnect the wire again."

The specter nodded and they were off. The new route was much longer, and the Bozog had the uncomfortable feeling that the Yugash was guessing the way, but they finally found the shaft. The Bozog was nervous at that opening; neither end was visible, and the big rod at its center faded into nothingness in either direction. The bridge looked awfully far away.

The wire, however, was a few meters above and about ten meters to the side. The Bozog headed toward it. The tendril from its sac reached out, gently took in the slack from the direction of the bridge. When it was satisfied that there was no more, it pulled—once, twice, three times. Again, once, twice, three times.

And then it scurried up the wall toward the bridge. If Renard had gotten the message, the Bozog had just a count of thirty.

Renard had sat waiting, seemingly forever, the tension so thick he almost passed out from it. When the wire had finally stopped unreeling after an eternity, he'd relaxed, calmed himself, prepared. Several jerky motions almost caused him to begin, but the thirty count was more than just a safety margin for the Bozog. When the second signal didn't come, he cursed silently to himself and settled back again. With nothing to do but wait, he imagined the horrors and depravities being perpetrated as he sat waiting in the corridor, but there was nothing he could do. Additionally, he often thought he heard noises, and the pistol rose, but nothing ever approached him.

Suddenly he was conscious of a change, something happening. It took a moment, then he realized that the uncoiled wire was being pulled taut. He held his breath and took gentle hold of the strand at his end. There were still quite a few meters on the coil.

There it came. One . . . two . . . three . . . One . . . two . . . three.

He counted slowly to thirty, silently praying that he would not be the link in the chain to fail.

All my life I've been waiting for this moment, he thought while counting. *This is what I was born to do, this one thing. In a few seconds, I will justify my existence* . . .

Twelve . . . Eleven . . . Ten . . .

"You are certain no Yugash was inside her?"

"Absolutely, Ben," the computer assured him. "Nor is there a Yugash in this room or on the bridge or platforms."

Yulin cursed himself for his lack of foresight. He should have questioned her under the hypno before transforming her. What the hell had she been trying to do? "Analysis of Mavra Chang's actions in coming here?"

"To place into operation a plan to stop you," Obie responded coyly.

"What plan?" he thundered. "What are they trying to do?"

"They are trying to destroy me," replied the computer.

Yulin was on his feet in sudden alarm. "The others! A decoy! Damn it! I should have guessed!"

"Bad mistake, Ben. You forgot to question Mavra Chang. Usually you only get one mistake in your line of work."

"Stop being so damned cheerful!" the minotaur stormed. "How do I stop them?"

"Well, your only chance is to—*Intruder! Intruder on bridge platform!*" Obie suddenly warned.

"Numbers one and three, with pistols, up here on the double!" he screamed; they scrambled to comply.

"Defense mode off, Obie. Door open!" He turned to the girls. "Shoot to kill anything you see!"

They went out the door.

As they did so, Renard dashed out with all his speed to the foot of the bridge and touched the electrified railing, feeling the voltage go into him. He was already heavily charged.

Here goes! He gave the wire all he had.

Far below, a tremendous explosion blew smoke and debris in both directions along the shaft with a deafening, echoing roar. Unprepared for a reaction of such magnitude, Renard fell backward when the concussion struck him.

A tremor shook the control room hard enough to topple equipment. The lights flickered on, off, on . . . then off. The door popped open, as it was designed to do in any power failure, and the dim auxiliary lighting cast a feeble glow here and there throughout the Underside.

Yulin's night vision allowed him to see the control panel, now dark. He flipped the transmitter switch so hard that it broke.

"Obie! Obie!" he screamed. "Answer me! *Damn it, answer me!*"

But there was no reply. From the distance he heard what seemed to be secondary explosions. Frantically, he looked around, his dreams collapsing about him in the dark.

The two girls on the bridge suddenly stopped running and looked around, puzzled, blank expressions on their faces.

The moment power was lost it was as if a veil had lifted from the women below. They'd barely had time to scream in terror when suddenly they were changed, became disoriented. But not for long.

"Vistaru!" Wooley screamed. "Get a pistol! We've got the bastard now!"

"Behind you!" came another woman's voice, and two figures headed for the stairs, joined by two others.

Vistaru looked back nervously. "Who the hell are you?" she challenged.

"Nikki Zinder!" the other yelled. "Stand clear! Ben Yulin's *mine!*" she snarled so viciously that the other two let her pass.

Yulin heard them coming, and instantly realized what had happened.

Physical changes were accomplished by biological redesign; they were permanent unless changed by Obie, the Well, or a similar agency. But mental—at-titudinal—controls and changes were impositions by the computer, held in place by the computer's contin-ued operation.

Yulin no longer had slaves, he had old enemies.

He threw his chair down the stairs with great force, and the women jumped out of the way to avoid it. Yulin took advantage of their momentary confusion to run out the door.

The two women on the bridge had not previously had strong personalities, having been but animalistic savages, yet they retained the language and skills Obie had programmed into them in the same way that Mavra had retained the plans for New Pompeii. But for a few fleeting memories, the two felt as if they had just been born. They were totally confused.

Realizing their probable state, Yulin raced in their direction. One seemed to be puzzled by her energy pistol and he lunged toward her. Almost upon them, Yulin encountered the Agitar form of Renard running toward him. The minotaur was going to be beaten to the girl and the gun.

He stopped, frantic now, and looked back. Four of his former love-slaves were heading toward him, all armed, all grimly determined. From the opposite di-rection, Renard rushed past the women, pistol drawn.

Yulin opted for Renard. With a snarl he turned and ran into him; both went sprawling.

Yulin rolled, jumped to his feet, and grabbed Renard's pistol. Smiling now, he passed the two women, grabbing another pistol, and backed along the side of the bridge.

The lights in the main shaft were flickering, and there were more rumblings and bangings from below.

"Standoff!" Yulin yelled at them over the din. "Let's everybody stay calm!"

"Give it up, Yulin!" Nikki Zinder screamed, almost drowned out by the din from the shaft. The scene was eerily unreal in the dim and flickering light.

The minotaur laughed. "Just stay away" He continued to back along the shaft, and they continued to match him, coming warily forward.

Renard ran into the control room.

"We've got to get him," Wooley called from in back. "If he gets to the ship we're trapped—and he can build another Obie."

But they were bunched a little too close. A single shot from him could take them, but not, perhaps, before one of them also fried him.

As Yulin said, it was a draw, and he was backing along the side of the bridge.

He risked a quick glance back. Almost across now. Once in the corridor, he could outrun them to the car. Just a little farther . . .

Suddenly an orange tentacle lashed over the side of the bridge behind him, wrapped itself around his neck, and pulled him with a jerk up and over, then let go. Yulin felt himself lifted, turned over, then dropped down into the shaft.

He screamed in horror for some time. But thanks to Coriolis effect, he was smashed to death against the shaft long before he struck bottom.

The Bozog climbed up and over the bridge and down onto it, the pale-red cloak of the Ghiskind following.

Wooley saw what happened and applauded. There was more rumbling, booming, and flickering, and she grew suddenly businesslike.

"Vistaru, Zinder, go with the Bozog and the Ghiskind! Get both elevator cars open and ready! Com'on, Star! Let's help Renard get the others!" They ran back to the open, dark doorway.

"Renard!" Wooley screamed.

"Here!" he yelled. "Damn it! Come and help! I can't see a blasted thing!"

They could, and Vistaru gently herded the confused and blank other women up the stairs and out the door.

"Come on!" she yelled.

"Mavra! We've got to find Mavra!" Renard screamed.

Wooley looked around with her exceptional night vision. "I don't see her! Mavra!" she screamed. "Mavra!"

Suddenly the whole control room shook with a thunderous wrenching, and part of the far balcony collapsed.

Wooley grabbed Renard. "Come on! Get out of here!" she yelled at him. "We need you to get the others out!"

He looked desperate, tragic. "But—Mavra!" he screamed back.

"She's got to be dead, or unconscious, or something!" Wooley snapped back. Another spasm shook them and the shaft lights stayed out. "Come on! We've got to get out of here or we'll all die!"

With her deceptive strength she picked him up and raced up the stairs. At the top, she looked back, and there seemed to be tears in her eyes.

"Forgive me once more, dear Mavra," she whispered, more to herself than to Renard, although he heard.

Then she was off across the bridge.

Both cars were packed with bodies, and they stopped and started several times and moved jerkily. Despite moments when they seemed stuck, doomed to die of asphyxiation, both made it to the surface.

Renard, though still in shock, realized it was now his show. "To the ship!" he yelled. Time for mourning later.

Aboard the Shuttle

THE SHUTTLE HAD ORIGINALLY BEEN DESIGNED FOR humans. The Bozog engineers had adapted it for the flight from the Well World to New Pompeii—and though there were now eleven humans and only three nonhumans aboard, they managed. The shuttle had been designed for up to thirty people, and the rear area still had its seats—with two to spare.

The Bozog and the Ghiskind remained with Renard on the bridge. The Agitar struggled to get ahold of himself. "Ghiskind, look in back and make sure everybody's seated and strapped down," he snapped. The red specter drifted back, looked, came back, and its hollow-hooded head nodded.

"E-release," Renard muttered. "Now—oh, yeah. Hold tight!" He checked his own straps and reached over to a keyboard, punching the code in.

Nothing happened.

He cursed, then thought a bit, trying to figure out what he had done wrong. Suddenly, he had it.

"E-lift," he punched.

The ship broke free and rose at near maximum power.

"Code please," a pleasant, mechanical voice came at them over the ship's radio, startling him. "Correct code within sixty seconds or we will destroy your ship."

"The robot sentinels!" he cried. "We forgot about them!"

But Mavra hadn't. She'd had him program the entire sequence.

"The Decline and Fall of Pompeii," came her recorded voice over the radio. It was, Renard thought with some relief, a truly appropriate title.

Now the ship slowed, came almost to a standstill. Before him, the screens showed a meaningless series of figures and lots of circles, dots, and other shapes.

The shuttle began to move forward again.

He sighed and relaxed. "That's that for now," he told the others. "She said it would be a day or two before we'd be in range of anybody, unless we run into someone coming our way first."

He walked back to the passenger compartment.

"Goddamned bushy horse's tail!" one of the women swore. "Feels like you're sitting on a rock, and it's so long you sweep the floor with it!"

Another laughed. "I guess we got off lucky," she said cheerfully. "He hadn't thought of the tails until he got the people in from the forest."

Renard was confused. Except for slight differences in coloration, and the occasional tail, they all looked alike.

"Who's who?" he moaned.

One laughed. "I'm Wooley, Renard, so relax. This is Star—ah, Vistaru, that is. And these two over here are Nikki Zinder and her daughter, Mavra." She choked up, but recovered quickly.

He didn't. "Nikki Zinder . . ." he mumbled. "Her daughter . . ."

The girl stared at him unbelievingly. "Are you really my father?" she asked.

He shook his head slowly. "No, somebody else was, somebody human. I have his memories, and his personality, but I'm something else now."

That seemed to satisfy her, and Nikki, who'd tensed at the question, visibly relaxed.

Renard looked at the others, anxious to change the subject. "What about them?" he asked, looking at the seven other girls.

Wooley undid her straps and walked to him. She was taller than he and her tail trailed like a bird's plume.

"We've explained to them that they have all lost their memories for good," she whispered to him, "because of the machine. They'll be okay."

That relieved him, and his body reminded him of a different need. "We've got at least a couple of days on this tub," he pointed out, "and very little to eat."

She shrugged. "We can hold out if we have to. Actually, there's enough organic stuff in the padding and old packs. We can all have something, I think. You're the one that will probably have the most problem."

He chuckled and looked at his passengers. "Live on love, huh?" he cracked.

By the time contact was made two and a half days out, they had all practiced what was to be said—and what was not to be said—and their courses of action.

"This is the Com police," a stern male voice came over the radio. "Identify yourself by number and destination."

Renard sighed. "This is a refugee ship from New Pompeii, a planetoid formerly owned by New Harmony," he replied. "I am not a pilot and there is not one aboard."

That seemed to disturb the police a bit. There was some anxious checking against police computer files.

"Stand by, we will match you and board," the police ship stated.

"It's in your hands," he responded. "However, first I think I better warn you about a few things."

He proceeded to tell them of Antor Trelig's party, of Obie, the Well World, everything. The only details omitted concerned how to reach the Well World.

The police didn't believe, of course, but they recorded the information anyway; then they matched the ships, locked, and two armored cops boarded.

One look at the passengers and they had less reason to doubt.

Com police were an odd group: the wild ones, the undomesticated, the lovers of freedom and the restless. They were carefully recruited in midlife, usually after having been caught red-handed at something nasty.

In exchange for voluntarily undergoing some loyalty conditioning, they were paroled—to police the rest, to protect the Com and the frontier from others just like them.

They generally knew a hot potato when they grabbed it. The taped conversations were coded, sealed, and sent directly to the eleven-member Council Presidium, which made decisions when the full Council could not be summoned—or when it shouldn't be.

Three Council members were out to the ship in less than fourteen additional hours. They were Com, all right, yet each maintained his own strong character. One, a woman apparently approaching middle age, had an especially regal bearing.

"Some twenty-two years ago," Councillor Alaina said, "before I had this last rejuve, I hired Mavra Chang to attend Antor Trelig's little party as my agent. I never heard from her again, of course—but, since New Pompeii disappeared, taking dear Antor with it, I was satisfied." She looked around at the odd little group of human women and aliens. "And now I see she succeeded after all."

They all had tears in their eyes, and even the Bozog quivered a bit. Only the Ghiskind, as usual, was impassive.

"When I heard the police report, I didn't believe it —but here you all are, even Nikki Zinder!" She turned to Vistaru. "And you—an unexpected pleasure, Star Tongue. One of your sons is an invaluable Chief Counselor."

"The kids," Wooley murmured to herself. "It'd be interesting to see the kids again."

"And now we must decide what is to be done," Councillor Alaina continued. "We owe you all a great deal."

Renard slapped himself. "The sponge cure!" he blurted.

The refugees looked startled, and he nodded. "Obie —the computer—gave it to Mavra. She recorded it in the ship's log."

Alaina nodded to a Com policeman. "Get it," she

ordered. "Secure it." She looked preoccupied, as if watching new vistas unfold. "If that cure holds up," she continued, "It'll break the back of the syndicate. The changes will be revolutionary."

"It'll work," the Agitar assured her. "Mavra said it would."

A grim expression marred the Councillor's normally impassive features. "Mavra Chang. Yes. So sad. You're sure we can't go back for her?"

"Studies show most power has failed," a policeman put in. "The plasma shield itself is weakening. If anybody's still there, they're dead now for sure."

She nodded. "I thought as much. But her name shall live on in our histories. She shall be celebrated among the greats. We will not forget her."

"None of us will," Renard replied sincerely.

They sat about half a light-hour off New Pompeii. On the screens the planetoid showed clearly as a small ball.

"Everyone thinks that you need the weapons locker to destroy a planet," Alaina noted. "But you don't. That takes a vote of all the Council, and we can't put this to the Council until we've substantially laundered it. No use informing the universe that such a thing as Obie is possible. Somebody else would surely build one."

All agreed.

Four ships showed on the screens, Com police cruisers towing huge objects with tractor beams.

"What are they?" Wooley asked, fascinated.

"Antimatter, my dear," Alaina replied. "It's all over the place, you know. Always has been. Calculate the mass of the object you want to destroy, grab some antimatter of equal mass, bring the two together, and they cancel each other out. Took a century even to create a tractor beam that wouldn't react with the stuff. The police craft will follow a trajectory that will have the antimatter asteroids strike New Pompeii at the same time. Should be quite a flash, and that will be that."

They watched as the ships moved by, curved, swung the asteroids around and let them fly.

And then scrammed like hell.

While they waited for the missiles to reach their target, Alaina discussed other things.

"Makes you wonder," she said, looking at Renard, the Bozog, and the Ghiskind. "If you three can exist, how many others might? Maybe just over the next solar system, so to speak. Perhaps within our lifetime two of our cultures will meet. How I'd love to see that!"

"If you'd been on the Well World you'd have your fill of alien races pretty quickly," Vistaru responded.

She shrugged. "I've always wondered. Perhaps such a clash will be the ultimate problem. Perhaps the other beings will be antimatter? *That* would be frustrating!" She laughed, then changed tone.

"Have you thought about your own futures?" she asked them.

"We—the Bozog, the Ghiskind, and I—can return to the Well World," Renard replied. "We've told you that. Just get us to a Markovian world. That's what we have to do, of course. There's no place for us in this part of the universe."

She nodded, and turned to the others. "What about you, Tonges?"

Wooley smiled. "Nikki Zinder has never had a chance to be a real person, live a real life. Her daughter even less so—and the others, well, they can learn to be people. It will be interesting to see how the family's come along. And, well, Star and I really did love each other, you know. It'll be fun being together again after twenty-two long years."

"And we owe Mavra something," Vistaru put in. "Both of us keep thinking, if only we had stayed a little longer, if only we'd made sure that Vash's children all got out. If only we hadn't left them. She had such a horrible life—maybe we can help these other women, instead of letting them wind up in a hole, like Mavra. I think we owe that much to her, to them, and to ourselves."

Alaina nodded. "I think I can understand. Bodies like those can be wonderful, or the biggest curse you can have. And I'll help. Mavra's fee was agreed to, recorded, and never paid. I think you could do a pretty good job with a million, couldn't you?"

Wooley's eyes went wide. "A *million?*" She laughed suddenly. "Wow! We'll buy our own frontier world!" She looked at Vistaru. "You know, it's crazy, isn't it? We had lives once, then second lives on the Well, then third lives back here, fourth back on the Well, now fifth—I wonder if that means we're going to keep living forever? We can always return to the Well again in the future."

Vistaru laughed. "Yeah, but take it easy. You aren't my husband any more. You're superwoman now."

"I started out a woman," the other pointed out. "Not much of one, I admit. Maybe it's time for Wu Julee to find out what it's really like."

Vistaru nodded. "It can really be wonderful," she said softly.

"Look!" Renard yelled. "The asteroids are about there!"

As he spoke four smaller dots converged on the large ball. A tremendous flash of energy blurred their vision momentarily, then there was nothing.

Scans revealed no trace of New Pompeii, not the slightest speck of dust.

Alaina sighed. "That's it, then. Let's get out of here."

The ship throbbed to life and started moving. There were tears in Renard's eyes and all were silent.

"Good-bye, Mavra. Forgive us."

And even the Yugash's hood bowed.

An Unnamed Star in M-51

SHE STOOD AND STRETCHED ALL FOUR LEGS IN THE darkness. She was used to working in the dark, and her nose quickly found some edible fruit and some stale bread. It would do, and the fruit provided needed water. She'd gone through the last of the preserved foodstuffs the day before.

She wondered why she was still alive. She wondered why she persisted in postponing the end.

The lights came on. That, in itself, was no surprise. She'd been expecting it any time now, ever since she'd experienced the familiar blackout and that long dropping feeling a few hours before.

She turned her downward-facing head and looked around. The place was a mess. Much of the structures had collapsed, including part of the far balcony.

The explosions, hisses, and rumbles had stopped several days earlier, but they had been replaced by the sounds of hammering and welding and lots of clanking. She'd actually gone out to see what was making them, but except for discovering some emergency lighting still going in the main shaft area, there was nothing that could be seen. Whatever was going on was going on far below her, she was sure.

"Hello, Mavra," Obie's soft, pleasant tenor sprang suddenly out of the air near her. She almost jumped out of her skin.

"Obie!" she responded, almost scolding in tone.

285

She was about to say more, but suddenly realized that while it could talk to you you had to broadcast to it.

The computer seemed to realize her thoughts. "No, it's not necessary to transmit any more," he informed her. "There's nothing left to transmit with anyway. Things have changed a great deal in the last few days. *I* have changed, too, Mavra."

She felt numbed, as though in some sort of half-sleep. Nothing seemed quite real, and she only half believed in her continued existence.

"All right, Obie—just what did you do? And how?" she called.

The computer actually chuckled. "They decided to destroy me by pushing four antimatter asteroids at me. I just used the big dish and translated two of the asteroids into normal matter—for us, that is. Then, two and a half milliseconds before they all collided, I translated here. They met with a nice flash and it looked like we were all blown up as the two antimatter asteroids met my newly transformed matter asteroids."

"Two milliseconds?" she responded, aghast. "Wasn't that cutting it a little close?"

"Two and a half," he corrected. "No, it was just right. You see, the amount of change their instruments could detect is five milliseconds, so I provided for a safety margin. Plenty of time, really."

Mavra decided to avoid further conversation on that subject. Anybody who could talk about two and a half milliseconds as plenty of time was not somebody she could directly relate to on that level. Instead she said, "I thought we destroyed you. The bomb went off, didn't it?"

"Oh, yes," Obie replied cheerfully. "The bomb went off all right. It's just that the deck was stacked. The bomb didn't remove control, it removed blockages to control, just as we'd planned it."

"We?" she came back, puzzled.

"Dr. Zinder and I, of course," the computer told her. "You see, from the start Trelig was afraid somebody might get their hands on me. So, if that happened, he wanted bombs that would destroy me planted in key areas. The trouble was, the people he was most afraid of were people like Yulin, who could operate me properly. So, he forced Dr. Zinder to do it. They were all proper and checked. But they all had electrical triggers. In other words, I had to pass on the triggering voltage myself, and, as I told you on the radio, I was programmed absolutely never to assist in my own destruction. Dr. Zinder knew I could not accept the order to initiate those voltages. He placed the bomb where it would have to blow outward, destroying the two modules that separated my voluntary circuits from the involuntary and life-support areas. A simple matter, really. Only, it had to be triggered from outside. So, when things went all wrong and we wound up jammed around the Well World, I had to create a situation where that bomb would be detonated."

Now she was fascinated. "How did you do that?"

"Well, for one thing, in the plans I placed in all the agents' heads, that's the only bomb detailed. It's the one that comes up when you think of the destruction of New Pompeii."

She nodded. "So you played the odds—but, do you mean you did that before you even knew about the Well World and us going there?"

"Percentages," he explained. "The odds were heavy we'd die when Dr. Zinder and I double-crossed Trelig and reversed to the Well World. But, if we didn't, then I'd still be under the control of Trelig or Yulin or both. That meant those able to do so would try and destroy me. So, I included the contingency—and it worked!"

"After twenty-two years," she noted.

"It was sufficient," he replied. "Besides, in that time I learned a lot. And now I'm an individual, Mavra— a totally self-sufficent organism. I control and see and perceive everything on this planetoid. I am Topside as well as Underside. And nobody can ever force orders into me again. This world *is* me now, Mavra—not just this room. Everything. The big dish and the little dish, too."

She wasn't sure she shared his enthusiasm. No one should have such power, she thought.

"My apologies, too, for not getting to you sooner, but all of my energies were taken up in simulating my total breakdown while at the some time using my service modules, which I'd never had conscious control of before, to repair and modify myself. And now I'm a person, Mavra—an independent organism!"

"But you're a small *planet*," she pointed out.

That didn't disturb him. "So? Considering all the other creatures you have seen, and the oddity you are now, what's one more kind of person? What somebody looks like, what somebody is externally, isn't important. It's what that individual is on the inside that counts. Surely that is the lesson of the Well World. Aren't the different life forms there simply exaggerated examples of what is seen in human society? Too fat, too thin, too short, too tall, too dark, too light. Be concerned with the contents, not the package. It's easier on the Well, isn't it? Everybody's expected to look different there, yet all of them, no matter how alien, sprang from the same Markovian roots."

She sighed. "I suppose so," she said wearily. "What will you do now? And where are we, anyway?"

"To answer the last first, we're in M-51, orbiting a lonely star, about thirty-five million light-years from anything that thinks. I picked it out of the Well years ago in case I needed a place to go. As for the other . . ." He paused, seemingly hesitant to voice his next thought. Quietly, he said, "Why didn't you go with the others, Mavra? Why did you decide to die? It was your intention all along, wasn't it?"

"Yes. The Well isn't for me. I survived to complete the commission, to make certain that New Pompeii would never be in the hands of such as Trelig or Yulin. So after that, what? All my life I've prided myself on my independence. To return to the Well World is to be made into something random, maybe even a whirling flower or a thinking clam or maybe a Wuckl or an Ecundan. Someone else's choice. And even if it's a good one, your universe is the Well World, your existence confined to an area no bigger than New Pompeii. As for the Com—for a while I'd be a hero, but soon I'd be yesterday's hero. Then I'd be just a freak, a four-legged woman with a tail. Maybe a nice compound for the heroine somewhere, like in Glathriel, or a circus, or some form of luxurious zoo. No freedom, no ship, no stars, no self-determination. What other choice did I have? Even what little I have left, my own life and accomplishments, turn out to be a lie. I don't owe you and you don't owe me, I always believed. But the beggars took me in because they were asked to, and helped me because they were asked to or paid to. The same one who did that sent my husband to me to get me out of the whore house."

"But he did care for you," Obie pointed out.

"I think he did—but that's not the point. He would never have been there without Brazil. Even if we met, once, by chance, I'd just have been another bar girl. Now that I've thought it out, I wonder if *any* of it was for real? How many times did I escape because of outside interference? So many things broke right. So many things *always* broke right. Little things, big things, but they add up to my life. Even you—you programmed me as your agent for your own ends, and I did exactly what you wanted done, while my grandparents and Brazil's friend Ortega looked after me on the Well World."

"You underrate yourself," Obie scolded. "You did it all yourself. Opportunity is not accomplishment. You did it, by ingenuity, by resourcefulness, by guts. You really *are* as good as you thought you were, and you have the potential to be much better."

She shook her head. "No. Even if I accept all that, there's Joshi. I liked him, and he was useful to me.

He was something I needed. But I'm sure I never would have . . ." Her voice faltered. "Never—do what he did, for him. He gave his life to save mine! Why?"

"Perhaps he loved you," the computer replied kindly. "Love is the most abused word in history. It is, simply, caring more for others than you do for yourself. It's a measure of greatness that flashes rarely in an otherwise pretty sordid universe. This is the quality that the Markovians lost, for godhead is inherently selfish. They lost the capacity to care for others, to give as well as receive, to love others as they would be loved. Their curse was the hollow emptiness left inside them when the ability to love was lost. Such was their tragedy that they could no longer even comprehend it."

She sniffed in derision. "And me? It's not within me, Obie. Others have loved me, I suppose—Brazil, my parents and grandparents, and most especially Joshi—but I never returned it, couldn't return it. I don't know how. I don't even understand you now."

"When Joshi died, you cried," Obie reminded her softly. "Now you are lost and wallowing in self-pity, yet it is within you to grow, to learn it, Mavra Chang."

"Another of those quantitative measurements you make when I run through you?" she retorted.

"It cannot be quantified," Obie replied. "That's why the Markovians couldn't discover it. That's why the Gedemondans will fail as well. They have sealed themselves off from the rest of mankind, in whatever form. All their energies are directed to isolating, to *quantifying* the element. And in that very act they reject their own potential for giving to others." He paused for a moment.

"So, like the Markovians, you are forced to face the nonquantifiable, something you can't touch, measure, or define except by example, and your own selfish nature eats you alive so your ego can be shattered. You want to die, as the Markovians finally wanted to die, but without even their noble motives. It is ironic that their very sacrifice was an act of that quality they, too, believed they no longer possessed."

She laughed mirthlessly. "I can't see the profit, the reason. As a beggar, I learned that most charity is really guilt. I *deserve* to die."

"But you don't," Obie responded. "You could have killed yourself a thousand times, just in the last three days. Is that why you wish to retain that most inconvenient form? Punishment for the guilt you feel? Here! I give you choices, and they are freely given. You wish to be an animal? I shall place you where you want, as you are or as you wish to be. Want to be a queen? Just name the race. Anything you want, any place you want, alive, dead, productive, destructive. What is your wish? I will see that it comes about! Or —join me in exploring the nearly limitless stars, in helping where I can, in learning as well. In meeting the challenges to come. Very soon our human relatives will meet with not one but several other alien cultures. Are they to clash and condemn themselves, or mesh and grow? Do you want to join me in working at such grand projects, or will you allow your guilt and self-pity to place you in a hell most assuredly of the worst kind because it is of your own device? Tell me. Take your time—we have a lot of it, perhaps all there is."

The words of the Gedemondans again floated through her mind.

First you must descend into Hell. Then, only when hope is gone, will you be lifted up and placed at the pinnacle of attainable power, but whether or not you will be wise enough to know what to do with it or what not to do with it is closed to us.

She'd once defined hell as the absence of hope, and Obie had added guilt and self-pity, so hell she had attained indeed.

She shook her head slowly in puzzled wonder, not able to comprehend or control new feelings that were rising inside her. For a long while she was silent. At last she looked around at the wrecked control room, at the air around her.

"Partners?" she asked softly, hesitantly.

"Partners!" Obie shouted joyfully.

Appendix I: Races of the Southern Hemisphere

Only those hexes that have people or geography in this second half of the book are listed. Those from *Exiles of the Well of Souls* are listed only if they and/or theirs actually also appears in Volume II. Names are as one would hear them. Pronunciation is left up to the reader; if you want a rule, treat it as you would Polish—pronounce every letter and syllable.

H = High-tech hex. All technology works here if you invent it and can develop it.

S = Semitech hex. Steam and internal combustion work, but not electrical, atomic, or more sophisticated systems.

N = Nontech hex. No machine not directly or indirectly powered by muscle works here. Oil and gas still burn and can be used directly for light and heat, but they won't move a piston.

A parenthesis around the tech designation—e.g., (S)—indicates that it is a water hex.

The letter M following a tech designation—e.g., NM—means the hex has what would be regarded as magical capabilities by those who don't have them.

Atmospheric composition and pressure vary widely, but there is no hex listed here in which others could not live without artificial aids.

AGITAR	H	Diurnal	Males satyrlike; females reverse animalism of males but are smarter. Males can store and discharge high electrical voltages without harm. The pegasus is native to Agitar.
ALESTOL	N	Diurnal	Moving, barrel-shaped plants; carnivores that shoot a variety of noxious gasses.
AMBREZA	H	Diurnal	Resemble giant beavers. Used to be N until they beat the Glathriel in a war and forced them to swap hexes.
CZLAPLON	H	Diurnal	Look like a giant ball of tangled nylon cord with a little head and internal brain case. The captain of the *Toorine Trader* is a Czlaplon.
DAHIR	N	Diurnal	Huge lizardlike creatures who can change color to blend almost invisibly with any background. The Parmiter's henchmen are Dahir.

DASHEEN	N	Diurnal	Basically minotaurs. Females are much larger and dumber than males, which they outnumber 100 to 1, but males are dependent on female's milk for calcium and lactose.
DILLIA	S	Diurnal	True, classical centaurs. Peaceful folk who hunt, trap, farm. Can eat anything organic but are basically vegetarians.
ECUNDO	S	Diurnal	Creatures of rubbery texture but much like giant scorpions. Carnivores who live in the ground and eat giant guinea piglike bundas fresh and raw. Nasty, vile tempers.
EVEROD	(N)		Giant clamlike creatures with hundreds of long tentacles. Deep water, nobody knows much about them, but they have trade through Zone.
GEDEMONDAS	N	Diurnal	Large, thin, hirsute apelike creatures with round feet and hairy snouts, they live in volcanic caverns under cold, high mountains and think a lot.

GLATHRIEL	N	Diurnal	The ancestors of humanity, more Oriental in stature and Negroid in features. Very primitive since the Ambreza gassed them back to the stone age.
HOOKL	(N)		Off-camera in the book, they are giant sea-snakes who can combine into squidlike amalgums.
JOL	(N)		Off-camera in the book, they are water-breathing relatives of the sea lion.
KYRBIZMYTH	N	Diurnal	Plants, each with a brain, who move by mindswapping. They sleep nights, but better hadn't touch if you don't want to join them. Even so, they trade much in something.
LATA	H	Nocturnal	Very small hermaphroditic humanoid pixies who can fly like a bee, have nasty stingers, and can glow by chemical secretions on the skin. Mentally as well as outwardly akin to humans, internally they tend more to resemble the cockroach.

MAKIEM	N	Diurnal	Large reptiles resembling giant toads, they need some water daily though land-dwellers. Cold-blooded and can climb walls and leap like mad.
MUCROL	S	Diurnal	Doglike carnivores who live in packs around desert waterholes protected by steam-powered tanks. Lack political cohesion.
NOCHA	(S)		Off-camera in the book, they resemble starfish and live in cities composed of shells.
OOLAGASH	(H)		Tentacled sea-horses restricted to great depths; managed to get to atomic stage without some obviously impossible intermediary stages.
ORARC	S	Diurnal	Weasellike, these are the signalmen of the *Toorine Trader* and good cannoneers as well.
PARMITER	H	Diurnal	Tiny monkeys with owl-like faces and beaks. What they lack in stature they make up in nastiness; a race of wild and crooked freebooters.

TWOSH	S	Diurnal	Large pink bowling pins with big brown eyes. Only two limbs, which double as arms and legs. Highly resourceful due to their physical limitations.
ULIK	H	Diurnal	Six-armed creatures, humanoid above the waist but with walruslike faces, big moustaches, and six arms. Below the waist are five to ten meters of very large colorful snake.
USURK	(H)		Off-camera in the book. Can be sociable, but can you imagine a tentacled piranha with a jet assist?
WUCKL	H	Diurnal	Legs like an emu's, body a hairy oblong, long arms that bend every which way, long soft hands, a tremendously high, infinitely movable neck, and a birdlike head with a four-way beak. Peaceful vegetarians who are incredibly good psychic surgeons.
WYGON	S	Diurnal	Six-stemmed creatures seemingly made of pipe cleaners, they are fast and bright. Tbisi, First Mate of the *Toorine Trader*, is Wygonian.

XYRICIS	N	Nocturnal	Giant armadillos, they trade with many hexes. The Tindler was a far-traveling Xyricis.
YIMSK	(N)		Off-camera in the book. Plankton-eaters mostly of deep water, who somewhat resemble the nautilus.
ZANTI	(H)		Off-camera in the book. These shocking relatives of the electric eel have managed to build quite an effective and modern culture on the sea floor; their coop trade with Wuckl gives the latter fishing rights in exchange for some goods not possible to manufacture under water.

Appendix II: Races of the Northern Hemisphere

The key is the same as for the Southern Races in Appendix I. All names in the North are Southern approximations, hence compromises. Even their seas, mountain ranges, etc., have no common names unlike the standard system in the South, so Southern designations are used throughout. None of the following hexes have atmosphere in common with the others or close to that of any Southern hex, although a few inhabitants, notably the Bozog and Yugash, can travel without protection because they don't breathe in the normal sense of the word.

ASTILGOL	N	Diurnal	The legendary Diviner and The Rel were Astilgolians. Symbiotic creatures resembling a set of hanging crystal chimes on which is set an invisible bowl with little flashing lights. Silicon eaters.
BOZOG	H	Diurnal	Two eggs sunny side up, full of gritty little balls, and with cilia beneath. Can form the liquid in their sacs into tentacles, etc. and can stick to walls.

CUZICOL | N | Nocturnal | Metallic yellow flowers with hundreds of sharp spikes, they stand on two spindly legs. One operated on Mavra and Joshi in the Yaxan Embassy.

MASJENADA | S | Diurnal | Blown glass swans without heads or feet, they can combine and alter their body material, and have the annoying habit of flying through each other with no ill effect.

OYAKOT | H | Diurnal | Like enormous drab puff-balls with spikes, they are actually a very pleasant, normal sort of folk. They like their oxygen frozen.

PUGEESH | S | Nocturnal | Little brown disks surrounded by ten thin tentacles. Tribal and easily frightened if they fail to kill you; can induce dreamy lethargy but melt in any heat.

UBORSK | S | Diurnal | Amorphous sanddwellers who have become middlemen in the trade between Bozog and Wohafa.

UCHJIN | N | Nocturnal | Hard people to talk to, they resemble smears of paint dripping in midair.

WOHAFA	H	Diurnal	Balls of bright yellow light out of which shoot hundreds of lightning-like tentacles. Able to turn energy into matter and one kind of matter to energy and back to something else, making them everybody's favorite trade partner.
YUGASH	H	Diurnal	These creatures of stable energy that resemble pale red hooded cloaks without wearers and fade in bright light can take over your body if you let them—or don't watch them carefully.

About the Author

JACK L. CHALKER was born in Norfolk, Virginia on December 17, 1944, but was raised and has spent most of his life in Baltimore, Maryland. He learned to read almost from the moment of entering school, and by working odd jobs had amassed a large book collection by the time he was in junior high school, a collection now too large for containment in his present quarters. Science fiction, history, and geography all fascinated him early on, interests which continue.

Chalker joined the Washington Science Fiction Association in 1958 and began publishing an amateur SF journal, *Mirage,* in 1960. After high school he decided to be a trial lawyer, but money problems and the lack of a firm caused him to switch to teaching. He holds B.S. degrees in history and English, and an M.L.A. from the Johns Hopkins University. He taught history and geography in the Baltimore public schools between 1966 and 1978, and now makes his living as a freelance writer. Additionally, out of the amateur journals he founded a publishing house, The Mirage Press, Ltd., devoted to nonfiction and bibliographic works on science fiction and fantasy. This company has produced more than twenty books in the last nine years. His hobbies include esoteric audio, travel, working on science-fiction convention committees, and guest lecturing on SF to institutions like the Smithsonian. He is an active conservationist and National Parks supporter, and he has an intensive love of ferryboats, with the avowed goal of riding every ferry in the world. He is single, and still lives and works in Baltimore.